KENNETH MACMILLAN

The Man and the Ballets

Also by Edward Thorpe

The Other Hollywood
The Night I Caught the Santa Fé Chief
The Colourful World of Ballet (with Clement Crisp)
MacMillan's *Isadora*: the creation of a ballet
Chandlertown

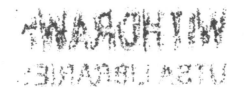

KENNETH MACMILLAN

The Man and the Ballets

by EDWARD THORPE

With a foreword by Dame Ninette de Valois

HAMISH HAMILTON   LONDON

The author and the publisher gratefully acknowledge their debt to the photographers whose work appears in this book, especially:
Catherine Ashmore
Clive Boursnell
Anthony Crickmay
Zoë Dominic
Collection of Nicholas Georgiadis
Leslie E. Spatt
Michael Werner for the Barry Kay Archives

First published in Great Britain 1985
by Hamish Hamilton Ltd
Garden House 57–59 Long Acre London WC2E 9JZ

British Library Cataloguing in Publication Data

Thorpe, Edward
  Kenneth MacMillan : the man and the ballets.
  1. MacMillan, Kenneth   2. Choreographers –
  Great Britain – Biography
  I. Title
  792.8'092'4   GV1785.M25/

ISBN 0 241 11694 5

Photoset by Rowland Phototypesetting Ltd
Bury St Edmunds, Suffolk
Printed in Great Britain by
Billings and Sons Ltd,
Guildford and Worcester

CONTENTS

Foreword by Dame Ninette de Valois   vii
Author's Note   xi

Chap. 1: Childhood: happy and unhappy times   1
Chap. 2: Student of the ballet   6
Chap. 3: Ambition achieved: first performances   10
Chap. 4: Stage fright and a new beginning   16
Chap. 5: Last performances: dancer into choreographer   22
Chap. 6: The first commission   28
Chap. 7: Company choreographer   32
Chap. 8: From success to success   38
Chap. 9: The first failure   42
Chap. 10: Farewell to fantasy   47
Chap. 11: A muse discovered, a rite created   55
Chap. 12: Difficulty in London, success in Stuttgart   67
Chap. 13: A major triumph   79
Chap. 14: 'A masterpiece' – but 'parting is such sweet sorrow'   85
Chap. 15: Berlin beginnings: Expressionism and a brilliant *Beauty*   92
Chap. 16: Goodbye to Berlin – and to alcohol   101
Chap. 17: Director of the Royal – a difficult start   109
Chap. 18: 'She likes you, too'   119
Chap. 19: Death of a friend, birth of a baby, creation of *Manon*   127
Chap. 20: A popular success and an honour bestowed   139
Chap. 21: A nasty accident and a resignation   150
Chap. 22: A hectic year – a succession of successes   158
Chap. 23: From haute couture to psychiatric clinic   176
Chap. 24: *Gloria* and *Isadora*   186
Chap. 25: A lot of television   200
Chap. 26: A new muse and a knighthood   210

Envoi   218
Chronology of ballets   219
Index   223

for Deborah and Charlotte

Foreword

Kenneth MacMillan's work is as varied as it is fearless, and can be at times bold to a point of folly; he takes everything in his stride, a stride that is objective and not susceptible to outside influences. A MacMillan failure is as positive as a MacMillan success – perhaps the proper outcome of the work of any choreographer of distinction under the age of sixty.

His sense of beauty is as it should be; for beauty is more than often obscure, a light diffused, rising to the surface as a part of the whole. Take, as an example, the scene in *Mayerling* where the Empress and her son meet in her boudoir on his wedding night. Behind the Empress's sofa hangs a rigid line of grandly attired dummies. Symbolic, perhaps; some members of the audience may find this a tough birthmark of a dying era – others are disturbed. Yet, eventually, a wonderful atmosphere is created by the choreography; there is a mixture of suspended emotion and an inevitable acceptance of fate that forms a strange partnership with the background. Distraction for distraction's sake is annihilated.

MacMillan produced, in a little over a decade, four full-length ballets for the Royal Ballet – *Romeo and Juliet*, *Anastasia*, *Manon* and *Mayerling* – not to mention certain one-act works of importance such as *Song of the Earth* and *Gloria*. It is his approach to his first four full-length ballets that matters, and the success that they have met with – despite a controversial attitude towards them by some critics. The overall aim quite simply lay in the fact that they were full-length ballets of today, not yesterday. *Manon* is already an accepted classic; *Mayerling* is much admired by a very wide public. The documentary television film version of *Mayerling* (which won the Prix Italia in 1977) is, on the part of the producers, an inspired transfer from stage to small screen. For the first time in a filmed ballet there is a suggestion that the theatre version could take notice of certain points, and profit from the approach. *Anastasia* has been aptly described by Mary Clarke as 'a flawed masterpiece', and perhaps one day MacMillan may have the time to set about solving *Anastasia*'s problems. The ballet has style and atmosphere, yet more than atmosphere is needed to solve the musical problem, and bury a campaign of slaughter on the part of certain critics in the past.

On the subject of criticism in general I have experienced understanding and satisfaction in the following summing-up of MacMillan after a very adverse criticism of *Manon* on the part of an American critic: '. . . I don't think he (MacMillan) was being pretentious, and the insults that were showered upon him for missing the mark themselves missed the mark . . . MacMillan's taste, music-al instinct, and technical skill place him first among the British and European choreographers whose careers began in the fifties . . . *Manon* shows a lack of confidence, the steely bravura of *Anastasia* is missing – but at forty-four MacMillan is just entering his maturity, and I think we have a right to expect him to fulfil it . . .' (Arlene Croce, 1974).

The above shows a sense of balance in relation of the part to the whole, and therefore one accepts the critic's personal reaction without any negative feelings.

It is important to note that the full-length ballet takes many years to settle down. What is true of the nineteenth century productions will be true of our twentieth century works. They need now, as in the past, time to submit to a dispassionate view of their shortcomings. Meanwhile, history will repeat itself, and all the great choreographic moments within these twentieth century ballets will forge ahead intact, bestowing a form of eternal inspiration for the dancers, and give them an opportunity of an individual interpretation within a framework of skilful and imaginative choreography. As an example: the three leading roles in *Manon*, as they are today, will outlive any corps de ballet developments or changes that time may impose on other parts of the production; and to recall a further example – this time from the past – take the Garland Dance in Act I of *The Sleeping Beauty*: it has known countless developments, but the Rose Adagio goes on forever as a challenge to all aspiring ballerinas.

It must be remembered that, if a choreographer tumbles from the height of a full-length work, he may well crack his skull and have to make a struggling return; if he collapses from the top of a twenty-minute effort he suffers from what is known as a 'feather fracture'; yet I hasten to add that work on a long or short new ballet is infinitely preferable – whatever its fate – to what nowadays appears likely to happen. The most unfortunate group of the nineteenth century full-length works show some danger of being reinstated – suggesting that balletic popularity can suffer from a form of sinister inflation. Time may have lifted, in isolation, a successful *pas de deux* or short *divertissement* (in spite of the accompanying music) from these particular works; thus it appears that even time seems to have been aware of the dangers of the whole.

I think that the full-length ballet of this generation has been as strongly expressed in Britain as anywhere. I speak of the work of Ashton, Cranko and MacMillan, with many ballets of world-wide reputation to their credit. Their collective full-length works, pro-duced in so short a page of history, must amount to twelve or fifteen in number. Strange? It was more likely to be inevitable. In the first half of the thirties the Royal Ballet (then Sadler's Wells Ballet) staged five full-length classics of the nineteenth century. *Casse Noisette* (*The Nutcracker*) in full, had its first European performance. When we first visited the United States of America we were the only company performing a full-length *Sleeping Beauty* and *Swan Lake*. Diaghilev with his foresight announced that 'the classics will return'. This remark was made at the time that he was bankrupted by his ravishing *Sleeping Beauty* production.

I have not as yet dwelt upon MacMillan's first full-length production for the Royal Ballet, *Romeo and Juliet* (1965). It has been seen a great deal abroad and has been given at least two hundred performances in London. It is the writer's opinion that any production of *Romeo and Juliet* owes much to Lavrovsky and Prokoviev. Scenically and choreographically the original may have been surpassed many times, yet all of today's productions bow, intentionally or unintentionally, to the basic craftsmanship and unified development of the original Russian production, wherein was carried the successful nineteenth century developments to be found in the Tchaikowsky-Delibes period. Prokoviev's *Romeo and Juliet* is a yardstick by which composers, choreographers, designers and scenario-writers may well study the *structure* of a full-length ballet for some time to come. There have been, of course, many interesting if diverse readings of this work.

There spring to mind two productions of *Romeo and Juliet*: Frederick Ashton's for the Royal Danish Ballet and Kenneth MacMillan's for the Royal Ballet of Britain. The answer to these productions lies in the approach of Coleridge, writing on the subject of Shakespeare's lovers:

> All is youth and spring – youth with its follies and its virtues, its precipitancies; it is one and the same feeling that commences, goes through and ends the play. . . . The old men, the Capulets and the Montagus, are not common old men; they have an eagerness, a heartiness, a vehemence, the effect of spring; with Romeo his change of passion, his sudden marriage, and his rash death, are all the effects of youth – whilst in Juliet love has all that is tender and melancholy in the nightingale, all that is voluptuous in the rose, and whatever is sweet in the freshness of spring; but it ends with a long deep sigh like the last breeze of the Italian evening. . . .

Has the triumph of MacMillan's *Gloria* opened out still further creative works of such like distinction? *Song of the Earth* is still with us and perhaps the future will produce from him some other great choral work. Is not this the logical development in a theatre that houses both opera and ballet? For what theatre without this combination could embark on such special and demanding productions? MacMillan may possibly look to opera for further inspiration and I suspect that he is not uninterested in the film world. He undoubtedly sees the ballet as a whole; hence the reply that I received after a complaint, on my part, concerning scenario obscurities: 'When I go to the opera I go to listen to the music and study the production; if the libretto is not clear to me I can always read it again at home.' Is he sometimes living out what he logically thinks applies to his own world of ballet, an approach that he feels is not the exclusive property of opera?

Ninette de Valois

Author's Note

It may seem premature to write the biography of a choreographer who is still only in his fifties, still highly prolific and at the height of his powers. But a few years ago, when I had been asked to write an extended article about Kenneth MacMillan, I found that there was little or no background material available. Yet here was a choreographer who, for more than thirty years, had enriched the Royal Ballet's repertoire with many important works, had directed that company for seven years, had directed the Berlin Opera Ballet for three and was generally regarded as one of the most innovative – and controversial – choreographers of this century. Clearly there was a need to chronicle his career to date.

That need became more apparent as soon as I began my research. MacMillan had kept no record of his own works, no diaries, no journals, no press-cutting books; he often found it difficult to remember details of this or that production, the reason for this choice of music, that choice of designer, for he is the sort of artist for whom the present is paramount. He does not dwell on the successes, or failures, of the past.

Time corrodes memory. It is also the constant companion of Shakespeare's 'fell sergeant, death', and one has to face the reality that some of those people who remember MacMillan in his early days are now in advanced years: their personal reminiscences might easily be lost forever. During the writing of this book his first ballet teacher, a most important person in the development of his career, Phyllis Adams, died in Gt. Yarmouth. And death can strike cruelly and unexpectedly. Barry Kay, who designed some of MacMillan's most important and successful works, died suddenly – and prematurely – a few weeks after this book was completed.

I am deeply indebted to a number of people for their help in piecing together details of MacMillan's past. First and foremost I am most grateful to Dame Ninette de Valois, not only for so readily contributing a Foreword to this work, but for being so generous with her time, discussing MacMillan's early days in (what was then) the Sadler's Wells School and the Sadler's Wells Theatre Ballet.

Two years before she died I spent some interesting and entertaining hours with Phyllis Adams, who recalled MacMillan's first approach to her in 1943 and who gave me an illuminating account of his eighteen months with her as a pupil. I remember her with gratitude – and can well understand why MacMillan held her in such esteem and affection.

Nicholas Georgiadis, the first designer with whom MacMillan

collaborated and who has continued to provide magnificent designs for MacMillan ballets ever since, was most helpful in providing information about productions that I never saw, such as the Berlin *Swan Lake*. So was Barry Kay who also provided information concerning works that were produced in Berlin and Stuttgart, as well as absorbing anecdotes about the *soirée MacMillan* given by the Paris Opera Ballet.

Elizabeth Dalton, who has designed MacMillan ballets in Britain and Germany, gave me a graphic description of how he was taken ill in Munich – alarming moments when no other person was present.

Several people have been extremely kind in putting private archive and reference material at my disposal, notably Clement Crisp who was unfailingly helpful – and prompt – in providing articles and reviews from his personal collection. Robert Penman, with great generosity, gave me photocopies of all his own research material gathered for his thesis on MacMillan. William Poole, librarian at the Royal Academy of Dancing, made me welcome on many occasions while giving me access to the R.A.D.'s extensive records.

I am very grateful to Sarah Woodcock and Graham Brandon of the Theatre Museum for their assistance in finding and printing photographs of early MacMillan works.

I made many calls upon the Royal Ballet Press Office and the Sadler's Wells Royal Ballet Press Office: to Janet Judd, Lucy Corbett, Jose Phillips and Sue Merritt my heartfelt thanks for their invaluable help and patient understanding. I must also thank Katharine Wilkinson of the Royal Opera Press Office for digging out obscure information, and Boris Skidelsky and Francesca Franchi of the Royal Opera House Archives for their helpful assistance.

To David Palmer I am indebted for providing private reference material; to Tanya Bruce Lockhart for clarifying details about television programmes; to Norman Frisby of the Granada Television Public Relations Office who was most efficient in supplying dates of rehearsals and transmission and to Joan Riley, picture editor of Granada TV. I am also indebted to Keith Gray, Stage Manager for the Royal Ballet at Covent Garden, who provided incidental details about MacMillan's first venture into the 'straight' theatre and to Philip Gammon, Royal Ballet pianist, who provided the answers to musical questions.

A number of people who have known MacMillan for many years, both personally and professionally, reminisced at length and provided interesting information about his life and career. Among them were Peter Wright, Director of Sadler's Wells Royal Ballet; Peter Williams, Editor of *Dance and Dancers* from its inception in 1950 until

1980; Mary Clarke, Editor of the *Dancing Times*; and Geoffrey Solomons, the friend who was instrumental in MacMillan meeting his wife, Deborah.

I have had illuminating conversations with a number of dancers and ex-dancers who have been closely involved with MacMillan ballets, including (alphabetically): Mikhail Baryshnikov, Bryony Brind, Fiona Chadwick, Lesley Collier, Richard Cragun, Anthony Dowell, Wayne Eagling, Leslie Edwards, Christopher Gable, Marcia Haydée, Maryon Lane, Gerd Larsen, Natalia Makarova, Monica Mason, Merle Park, Galina Samsova, Peter Schaufuss, Lynn Seymour and David Wall. I am grateful to them all. Above all, I am grateful to MacMillan himself, and Deborah, for the patience they have displayed in the face of endless interrogation at inconvenient moments.

Throughout the book I have quoted fairly extensively from the reviews of a number of critics to indicate the general reception given to the most important ballets; sometimes the critics have been more or less unanimous, more often they have been diametrically opposed. For obvious reasons it seemed better to refrain from quoting from my own reviews.

Finally, I have consistently referred to the subject of the biography by his Christian name. When writing of him as a child and a boy it seemed natural to do so; it seemed equally natural to do so when I reached the point where he had embarked on his career. I hope it will help the reader to feel he has become acquainted with the man and the artist.

Edward Thorpe
London, 1985

Childhood: happy and unhappy times

As the train rattled south through the darkness the small boy stared out of the window at the bonfires. Some were quite close to the track, close enough to see, now and then, a fountain of sparks rising into the sky, the glare from the flames illuminating the faces of the bystanders like demons. Other fires were far away, flickering pin-points of light. Sometimes a rocket would flare upwards, tracing a golden arc that culminated in a brief sunburst. It was 1935: the bonfires and the fireworks were celebrating the Silver Jubilee of King George V and Queen Mary and the excitement of the train-ride through the pyrotechnically illuminated night has remained as one of the earliest childhood memories of Kenneth MacMillan who was then in his sixth year. What he did not realise at the time was that the journey that he and his family were making was a 'moonlight flit' from Scotland where his father had become bankrupt after a disastrous attempt at chicken-farming.

*

William MacMillan was a disillusioned man. He had been gassed in the First World War and the horror and stupidity of that conflict and its aftermath – the economic depression, mass unemployment and the farce of the League of Nations – had moved his political convictions far to the left. So much so, in fact, that he had seriously considered emigrating with his family to the Soviet Union. As a Scottish miner he had seen, literally, the blackest side of the workers' struggle for decent living conditions; that, and the respiratory difficulties he suffered as a result of his war service, no doubt motivated the move into chicken-farming. But the need for a clean, healthy, open-air life was not accompanied by the necessary business acumen and financial ruin followed.

Kenneth, the youngest child in the family, remembers little of his early life in Dunfermline in Scotland where he was born on December 11, 1929. He does recall being taken by his mother to his first school: as he watched her through the window, walking away, leaving him in a roomful of unsmiling strangers, he burst into tears and was immediately dubbed a cry-baby by the teacher. Less than a year later he was on his way south.

The MacMillan family left Scotland in two groups: Kenneth travelled with his mother and older brother, George, while his father and elder sisters, Jean and Betty, went by road in the small family car. They were reunited in Gt. Yarmouth where the maternal grandparents lived. The car was subsequently sold for £5.

Fifty years later Kenneth retains equally few memories of the period between his arrival on the bleak Norfolk coast and the outbreak of the Second World War four years later. What he is certain of is that they were a poor family, living in a small Victorian terrace house in the narrow streets near the town market. His father was forced to take a variety of uncongenial jobs before finally settling down as a chef. Kenneth himself lived a solitary life, finding little in common with the rest of his family but feeling closest to his mother and sister Jean who suffered from acute deafness. His own introspective disposition and shy manner seemed to find a bond with the young woman (Jean was fifteen years older than Kenneth) whose contact with everyday life was severely hampered by her disability. A look, a smile, a mimed gesture from her younger brother would often serve as her closest communication with family affairs. His relationship with his brother George was a distant one – mainly through the five-year difference in ages – and Kenneth's strongest memory of filial affection is having to keep a look-out while George seduced his girlfriends under the sea-front jetty.

Actual separation from the family came with the war in 1939. Like thousands of other children, Kenneth was evacuated to a part of the country considered less vulnerable to air attack. The pupils of his junior elementary school were sent to a small village near Melton Mowbray, Leicestershire, but within three weeks – during which the expected air-raids had not materialised – he was writing home threatening suicide if no-one came to fetch him. The letter had the desired effect and in a short time he was once more back in Gt. Yarmouth.

During the first few months of the war organised education was virtually at a standstill, with the regular schools still requisitioned as 'emergency centres' (rumour had it that they were filled with mass-produced coffins), and so Kenneth spent some time taking classes in a private 'school' run by an enterprising woman in the back room of an ice-cream parlour.

Despite interrupted and haphazard tutelage, Kenneth was a bright scholar. After his eleventh birthday he took the scholarship examination for the local grammar school and was successful in gaining a place. This school had been evacuated to Retford in Nottinghamshire, and so once more Kenneth found himself leaving home. This time it was a happier experience; the foster parents he lodged with were a sympathetic couple and Kenneth was as happy with them as he was in his own home environment. His main recreations during this period were amateur theatricals, undertaken with a close school-friend, and going to the cinema. Back in the mid-1930s, as a child of six or seven, he had been taken to see and had been fascinated by the early Fred Astaire-Ginger Rogers musicals – *The Gay Divorce, Roberta, Top Hat.* He spent hours trying to emulate the elegant tap-dancing routines, not without success. Dressed in short trousers with braces over a thin, shirtless torso and with child's sandals on his feet, he danced on the broad window-ledge of a neighbourhood public house, improvising a 'tap' dance that, because of his footwear, was more in the nature of a soft-shoe shuffle. The bar-room regulars readily gave him pennies for his performances. Astutely exploiting his waif-like appearance in the same clothes, he used also to enter a talent show on the sea-front, winning the juvenile section each time. During his schoolboy years in Retford he took some proper tap lessons, paid for from his pocket money, and he went to see every film that came to the local cinema (he remembers that for each visit he had to obtain written permission – an 'exeat' – from his foster-parents), thus consolidating a love-affair with the medium that has lasted all his life.

*

After the 'phoney war' of 1939–40 was over Gt. Yarmouth had been subjected to numerous air-attacks, but evacuees were still sent back there for the school holidays. Arriving home for the Easter vacation in 1941, after a slow and arduous cross-country train journey, Kenneth was met with the traumatic news that his mother had died in the night.

For some time Edith MacMillan had been a sick woman, subject to what were then called 'fits'. Kenneth remembers being aroused at night by her moaning and being admonished not to talk about it; such illnesses, in those days, carried with them a social stigma. Her condition was not, in fact, epileptic but a fatal disorder of the kidneys and so, at the age of eleven, her youngest son was bereft of the parent with whom he had most rapport. With the passing of the years MacMillan senior's disillusion had grown into something more rancorous, and after the death of his wife he became even more withdrawn and remote from his family. For Kenneth, his deaf sister and his foster-parents in Retford were now his closest adult associates.

As the war neared its end in Europe the grammar school returned to Gt. Yarmouth. Kenneth was now fourteen and inevitably his own future was frequently in his mind. An East Anglian fishing port – even in peacetime – is no great stimulus to the imagination when considering careers; most of Kenneth's school colleagues were

3

William MacMillan, Kenneth's
father, was a Scottish miner. After the
First World War, his disastrous
business enterprises led to a
precipitate flight from Dunfermline
to Gt. Yarmouth, where Kenneth
grew up.

Edith MacMillan, Kenneth's mother.
A photograph taken when she was
still a teenage girl about to enter
service. Kenneth was very close to his
mother who died when he was eleven.

Intimations of a theatrical career: a
snapshot of Kenneth aged about
eight.

Early teens: Kenneth's secret
ambition was to become a dancer.

thinking in terms of engineering, accountancy, banking, law and commerce, none of which was remotely appealing to Kenneth. His interest in the theatre had already crystallised into something more specific: dancing.

Making use of the tap lessons he had paid for, he had joined an amateur concert party (the Empire Orpheans) which, during the school holidays, regularly gave performances at United States Air Force bases in Norfolk. Kenneth recalls that his costume was a red tail suit and, in the absence of proper tap shoes, cricket boots with metal tips fixed to the toes and heels. His routine was improvised to 'An American Medley' played by an accompanist on an upright piano, and today Kenneth shudders at the memory, amazed now that he had the confidence to go through with it. But the entertainment seems to have been popular and the strongest recollection is of the big meals – egg-and-bacon suppers and gifts of chocolate – provided by the American hosts.

Kenneth's father disapproved of the theatrical venture – mainly because he often did not return from the remote air force bases until the early hours of the morning. But Kenneth was beginning to form other plans. Long hours spent in the reading rooms of public libraries had brought to his notice a magazine called the *Dancing Times*. Devouring every page of every issue, he had become aware that tap dancing was not the only form of dance that drew audiences; there was something called ballet, too, something that, from the photographs he saw, seemed to offer an even wider means of dramatic expression. From the articles and advertisements it was apparent that ballet offered a potential career for a young man, however arcane and esoteric it might seem to his family and school-teachers. But whatever anyone might say, whatever astonishment and ridicule they might express, whatever dissuasion they might attempt, Kenneth now knew, *knew* with a conviction that was as strong as any religious revelation, that he was going to be a professional ballet dancer. And that secret knowledge gave him the courage to take the next momentous step.

2

Student of the ballet

For nearly an hour Kenneth rode his bicycle up and down in front of the impressive Edwardian mock-Tudor house facing the Gt. Yarmouth seafront. Finally summoning his courage, he propped his machine against the kerb, opened the gate, walked up the front path bordered by carefully kept lawns and neat flower beds and rang the front door bell. The door was opened by a small, pleasant-looking woman who smiled at him.

'I want to be a ballet dancer,' Kenneth said.

'Then you'd better come in,' the woman answered, ushering him into the front hall.

'I want to get a scholarship to the Sadler's Wells Ballet School,' Kenneth continued, at once. He did not want anyone to think his ambition stopped at Gt. Yarmouth.

'Well, first we'll have to find out if you're good enough, won't we?' said the woman with practical common-sense.

Her name was Phyllis Adams and she had established her school in Gt. Yarmouth after completing her own classical ballet training in London during the late 1920s. Her teachers at Flora M. Fairbairn's Mayfair School of Dancing had been Anna Pruzina and Laurent Novikov, while Tamara Karsavina and Stanislas Idzikowsky were also occasional visitors so that her own training had been directly influenced by both the Kirov and Bolshoi pedagogy.

Nearly all Miss Adams's pupils had been evacuated during the war and her school was closed. Kenneth had heard of it after making extensive enquiries about the possibility of local ballet tuition. Their first meeting established that Kenneth had natural ability as a dancer, and this was the beginning of a deep friendship which was to last until Miss Adams's death in the early 1980s.

Kenneth had nothing with which to pay for his ballet classes except his very limited pocket money but Miss Adams was so impressed – indeed, excited – by a young male wanting to become a classical dancer without ever having seen a ballet that she gladly taught him without charge. He had, she said, an immediate and instinctive grasp of technique and had only to be shown once to understand the movement or step. There was no music and for an exercise *barre* he held on to the central drawer of a large, curious piece of oak furniture, part dresser, part book-case, part chest-of-drawers.

Kenneth's regular visits to Miss Adams were the happiest hours of his weekly routine. Rapidly, the visits extended in number and duration until he was virtually an adopted member of the household. (Miss Adams's married name was Roche and she had four children, three girls and a boy: Wendy, Merry, Andrea and Martin – all younger than Kenneth although Wendy often took class with him.) Indeed, it is no exaggeration to say that Miss Adams, as well as teaching Kenneth and encouraging him in his ambition, also became something of a surrogate mother to the lonely boy, for by this time Kenneth's brother George was in the army and his sisters were at work all day.

Despite the problems of rationing, Kenneth often shared family meals with the Adams family whose friendship did much to break through his natural reserve. To this day Wendy recalls Kenneth's physical exuberance, released by his ballet classes, finding an outlet in performing *grandes jetés* down the street on his way home.

No-one in Kenneth's family seemed to appreciate that these 'dancing classes' were actually concerned with classical ballet, far less that he was determined on a professional career as a dancer. For fear of ridicule, he also took great care not to let any of his school colleagues know the nature of his dance lessons or his plans for the future. His rapid progress produced a concomitant impatience to attain his ambition of getting into the Sadler's Wells School, and when he read in the *Dancing Times* an announcement about forthcoming auditions he precipitated the situation by forging a letter of application from his father.

Addressing the letter to the Principal of the School (Ninette de Valois as she was then) he wrote: *Dear Madam, My son, who is nearly fifteen, wants to be a ballet dancer and many people think he is very talented*, and signed the letter in his father's name. Whether or not the forgery actually deceived anyone it is difficult to say (the handwriting was distinctly youthful) but at any rate an audition was granted.

*

After a slow and tedious early morning journey by 'milk train' from Norwich Kenneth, accompanied by his sister Betty, arrived in time at the New Theatre (now the Albery) but was late for class having lost his way trying to find the room used as a rehearsal studio. Kenneth still remembers his acute embarrassment and anxiety when de Valois commented on his lateness. He was placed at the *barre* between Margot Fonteyn and Beryl Grey and finding himself situated next to these two renowned dancers made him even more nervous. His natural ability, however, impressed de Valois and her subsequent letter to Phyllis Adams, provisionally accepting him for the Sadler's Wells School, is worth quoting in full:

Dear Miss Roche (sic)   8th January 1945

Re. Kenneth MacMillan

I gave your pupil an audition the other day and was extremely impressed with the boy from every angle. He was well-grown, well-made, has a good presence and is obviously intelligent.

What he has managed to do in one year nine months is quite extraordinary. I think his parents would be very wrong to stop him taking it up. I have to go to France with the company for the next eight weeks and would suggest that we hold over the matter of his Scholarship, maintainance etc. until the Summer Term which would start somewhere about May.

I would most definitely like to take him on, but it is almost impossible for me to arrange, at such short notice, matters with his parents, also, London is pretty 'lively' at the moment at nights. [A reference to V-bombs; official censorship forbade any direct mention of the situation.] I do not feel he has anything to lose by waiting another eight weeks or so.

For your information the maintainance grant is given when the parents have submitted to some form of 'Means Test'. Actually, the tuition would be free anyway, it is only the question of his board and lodging in London. You have my permission to show this letter to his parents, and I thank you for bringing to my notice such a talented youngster.

Yours Sincerely
Ninette de Valois

This letter was Kenneth's passport to his chosen profession. His father agreed – reluctantly – to Kenneth's going to London and attending the Sadler's Wells School. At school the Headmaster made an announcement during morning assembly about Kenneth being awarded a scholarship and far from being ridiculed he was held in some awe by his classmates.

*

The weeks of waiting before Kenneth could take up his scholarship seemed to him the most tedious of his life but in the late spring of 1945 he was finally back in London, boarding in a large Victorian villa in Hornsey Lane, in north London, which was run as a student lodging house by the mother of one of Kenneth's colleagues, Michael Boulton. From nearby Highgate underground station the Northern Line took them direct to the Angel, Islington, close to Sadler's Wells Theatre where classes were held.

The tuition was very different from the intimate family atmosphere of Miss Adams's kitchen but Kenneth was more than happy to accept the formal disciplines of the school, finding great personal satisfaction in the daily challenge of the training, filled with ambition for the future, happily forming new friendships, excited by life in the capital and in particular by the artistic activities it offered. Within a few weeks of his arrival in London the whole country was celebrating Victory in Europe and together with thousands of others Kenneth celebrated V.E. day in the West End, swept along by the delirious, drunken, singing, dancing crowds; the euphoric mood seemed to augur a bright future for everyone.

Looking back, Kenneth now thinks of that year in the Sadler's Wells Ballet School as one of the happiest times of his life. He worked hard at his technique under the tuition of Ninette de Valois herself and Vera Volkova, received regular scholastic teaching – which bored him – and spent most of his evening watching the Sadler's Wells Ballet from the stage wings of the New Theatre. The first ballet programme he ever saw was Frederick Ashton's *Facade* followed by *Giselle* with Beryl Grey and Alexis Rassine in the leading roles. Despite his excitement, it seemed as familiar as if he had been watching ballet performances all his young life.

Each night four students were allowed to watch from the wings; competition for these privileged places, dispensed on a first come, first-served basis, was fierce and Kenneth found himself getting to the theatre earlier and earlier each day, waiting patiently from 3.30 in the afternoon until the performance began at 7.15. There were very few programmes that he missed; if he did, it was because of the continuing attraction of the cinema. He rarely went to the theatre: for one thing it was (relatively) expensive and for another 'live' theatre for him meant ballet.

During this period, plans were well advanced for the Royal Opera House, Covent Garden, to be reopened (during the war it had served as a dance hall) as a permanent home for the Sadler's Wells Ballet. Kenneth remembers standing in the empty auditorium, thrilled by the seeming vastness of the stage, then being reconstructed. The opening night of February 2, 1946, with Margot Fonteyn and Robert Helpmann in a splendid new production of *The Sleeping Beauty*, is now well-documented history. But there was no room for the Sadler's Wells Ballet school students at the opening performance; they had to wait until the second night which, although it may not have had quite the same sparkle and splendour, Kenneth recalls as an occasion of tremendous excitement. As he watched the dancers of the company performing Petipa's masterpiece, his greatest aspiration, then, was to become one of them.

Later that same year the Sadler's Wells Theatre was reopened as a permanent home for the Sadler's Wells Opera Company for which de Valois had been asked to provide a troupe of dancers who were known, initially, as the Sadler's Wells Opera Ballet. As well as

9

performing in the operas, the dancers were to give occasional ballet performances (just as the original company had done for Lilian Baylis back in 1931) but it soon became apparent that the company could operate as a touring section of the main company, giving performances in regional theatres which were too small to accept the big productions designed for Covent Garden. The company's name was changed to Sadler's Wells Theatre Ballet and with a specially arranged repertoire of works mainly by Frederick Ashton, de Valois and Andrée Howard it soon began to earn itself a considerable reputation.

At the end of the summer term in 1946 Kenneth was one of several young students who auditioned for the newly-formed company and were accepted. Kenneth was elated. At last his ambition had been realised: he was a professional ballet dancer. Not yet at Covent Garden, of course, but still within the organisation of Britain's foremost ballet company and he felt it could only be a matter of time before he appeared at the Royal Opera House. Meanwhile, he still had to work hard at his technique; he remembers that when he was accepted into the company he could not execute a double *tour en l'air*. With Anne Heaton, Donald Britton, Sheila Nelson and Greta Hamby, he had a celebratory 'brunch' at Lyon's tea-shop on the corner of the Angel, Islington. Food rationing was still in operation and the meal was necessarily frugal but for all those eager young dancers setting out on their careers it was an occasion to remember.

3

Ambition achieved: first performances

The first public performance that Kenneth gave was in the dances accompanying the Sadler's Wells Opera production of Smetana's *The Bartered Bride*. At the same time rehearsals were going forward for the first all-ballet programme to be given by the newly-formed Sadler's Wells Theatre Ballet.

During this hectic and exciting period Kenneth received news from home that his father was seriously ill. During the brief weekends when he was not rehearsing Kenneth made the tedious rail journey back to Gt. Yarmouth to give what support he could to his sisters. Back in London, as the first night approached, he received a telegram saying that his father was dying from pneumonia. He hurried back to Norfolk again and reached home just before his father died; then he rushed back to London to make his balletic debut in a triple bill that consisted of *Promenade* by de Valois, *Assembly Ball* by Andrée Howard and the second act of *Casse Noisette* (*The Nutcracker*) as it was then called. Although Kenneth had never felt really close to his father the loss of his second parent naturally cast a veil of depression over his success at finally becoming a ballet dancer.

At that time, of course, Kenneth was just a member of the *corps de ballet* and much concerned with improving his technique. He found most difficulty with partnering; being tall himself he was frequently given tall – and heavy – girls to partner. As a solo dancer he was developing a fine classical line and finish with good turn-out and a well-stretched foot – all attributes that please the purists. He also possessed a strong stage presence that attracted critical attention even among a company that was loaded with talented young artists.

The first recorded major role that Kenneth danced was Floristan in the company's production of Michel Fokine's *Carnaval* in May 1947. [Later he also danced the role of Eusebius.] He was soon performing other solo roles in the regular repertoire as well as in new works such as Ashton's *Valses Nobles et Sentimentales* in October 1947 and Anthony Burke's *Parures* in January 1948.

In the routine of daily classes, rehearsals and performances, in the excitement of new London seasons and in the frenetic day-to-day life on tour in the provinces, friendships were formed and relationships developed that later matured into artistic collaboration and achievement. In those early days of the company's existence Kenneth's closest colleagues were Margaret Hill, Maryon Lane, David Poole and – perhaps most important of all in the subsequent development of his career – John Cranko.

Cranko had come to London from Capetown, South Africa, where he had studied as a dancer and also done some choreography. For a short period he attended the Sadler's Wells Ballet school and then joined the Sadler's Wells Theatre Ballet. Almost immediately he began choreographing and one of his earliest works was *Children's Corner*, a light-hearted ballet to music by Debussy. The ballet was first produced for a Royal Academy of Dancing workshop performance and almost immediately taken into the Sadler's Wells Theatre Ballet repertoire and given its first performance on April 6, 1948. Although slight, the work was well received – one critic wrote of its 'musicality and gay humour' – and in it Patricia Miller and Kenneth danced a character duet as 'Mlle. Piquant and her Great Admirer' which was the first role that Kenneth ever created.

The carefully tailored repertoire of the Sadler's Wells Theatre

Kenneth established a reputation as an outstanding classical dancer as well as an artist with a strong stage presence.

Above left: Partnering Yvonne Barnes in Frederick Ashton's *Valses Nobles et Sentimentales* (a score that Kenneth was to use himself nineteen years later) created for what was then Sadler's Wells Theatre Ballet.

Above: Partnering Stella Claire in Fokine's neo-Romantic classic *Les Sylphides. (Ian Gibson-Smith.)*

Left: With Patricia Miller in John Cranko's *Children's Corner. (Gibson-Smith.)*

Opposite: This photograph reveals Kenneth's impeccable classical line and beautifully stretched feet as Prince Florestan in the famous production of *The Sleeping Beauty* designed by Oliver Messel for the Sadler's Wells Ballet at Covent Garden. *(Hans Wild.)*

Ballet and the exhuberance, vitality and youthful spirit of the company soon brought it great popularity, not only in the provinces but also among discerning London audiences. It must be remembered that, by 1948, the capital had not only been graced by regular seasons by the two Sadler's Wells companies at the Royal Opera House and Sadler's Wells Theatre, but had also received visits from Colonel de Basil's Original Ballet Russe, (American) Ballet Theatre [the prefix 'American' was added to the company's title in 1957] and Les Ballets de Champs Elysées. These companies stimulated audiences with new productions and new standards of dancing and also influenced British dancers, designers and choreographers – Kenneth among them. Sadler's Wells Theatre Ballet accordingly played its part in a national upsurge of interest in ballet that had begun when the Sadler's Wells Ballet had undertaken extensive tours during the war years.

As the young dancers of the Sadler's Wells Theatre Ballet progressed in technique and experience, so several of them were promoted to the 'senior' company at the Royal Opera House. Among them was Kenneth whose transfer was effected in the autumn of 1948. It was another major step in his career: at last he was dancing on that famous stage. All the time he continued to learn – not just the balletic technique and dramatic expression needed for the roles he was given but also in the much more complex elements involved in creating a ballet; structure, the integration of choreographic patterns with musical development, the use of space, the delineation of character and so on.

One of the first ballets in which Kenneth remembers assimilating all these points and consciously learning from them was Ashton's *Scènes de Ballet* which had received its premiere earlier that year. A plotless work that is nevertheless a homage to the classical style developed in Imperial Russia by Marius Petipa, it is danced to a typically difficult, rhythmically elaborate score by Stravinsky. Ashton has said that the ballet's composition was based on geometric theorems and its highly complex choreographic structure is a masterful interpretation of the music. It also presents a considerable technical challenge to all the dancers (a principle couple, four male soloists and a *corps de ballet* of twelve women) not least to the men who, in 1948, were faced with virtuoso demands at least as difficult as any of the major classics then in the repertoire.

On December 23, 1948, Ashton's first full-length ballet, *Cinderella*, received its premiere. Ashton himself and Robert Helpmann danced the roles of the Ugly Sisters – a brilliantly funny duo *en travesti* – and Kenneth understudied the Helpmann part and subsequently played it at several performances with success. By then he was also dancing

14

other solo roles in the repertoire and his excellent classical technique brought him acclaim. He performed the Bluebird *pas de deux* with Rowena Jackson (surely one of the tallest pairs ever to perform this famous virtuoso duet) and hated it. In the solo male role in *Les Sylphides* he partnered Beryl Grey – another tall ballerina – but broke a rib partnering Pauline Claydon who was one of the lightest dancers in the company. Yet his greatest success as a classical dancer was as Florestan in *The Sleeping Beauty*. He danced the role when the company gave its memorable first performance in New York on October 9, 1949, but on that night the applause throughout the evening was so great that when the conductor, Constant Lambert, began the coda to Kenneth's solo Kenneth could not hear the music and missed his entrance altogether.

Although the arduous flight from London to New York [via Reykjavik in Iceland and Gander in Newfoundland by propeller-driven Boeing Stratocruiser] initiated Kenneth's intense dislike of flying, that season in the city and the subsequent long transcontinental tour confirmed in him the fascination with the United States of America that had begun in childhood with American feature films and has continued to this day. The brilliance and excitement of that first night in Manhattan has remained with Kenneth as a series of vivid but disconnected scenes. Following the glittering reception given for the company by Mayor O'Dwyer at his official mansion Kenneth remembers dancing down Broadway in the company of John Cranko and Alfred Rodrigues and then, somehow, attending another party with Alexandra Danilova.

Back in Britain, new works began to enter the Sadler's Wells Ballet repertoire fairly regularly and Kenneth not only danced a variety of roles [during 1948–49 he also made guest appearances with the Sadler's Wells Theatre Ballet] but continued to absorb the techniques of creating ballets by working with and watching several distinguished choreographers. In April 1950 George Balanchine produced his *Ballet Imperial* for the company and Kenneth made a notable debut in one of the casts, dancing the *pas de trois* with Beryl Grey and John Field. In May 1950 he was in the cast of Roland Petit's *Ballabile*; in April 1951 he was in Ashton's *Daphnis and Chloe*; in July 1951 he was in Ashton's *Tiresias*; in December 1951 he was in Léonid Massine's *Donald of the Burthens*.

But at each of Kenneth's performances something began to manifest itself more and more frequently, more and more intensely. Dancers often develop physical weaknesses through the fierce bodily disciplines to which they are constantly subjected – weaknesses that are apt to recur and hold up their progress. Kenneth was now subject to something far more distressing than a torn muscle or a fractured foot, something that was about to create a terrible personal crisis: stage-fright.

As with agoraphobia, or claustrophobia or vertigo, it is difficult to convey to those who have not suffered it just what a nervous strain stage-fright imposes on the system. When it affects one's profession then it becomes far more than an inconvenience – an avoidance of lifts or subway trains or department stores – and strikes at the very basis of life. With Kenneth, each performance became more and more of an ordeal until merely contemplating his entrance created in him a state of unbearable tension verging on terror. His stage-fright had reached the point where he was considering giving up the work he loved and which he had striven with such single-minded determination to achieve. In practical terms it had become so serious that although he had rehearsed Andrée Howard's *A Mirror for Witches* (an ironic title considering the spell which had fallen upon him) he was too stricken with his mental malady to dance on the opening night.

In despair Kenneth went to de Valois with his problem and, typically, she proposed a solution which led, indirectly, to the most important development in his career.

4

Stage fright and a new beginning

Ninette de Valois suggested that Kenneth should take three months off from dancing. During this rest period from the pressures of performance she thought that he might well overcome the nervous tension that had already kept him from several scheduled appearances. In any case the winter season was half over; within a few weeks the company would be taking its annual holiday and the following autumn would be time enough for conclusive decisions. De Valois also thought that Kenneth might be happier if he rejoined the Sadler's Wells Theatre Ballet. Apart from a more intimate, convivial company atmosphere – engendered by the exigencies of touring together as opposed to the dispersal of the dancers at the Royal Opera House – there would be more opportunities to dance new roles in the repertoire of the touring company.

Kenneth agreed – and then found himself with time on his hands which is very pleasant if there is plenty of money to spend. But dancers – even soloists – have always been poorly paid and Kenreth's salary did not allow him to take much advantage of his 'holiday'. Besides, almost all his friends were busy within the company so he was rather lonely, too. He read a great deal, paid visits to art galleries and museums, went to the theatre and cinema occasionally, when he could afford it, and watched a lot of ballet performances. Then something happened that was to act as a catalyst – albeit with a delayed action – on his career.

During the company holidays John Cranko had arranged to go down to Henley-on-Thames to present a short season of ballets of his own devising. The small Kenton Theatre there had been booked by the artist John Piper and his wife Mifanwy who were living locally and had agreed to be responsible for the decors. Cranko had recruited a number of dancers from the Sadler's Wells Theatre Ballet, Ballet Rambert and London Festival Ballet and he approached Kenneth with an invitation to join them. Kenneth was interested, even excited. The possibility of his being struck with stage-fright seemed remote: dancing with a small group of friends in a tiny provincial theatre was far removed from the responsibility of appearing at the Royal Opera House as a member of Britain's foremost ballet company. Not that there was anything amateur about the Henley season – all the participants were highly pro-fessional – but Kenneth recalls that the venture possessed a feeling something similar to the youthful enthusiasm created in those Judy Garland-Mickey Rooney 'let's put on a show' films. Before he could accept Cranko's invitation, however, he had to obtain de Valois's permission, which was readily given.

The season, within its limited compass, was a success. Cranko produced several of his small-scale works, including *Tritsch-Tratsch*, *The Forgotten Room* and a scaled-down version of *Pineaple Poll* which had had such a triumph when it was first produced for the Sadler's Wells Theatre Ballet in 1951. There was also a work entitled, simply, *Dancing*, to swing music by George Shearing. It was a plotless ballet in which Kenneth had the leading role which was not only rewarding in itself but interested Kenneth because he saw how Cranko went about choreographing for dancers with whose style and technique he was familiar. The score attracted a young man in the audience who was a jazz fanatic; he became a friend of the company and introduced Kenneth to his huge collection of records. In fact, the whole season seemed to have had a therapeutic effect on Kenneth: he had found new confidence as a dancer as well as a personal satisfaction in performing in several of Cranko's works which had also further consolidated their friendship.

*

As part of the process of recovering from a serious bout of stage-fright at the Royal Opera House, Kenneth danced with a small ad hoc group, formed by John Cranko, which gave a season in the tiny Kenton Theatre, Henley-on-Thames, with decors by John Piper. This rare photograph shows Kenneth with Sonya Hana (who later married Peter Wright, Director of Sadler's Wells Royal Ballet) in Cranko's work, *Dancing*, to a jazz score by George Shearing.

Kenneth looked forward to rejoining his old company but before he did so something happened that might well have destroyed not only his future as a dancer and choreographer but even his life. Driving through the Midlands en route to the Edinburgh Festival at which the company was to begin its autumn season, Kenneth, Margaret Hill, Pirmin Trecu and Cranko (who was at the wheel) were involved in a terrifying crash. Failing to negotiate a sharp bend which followed immediately after a hump-backed bridge, the car rolled over three times before landing on its roof. Although the car was smashed to pieces, miraculously none of the occupants was seriously hurt although they had to be extricated from the wreckage by an A.A. patrolman.

Within a few months of Kenneth's return to the company he had had his first major leading role created for him, the eponymous part of Sherlock Holmes in Margaret Dale's comedy ballet *The Great Detective* which had its first performance at Sadler's Wells Theatre on January 21, 1953. The ballet itself received unenthusiastic reviews but Kenneth gained good notices from several critics for his portrayal of Sir Arthur Conan Doyle's famous hero. Gratifying as this was, he had a much greater reward from an occasion that followed a mere eleven days later.

The Sadler's Wells Theatre Ballet was, at that time, bursting with a creative spirit trying to find an outlet. David Poole, one of the company's principal dancers and a close friend of Kenneth, proposed to him that they should form a choreographic group to present workshop performances that would serve as a proving ground for the embryo talent within the company. With his successful participation in the Cranko season at Henley as a stimulus, Kenneth agreed to co-operate; although he felt he was not yet ready to tackle choreography himself, he was happy to assist his friend in the hard organisational work that the venture would entail. De Valois, always ready to encourage new talent, gave her assent to occasional Sunday performances at the Sadler's Wells Theatre, and the first programme was arranged for February 1, 1953. (Rehearsals for Margaret Dale's new ballet, as well as for the regular repertoire had, of course, been proceeding simultaneously.) A week before the workshop performance one of the choreographers dropped out through illness. In desperation Poole appealed to Kenneth to fill the gap and, with many misgivings, he agreed. Both of them were anxious that the workshop should be of a sufficiently high standard to justify the expense of the experiment, but the time available to create and rehearse something worthy of the project seemed to Kenneth to present him with an insuperable problem.

Looking back today, Kenneth cannot remember exactly how he

came upon the idea of a work based on dreams and their effect on the psyche. He feels that he may have been thinking that one day (when he could afford it!) he might undergo psychoanalysis; certainly the unhappy experience of stage-fright, of how the imagination, subject to anxiety, can affect the body and its movements, must have been in the forefront of his mind. In retrospect it seems significant that, even then, with his very first attempt at choreography – and that produced under pressure – he chose to express a definite thematic idea rather than the simpler expedient of devising a plotless work of pure dance. It was a pointer in the direction that the greater part of his work would take, with the emphasis on using ballet as a means of dramatic expression.

The theme of his first work, then, was the effect of dreams on human behaviour. There were three solo dancers (David Poole, Maryon Lane and Margaret Hill) who, at the beginning of the ballet, were discovered asleep within a simple set that consisted of a rostrum and a small flight of steps. Each dancer had a variation depicting three states of mind induced by the dreams: Anxiety, Monotony and Premonition. As music Kenneth chose a 'symphonic jazz' score by Stan Kenton – a direct result of his introduction to this form of music during the Henley season – and he called the ballet *Somnambulism*.

Kenneth and the three soloists worked feverishly to complete the work in time. Maryon Lane, who was dancing Premonition, recalls that rehearsals took place at Sadler's Wells Theatre in a room cluttered with large skips and wardrobe baskets so that the effective floor space was only about eight square feet. Even so, she says, Kenneth seemed absolutely sure of what he wanted and what the theatrical effect would be; each movement that he invented had a clear motivation behind it and developed in direct relation to the music.

On the day of the performance there was another potentially disastrous situation: Margaret Hill was sick and unable to go on. At such short notice the only alternative was for Kenneth himself to replace Margaret Hill whose solo represented Anxiety. This, in itself, presented a problem in that the dance had, of course, been devised for a woman and the choreography was, therefore, considerably different from what he would have created for a man. [When the ballet went into the company's repertoire three years later at least one critic seemed puzzled as to why the role had been given to a woman.] In the event Kenneth improvised the dance – and his own anxiety must have aided his interpretation of the theme!

To Kenneth's utter surprise *Somnambulism* was the great success of the evening. The audience were vociferously enthusiastic – 'the first time in my life I had ever been cheered,' he says – and back-stage

Margot Fonteyn congratulated him on his triumph. Kenneth felt not only an enormous sense of elation but also of *revelation*: he had finally discovered his real vocation. And for once the critics were in agreement that a new choreographer had emerged, fully armed, from the temple of Terpsichore.

5

Last performances: dancer into choreographer

Although Kenneth's success with *Somnambulism* had convinced him that he had a real talent for choreography which had opened up a whole new dimension of his art, he still continued to dance as a soloist with the company. His roles in the repertoire included Siegfried in *Swan Lake* Act II; the principal man in Ashton's *Les Rendezvous*; Damon in Cranko's *Pastorale*; Captain Belaye in Cranko's *Pineapple Poll* and the Fencing Master in de Valois's *The Rake's Progress*.

In June, 1953, Alfred Rodrigues's second ballet for the company, *Blood Wedding*, was given its first performance. A melodramatic story based on a play by the Spanish poet Federico García Lorca, the synopsis stated: 'The Moon, condemned to eternal coldness, longs for blood to warm his heart. Death seeks to aid him by bringing two former lovers together on the eve of the girl's wedding.' The ballet was a great success and its strong dramatic theme of jealousy and murder made it a useful work as the centre piece in a triple bill. It is never easy to make a theatrical impact with purely symbolic roles but Kenneth's chilling portrayal of the Moon, making effective use of his strong stage presence, brought him further excellent notices from the critics.

Just over a week after the premiere of *Blood Wedding* the Choreographic Group gave its second programme. Kenneth was naturally anxious to follow up the success of *Somnambulism* with something of equal importance but so much of his time had been taken up with rehearsals of Rodrigues's ballet that his proposal to use George Gershwin's Piano Concerto in F had to be abandoned as too ambitious in the time available. In fact, time was so short that he had to settle for a *pas de trois* arranged for Sara Neil, Annette Page and Donald Britton. Once more – mainly for expediency – he used jazz music by Stan Kenton. He called the work *Fragment*. Despite its brevity it reinforced critical opinion about his choreographic talent. In particular the reviewers remarked on how he had provided Donald Britton with solo material that showed his technical abilities to advantage.

During the summer holidays Kenneth began to consider what he should do for the next Choreographic Group programme which was scheduled for January of the following year. There seemed, then, plenty of time to produce something on a larger scale but, with the holidays over, his work as a company soloist continued to be as demanding as ever.

At the Edinburgh Festival in September Walter Gore produced a new ballet, *Carte Blanche*, based upon circus characters and Kenneth was in one of the successive casts, dancing a divertissement called *Romanza*. At about the same time his idea for a Choreographic Group work began to crystallise. It concerned a troupe of travelling pierrots among whom is a young girl abandoned on the steps of a grand house where she is caught up in the gaiety of a masked party; the host falls in love with her but when, at the unmasking, she is revealed as bald she is rejected and left to take up her life as a sad little clown. The ballet, *Laiderette*, took its title from this character. The theme of rejection, with its central figure something of a social outcast, was one that would often recur throughout Kenneth's subsequent career. It does not need any great deductive powers to see that his own somewhat lonely formative years were – consciously or not – the empathetic thread upon which he would string this succession of characters.

The context of the story, a group of itinerent clowns, is one which has provided many choreographic themes – indeed, the street entertainers of the *Commedia dell'arte* were one of the foundations of theatrical dance in Western Europe – so it is probably coincidence that Kenneth had not only just completed Gore's *Carte Blanche* but was currently engaged in rehearsing yet another ballet with clown characters, this time Cranko's *The Lady and the Fool*. In this work a grand society lady (La Capricciosa) rejects her elegant suitors (at another ball) in preference for one of two street clowns (Moondog and Bootface); all three find happiness in a nomadic *ménage à trois*.

Cranko's approach to his theme was typically more romantic – not to say sentimental – than Kenneth's (if *he* had devised the scenario for *The Lady and the Fool* we can be sure there would not have been such a happy ending). At any rate, the role of Moondog, the taller and more dominant clown, provided Kenneth with what was probably his best created role. There was a comic, but touching, acrobatic duet for Moondog and Bootface (Johaar Mosavaal) in which they squabbled over possession of a rose, and a long, romantic *pas de deux*

23

for Moondog and La Capricciosa (Patricia Miller) which displayed both dancers' classical capabilities. The ballet had a great popular success and was later produced for the company at the Royal Opera House; in recent years it has been revived for what is now Sadler's Wells Royal Ballet.

Shortly after the premiere of Cranko's ballet, *Laiderette* was performed by the Choreographic Group on January 24, 1954, with Maryon Lane in the title role, David Poole as the Host and Johaar Mosavaal as the Mask Seller. After the performance of *Fragment* at the previous Choreographic Group evening de Valois had said to Kenneth that it was about time he stopped using jazz scores and so, at the suggestion of David Poole, he chose for his new work the Petite Symphonie Concertante for harpsichord, harp, piano and orchestra by the Swiss composer Frank Martin. The somewhat rudimentary set was made up from the façade of a house with a balcony used for one of the Sadler's Wells Opera productions. Once again Kenneth's ballet was the big success of the evening and received great acclaim – 'here was a work of near-genius,' wrote one critic and another referred to Kenneth as 'a choreographer of major dimensions'. Such extravagant praise for a workshop production is an indication of the immense impact the choreography had on a sophisticated audience. *Laiderette* proved that *Somnambulism* was no fluke but the work of a young choreographer endowed with great natural talent already disciplined and refined by an intellectual apprehension of his art.

Laiderette was such a success that de Valois immediately wanted to take it into the Sadler's Wells Theatre Ballet repertoire but the inclusion of a harpsichord in the score proved a stumbling block: it was impractical for the orchestra to take such an instrument on tour and so the idea of giving the ballet a proper production had to be abandoned. Kenneth's acute disappointment was softened somewhat by a B.B.C. proposal to televise *Somnambulism*. The Sadler's Wells Theatre Ballet was about to embark on an eight week tour of the provinces after which it was to undertake its first visit to South Africa but, despite the tight schedule, Kenneth managed to cram in his stage performances on tour with a close involvement with the B.B.C. venture.

The television version of *Somnambulism* was retitled *The Dreamers* and although it retained something of its original simplicity of setting the production itself was much more elaborate than the necessarily improvisatory presentation that it had received by the Choreographic Group. Kenneth was able to supervise the choreography without having to dance himself – although he retained the three leading roles for two men and a girl rather than his first intention of two girls and a man. The dancers were Pirmin Trecu in the first sequence,

Above: An early B.B.C. television performance of the third act of *The Sleeping Beauty* with principal dancers of the Sadler's Wells Ballet. From left to right: Anne Negus, Beryl Grey, Kenneth MacMillan, John Field (seated), Gerd Larsen, Rowena Jackson and Alexis Rassine. (*Paul Wilson*.)

Right: A study of the young dancer.

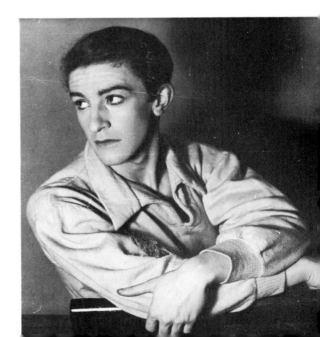

Lament; Maryon Lane in *Abstraction* and David Poole in *Monotony*. The large B.B.C. studio allowed the designer, Michael Yates, to create the impression of a vast, shadowy hall atmospherically suitable to a 'dream' interior, and the jazz score was played by Ted Heath and his orchestra whose 'big band' sound was then very popular. The theme of nightmarish dreams was ideal for the television medium and the production, by Naomi Capon, achieved a strong effect on the small screen, receiving enthusiastic reviews in the specialist dance magazines and in the general press. Kenneth's name had now reached a wide audience.

*

Eight days after the television transmission of *Somnambulism* the company departed for South Africa. They travelled by ship and the two-week voyage, during which they were blessed with calm weather and sunshine, was a welcome holiday. Daily class was held every morning on the sun deck after which the dancers were free to enjoy the leisurely ship-board life. They carried off all the prizes at the fancy dress dance and gave an impromptu cabaret for the other passengers. Kenneth also took part in a short amateur film made by David Gill (who has since achieved a distinguished career in film-making) in which he was a thief stealing jewels from a passenger's cabin. In Cape Town the company enjoyed a civic welcome and then flew directly to Johannesburg. On stepping off the plane Kenneth was stung on the eyelid by some hostile insect but despite a bad swelling he was able to dance on the opening night, performing the male role in *Les Sylphides* and partnering Annette Page.

During the seven-week season in Johannesburg Kenneth created what was to be his last role as a dancer in *Café des Sport*, a new ballet by Alfred Rodrigues who was a native South African. The comic scenario was built around the theme of a bicycle race passing through a small French Mediterranean port. Among the characters frequenting the café of the title were two opposing groups of artists, the Hedonists and the Essentialists, but Kenneth, who was the leader of the latter group, does not recall the role with any great pleasure although the ballet itself was briefly popular.

The Sadler's Wells Theatre Ballet's South African visit was an unqualified success with full houses every night; the critics, too, were magnanimous in their praise and Kenneth was among the male soloists particularly commended for the strength of their dancing. The company enjoyed another fortnight's 'holiday' during the voyage home but on reaching London the euphoric mood was quickly shattered by a dispute between the Sadler's Wells Theatre Ballet management and Equity over dancers' pay (many dancers, even after two years in the company, were still receiving the minimum rate of £7 per week which, even in the mid-1950s, was very little) and the autumn season at Sadler's Wells Theatre was cancelled. [The dancers reduced their original demand for a £2 increase to £1.10s.]

During the weeks that followed, when the dancers received no salary at all, Kenneth was desperately broke. At that time he was living in the Bayswater home of Margaret Hill's mother and he remembers how Margaret Hill and he used to go into Hyde Park and collect empty Coca-Cola and lemonade bottles for the few pennies they were worth on return to an off-licence. When the dispute was over, however, he was promoted from soloist to principal.

Additional good fortune attended Kenneth when the B.B.C., following the success of *The Dreamers*, approached him to provide the choreography for a three-part series specially designed for childrens' viewing. Eventually called *Punch and the Child* the programmes demonstrated how highly-stylised ballet steps grew from everyday movement. (Not wholly true!) The series was also intended to instruct its young audience how ballet dancers trained to develop their bodies to respond to the severe demands made by the classical style – the *danse d'école*. The first programme was transmitted on November 29, 1954, beginning with a practise demonstration by two dancers, Maureen Bruce and Donald Britton, with Peggy van Praagh (at that time Assistant Director of the Sadler's Wells Theatre Ballet) as compere. Kenneth had devised a simple story of a family, Father, Mother and small Daughter, at the seaside. The parents would not let their child watch the Punch and Judy show but she rushed into the tent and was confronted by Mr. Punch. The two succeeding episodes covered the child's adventures with Mr. Punch and a character called Pretty Polly – with Kenneth as a policeman wearing enormous boots. The series was again produced by Naomi Capon, was enormously successful and set a standard for televised dance which, for all the technological advances of the last twenty-five years, has rarely been equalled.

While the series was in production Kenneth had been tremendously busy considering another commission, a commission so momentous in effect that it was to end his dancing career and complete his conversion into a full-time professional choreographer.

6

The first commission

Following Kenneth's disappointment over a full-scale production of *Laiderette*, de Valois considered commissioning a work from him for the Sadler's Wells Theatre Ballet and when the company returned from South Africa (and the dispute with Equity was over) she did so. Of course Kenneth was thrilled to have his talent rewarded by this official recognition but the sheer importance of the undertaking was somewhat daunting to him: unlike the embryonic works produced for the Choreographic Group, this ballet would represent his professional debut as a choreographer, exposed to the highest standards of criticism, and whatever he chose to do just had to be right.

Some years before, while browsing in a record shop in New York when he was with the Sadler's Wells Ballet, Kenneth had bought a recording of Stravinsky's ballet score *Le Baiser de la Fée*. He loved the music (written by Stravinsky in homage to Tchaikovsky) and although he was aware of the awkwardness of the fairy-tale scenario, based on Hans Andersens's *The Ice Maiden*, he was, he says, 'prepared to swallow the libretto in order to make something of the music'. The ballet had first been choreographed by Bronislava Nijinska for Ida Rubinstein's company in Paris in 1928 and had also been produced by Ashton as his first work for the Sadler's Wells Ballet after his appointment as resident choreographer in 1935 (the role of the Fiancée was the first part Ashton created for Fonteyn). Kenneth was unaware of this latter history of the work when he made his proposal to de Valois and she did not mention it. But once again the score proved to be the obstacle – it was altogether too elaborately orchestrated for the touring company. Kenneth had to think again. His solution was quick and simple. On the reverse side of the record was Stravinsky's *Danses Concertantes*, much more sparingly orchestrated, and this was the music he decided to use. The fact that there was no scenario attached provided him with both a degree of freedom and a challenge to his choreographic imagination. As de Valois said to him, 'Now you have to prove yourself with the steps you invent.'

Kenneth could hardly have chosen a more difficult score upon which to create his first plotless ballet. The music of *Danses Concertantes* is Stravinsky at his most cerebral and acerbic, full of complexities of rhythm and metre, of rapid changes of pace, mood and expression. Although the five movements are headed March, Pas d'action, Théme Varié, Pas de deux and March, there is little to suggest that the music was written for dancing; it is more like a concerto grosso for twenty-four instruments, a chamber work that stands by itself as absolute music.

To match this capricious score Kenneth worked out a sharp, spiky choreographic style with much use of pointing fingers, angled *port de bras*, heads turned in profile and swift changes of direction, all of which demanded the utmost precision in execution. The result was a very sophisticated distortion of the classical dance vocabulary, a brilliant and effective visual parallel to the jagged musical forms. Once again Kenneth chose those dancers in the company whose work he most admired and with whom he had established a personal rapport. There were six principals, three men and three women used in various combinations, and a supporting cast of two men and six women.

Because Kenneth had always found double work to be the most difficult of his dancing career (although he had eventually become a strong and considerate partner) he had deliberately avoided creating anything resembling an extended *pas de deux* in his previous ballets. Now he had to accept the challenge and *Danses Concertantes* included both a sustained *pas de deux* and a *pas de trois*. Not that either passage conformed to anything resembling a classical duet or trio: the contiguities between ballerina(s) and partner were sharp and fleeting, the dancers seeming to fly apart almost as soon as they came together only to re-establish contact again like rapidly galvanised particles. Supported pirouettes became violently twisted, limbs were placed in opposition rather than harmony, there was an emphasis on acute angles. The *pas de deux* for Maryon Lane and David Poole included a number of unusual lifts. The *pas de trois* for Sara Neil, Gilbert Vernon and Annette Page was equally inventive, culminating in a witty exit for all three dancers. Maryon Lane remembers that although Kenneth was busy devising this distinctive choreographic style he cleverly incorporated those particular technical abilities and expressive qualities that showed her dancing to advantage. 'It is always so satisfying to have a solo created for you,' she says, 'and *Danses Concertantes* was one of those ballets that you loved to do – a work that you could happily go on performing all your professional life.'

For Donald Britton, Kenneth created another brilliant solo, technically very difficult, ending in a 'star-fish' position with the head and torso twisted and the arms and legs radiating at extreme angles. Throughout the ballet the continual flow of idiomatic movement owed nothing to the work of any other choreographer; it was invented purely to reflect Stravinsky's splintery score and in doing so revealed a marvellously sustained creative imagination.

Above: *Danses Concertantes* was Kenneth's first commissioned work. It established a collaboration between choreographer and designer – Nicholas Georgiadis – that has lasted throughout the careers of both men. For Stravinsky's cerebral, spiky score Kenneth devised idiomatic choreography with much emphasis on hand movements, sudden changes of direction, angled *port de bras* and off-balance manouevres that made a perfect parallel to the music. The dancers in this photograph are the leading sextet of the original cast with, centre, Maryon Lane surrounded by, left to right, David Poole, Bryan Lawrence, Gilbert Vernon, Donald MacLeary and Donald Britton. (*Theatre Museum, V. and A. Museum.*)

Right: A studio portrait: every inch the intense young choreographer. (*Paul Wilson.*)

Kenneth now had to consider a specially commissioned decor for his ballet. He was anxious to use a painter or designer whose work he found sympathetic to his own ideas and to this end de Valois offered to introduce him to Sir William Coldstream who was then the Principal of the Slade School of Fine Art and so, one morning, Kenneth and de Valois entered the building in Gower Street together. After wandering up and down the corridors for some minutes Kenneth said, 'Madam, there seem to be an awful lot of nurses about the place.' There were indeed; instead of the Slade School they had entered University College Hospital which is adjacent.

When they had at last found the proper entrance and the introduction to Sir William had been effected, Kenneth was taken to examine the work of several students in the Theatre Class and finally chose as his designer a young man, Nicholas Georgiadis, who had recently arrived in London from his native Greece. The choice was to prove the beginning of a long and rewarding artistic association between choreographer and designer.

For *Danses Concertantes* Georgiadis designed what might be called an ante-room in a fantasy palace, suggestive of lofty, formal architecture, the pervasive colouring green and blue with applied decoration in black using occasional motifs of small, winged sphinxes which were repeated on the backs of six chairs arranged up-stage, left and right, in two rows of three and which, during the ballet, were used by the dancers.

The costumes were leotards for the men, decorated with a pattern of lines and arrow-heads which accentuated the pointed, spikiness of the choreography, and short-skirted tunics for the women, somewhat less heavily decorated but with an emphasis on bust and hips. The colours of umber, turquoise, chartreuse, blue and orange contrasted sharply with the effective use of black throughout the designs. All the dancers wore black 'urchin-cut' wigs, the men's topped with jewelled pyramids and the women's with rather more elaborate winged devices. The overall effect was both highly fantasticated and immensely chic.

Danses Concertantes received its first performance on January 18, 1955, at Sadler's Wells Theatre. Rarely can a first professional work have received more rapturous acclaim from an audience or such unanimous praise from the critics. The performance, too, brought fresh verbal bouquets for the dancers involved; one critic wrote 'I do not think that the ballet could ever be better danced than it was on its first performance,' and thirty odd years later that still stands as a viable verdict. With *Danses Concertantes* Kenneth had fully justified de Valois's faith in him – the first choreographer produced entirely by the Sadler's Wells Ballet. Almost immediately Kenneth decided he wanted to give up dancing and concentrate on a choreographic career. De Valois fully understood and Kenneth was duly appointed as a resident choreographer to the company. For attaining this exalted position Kenneth accepted a cut in his weekly salary from £14 to £13.

7

Company choreographer

With his retirement from dancing and his new status as a company choreographer Kenneth was left with a considerable amount of time on his hands. With no daily classes, or rehearsals, or performances to give, he was back in that empty world he had briefly experienced during the period of stage-fright. Of course, he did have to think about his next work and that pre-occupied his mind without providing a substitute for the daily physical discipline that had been his routine for more than ten years. He took to haunting gramophone record shops and asking to hear various recordings; money was still short, however, and he could rarely afford to buy anything even if he liked the music. The assistants soon came to recognise him and it was not long before his requests were refused.

In the mid-1950s one of the chief sources of social contact for members of the theatre was the Petit Club Français in St. James's Place, S.W.1, which had originally been established as a 'home-from-home' for the Free French forces during the war. There it was possible to meet for a drink after or before a show and, more important for the performing artists, an excellent restaurant provided good meals at reasonable prices. The only alternative for hungry dancers after a tiring evening (apart from going home and cooking for themselves) were the Lyon's Corner House restaurants or expensive establishments in Soho and hotel restaurants – far beyond the pockets of most of them. Kenneth was a regular diner at the 'French Club', as it was popularly known, and enjoyed relaxing there with his friends, exchanging news, ideas and gossip.

*

The suggestion for Kenneth's next ballet came, in fact, from his friend Cranko. It was an idea that Cranko had himself considered but subsequently felt was more suited to Kenneth's talents. It was a story ballet, the narrative taken from a Brothers Grimm fairy tale, *Jorinda and Joringel*, concerning a boy and girl who play outside the house of a Bird Woman, a witch. While the boy sleeps the witch entices the girl into the house which is full of exotic birds. The birds are in fact enchanted children and the witch makes captive her new prey. While the witch sleeps (what a narrative convenience those careless slumbers are in fairy tales!) the boy enters the house and releases the birds who peck the witch to death, whereupon the children return to human form. The macabre quality of the tale appealed to Kenneth and he set about reducing the Grimms' story to a ballet scenario. The boy and girl were turned into young lovers and the children into young men and women; that apart the simple tale of evil enchantment and rescue, with a cruel retribution for the witch, needed little alteration.

The problem was the music. It was John Lanchbery, who was then Musical Director and Conductor for the company, who suggested using a selection of piano scores by the little-known Spanish-born composer Federico Mompou whose output consisted solely of piano pieces and songs. Mompou's description of himself as a 'primitive' was somewhat at odds with composers such as Monteverdi, Bach, Chopin, Fauré and Stravinsky who, he asserted, had influenced his work. Moreover, in defining his musical creed as 'a reaction against unimaginative abstract music and a return to expressiveness and lyricism', he revealed himself more of a sophisticated romantic than a primitive. But whatever label one cares to apply, there is no doubt that his music, cleverly arranged and orchestrated by Lanchbery, proved ideal for *House of Birds* which was the title Kenneth gave to his new ballet.

Once again Kenneth asked Georgiadis to do the designs and once again the result was a highly effective collaboration between choreographer and artist. Georgiadis created an atmospheric set in two scenes – the exterior and interior of the Bird Woman's house. The interior was particularly successful, especially when, in the scene in which the young woman is enticed inside, it was lit from behind to reveal the dazzling hues of an exotic aviary. Georgiadis's graphic style – a Klee-like linear use of black with sparing touches of white high-lighted with splashes of vivid colour, yellow, orange, pink, green and blue – served to create a fascinatingly sinister but beautiful setting for the allegory, just as Georgiadis had done for the astringent abstractions of *Danses Concertantes*.

The grace and beauty of the classical ballet vocabulary has, of course, often been used by choreographers to simulate avian movements but in *House of Birds* Kenneth was concerned not with free flight but with creatures in captivity. The birds' struggles for freedom, the dance of the young woman when half transformed into a bird and the attack on the Bird Woman were portrayed with a chilling inventiveness. For the Bird Woman herself Kenneth used the awkward, jerky, menacing movements that birds display on the ground and Georgiadis's black and white skeletal costume with touches of scarlet and a hideous mask with a venomously hooked beak made her a truly terrifying creature.

Against this nightmarish apparition Kenneth contrasted the warm physical relationship of the lovers, combining many complicated but beautiful lifts in their various duets. (The dancer-choreographer who had felt that his weakest technique was in *pas de deux* had come a long way in a short time.) Once again his chosen dancers – Maryon Lane and David Poole as the Young Lovers and Doreen Tempest as the Bird Woman – excelled in the roles that had been written for them and once again Kenneth's new ballet, given its first performance at the Sadler's Wells Theatre on May 26, 1955, was a triumphant success, pleasing audiences and critics alike. One critic called the choreography 'as unforced and fluent as a master's' and went on to comment that it 'brought the unusual and fantastic to our stage, which British ballet has long needed'.

*

At this time Kenneth's life became somewhat hectic. Less than two months after the first performance of *House of Birds*, Ballet Rambert gave the first 'proper' London Performance of *Laiderette* on July 4, 1955, during a season at Sadler's Wells Theatre. Dame Marie Rambert had loved the work when she had first seen it given by the Choreographic Group and when it became known that the Sadler's Wells Theatre Ballet was unable to mount it was delighted to take it into the repertoire of her company. For his part Kenneth was delighted, too, that his second ballet should be given a full-scale production although, initially, he was somewhat nervous about working with dancers he did not know in a company that was unfamiliar to him. His creative ideas, however, fitted naturally into place with a company which had been responsible for important dramatic works by Ashton, Antony Tudor and Walter Gore. Moreover, the combination of friendliness and professionalism that he found in Ballet Rambert soon put him at ease.

For the first time Kenneth used a designer other than Georgiadis. He had met Australian-born Kenneth Rowell when he was designing Gore's *Carte Blanche* two years before and had also liked the work that Rowell had done for Cranko's *Variations on a Theme*, also for Ballet Rambert. Rowell's designs for *Laiderette*, while making a sharp visual distinction between the ragged pierrots and the chic rich, invested the whole work with an air of fantasy which, at the end of the ballet, left the audience with the question: did it really happen or was it just the dream of a tired pierrot?

The eponymous role of the bald pierrette was danced by Patricia Ashworth. She did not possess the razor-sharp technique of Maryon Lane but in the words of one critic she '. . . succeeded in the ballet extremely well. She gave the part a peculiar intensity, high-pitched and nervous. Her ugliness was to be pitied but was never pitiable.' As the Host, who is first attracted to her and then rejects her, Ronald Yerrill had 'a powerful stage personality which in this (ballet) was appropriately unsympathetic. As a whole the ballet was possibly not as well danced as in the original production, but it came over rather better theatrically.' The reviewer concluded by saying, 'With these early MacMillan ballets one has the privilege of seeing the first steps of a choreographer who potentially can shape the future of ballet in this country.' *Laiderette* remained in the repertoire of Ballet Rambert for many years.

*

Kenneth's next commission came from the BBC, an invitation to choreograph a whole dance programme. Devised by Margaret Dale who, not long before, had abandoned a very successful career as a dancer in favour of directing dance from behind T.V. cameras, the programme was conceived as light entertainment, a pot-pourri of dance styles ranging from classical ballet to jazz, linked by a commentary spoken by the actor John Neville wearing an opera cloak and a top hat. The music was selected from those works in the B.B.C. archives that would not entail broadcasting fees, and consequently it varied from Jacques Ibert to New Orleans blues – a consideration that had probably initiated the whole idea. The cast was drawn mainly from both Sadler's Wells companies but also included Violette Verdy who was at that time a leading dancer with Roland Petit's Ballets de Paris.

The suite of nine dances that Kenneth created (under the curious title of *Turned Out Proud* – perhaps intended as a pun on the ballet term 'turned out') included a duet for Annette Chappell and Sonya Hana as Oriental twins (not Siamese!), a *pas de deux* for Verdy and Gilbert Vernon, a character number for Sheila O'Neil and a *pas de cinq* for Julia Farron and four men. For Verdy there was also a solo number of great technical difficulty. A critic wrote that 'the unceasing invention of MacMillan's choreography is continually amazing' and concluded that 'this is obviously the way that television ballet should go, let us have more of this kind of ballet programme,' – a plea that has produced little response over the last thirty years or so.

The programme was transmitted on October 23, 1955, and its success was doubtless instrumental in Margaret Dale coaxing Kenneth to appear actually as a dancer in another programme given on December 30 of that year. It consisted of the clowns' disputatious duet over a rose from Cranko's *Lady and the Fool* followed by Ashton's *Les Patineurs*. Although the ballets had nothing in common, on screen they were cleverly linked by the rose motif. At the beginning of the programme the rose was seen slowly revolving; during the clowns' dance the rose was crushed and at the end the falling petals turned into the snow of *Les Patineurs*. At the conclusion of that ballet, with the Blue Skater performing his endless pirouettes, the spinning figure faded into the opening shot of the revolving rose.

Kenneth's recreation of the role of Moondog in the clown duet (retitled *La Commedia* for the television transmission) was called by one critic 'a highlight of the programme', and he added that 'it was difficult to convey the absurdly moving quality of his dance and mime.' For his part Kenneth not only enjoyed playing the role again but the experience consolidated his interest in the techniques of filming.

The appearance on television may have had something to do with Kenneth appearing as a dancer 'in the flesh' only a week later. The 1956 Sadler's Wells Ballet season at Covent Garden included a revival of Ashton's *Cinderella* and on January 7, 1956, Kenneth re-appeared at the Royal Opera House, taking over Robert Helpmann's role as one of the Ugly Sisters opposite Frederick Ashton. Again, Kenneth enjoyed himself: the role made no great technical demands on him and of course it was fun to do. One critic wrote, 'Ashton's compassionate . . . ugly sister has found a fine partner in MacMillan's termagant – a virago who, if she could not launch a thousand ships, would at least sink them.'

*

At this very same time Kenneth was preparing to make the final step for an aspiring young British choreographer: the creation of a work for the Sadler's Wells Ballet at the Royal Opera House. Some four months before that was to happen, however, his first choreography to be seen on the Royal Opera House stage were the dances he was asked to arrange for the bacchanale in a new production of Wagner's *Tannhäuser*. They were also Kenneth's first essay in explicit erotica and, although the scene achieved something of a mild *succès de scandale* because of the 'lascivious entwinings' he devised for Julia Farron and Gilbert Vernon who led the Venusberg revels, he thinks that, compared to what is legally permissible and artistically accept-

36

able today, it would seem rather tame – if not downright comic. His inventive powers were severely limited by the fact that the bacchanale took place on a steep ramp; nevertheless the dance was sufficiently sensuous to provoke a newspaper reporter in the popular press to ask whether the Lord Chamberlain had seen it as 'it was something the Folies Bergère would not dare to put on'.

For his first major work at the Royal Opera House Kenneth concocted a scenario of his own, the story of a hypnotist whose powers not only affect the lives of his audience but also his own and that of his assistant. In a shabby but ornate back-street theatre a hypnotist gives his performance; the climax fails, however, and the hypnotist takes his revenge upon a jeering audience. The rich and the poor intermingle, among them a young couple who fall in love; a soldier sees himself as a hero and a faded beauty attracts four suitors. The hypnotist also falls for her charms and discards his assistant who, at the end of the ballet, is left circling the stage banging her drum like a mechanical doll.

Once again it was a story with macabre overtones, a melodrama that gained extra atmosphere from being presented as a theatre-within-a-theatre. For the first time Kenneth was to work from a commissioned score – so often cited as the ideal arrangement for the creation of a fine ballet but, in actual practice, presenting its own difficulties. The ideal is much more likely to be attained if choreographer and composer know one another or are aware of, and in sympathy with, each other's work. In this case, Kenneth was a stranger to Humphrey Searle who was the composer suggested by de Valois. Kenneth gave him the scenario he had sketched out with the approximate durations for each dance sequence. The piano score which Kenneth subsequently received was longer in some sections than he had anticipated but Kenneth accepted it without demur – probably because he was somewhat intimidated by Searle's considerable prestige as a successful composer and thus felt some diffidence about asking for cuts which he felt were really necessary.

One of the Sadler's Wells Theatre Ballet principals whose work Kenneth had always admired and for whom he had created several important roles, Maryon Lane, had recently joined the Covent Garden company as a soloist, and so he was able to continue his artistic association with her, casting her in the important role of the Hypnotist's Assistant. Leslie Edwards, the company's leading character dancer, was the Hypnotist, Nadia Nerina the Faded Beauty, Anya Linden the Poor Girl, Desmond Doyle the Rich Man and Brian Shaw the Soldier. The ballet, entitled *Noctambules*, was given its first performance on March 1, 1956, and Kenneth's choreography was described as 'often shockingly original', and 'a notable success', and he was also praised for having successfully created for 'opera house dimensions'. Nicholas Georgiadis who, once again, had been Kenneth's choice of designer, was also lavishly praised for his sets and costumes. As with *House of Birds* his setting of the decaying theatre was marvellously atmospheric, sinister but decorative, while the various characters in the ballet were delineated by their costumes without being overloaded with fussy bits and pieces.

Ironically, it was Humphrey Searle's score which received what adverse criticism there was. The music was described as being too insistently dramatic – 'by continually piling climax upon climax he has given . . . no climax at all'. For Kenneth there had been one or two sharp lessons on working with a commissioned score – although, in later ballets which also made use of an 'ideal' collaboration, there were more shocks to come. For the time being, however, he could congratulate himself not only on having had three brilliant successes in a row but also in having surmounted the considerable obstacle of creating on a big scale for a big company; had he kept a book of press clippings (which unfortunately he did not) he could have begun it with columns of fulsome praise.

8

From success to success

A string of successes makes it increasingly difficult for any artist to maintain the standard, let alone reveal a progressive improvement, in subsequent new works. The situation is full of pitfalls – an open invitation merely to repeat a successful formula, to be over-ambitious or just downright complacent. Kenneth was aware of these dangers, of course, and consequently felt the necessity for his next work to be different in mood, if not in choreographic style, from what he had done previously. In the event, what he did was largely dictated by circumstances.

While Kenneth was busily establishing himself as an important new choreographer, his friend John Cranko had also been extremely active. He had been planning a new one-act work for the Sadler's Wells Theatre Ballet at the same time that he was working on what was to be the first original full-length work for a British company, *The Prince of the Pagodas*. This long work had a commissioned score by Benjamin Britten and decor by John Piper and was occupying much of Cranko's time. Meanwhile, the decor for his work for the Sadler's Wells company had already been designed by Desmond Heeley. [Kenneth thinks that this was for his subsequent ballet *The Angels*.] When it was decided to postpone this ballet, Kenneth received a call from de Valois asking if he would create a work suitable for the Heeley designs. Thus, to a great extent, the atmosphere for Kenneth's new ballet was already dictated for him.

The decor that Heeley had created was a romantic forest of white scaffolding set against a turquoise sky. The effect was modern and, because of the colours, light in feeling with nothing sinister, dark or oppressive or, for that matter, too precise in location. It would have been suitable for a plotless work but Kenneth chose a distinct theme although there was no story or narrative thread attached to it.

For some time Kenneth's association with Margaret Hill, sharing the same apartment in her mother's house, had been a close, if not intense, personal relationship. He was consequently very aware, very bound up with, her disposition, her character, her attitudes to life and her profession. He says that as she had been a dancer with Ballet Rambert before joining the Sadler's Wells Theatre Ballet, she always had the feeling of not 'fitting in' with the same easiness as those dancers who (like Kenneth) had been with the Sadler's Wells School and graduated into the company. She was, he says, always making attempts to join in whatever extra-mural activities there may have been but the more she tried to be one of them the more she retained the feeling of being an outsider. Whether consciously or not, Kenneth's own somewhat solitary and lonely childhood gave him an empathy for Margaret Hill's situation; it also gave him the leading character for his new ballet. He decided to create it around a solitary dancer, anxious to join in the activities of others but, ultimately, always finding herself alone.

There then began a hurried, if not frantic, search for suitable music – there was not time to commission a score even if Kenneth had felt inclined to do so. After a round of the record shops he came across a recording of Malcolm Arnold's *English Dances* which he immediately found attractive. But the score was too short. Accordingly, Kenneth wrote to the composer asking if he would write two more movements. With typical good humour and alacrity, Arnold agreed to do so, providing a Polka and a Sarabande.

With the theme in mind, the choreography came comparatively easily. There was no doubt who was the 'star' of the ballet but Kenneth wrote interesting and rewarding roles for several other leading dancers of the company including Sara Neil, Donald Britton, Michael Boulton and Donald MacLeary. The title of the new ballet was *Solitaire* with the sub-title 'A Kind of Game for One'.

Before the first night of *Solitaire* the Sadler's Wells Theatre Ballet had mounted a full-scale revival of Kenneth's first work, *Somnambulism*, at Sadler's Wells Theatre on May 29, 1956. In the three-and-a-half years since the ballet's first performance with the Choreographic Group Kenneth had fully established himself as a major choreographer, and it was understandable that with *Danses Concertantes*, *House of Birds* and *Noctambules* in the repertoires of the two Sadler's Wells companies, as well as Ballet Rambert's production of *Laiderette*, the critics were not as ecstatic over *Somnambulism* as they had originally been. Even so, the work was welcomed and the three soloists – Margaret Hill (in the role originally written for her) David Poole and Anne Heaton (replacing Maryon Lane who had joined the Covent Garden company) – all received complimentary reviews.

The first night of *Solitaire* came only nine days later and it was immediately acclaimed as yet another MacMillan success – one eminent critic going so far as to proclaim that Kenneth was a genius: 'There comes a time when any critic tires of ifs and buts and maybes, and wants to climb on the bough of an assertion. For this critic the time has come with *Solitaire*. Kenneth MacMillan is a choreographic genius capable of transforming the ballet of our day.' Audiences were equally enthusiastic, no doubt delighted to discover that there was another side to Kenneth's creative abilities, witty and lighthearted, not perpetually obsessed with the macabre.

There was, in fact, a distinct air of melancholy beneath the surface gaiety of the ballet. At curtain rise the central character of the girl was discovered alone on stage, seeming to recall, somewhat wistfully, past pleasures. With each section of the music she was joined by various other characters with whom she became involved in varying degrees of acceptance, but at the conclusion of each sequence she was left alone. There was nothing as definite as rejection, just a gentle good-bye from transient aquaintances. At the final farewell there was a sense of resignation by the girl, of being alone but not lonely, surviving on memories.

Margaret Hill also received eulogistic reviews with such comments as 'the warmth and tenderness of her personality hold the whole ballet together,' and 'hers was a remarkable performance, piquant, appealing and beautifully danced.' Ironically, Kenneth thinks that her success in the role accentuated her feeling of being an outsider in the company – although he stresses that this was her own individual reaction; her colleagues were all as friendly as ever and delighted at her reception.

The tremendous success of *Solitaire* was but part of a personal triumph for Kenneth on that night, for the whole programme was devoted to his works: *Somnambulism*, *Danses Concertantes*, *Solitaire* and

House of Birds. It was an innovation for the company to give a complete evening to one choreographer, and nothing could have demonstrated more forcefully the consistent success he had achieved in such a short time.

*

During the summer holidays two principals of the Sadler's Wells Ballet at Covent Garden, Nadia Nerina and Alexis Rassine, undertook a tour of the provinces with a programme called *Ballet Highlights* for which Kenneth provided a new *pas de deux*. Using Stravinsky's short score *Fireworks*, he created a bravura display piece which made great use of Nerina's virtuosity. It was tailored to the technique of both dancers, of course, and the critics found it the most interesting item in the programme which otherwise consisted of familiar *pas de deux* and solos.

During the same summer recess *The House of Birds* was rehearsed for a television transmission which went out on the B.B.C. network on September 16, 1956. With new casting – Sara Neil and Michael Boulton as the young lovers and Margaret Hill as the Bird Woman – the critics thought that the sinister atmosphere of the ballet had been successfully transferred to the small screen although, in those pre-colour days, Georgiadis's sets and costumes were thought to have suffered in the black and white presentation. The production was staged by Margaret Dale who was doing so much in pioneering dance on television.

Kenneth's next created work was another small-scale *pièce d'occasion*, thrown together in a hurry, this time for a gala in aid of the Lord Mayor of London's National Hungarian and Central Relief Fund (following the Hungarian uprising against Soviet occupation forces of that year) organised by Frederick Ashton at Sadler's Wells Theatre on December 10.

Dancers from all the (then) major companies (Sadler's Wells Ballet, Sadler's Wells Theatre Ballet, Covent Garden Opera Ballet, Sadler's Wells Opera Ballet, Ballet Rambert and London Festival Ballet plus a famous British ballerina, Alicia Markova, whom one critic called 'a one-woman company in herself,') took part. The programme consisted of the usual gala fare, famous *pas de deux* and solos with a mixture of ensembles like the polka from *The Bartered Bride* and small works like Andrée Howard's version of Schubert's *Death and the Maiden*. The one specially created work was a *pas de trois* devised by Kenneth to Ibert's Divertimento from his music for *The Italian Straw Hat*. The ballet was a zany divertissement called *Valse Excentrique*, a trio of Victorian bathers, Brian Shaw and Alexander Grant in long bathing suits and sporting handle-bar moustaches with Anya Linden as a bathing belle comically manoeuvred between them. It came towards the end of a long programme of serious works and the audience, relieved at the chance to laugh, gave the three dancers a show-stopping reception.

9

The first failure

During August, 1956, American Ballet Theatre gave its third season at Covent Garden as part of an extensive European and Middle Eastern tour. Towards the end of the London engagement Lucia Chase, the Director of the company, told Peter Williams, editor of *Dance and Dancers*, that she would like to take back to America a new ballet by a European choreographer. He immediately suggested Kenneth. As Peter Williams subsequently wrote in his magazine: 'America had not seen the creations of this distinguished young choreographer, so it seemed right that its first major ballet company should also be the first to present him in New York.' And so, on August 31, in Margot Fonteyn's dressing room at the Royal Opera House, Lucia Chase met Kenneth for the first time.

That initial meeting was purely exploratory, but auspicious. Kenneth had several ideas for new works and one in particular, loosely based on a story by the American writer Carson McCullers, seemed appropriate as it would provide an excellent role for American Ballet Theatre's outstanding dramatic ballerina, Nora Kaye. Two days later, after the company's final performance at Covent Garden, Lucia Chase invited Kenneth to meet Nora Kaye for dinner at the Savoy. For Kenneth this was a particular pleasure as he had been a great admirer of this dancer ever since he had first seen her during Ballet Theatre's first visit to London in 1946. He had always been attracted by those dancers possessed by a strong stage presence and in roles such as Hagar in Antony Tudor's *Pillar of Fire* as well as Classics like *Swan Lake* and *Giselle* Nora Kaye was an exceptionally compelling artist.

Peter Williams remembers that dinner at the Savoy as a successful social occasion; Kenneth was his usual rather shy self but Nora Kaye, a more extrovert character, kept the conversation going although no one talked much about what must have been uppermost in their minds, Kenneth's creation of a new ballet for the company.

Next day Ballet Theatre left London for the next part of its tour. Lucia Chase flew back to New York 'to talk to the money-bags', as she put it, about raising the funds for the new work. And soon afterwards Kenneth also left London with Margaret Hill for a holiday in St. Tropez.

With the summer holidays over, cables began to pass back and forth across the Atlantic. Lucia Chase had been successful in raising the money, permission had been obtained from de Valois for Kenneth to take leave of absence to work with Ballet Theatre. Kenneth wanted Georgiadis to do the sets and costumes, and after Lucia Chase had seen some of Georgiadis's designs she readily agreed. Kenneth had originally suggested commissioning Henri Dutilleux to compose the music but as time was now short (Ballet Theatre wanted to premiere the new work during its European tour before showing it in New York) it was decided to use an existing score. Undeterred that the music had already been used by Frederick Ashton, by John Cranko and, in America, by Lew Christiansen (if in fact he was aware of it) Kenneth chose Benjamin Britten's *Variations on a Theme by Frank Bridge*.

It was arranged that after the company had completed its Middle Eastern tour of Israel, Syria and the Lebanon, Kenneth should rehearse the new work at Monte Carlo where the company were scheduled to give a Christmas season; the world premiere was arranged for January at the San Carlos Opera House in Lisbon. Everything seemed to be progressing smoothly, Kenneth was working out the details of the narrative, Georgiadis was making preliminary sketches, when the 1956 Israeli-Egyptian crisis over Suez occurred. Ballet Theatre's planned tour of the Middle East was hurriedly cancelled. It looked as if the company would be returning to the United States, in which case it would have been impossible to present the new ballet. Lucia Chase, however, was determined that Ballet Theatre should continue with its planned European tour and the company's European representative successfully rearranged the programme so that Ballet Theatre should visit Italy and Holland before Monte Carlo. Kenneth and Georgiadis joined the company in Rotterdam early in December, then travelled to the Cote d'Azur a week or so later.

The beautiful theatre in Monte Carlo – permeated by its historic association with Serge Diaghilev and his Ballets Russes – was also splendidly equipped for the purposes of creating a ballet: fine rehearsal rooms and studios, wardrobe workrooms and scene-painting shop. But almost immediately difficulties began to crop up: the scenery could not be made in Monte Carlo because the theatre was too busy preparing for the opera season; rehearsal time for the new ballet was extremely limited owing to the demands of the touring repertory; the theatre workrooms could not make the costumes and alternative arrangements had to be hurriedly made. Even so, Kenneth managed to make considerable progress with the choreography and, although some ensembles for the *corps de ballet* had not been completed, a run-through rehearsal was given at the end of December for Lucia Chase (who was seeing it for the first time) and a number of distinguished guests including Princess Antoinette of Monaco. Everyone agreed that, even in its incomplete state, without the benefit of costumes, setting and lighting, the ballet had a great dramatic impact. After a lot of discussion Kenneth finally decided to call the ballet *Winter's Eve*, a suitably chilling title for a story that concerned a blind girl falling in love with a young man unaware of her affliction. When they meet the air becomes full of fluttering birds which represent her soaring emotions. She accepts his invitation to a ball; while partnering her he realises she is blind and the birds return, this time menacing and angry. The girl strikes out at them and accidentally blinds the young man. United in their blindness they become separated in the dancing and the girl is left to face a bleak, empty future.

A week or so after the special rehearsal for Lucia Chase and her guests, the choreography was finished and Kenneth, disliking air travel, made the lengthy train journey from Monte Carlo to Lisbon. At the Franco-Spanish border he was held up for a whole day because he had neglected to apply for a visa for crossing Spain. When he eventually arrived in Lisbon it was for a disastrous dress-rehearsal at which everything went wrong. The very purpose of dress-rehearsals, however, is to rectify technical problems and mistakes and, perhaps, make minor artistic changes. On this occasion Kenneth did not need to alter the choreography and the first night, a glittering social affair with the President of the Republic and distinguished members of the Diplomatic Corps present, was a tremendous success.

As the tragic lovers, Nora Kaye and John Kriza scored a personal triumph and the ballet received many curtain calls. The next day the Lisbon critics were complimentary about Kenneth. The critic of the leading daily said that the work 'stood out in the history of ballet in Portugal' and that the collaboration between the artists concerned was 'worthy of the artistic direction of Diaghilev'. Other critics were unanimous in praising Kenneth's inventive powers, especially for the choreography he had created for the blind girl.

*

On the same day as *Winter's Eve* received its world premiere in Lisbon, in London there was the momentous announcement that Her Majesty Queen Elizabeth had been pleased to grant a Royal Charter to the Sadler's Wells Ballet, the Sadler's Wells Theatre Ballet and the Sadler's Wells School, all of which were to be known henceforth under the umbrella title of the Royal Ballet.

From Lisbon Kenneth made the long train journey back to London and then the bleak winter journey across the North Atlantic by sea to New York. He was delighted to be back in that city again, a city which he had always found stimulating, mostly because of the theatrical offerings of Broadway.

Winter's Eve had its American premiere on February 10, 1957, at the Metropolitan Opera House. The American critics were far more critical than those of Lisbon, more experienced, and far more analytical of the ballet. They were by no means unanimous in their opinions, but for Kenneth it was a salutary experience to receive anything other than praises. Today he still thinks of it as his first failure.

The critic of the New York *Times* found the story 'painful' and felt that the ballet had 'everything the matter with it'. He also felt that Kenneth's inventive ability was both his greatest asset and danger, that he ran the risk of turning out endless original movement without developing it. The *Herald Tribune* critic devoted two long notices to the work. He said that 'MacMillan has extended the vocabulary of ballet into a freer form of expression and emotional revelation', and went on to praise the freshness of the choreography both for the soloists and the ensemble. The critic of the *Post* considered that the ballet was 'a poignant work' and that the story was expressed with a theatrical brilliance which lifted the piece above its personal tragedy into a deeper and more compelling introspection.

Kenneth was considerably downcast by the New York reviewers' verdicts and felt that he had 'failed' both Lucia Chase and Nora Kaye – despite the fact that Nora Kaye and John Kriza both received enthusiastic reviews for their performances.

*

Soon after the New York premiere of *Winter's Eve* the Directors of Ballet Theatre were planning a number of workshop performances of new ballets to be given on four consecutive Mondays at the off-Broadway Phoenix Theatre. In the event the company presented no less than fifteen works by fourteen choreographers. Still feeling that he owed the company something after the 'failure' of *Winter's Eve*, Kenneth undertook to provide a new ballet for the workshop season.

Once again Kenneth devised his own theme, a woman's journey towards death, partly inspired by an exhibition of pictures by

Charles Munch illustrating Matthias Claudius's poem *Death and the Maiden*. Rejecting the obvious choice of Schubert, Kenneth selected Bartók's *Music for Strings, Percussion and Celeste*, and gave the four movements the subtitles *Premonitions, Three Messengers of Death, Journey* and *Judgement*; the work itself was entitled *Journey*.

The role of the woman was, of course, created upon Nora Kaye but the ballet also starred three of the company's leading male dancers, John Kriza, Eric Bruhn and Scott Douglas, with a supporting ensemble of three girls and twelve men.

Journey was performed on May 5, 1957, and was very well received. One critic wrote that it was 'replete with some of the most inventive and unusual dance movements to be seen in a ballet in several seasons in New York', and concluded 'in every sense this is a far more important work than MacMillan's *Winter's Eve* of earlier this year.'

It is of incidental interest to note that the second programme of that Ballet Theatre workshop season included Herbert Ross's sexually sensational adaptation of Jean Genet's *The Maids* which some critics found upsetting but which Kenneth was responsible for bringing into the repertory of the Royal Ballet New Group (as it was briefly called) some fourteen years later when he had become Director of the Royal Ballet.

On April 29, 1957, a week before *Journey* received its first performance, the Royal Ballet had been specially flown out to America by N.B.C. to give a single televised performance of Ashton's *Cinderella* in which Kenneth once again played the Helpmann role of the Ugly Sister.

With the critical acclaim of *Journey* exorcising the equivocal response to *Winter's Eve*, Kenneth settled down to enjoy his stay in New York, stimulated, as always, by the great variety of entertainment that that hectic city has to offer. But it was not long before his idyll was interrupted.

The Royal Ballet at Covent Garden (there was, at this time, a continuing rumpus over the fact that both companies were called the Royal Ballet which had led to a lot of confusion) was due to undertake a long transcontinental tour of North America starting in New York in September 1957 and ending in Montreal in January the following year. Most of that time there would be no ballet at Covent Garden but the Royal Ballet based at Sadler's Wells theatre was due to make its first appearance at the Royal Opera House from December 26 until January 17 1958. For such an important season it would be desirable for the company to show something new and in any case hardly any of its regular repertory would fit on to the large Covent Garden stage. Accordingly, de Valois sent Kenneth a peremptory telegram saying, in effect, 'come home at once!' Reluctantly,

Kenneth said farewell to the delights of New York, his friends in Theatre Ballet and, in particular, to Nora Kaye in whose apartment he had been staying and sailed for England in the R.M.S. *Queen Mary*.

It was proposed that during its Covent Garden season the Royal Ballet should give a triple bill of new ballets by Peter Wright, John Cranko and Kenneth so that, not long after his return Kenneth found himself searching for new material. What he eventually decided upon was to prove a complete breakaway from the style and content of his previous work, the rather French-influenced ballets of his first three choreographic years, the macabre fairy-tale of *House of Birds*, the bittersweet romanticism of *Solitaire*, gave way to something more akin to the abrasive realities of the new wave of British playwrights such as Osborne, Pinter, Wesker and Arden.

10

Farewell to fantasy

Kenneth found the subject for his newly commissioned ballet while reading Kafka's symbolic short story *The Burrow*. Although the author's characters are rabbits in a warren, it is a study in fear and claustrophobia and in adapting the theme Kenneth merely changed Kafka's anthropomorphised quadrupeds to human form.

In the original story the animals are in terror of the hunters' feet pounding above their warren; in the ballet it is the midnight knock on the door, so familiar from modern police states, that the characters dread.

Although the figures in *Noctambules* were recognisable types, the theme was more of a fantasy; in *The Burrow* (Kenneth kept the Kafka title for the ballet) the setting was much closer to reality, the characters far more delineated as individuals, people at the mercy of a repressive regime, a chilling reminder of the holocaust that had just passed, of the tyrannies that still existed. It was not only a step forward for Kenneth to be dealing with such a subject but also for ballet itself – the first of many works in which he has shown that the medium is capable of representing the happiness, the heartbreaks and the horrors of contemporary life, that it is not confined to being 'moving sculpture' or elegant whimsy or vague symbolism.

Once again Kenneth chose Georgiadis to do the designs. While the dramatic situation could find its parallel in any one of a number of totalitarian states, and telling the tale as a straight play might have required a wholly realistic set, the medium of classical dance needed something more stylised yet, at the same time, highly atmospheric. Georgiadis produced a claustrophobic feeling by enclosing the set with a sharply sloping ceiling. His colours were sombre browns and greys, the surfaces harsh, the few functional elements – a door, a single window covered with a dirty cloth, a naked electric light bulb – a bleak realisation of a cramped garret or dank cellar.

The colours of the costumes echoed the drabness of the decor with an occasional smudgy orange on the womens' clothes to relieve the cheerless effect and splashes of black and white to suggest a pattern or indicate texture. The silhouettes were vaguely modern, the men, in trousers with pullover-shaped tunics worn over shirts, the women in knee-length dresses, sometimes with a suggestion of a blouse and skirt and some of them with head-scarves. There was a recognisable personal style from Georgiadis's previous work for Kenneth but nothing, this time, that looked brilliant or chic.

After his experience with the music for *Noctambules*, Kenneth decided against a commissioned score. Once again he haunted the record shops and, following the success with the Frank Martin score for *Laiderette*, made a point of searching for that composer's music – although Martin has a very limited output. Eventually Kenneth decided upon the *Concerto for Wind Instruments, Percussion and Strings*.

Kenneth's invented characters – who were not to be found in Kafka's prototype rabbits – were the Woman, the Joker, the Outcast, Two Adolescents, Two Young Girls, a Child, Two Women and a supporting *corps* of Men and Women. An accompanying programme note, written by Arnold Haskell, stated: *There are many today who live in hiding, sealed off in some room. Such a room is a small world in which life burns more intensely; the flickering of a light-bulb may bring despair. The ballet introduces us to such a world; there is the woman close to breaking-point; the man who is an outcast – even the victims of intolerance are intolerant – the over-cheerful man, whose humour is a bludgeon; the child, unconscious of fear but quick to seize the mood; and the lovers who can never be alone. A knock on the door and their world is shattered.*

Anne Heaton, an outstandingly dramatic dancer, was cast as the Woman, a neurotic creature of faded prosperity if not gentility, finding herself not only in a nightmarish situation but also one with which she was socially unfamiliar. Donald Britton played the Joker whose relentless humour and constant grin first amused and then drove the other characters to distraction. When the Woman's control snapped and she slapped the Joker's face the Outcast – in his own psychological prison within a prison – erupted into mirthless laughter. It was a chilling moment in a ballet that, while it was mostly concerned with the creation of atmosphere rather than developing a narrative, was filled with dramatic incident.

For the two adolescent lovers, Lynn Seymour and Donald Mac-Leary, Kenneth created fragmentary dances rather than a set-piece *pas de deux*; in a squalid setting love still existed but the encounters were necessarily reticent and fleeting in a situation that precluded privacy. This was the first time that Kenneth had worked with Seymour. He saw her rehearsing in Peter Wright's *A Blue Rose* and was immediately attracted by the soft, deliquescent quality of her movement combined with her strong stage presence. It was the beginning of a professional relationship in which Kenneth would create a whole string of marvellous roles for a young artist who was to develop into a great dramatic dancer.

The role of the Child, taken by Noreen Sopwith, provided a foil for the corporate *angst* of the adults, precocious, knowing, yet comparatively unaffected by the oppressive atmosphere, the threat beyond the door.

The ballet was given its first performance by what was then colloquially called the Royal Ballet 'second company' at the Royal Opera House on January 2, 1958, in a triple bill that included *A Blue Rose* and Cranko's *The Angels* (the original decor of which Kenneth had utilised for *Solitaire*). Although the contemporary theme of *The Burrow* came as something of a shock to both audience and critics it was received as a brilliant piece of danced drama with rave reviews from most national newspapers. Almost without exception the critics assumed that Kenneth had based the ballet on *The Diary of Anne Frank* (the journal kept by the young Dutch-Jewish girl who for some time escaped the Nazi persecution by taking refuge in an Amsterdam attic before finally being sent to her death in a concentration camp) but in fact Kenneth had never read the work nor seen its stage adaptation.

Once again Kenneth was hailed as the most brilliant and inventive of young contemporary choreographers, tackling a modern theme with imagination and with a choreographic style that not only illustrated the story in a vivid and compelling manner but owed nothing to anyone else. His dexterity in fashioning a powerful narrative from an existing score was also once more commented upon. All the leading dancers were praised for their individual performances which helped them to re-establish the strong company identity that had tended to become blurred after an abortive attempt to overlap, if not amalgamate, the Sadler's Wells and Covent Garden companies following the granting of the Royal Charter.

*

Elated by his latest success and feeling that his creative abilities were once again in full flood, Kenneth before long embarked upon another new work, this time for the Covent Garden company which returned from its exhausting five-month American tour in mid-Febraury, 1958.

Only a few months before, the New York City Ballet had premiered George Balanchine's ballet *Agon* to a new score written by Stravinsky. Although the title means 'contest' in Greek there is practically nothing in the music to suggest any form of competition or struggle even on a competitive, concertante manner between the orchestral forces. The score was, in fact, derived from a seventeenth century French dance manual. It used a fairly large number of instruments, including mandolins, in small groups and the structure was built up from short, epigrammatic sequences linked to each other through the musical material; structurally, however, there was no discernable climactic episode or sequence.

The suggestion that Kenneth might use the score came from Dame Ninette (she may have seen the Balanchine version – totally plotless, of course – during the Royal Ballet's tour of America) and there is no doubt that it was the most challenging and difficult music that Kenneth had, up until then, ever attempted to choreograph – far more so than that composer's *Danses Concertantes*.

Without devising anything so distinct as a narrative theme, Kenneth, with the visual aid of yet another of Georgiadis's designs, hinted at a location and a mood which gave some substance to the choreography. The decor, black lines on an orangy-gold backcloth, vaguely suggested the facade of a house (one critic considered it was meant to be a 'bordello') with a number of mysterious silhouetted figures watching from a terrace or balcony, with the stage area itself as a meeting ground for the various groups of dancers made up from a total of fourteen.

Accompanying the opening and closing fanfares of the score were a pair of soloists, Dierdre Dixon and Ronald Hynd, who, dressed in turquoise, acted as 'chorus figures', presenting the other dancers, in yellowy-orange hues, led by Anya Linden and David Blair, in a series of brief solos and variations that, following the music, rapidly dissolved into one another.

The dancers' meetings that parallelled the music seemed, to some, like brief, laconic encounters between lovers whose feelings for one another were no longer motivated by affection. One critic thought that the various *pas de deux* expressed 'resignation, suppressed anger, pathos and futility', and certainly the general mood of the ballet was one of cynical, world-weary sophistication. Others saw the work as totally abstract, generally taken to mean plotless.

In general the audiences gave the ballet a lukewarm reception, no doubt disappointed that there was no overt virtuosity or climactic *pas de deux*; surprisingly, however, it received considerable acclaim in the daily press. Most critics realised that Stravinsky's score was difficult – both for the choreographer and the audience – in that it had little apparent melody or exciting rhythms but was dessicated and fragmented to the untrained ear. Even so, it was remarked that Kenneth's choreography had 'the same outer jerkiness and inner flow as the music', and that there was 'the right weight of dance to support the orchestration'.

The first night at Covent Garden was not enthusiastically received. One dance-magazine critic commented that the ballet was 'difficult for the dancers', having noted them 'counting with grim absorbtion', and concluded that the work was 'sophisticated, but signified nothing'. The most severe criticism, however, was reserved for the orchestra which was deemed 'unable to come to grips with Stravinsky's difficult score'. (Probably, one is inclined to think, because of inadequate rehearsal time.) It is interesting to note that the distinguished Swiss conductor, Ernest Ansermet, so closely associated with Diaghilev's Ballets Russes, remarked that it was 'the first truly abstract ballet' that he had ever seen.

In retrospect Kenneth thinks that he was insufficiently experienced to tackle such a complex, uningratiating score and his approach today would be very different. Even so it would seem that his apprehension of its musical qualities revealed a very acute sensibility; it would have been all too easy to match the music with a sharply stylised set of dances, a repitition of his success with *Danses Concertantes*.

*

After the failure of *Agon* to achieve a popular success (it received ten performances at the Royal Opera House, nine on tour) there followed something of a creative hiatus in Kenneth's career, lasting almost eighteen months, which is not easy to explain, even in terms of his other activities.

Early in 1959 Kenneth was approached by John Osborne to choreograph the dances in his satirical new musical, *The World of Paul Slickey*, which dealt mainly with the (then) difficult and delicate subject of sex change and the activities of a rather scurrilous newspaper gossip columnist. Kenneth had admired Osborne's early plays, *Look Back in Anger* and *The Entertainer*, in which the author's abrasive reflections upon contemporary society had had a distinct influence upon the new direction taken by Kenneth's choreography in *The Burrow*. The invitation to work with Osborne was gratifying.

During their initial meetings Kenneth found Osborne's personality stimulating, and the two men established quite a strong friendship.

At the same time Kenneth was preparing *Danses Concertantes* for the Royal Ballet's Covent Garden repertoire. For this production the main roles were danced by Maryon Lane (in her original part) with Desmond Doyle, and Donald MacLeary and Pirmin Trecu in the male roles originally danced by Michael Boulton and David Poole. Georgiadis had made minor alterations to the costumes including small tutus for the women which were generally disliked, one critic going so far as to say he would 'never forgive' the designer for doing such a thing.

The ballet itself (which had its Covent Garden premiere on March 13, 1959) was well received by the critics of the specialist dance magazines who considered that it gained considerably by being 'opened out' on the large stage, while the national press gave both the work and the dancers unanimously rave reviews.

Having spent all his professional life within the somewhat rarified, enclosed world of the Royal Ballet, familiar with its hierarchy, its distinct artistic policy and the ordered progress of its artists, Kenneth was intrigued by the free-for-all hurly-burly of the commercial theatre. At the auditions for the Osborne musical literally hundreds of 'dancers' turned up, only a small percentage of whom had either the experience or the technical ability necessary for the production.

In his choreography Kenneth did his best to develop the narrative progression of the work in a way that had already been pioneered by various American musicals, in particular *West Side Story*, which had opened in London not long before, but he felt that what was required of him left him little chance to do more than create a number of set pieces.

Throughout the several weeks of rehearsal and the subsequent pre-London tour, the production was beset with numerous problems (not all of them concerned with the musical itself) one of which was that the work was inordinately long. Kenneth remembers that, at one performance in Brighton, the matinée ran into the time for the evening performance with the ensuing confusion of one audience trying to get into the theatre while the other was trying to get out!

The World of Paul Slickey opened at the Palace Theatre in London on May 5, 1959, to almost universally bad reviews. It ran for only a short time.

Kenneth's agent was then successful in obtaining another commercial contract for him, this time in the film industry: he was commissioned to do the dance sequences for a British rock-and-roll musical, *Expresso Bongo*, starring Cliff Richard, Yolande Donlan and

Sylvia Sims. Kenneth was excited to be working on a film, although the material was rather flimsy – he had to arrange a rock-and-roll sequence as well as a strip-tease number – but in no way could he use the choreography in a creative way to further the action. What he most remembers now is having to get up in the early hours of the morning for the drive down to the studios in order to be ready to start work at 9 a.m. and then hanging around all day for a 'take' that was not set up until late afternoon. Again, however, it was useful experience in another medium – and the fee seemed enormously inflated by Covent Garden standards.

It would seem, then, that Kenneth's involvement with the Osborne musical and the film were the main reasons for the long gap between *Agon*, premiered on July 20, 1958, and his next ballet. He remembers remarking to Beriosova that it had been a depressing period of inactivity. The new ballet was *Le Baiser de la fée* (*The Fairy's Kiss*), the Stravinsky score which, three years before, had been too elaborate for the Sadler's Wells Theatre Ballet. Now, with the resources of Covent Garden at his disposal, Kenneth thought that the time had come to tackle it.

The score itself is among the most mellifluous that Stravinsky ever wrote, being a personal tribute to Tchaikovsky and using several themes from Tchaikovsky's songs and minor piano pieces. The stumbling block, as Kenneth knew well, was the story, adapted by the composer from Hans Andersen's *The Ice Maiden*. Stravinsky called it 'an allegory', adding, in his homage to Tchaikovsky, 'This Muse has, in the same way, marked the ballet with the fatal kiss whose mysterious imprint is visible in all the work of that great artist,' which was nice and poetic but not helpful when it came to making the allegory into a comprehensible narrative.

Following the score, Kenneth constructed his ballet in four scenes. *The Lullaby in the Storm*, a prologue in which a mother struggles through a storm with her baby; the mother dies and the baby receives a kiss from the Fairy and is found by Villagers. *A Village Fete*, in which the child, now a Young Man, appears with his Fiancée; the Fiancée leaves and he has his fortune told by a Gypsy who turns out to be the Fairy. *At the Mill*, where the Young Man, guided by the Fairy, finds his Fiancée dancing with her friends; the Fairy disappears then reappears again when the Young Man is left alone; he mistakes the Fairy for his Fiancée but is unable to resist her power; she kisses him. *The Lullaby of the Land Beyond Time and Place*, in which the Fiancée looks in vain for her lost love; the Young Man, totally in thrall to the Fairy, is taken by her to the mysterious Land Beyond Time and Place there to live eternally.

Even from this condensed synopsis it will be seen that the story poses certain questions. Why should the Fairy lead the Young Man to his Fiancée? How does he confuse two such evidently different characters? If, as Stravinsky stated, it was an allegory, what did those characters and events represent? The word, after all, means 'the description of a subject under the guise of another subject' (O.E.D.). Undaunted by such literal questions, Kenneth accepted the fairy story anomalies and followed the dictates of the music which were difficult enough in that the score often seems to ignore the scenario. In the opening prologue, for example, the music implies desolation rather than the orchestral representation of a storm. There is no sense of a musical/narrative progression towards a climax and, indeed, in the final scene, where the Young Man is in eternal thrall to the Fairy, the score is very lovely but drifts on and on in an anticlimactic way.

For his designer Kenneth chose Kenneth Rowell whose decor for *Laiderette* had been so successful. Rowell eschewed every conventional visual association of stage fairyland and devised a number of semi-abstract scenes, even for the village, which suggested a bleak, rather threatening landscape, rocks, cliffs and caverns, grottoes and gorges, with tendrilled foliage that was decorative yet sinister. His drop-curtain was patterned with what one critic described as 'vast falling leaves' which, at the opening of the ballet, became luminous then melted into the turbulence of the storm. Although Rowell's palette was sombre, browns, greys and dull purple, there were some magical lighting effects as when, for instance, the village scene was back-lit and glowed like a stained-glass window.

The role of the fairy was given to Beriosova and the Young Man and his Fiancée were MacLeary and Seymour. The choreography was the closest Kenneth had yet come to using the 'pure' classical vocabulary, including *tours en l'air* for MacLeary. Up until then he had avoided the use of such steps, feeling that they were a choreographic cliché when it was necessary to express brilliance. Even so, there were many distinctive moments in the various *pas de deux*, including a sequence where the Young Man, lying on his back, supported the Fairy in a flying image on his raised knees, a position that Kenneth was to use to great effect in subsequent ballets.

Each one of the three main roles (there was also a male quartet representing the Four Winds in the opening storm sequence) was not only inventively characterised, but exploited the particular capabilities and qualities of the dancers. MacLeary was given a number of big, open jumps and fast pirouettes which not only expressed his youthful vitality but, by the use of such classical bravura, set him apart from the other village youths in the story. Beriosova had movements of a cold, icy beauty with slow extensions and high arabesques, while Seymour had a more developed role, from blithe insouciance in the first scene, dancing with her friends, to something more complicated and excited in the pre-nuptial dances at the mill to a final series of dance images that evoked her misery at being abandoned.

The ballet received its premiere at the Royal Opera House on April 12, 1960, and was enthusiastically reviewed. Most critics made mention of the intractable story and the dramatic difficulties inherent in the score, but felt that Kenneth had overcome them with sufficient ingenuity to produce a work that had moments of great beauty. In particular, the final scene combined the resources of composer, choreographer and designer to create, in the words of one critic, 'an apotheosis of serene power that is one of the most poetic and significant moments in modern ballet'.

The three principal dancers enhanced their reputations through the work: MacLeary was praised for his virtuosity and 'lyrical fire'; Beriosova for her 'classically faultless phrasing and eloquence', and Seymour for the 'mixture of piquancy and pathos, tenderness and warmth' that she brought to the role.

11

A muse discovered, a rite created

If *Agon* and *Baiser de la fée* represented a return to more usual balletic idioms after an excursion into contemporary life with *The Burrow*, Kenneth's next ballet, although it was set in a previous period, dealt once more with the facts of life – this time literally. And once again the source was modern literature.

He had been reading two novels, *The Ripening Seed* by Colette and *House of the Angel* by a South American writer, Beatriz Guido. Both books dealt, in rather different ways, with the awakening of sexuality in adolescents. This was the theme from which Kenneth formulated his own scenario about a house party involving a number of young people, two of whom, a teenage girl and her pubescent cousin, become involved with an embittered husband and wife.

In the first scene a Young Man is alone in the garden of the house; the Mother emerges with two of her daughters and they drape the naked statues. The Boy and his Young Girl cousin, who does not comprehend his sexual interest in her, are left alone. They are joined by other young people and the Girl is teased by them and further bewildered by their giggling prurience over the statues. Guests arrive, among them the estranged Husband and Wife, and they are greeted by the Mother and daughters. The Boy and Girl are briefly aware of the married couple; then, left alone together again, the Girl gives the Boy a fleeting kiss before running off.

In the second scene, inside the house, the Governess supervises a dancing lesson for the young people. The Boy is awkward and embarrassed when the Wife tries to help him; the Girl, half aware of the Husband's interest in her, shows off and flirts with him to the alarm and outrage of the Mother. Left alone together, the Husband and Wife quarrel, observed by the Girl and her cousin.

At night the guests, assembled in the garden, watch a cabaret by dancers dressed as two cockerels and a hen. There is an atmosphere of repressed sexuality. The Wife, sitting alone, shows the Boy she understands his sexual yearnings and leads him away. The Girl follows the Husband into the garden and tries to re-establish her innocent flirtation; at first he resists her attentions but his ensuing interest turns into a brutal rape. Numbed and wounded, the Girl returns to the house where the Wife embraces the Young Man whom she has seduced. She sees her anguished Husband and tries to console him. The Young Man attempts to do the same for the Girl when she reappears but she misinterprets his attentions as the prelude to another vicious assault and rejects him. Alone, she arches her body in pain and walks towards a frigid future.

To sustain this fairly elaborate story, with its central core of a sexual quadrille, Kenneth decided that this time, whatever the risks involved, he needed a commissioned score. On the radio he had heard some music by the expatriate Hungarian composer Matyas Seiber. He liked it and approached Seiber, who readily agreed to write the music for the ballet, composing to the timed breakdown that Kenneth subsequently gave him.

For his designer, Kenneth reverted to Georgiadis who created a series of gauzy, dappled settings that not only looked beautiful and mysterious – particularly the garden scene – but, with simple cane and bamboo furniture, effectively placed both the Edwardian period and the semi-tropical South American location. The costumes, too, with the womens' bustles and enormous hats and the mens' stiff wing collars and formal attire, accentuated the torrid atmosphere of suppressed sexuality beneath the rigid social conventions of the time.

Kenneth chose Lynn Seymour for the Young Girl. Her performances in *The Burrow* and *Le Baiser de la Fée* had more than fulfilled his expectations of her talent and since those ballets, with their created

Baiser de la Fée was the first ballet in which MacMillan paired Beriosova with Donald MacLeary, a splendid partnership (he matched them in several ballets) which has gone curiously unremarked. This photograph illustrates well Beriosova's high arabesque and pliant back. (*Zoe Dominic.*)

The rape scene in *The Invitation* shocked audiences in 1960. The photograph shows Seymour with Doyle as the Husband in the climatic sequence. (*Zoe Dominic.*)

roles, she had also gained further experience – and acclaim – by dancing the great classical tests of Aurora in *The Sleeping Beauty* and Odette-Odile in *Swan Lake*.

A young male dancer of exceptional promise, Christopher Gable, was cast as the Cousin, with Anne Heaton and Desmond Doyle as the Wife and the Husband. Everything went well during rehearsals, in fact it was a very happy time with Kenneth and Seymour consolidating the personal rapport they had established in the previous ballets. Kenneth was constantly stimulated by Seymour's ability to 'flesh out' the steps he created for her. They had a similar approach to, and feeling for, the way a character can be developed through the steps of the classical vocabulary and, for her part, Seymour was interested in the way that Kenneth did not merely wish to impose a 'glossy shell' of beauty or romance on a given character or situation; they both felt that, if ballet was to have any contact with everyday life, was to reflect contemporary problems, then some steps, some movements would have to look ugly, odd, unexpected. People, says Seymour, are like that.

The happy atmosphere was shattered when news came that Seiber had been killed in a car crash while on a visit to South Africa. From a practical point of view the tragedy posed no problems – the score had been completed – but Seiber's untimely death was a terrible shock to Kenneth and the cast.

The ballet was called *The Invitation* and was first performed at Oxford on November 10, 1960, and given at the Royal Opera House on December 30 that year when the Royal Ballet touring company, for which the work had been created, was in residence while the main company were on tour in America. The national press gave it rave reviews, the *Financial Times* critic stating that it was 'a work of major importance both for the Royal Ballet and as the development of a choreographer's great talent.'

Of course the subject matter, and the rape scene itself, led to some controversy. In an interview in *The Times* Kenneth had stated, 'I'm sick to death of fairy stories', and his determined use of literary sources to reflect the physical and emotional problems of flesh-and-blood characters prompted one or two critics to question whether ballet was the proper medium for such subjects. The idea that the art can, or should, concern itself only with what is conventionally pretty, beautiful, graceful and charming dies hard.

Some critics thought that the ballet was too long; one thought that the symbolism of the hen and cockerels cabaret was too explicit for the social milieu in which the ballet was set; another that there was an inconsistency of design between the 'pretty, decorative cloths and the realistic statues', and yet another that Seiber's score was too eclectic, that he had been 'too loyal to the dramatic dictates for the music to be distinguished in its own right'. These comments, however, amounted only to so much cavilling in relation to the general and generous acclaim that the work received.

There was absolutely no divergence of opinion about the performances that Kenneth had obtained from his cast, particularly that of Seymour as the Young Girl whose 'startling tour de force' established her without question as the Royal Ballet's outstanding young dramatic dancer. And for the critics and the ballet-going public, it confirmed a choreographer/dancer relationship which was as important as had been the mutual inspiration between Ashton and Fonteyn and which was to produce a succession of marvellous roles and marvellous performances for the next twenty years.

The other members of the erotic quartet were also lavishly praised: Christopher Gable (who was to continue his successful partnership with Seymour when they created the leading roles in Ashton's *The Two Pigeons* a mere two months later) as the Cousin leapt into the front rank of Royal Ballet male dancers; Anne Heaton was praised for adding another memorable portrait to her *galère* of neurotic women; and several critics commented on Desmond Doyle's ability to create and maintain sympathy for the Husband despite his brutal behaviour.

*

The success of *The Invitation* did much to raise even higher Kenneth's reputation as the most exciting individual choreographic talent of the time – but it did very little for his bank balance. He still recalls it as a period when he was perpetually broke although his life-style could hardly be considered – indeed, never has been – extravagant. He was living alone in a small *pied à terre* in Dover Street, in central London, which was adequate for his simple domestic needs and conveniently situated for work, theatres, cinemas and public transport. His need to work was therefore not only from a compulsion to create but also to pay the grocery bills. Yet it appears there was another hiatus of several months between the first performance of *The Invitation* and his next ballet – and then two commissions arrived almost simultaneously.

The first came from Elizabeth West who, with Peter Darrell, was the co-founder, in 1957, of a small regional ballet company, Western Theatre Ballet, based in Bristol. (In 1969 the company became the Scottish Theatre Ballet, since renamed Scottish Ballet, based in Glasgow.) Elizabeth West was preparing a triple bill of works by modern composers: Stravinsky's *Le Reynard*, Milhaud's *Salade* and Kurt Weill's *Seven Deadly Sins*. Kenneth was offered the Milhaud score but held out instead for the Weill work which interested him much more.

The ballet had first been produced, with a libretto by Weill's famous collaborator Bertolt Brecht, in 1933 with choreography by George Balanchine for a short-lived Parisian company called Les Ballets 1933. There had been two subsequent productions, in America and Denmark. The story concerns two young women called Anna – a dancer and a singer, two halves of the same character – whose pilgrimage in search of a fortune through seven American cities leads them to encounter one of the seven sins in each location. In typical Brecht-Weill manner, it is an allegory that has more to do with the frailties and foibles of human nature than any specific reflection upon American metropolitan society. The subject-matter had an obvious appeal for Kenneth.

The overall artistic conception of the triple bill was in the hands of Barry Kay. Kenneth had already met him socially, but this was their first professional collaboration, an association that was to become increasingly important as both men's careers progressed. Kay created a basic setting of rostrums while the main dancing space was left to the designers of each ballet, Kay himself for *Salade*, Arthur Boyd for *Le Reynard* and Ian Spurling for *Seven Deadly Sins*. (Coincidentally, all three designers came from Australia.) The setting was particularly interesting in that (in Britain at least) it was, perhaps, the first time that a ballet set had been constructed rather than relying on painted cloths and flats and Kenneth was very impressed with the way that Kay had handled a complex assignment, finding a basic system that would serve all three productions.

In the case of *Seven Deadly Sins* the constructivist idea was carried a stage further by Spurling who designed the costumes and set-within-a-set. The seven city locations and the relevant sins were announced on vast lettered cubes manipulated by the cast, rather like children's building blocks.

The first performance of *Seven Deadly Sins* took place on the stage of the Empire Cinema, Edinburgh, on September 4, 1961. The rehearsal period had not been without its difficulties: the stage crew, unused to the technical problems attendant upon a live performance, at one point walked out *en bloc*. By the first night, however, all the problems had been sorted out and, with Anya Linden and Cleo Laine as the two halves of Anna, supported by Laverne Mayer, Oliver Symons and Peter Cazalet in character roles, the ballet was the undoubted success of the triple bill (Kenneth had shrewdly guessed which was the most interesting material!). It was subsequently presented in London for a short, though equally successful, season at Sadler's Wells Theatre.

*

Eleven days after the Edinburgh premier, Kenneth presented another new work, *Diversions*, at Covent Garden which implies that he had been working on both ballets simultaneously. This time it was an abstract work and Kenneth, whose recollection of the ballet's provenance is now somewhat hazy, thinks that it came to him as a specific call to complete a triple bill with which to open the 1961/62 season and which already included two narrative ballets, Ashton's *Persephone* and Rodrigues' *Jabez and the Devil*. Certainly the score, Arthur Bliss's *Concerto for Double String Orchestra*, suggested by de Valois, was not suitable for the imposition of any narrative theme.

Kenneth's choreographic plan called for two leading couples plus four supporting couples. The choreography itself, by far the purest example of straightforward classicism in all of Kenneth's work, made fiendishly difficult technical demands upon the whole cast, not only in the steps themselves but also in phrasing, precision and musicality. But then Kenneth was writing for a company which, at that time, was technically very strong indeed. He recalls that, even in the *corps de ballet*, there were such superb technicians as Vergie Derman, Deanne Bergsma, Vivienne Lorrayne and Georgina Parkinson.

The steps for the leading couple, Svetlana Beriosova and Donald MacLeary, were romantic and serene, making much use of Beriosova's beautiful classical line, especially in arabesque. For MacLeary, the style might best be described as 'fluent athleticism', once again showing his polished virtuosity to advantage. The second couple, Maryon Lane and Graham Usher, being smaller in stature but equally accomplished in technique, were given double work and solos that were gay and buoyant, demanding tremendous speed with precision. (It is interesting to note that when the ballet was revived in 1979 Kenneth said he was amazed that, eighteen years before, he had dared to demand such sustained virtuosity from his dancers.)

As is sometimes the way, however, the technical difficulties were masked by the sheer beauty of the various *pas de deux* and framing ensembles. The designs by Philip Prowse were created on a shoe-string budget but none the less effective. The dancing area was totally blank, with black drapes at the back of the stage; the decor was all 'flown', suspended above the dancers' heads, representing large pieces of ruined, classical architecture, a crumbling pediment, a cracked architrave. The costumes, too, neat tunics for the men, bodices and short, tennis-style skirts for the women, with both sexes wearing gold fillets round the head and brow, were decorated in a manner that suggested classical figures from a frieze – more Etruscan, perhaps, than Roman or Greek – and executed in richly sombre colours, black, aubergine, ochre and cinnamon. The effect was both grand and darkly romantic, and not only showed the dancers' bodies to great advantage but, together with the decor, echoed the brooding melancholy of the score.

Once again Kenneth's ballet, produced quickly and intended as a foil for the other two works in the programme, proved to be the success not only of that triple bill but also of the season (both *Persephone* and *Jabez and the Devil* were soon dropped from the repertoire). Critics remarked upon the extraordinary lightness and freedom of the choreography and called it 'fluent', 'graceful' and 'aqueous'. Curiously, the score was not greatly liked, one critic saying that its 'neo-Elgarian' quality had 'a dark melancholy' which gave a 'dying fall' to the ballet. That, indeed, was part of the work's refulgent beauty but the writer intended it as a criticism. Yet again, several reviewers noticed how brilliantly Kenneth had written for the particular qualities of his chosen cast and audiences responded enthusiastically at each performance.

*

As soon as the first performance of *Diversions* was over Kenneth travelled to Copenhagen where the Royal Danish Ballet, one of Europe's major classical companies with a tradition second only to that of the Paris Opera Ballet, had done him the signal honour of inviting him to present a whole evening of his works. The three ballets chosen were *Solitaire*, for which Kenneth Rowell designed a new decor, *Danses Concertantes* and *The Burrow*.

Kenneth remembers the visit as an extremely happy one in which he was made very welcome by the whole company. He remembers, too, being very impressed by the male dancers though not so much by the women. (The Royal Ballet was, at that time, very strong in female dancers but had yet to develop more than one or two outstanding male technicians such as Donald MacLeary and David Blair.)

If *Diversions* had, as it were, been 'written to order', Kenneth's next ballet was a work that had been gestating in his mind for some time, a score that, for half a century, had presented a titanic challenge to choreographers: Stravinsky's *The Rite of Spring*.

Since the ballet's riotous first performance by Diaghilev's Ballets Russes in Paris in 1913, with choreography by Nijinsky, there had been two major reinterpretations: one by Léonid Massine in 1920, also for Diaghilev's company, and another by Maurice Bejart in 1959. Nijinsky and Massine had kept to Stravinsky's original conception of an ancient Russian tribal rite, the release of generative forces with the coming of spring (such an important season in that land, so much of which suffers a frozen winter) and the propitiation

62

Created quickly to fill in a triple bill, *Diversions* still stands as an example of pure classicism which, together with *Concerto*, demonstrates that MacMillan is as capable as any choreographer in the world in creating abstract ballets of sheer beauty of movement. (*Zoe Dominic*.)

In 1962 MacMillan selected a relatively unknown dancer, Monica Mason, just out of the corps de ballet, for the only soloist role in *Rite of Spring*. Her tremendous performance as the Chosen Maiden, notable for both its emotional intensity and unflagging strength, brought her great critical acclaim. (*Anthony Crickmay*.)

of the gods of the vernal equinox by the sacrifice of a young virgin. Bejart's version was based more upon a fertility ritual with a climactic union between a man and a woman. Kenneth's version was not specific in location but his tribe, which enacted the Stravinskian sacrifice, represented all aboriginal forces.

At the suggestion of de Valois, Kenneth contacted the painter Sydney Nolan to do the designs. Nolan had had acclaim for his depiction of harsh landscapes and folk legends in his native Australia, but his designs for the ballet were, again, more universal in conception, not representative of anything recognisably antipodean. The first half of the ballet, The Adoration of the Earth, had a back-cloth and wings that resembled brown marbling on stone; here and there the veining seemed like primitive cave-paintings of warriors and animals. For the second half of the ballet, The Sacrifice, the backcloth was changed to a huge mushroom shape, the dome swollen to seem like an enormous sun, its surface textured like an opal. When lit, it was coloured the white-gold of dawn, then progressed to the yellow-gold of noon and finally the blood-red of sunset. The costumes for both men and women were all-over body tights, or leotards, ranging in colour from pale orange through pink to deep red and figured, haphazardly, with grey and white smudges and what looked like the imprint of hands. Head-dresses for the women were white raffia-straw wigs tipped with black, and for the men smaller black wigs drawn up to the crown of the head with a top-knot, rather like Samurai warriors.

Kenneth kept to the two distinct sections of the score; the only solo role was that of the Chosen Maiden and he knew that this would be crucial casting. When he told de Valois that he wanted one particular dancer she thought he meant Beriosova, but in fact he had selected a young soloist, only recently promoted from the corps de ballet, Monica Mason. Kenneth had been impressed by the strength and assurance of her dancing and thought that her striking, rather exotic features were just right for the part.

Although Kenneth had rarely, if ever, worked out choreography in advance, when he began work on *Rite of Spring* he knew he intended to use large groups of dancers *en masse*, sometimes segregating the sexes, sometimes differentiating between the *blocs* of Adolescents, Men and Maidens. Floor patterns were based on simple geometrics – squares, circles, diagonals – with one spectacular serpentine sequence in which the dancers, grasping each other by the hips and in line behind one another fell backwards, like a row of dominoes, into a sitting position. At other times dancers grouped in a tight circle opened outward like a flower in bloom. In performance, some critics thought they detected the formations of dancers to be symbolic of an atomic explosion. Certainly, at that time, there was a growing and active anti-nuclear movement and the backcloth for The Sacrifice could represent not only the mushroom fertility symbol but also its reverse, the deadly mushroom cloud of an atomic explosion.

Many of the dancers' movements were simian in manner, with legs wide apart, feet parallel in the style of modern dance, hands and arms dangling or sometimes angularly raised as if grasping an overhanging bough or spear. The style was totally anti-classical although now and again an extended leg or jump might seem to have a distant affinity with an arabesque or jeté. Certainly the atavistic postures that Kenneth invented drew upon the almost limitless possibilities of the classical vocabulary and the physical prowess and virtuosity with which classically trained dancers are endowed.

Rehearsals were difficult to schedule as Kenneth needed practically the entire company, apart from the principals. Accordingly, he began by choreographing Monica Mason's final death-dance before beginning work with the company. Mason recalls that she was excused the final half hour of daily class in order to rehearse with Kenneth and the company pianist, Anthony Twiner. They worked for an hour each day for three weeks in a small studio called The Garden Room, going over and over and over the latter part of the score note by note, bar by bar, with Mason memorising the complicated counts. In addition she listened at home to the complete orchestral score, also played in endless repetition until Mason's sister remarked that even the family dog must know the music. The result was that by the first night Mason was able to dance her role instinctively rather than mechanically. She says that quite apart from her own feeling of 'possession' by the music, the whole cast were so intoxicated by the score that they reached a state of corporate frenzy which carried them beyond questions of stamina (the ballet, of course, is exhausting to dance) and imbued them with a feeling that they could go on and on.

Rite of Spring received its first performance on May 3, 1962, at a Royal Gala at Covent Garden attended by Queen Elizabeth the Queen Mother. It made a tremendous impact on the distinguished and vociferously enthusiastic audience. The critics, as always, were sharply divided in their opinions. The review in the *Dancing Times* called it 'a clever and almost elegant work; as a ballet it lacks dramatic power, fails to engage our emotions and ends on an anticlimax', and went on to say that 'the classically trained dancers were too lightweight' and that a modern dance style might have proved a better idiom.

The critic of *Ballet Today* thought that Kenneth was a 'strange choice' as choreographer for 'nothing in his previous work suggested he would have a flair for a violent, brutal, primitive theme' as he was 'faced with a task quite foreign to his temperament'. One can only assume that this reviewer had seen very little of Kenneth's work.

The critic of *Dance and Dancers* was much more enthusiastic. 'Looked at in detail,' he wrote, 'the style MacMillan has created for himself – which, incidentally, bears a passing likeness to his normal choreographic development – is an interesting alloy derived from many different ones . . . yet the final result suggests a most secure choreographic unity. As a mere realisation of the score the choreography is astonishingly effective. Time and again he hits upon a compelling visual image that shocks the mind into a new awareness of the music.'

The unquestioned success of the evening was Monica Mason's performance as the Chosen Maiden. The unflagging power of her dancing, the appearance of being totally possessed by her destiny, brought an ovation from the audience (as it always has; some twenty years later, Mason gave undiminished performances in the role). The *Dance and Dancers* critic wrote of the 'vital and vibrant ensemble dancing' and, of Mason, 'even if she does nothing else she has given one of British ballet's most memorable performances'.

*

Having delivered himself of this tremendously complex opus, Kenneth was content to rest upon his laurels although, during the following month, on June 28, he reproduced *Valse Excentrique*, originally created for a gala in 1956, for three dancers of Western Theatre Ballet (Clover Roop, Laverne Mayer and Oliver Symons) while in July, for the annual Royal Ballet School performance, he created a piece called *Dance Suite* to Milhaud's *Suite Provencale*, consisting of a *pas de trois*, *pas de quatre* and *pas de cinque*. One critic commented upon its 'attractive, folksy flavour' but the general feeling was that Kenneth's choreography was far too difficult for the graduate students, but as they included Kerrison Cooke, Vergie Derman and Richard Cragun – later to become *premier danseur* of the Stuttgart Ballet and one of the world's greatest virtuosos – no doubt he was justified in making such technical demands on them.

In his next major work he was to make equally great demands not only upon the principal dancers in his new ballet but also upon himself and in doing so confronted an unwonted – and unwanted – creative crisis.

66

Difficulty in London, success in Stuttgart

Irrespective of the somewhat equivocal critical reception of *Rite of Spring* Kenneth had had no doubts about what he had wanted to do or how he wanted it done; it was the outcome of a gestation period of some years and it was a massive demonstration of choreographic confidence. His next work, however, involved him in a creative struggle that was the exact opposite: the choreographic equivalent of 'writer's block'.

As Kenneth's contract stipulated a certain number of ballets per year, it was customary for him to have a 'standing order' with the resident ballet conductor(s) of the Royal Opera House to suggest scores that might serve as the basis for a ballet. Accordingly, John Lanchbery suggested Shostakovich's youthful First Symphony, composed when he was nineteen as his graduation thesis. Kenneth obtained a recording of the work, found it attractive and decided to choreograph it as his next ballet.

The symphonic structure, which was in no way programmatic, meant that the ballet would be plotless. But with Lynn Seymour as the leading female dancer (the other principals were Georgina Parkinson, Donald MacLeary and Desmond Doyle, with Deanne Bergsma, Vivienne Lorrayne, Monica Mason, Keith Rosson, Robert Mead and Anthony Dowell as supporting dancers) almost anything that Kenneth gave her to do took on a meaningful quality, and his sensitive reaction to her inherently dramatic presence began to formulate, if not a narrative, then significant relationships between the dancers.

With Seymour's presence so suggestive of mood and atmosphere, Kenneth's imagination conspired to work against him – it was just too productive of choreographic ideas. For example, one morning Seymour entered the rehearsal studio and, while listening to Kenneth and without conscious intention, assumed a sphinx-like attitude on the floor. Kenneth liked it so much that he immediately incorporated it into the choreography although, of course, the ballet was not about a sphinx or any creature associated with classical legend. Kenneth's teeming ideas became too prolific for progression: he remembers that he would work all day devising steps and movements and the next day he would abandon everything.

Seymour recalls the ballet as 'agony to work on' and thought that Kenneth was 'exorcising devils' in his choreography. Kenneth, despite the difficulties he encountered in creating the work, remembers the period as a happy one. But there is no doubt that *Symphony* – which was the simple title given to the ballet – did present him with problems.

Following what by then had become his regular practice, Kenneth went to the Slade School to find a designer for the new ballet and was much taken with the work of Yolanda Sonnabend whom he commissioned to do the sets and costumes. *Symphony* was not her first work for the theatre, as she had already designed Peter Wright's *A Blue Rose* in 1957. For Kenneth she produced two florid abstract designs, with a change after the second movement with rather more geometric designs on the dancers' body tights. They also wore head-dresses that have been described as looking like 'bathing caps' but Kenneth dispensed with them at the dress rehearsal.

It was ironic that, after all her hard work, Seymour was unable to dance on the first night, having succumbed to raging influenza; her place was taken by Antoinette Sibley who, although the official 'second cast', had had little rehearsal and had to learn the difficult and exhausting role in three days. MacLeary, too, had been plagued by a knee injury throughout rehearsals and was unable to dance full out on the first night.

The first performance of *Symphony* was given at the Royal Opera House on February 15, 1963 and, despite its plotless construction (and without Seymour), most critics seemed to find that it carried emotional undertones. It is interesting to note that in an interview given to *About the House*, the quarterly magazine produced for The Friends of Covent Garden, Kenneth had said, while the ballet was still being created, 'The more I look at my work the more it seems that, unwittingly, I choose the lonely, outcast, rejected figure. I don't set out to do it but it always seems to happen unconsciously – as a sort of *leitmotif*. It will be interesting to see if this emerges in the new work.'

Nothing so definite did emerge, although the critic of *Dance and Dancers* detected a 'desolate undertow' in the choreography. Although the steps rarely seemed to parallel the musical ideas – indeed the pace and phrasing of the movements often seemed in opposition to the mood of the music – the same critic thought that it was 'some of MacMillan's most sensuously lovely choreography', and went on to say 'He daubs both male and female virtuosity on the stage with the sublime casualness of a painter selecting a certain colour.'

Other critics noted Kenneth's use of a growing virtuosity among the company's dancers, particularly the men, and several of them commented upon the difference between Kenneth's and Massine's

68

approach to the same score (Massine had used the Shostakovich First Symphony for *Rouge et Noir* which, in fact, was never seen in Britain). The response in the national press was very mixed, the critic of *The Times* calling it a 'work of obvious distinction', while the *Daily Mail* was 'baffled' by it; the critic of the *Daily Express* felt that it was 'decidedly a ballet to be seen', although the *Daily Telegraph* thought that 'so rarely does he seem to be creating with it (the music) that one feels most of the time he is taking the line of most resistance.' Almost all of them, once again, commented upon his prolific invention.

The settings were admired for their purely decorative values although some critics felt that the designs were simply too powerful, too overwhelming. One critic described the first movement setting as 'a mass of blue and orange viscera circumscribed by black masses', and the second movement as 'huge slabs of molten orange rock rent asunder by white hot flame'. The performances of the dancers were commended, especially that of Sibley as it was known that she had learnt the role at short notice but, not unexpectedly, when Seymour finally danced the part most critics thought that she extended the on-stage relationships between the dancers, though just what those relationships were, or what emotional content was revealed, they were unable to say.

*

Marking off years as milestones of achievement can be a pointless and sometimes misleading exercise, but perhaps it is worth noting that the first performance of *Symphony* occurred ten years and two weeks after Kenneth's very first choreographic endeavour, *Somnambulism*. However one chooses to look at that decade, it certainly presents a remarkable record of choreographic development: ten years in which Kenneth had established himself not only as one of the leading British choreographers but had also won international recognition. In fact, Kenneth's next commission came from abroad.

Before that, however, Kenneth had revised *House of Birds* for the Royal Ballet Touring Company (one of its interim, though not always official, titles). Since it was last produced, some of the choreography had been forgotten and the new version, with Maryon Lane and Christopher Gable dancing the roles of the Young Girl and the Young Man, ended with an extended bravura *pas de deux* in which Kenneth exploited Gable's virtuosity. One critic, however, felt that this 'ten minutes of exhilerating pure dance' with its 'breathtakingly difficult partnering' tended to 'neutralise the ballet's sinister aftertaste'. Yet there is no doubt that it further enhanced Gable's rising

Las Hermanas was originally created for the Stuttgart Ballet in 1963 and taken into the repertory of what is now the Sadler's Wells Royal Ballet in 1971. This photograph of the S.W.R.B. production illustrates the marvellously atmospheric monochrome set by Nicholas Georgiadis who had also suggested Federica Garcia Lorca's play, *The House of Bernado Alba*, as the basis of MacMillan's ballet. (*Anthony Crickmay*.)

reputation. One critic called him 'the first heroic British dancer' who could 'slip into Soviet ballet without anyone being the wiser'.

In 1961 John Cranko had been appointed Artistic Director of the Stuttgart Ballet and within a short space of time he had assembled an accomplished group of young dancers and an interesting repertoire. In the late spring of 1963 Cranko invited Kenneth over to see the company and he was very impressed. A second invitation was issued: for Kenneth to create a ballet, which he was delighted to do.

The idea for the new work actually came from Nicholas Georgiadis: Federico García Lorca's play *The House of Bernardo Alba*, a study in social and sexual repression. The setting is Spain in the early twentieth century, although the rigorous disciplines of the Catholic church and the moral conventions of society were so strict that the characters in the story could have been living four centuries earlier. A widowed, crippled matriarch has five daughters, none of whom can be married until the eldest is wed. A prospective husband calls and after a strained encounter with the plain eldest sister he is seduced by the youngest. The jealous middle sister observes what is happening and rouses the household. The man is banished; the mother locks the doors of the house and confronts her daughters, the youngest of whom is sent to her room in disgrace. They all know they face a life of frigid spinsterdom. Painfully the matriarch climbs the stairs to the youngest daughter's room, pulls aside a curtain and reveals her lifeless body hanging from a rope. Such powerfully emotional stuff was bound to appeal to Kenneth – here was not one but a whole houseful of social outcasts.

The feeling of oppression and repression, social and sexual, in a hot climate was, to some degree, reminiscent of *The Invitation*, but whereas that ballet dealt with pubescent awakenings, *Las Hermanas* (The Sisters) as Kenneth titled the new ballet, dealt with mature women only too aware of, if not experienced in, adult passions. Kenneth had felt the need for a commissioned score for *The Invitation*, but he thought the compressed, enclosed drama of *Las Hermanas* could be encompassed by existing music. Previously, he had twice successfully used compositions by Frank Martin, once for the wistful *Laiderette* and once for the highly dramatic *The Burrow*; again he studied the compositions of the Swiss composer and this time chose the *Concerto for Harpsichord and Strings*. Despite the delicacy of the writing for the solo instrument he thought that the thematic ideas of the concerto were sufficiently dark-toned to illustrate the dramatic events of the ballet while the sound qualities of the harpsichord itself would do much to intimate the formalities of the feminine ménage.

As Georgiadis had suggested the source material, it was natural for Kenneth to choose him once more as the designer and Georgiadis produced a marvellous monochromatic set – black, white and grey – that effectively realised the ascetic atmosphere inside the house in contrast to the brilliant sunlight outside when the man makes his first formal call and the romantic starlight when he later encounters the youngest sister.

The ballet received its first performance in Stuttgart on July 13, 1963 and was enthusiastically received by the German audiences and critics. It was first performed in this country when the Stuttgart Ballet made its British debut at the Edinburgh Festival in the autumn of that same year. Almost unanimously the critics thought that *Las Hermanas* was the most interesting work that the company had brought with them although several had reservations about the ballet. The critic of *Dance and Dancers* conceded that it had 'power and atmosphere', but felt that Kenneth needed to 'formalise and translate his material into his own medium much more'. The music critic of the magazine thought that the score served as a 'suitable background for repression' but was 'never suggestive of the passionate heat which plays such a part in Lorca's play'. Every critic praised Georgiadis's designs and Marcia Haydée, who was the leading dancer of the company, as the Eldest Sister. Helga Heinrich as the Jealous Sister and Birgit Keil as the Youngest Sister both received good notices for their performances, as did Ray Barra as the Man. It is interesting to note that Haydée was surprised when Kenneth selected her for the role of the Eldest Sister. 'How could you tell I'd be right for the part,' she asked, 'when you'd only seen me as Swanilda in *Coppelia*?' to which Kenneth replied that he knew a dramatic dancer when he saw one.

Audiences in Germany had responded enthusiastically to *Las Hermanas* which is no doubt why Cranko asked Kenneth to mount *House of Birds* for the company before its arrival in Edinburgh, with Anita Cardus and Richard Cragun as the young principals. The macabre fantasy of the ballet was not to the German critics' liking, however. Kenneth thinks that this was due to a lack of Teutonic awareness of the *genre*. After its decline in the nineteenth century, classical ballet in Germany had not had the same renaissance as had occurred in most of Western Europe following Diaghilev's appearance with his Ballets Russes. Since the beginning of the century Germany had been much more influenced by the Expressionism of Kurt Jooss and by the free-dance styles of Isadora Duncan, Mary Wigman, Rudolf Laban et al, while during the second World War it was effectively severed from contemporary developments altogether. Consequently German audiences were not so attuned to the post-war allegorical/philosophical fantasies created by Cocteau, Kochno, Petit, Charrat etc. that had briefly influenced Kenneth and other

73

British choreographers in the forties and fifties. *House of Birds*, then, seemed to them rather silly even though it was based on a fairy tale by the Brothers Grimm.

Before the year ended Kenneth produced a short solo for Rudolf Nureyev to dance at the R.A.D. Gala at the Theatre Royal, Drury Lane. It was a fiasco. At the performance the stage was slippery, Nureyev lost a shoe, stopped dancing to remove the other and thereafter appeared to improvise the choreography. Looking back, Kenneth says, 'I was not proud of the choreography.' He thinks that part of the trouble was that he was inhibited and somewhat over-awed by being asked to create a solo for a dancer who, since his defection to the West two years before, had become a world super-star. Another odd aspect of the occasion was Kenneth's choice of music, Bach's *Fantasia in C Minor*. Altogether it is an incident he prefers to put out of his mind – except that, when reminded of it, he remarked, 'Perhaps I should go back to Bach.'

At the beginning of 1964 Kenneth began work on another ballet for the Royal Ballet Touring Company, this time finding inspiration in Darius Milhaud's score *La Création du Monde*. The music had originally been commissioned for Rolf de Maré's short-lived Ballet Suédois in 1923, with choreography by Jean Borlin. The subject of the work was a naive account of the Creation seen through negro eyes and Milhaud used one or two allusions to jazz in his music.

In his version Kenneth maintained the naive approach by sub-stituting children for negroes although, it must be said, they were somewhat sophisticated children, very much of their time, at the height of the youthful rebellions of the 'permissive' sixties.

At the beginning of the ballet a group of children array themselves in clothes from a dressing-up box, watched by a Butcher's Boy who circles round them on his delivery bicycle. The Butcher's Boy brings on the Great Deity, an old man who subsequently appears as a figure wearing a paper hat, carrying a wooden sword and with a Union Jack on his leotards. The Butcher's Boy becomes a huge green Apple. With these characters' reincarnations, as it were, advertising slogans are flashed on the backcloth, such as (for the Deity) *For my next creation . . .* and (for the Apple) *I was seduced by Granny Smith*. With the slogan *I was a teenage snake* a Serpent appears and then, with *New, Instant People*, the figures of Adam and Eve, their leotards covered with slang phrases for man and woman, such as Bird, Guy, Fella, Filly. Despite the efforts of the Deity/John Bull figure, Adam and Eve are inevitably lured to the Apple whose costume deflates as he is eaten. Defeated and dejected the Deity is left alone; the children return in their street clothes and the Deity is driven off.

With a pop-art setting by James Goddard, the ballet used the

74

allegory of Adam and Eve to make a cynical comment on the contemporary world of advertising slogans and media manipulation (the decor utilised headlines from the *Financial Times*), making its points with a zany, off-beat humour that loses much in the telling. Perhaps it was too off-beat, for the critics were mostly unenthusiastic and audiences – always unsure whether to laugh at the ballet unless they are given very distinct pointers – somewhat bewildered. In short, Kenneth's conception seems to have been a bit too clever.

The *Financial Times* critic called it a 'vastly theatrical piece' and went on to say, 'One is struck by the comic ingenuity of the conception and the skill with which MacMillan has placed it within the stylistic limits of both a child's game and the ephemera of advertising.'

The *Dance and Dancers* reviewer, however, was less sure of what Kenneth intended, referring to 'a ballet within a ballet within a ballet' and asked 'why should the Deity wear a Union Jack?' (surely he knew God is British?) and 'who is the Butcher's Boy who becomes the Apple?' There are always people who need a literal explanation for every character, every step, every gesture in ballet and *La Création du Monde* is but one of several works by Kenneth that have puzzled critics and audiences who like everything spelt out. Perhaps the Butcher's Boy should have had Celestial Delivery Service printed on his costume.

The ballet received its first performance at the Stratford Memorial Theatre on February 12, 1964 and the cast included Doreen Wells and Richard Farley as Adam and Eve, praised for dancing with 'classic grace and feeling'; Ronald Emblen as the Deity, Adrian Grater as the Butcher's Boy/Apple and Elizabeth Anderton as the Serpent.

*

Kenneth's next creation was a work that was part of a triple bill to celebrate the quatercentenary of Shakespeare's birth, the two other ballets being Ashton's *The Dream* and a revival of Helpmann's *Hamlet*. In fact, it was the first of Kenneth's ballets to be commissioned by Ashton who had succeeded de Valois as Director of the Royal Ballet in September 1963, and because of that Kenneth was especially anxious to produce a worthwhile work. He conceived the idea of a suite of dances exploring several of Shakespeare's references to love, and he called the ballet *Images of Love*.

'I am not a Shakespeare scholar,' Kenneth has said, and in devising and defining his chosen references he was limited both by his lack of academic knowledge and, more importantly, by the limitations of the medium itself; obviously, a poetic phrase, a

Created for the quatercentenary of Shakespeare's birth, *Images of Love* proved
an interesting disappointment – mainly because of the unsatisfactory music
which made MacMillan extremely wary of commissioned scores.
The most compelling of the nine episodes of the ballet was a *pas de trois*
inspired by Sonnet 144 beginning 'Two loves I have of comfort and despair
. . .' The sequence had the immensely strong casting of Rudolf Nureyev with
Christopher Gable as 'a man right fair' and Lynn Seymour as 'a woman
coloured ill' as shown in this photograph.
(*Anthony Crickmay.*)

philosophical thought, can only be superficially expressed in dance.

The quotations he selected for the nine episodes of the ballet were:

1. 'She never told her love, But let concealment, like a worm i' the bud, Feed on her damask cheek' (Viola to Duke Orsino, *Twelfth Night*, Act II Scene IV.) For this opening scene Kenneth cast Svetlana Beriosova with Donald MacLeary, supported by Georgina Parkinson, Deanne Bergsma and Monica Mason.

2. '. . . the remembrance of my former love Is by a newer object quite forgotten.' (Proteus, soliloquising, *Two Gentlemen of Verona*, Act II Scene IV.) This was for a trio of dancers, Nadia Nerina, Desmond Doyle and Keith Rosson.

3. '. . . while idle I stood looking on, I found the effect of love in idleness' (Luciano to Tranio, *The Taming of the Shrew*, Act I Scene I.) This scene used Georgina Parkinson, Desmond Doyle, Monica Mason, Deanne Bergsma, Derek Rencher, Keith Rosson, Vergie Derman, Rosalyn Eyre, Carole Needham, David Jones, Geoffrey Cauley, Paul Brown.

4. 'If you love her, you cannot see her.' 'Why?' 'Because love is blind.' (Valentine and Speed, *Two Gentlemen of Verona*, Act II Scene I.) This was a duet for Lynn Seymour and Christopher Gable.

5. 'Love, lend me wings to make my purpose swift' (Proteus, soliloquising, *Two Gentlemen of Verona* Act I Scene I.) A duet for Nadia Nerina and Alexander Grant.

6. 'When love begins to sicken and decay, It useth an enforced ceremony' (Brutus to Lucilius, *Julius Caesar* Act IV Scene II.) Another duet for Beriosova and MacLeary.

7. 'Two loves I have of comfort and despair' (Sonnet CLVIV.) A *pas de trois* for Seymour, Gable and Rudolf Nureyev.

8. 'I break my fast, dine, sup, and sleep, Upon the very naked name of love' (Valentine to Proteus, *Two Gentlemen of Verona* Act II Scene IV.) This scene used Alexander Grant with Georgina Parkinson, Deanne Bergsma, Monica Mason, Vergie Derman, Rosalyn Eyre and Carole Needham.

9. 'If music be the food of love, play on; Give me excess of it' (Duke Orsino, *Twelfth Night*, Act I Scene I.) This was for the full company.

The quotations span a narrow range of plays with a somewhat curious emphasis on one scene from *Two Gentlemen of Verona*, which play represented four of the nine sequences, with two from *Twelfth Night*, one each from *The Taming of the Shrew* and *Julius Caesar* and one taken from a Sonnet. Any cursory perusal of Shakespeare's works will discover a number of dissertations upon the nature of love, from *Love's Labour's Lost* to *Much Ado About Nothing*, from *Troilus and Cressida* to *Othello*, but Kenneth did not intend that the ballet should be a grand tour of love themes from important plays or even an exploration of different kinds of love – passionate love, platonic love, filial love, love of self, of power, of wealth. 'I was really reduced to one-liners,' he says, and those one lines that he selected gave him sufficient scope for the ballet he intended. In fact, the sentiment expressed within the context of the source material was sometimes transferred, for Kenneth's purposes, to another situation entirely. Shakespeare, then, was simply a springboard for a number of dances dealing with human relationships, a titular link with the festival programme.

John Lanchbery had played for Kenneth some music by a young composer, Peter Tranchell, which Kenneth liked, and accordingly he decided to commission Tranchell to compose a score for the ballet. Kenneth produced a breakdown of his requirements including an explanation of how he saw each of the nine sequences and then left Tranchell to get on with it – which proved a mistake.

Barry Kay was asked to design the decor and he produced an elegant, non-representational, purely decorative construction of slim gold tubes which, when lit, looked very beautiful.

As is the custom, rehearsals proceeded to a piano version of the score; it was not until the dress rehearsal that Kenneth heard the orchestral version and he was so appalled that he burst into tears. What had sounded perfectly acceptable on the piano now sounded exceedingly trite and superficial when played by the full orchestra. It was, of course, too late to alter anything, to pare it down, make it appear more astringent, less like music for a Broadway show. It was an experience that seared Kenneth's artistic susceptibilities and made him ultra-wary of commissioned scores for years to come.

Images of Love received its first performance at the Royal Opera House on February 4, 1964 and can be accounted a partial success. It was welcomed by the critics as an attempt to interpret a theme that Shakespeare himself had found as a perpetual stimulus and one that was treated in purely dance terms, rather than just making a ballet out of a Shakespeare play and parts of it were seen by most critics as providing something genuinely new and inventive.

This point was made by the critic of the *Daily Telegraph* who wrote, 'One third of the ballet is heroic in size and meaning, the rest – well, let the rest be silence.' Another critic felt that 'it lacks overall shape but there are episodes of choreography that shine out with inspiration', while yet another thought it 'an important and enthralling ballet, meaty all through, without a moment where one does not want to look and look and look'.

Undoubtedly the *Twelfth Night* episode about the lady who never told her love, for Beriosova and MacLeary, was one of the most successful, as was their cold, formal relationship in the *Julius Caesar* quotation, but the most inventive – and, for its time, rather daring in the relationships that it explored – was the *pas de trois* for Seymour, Gable and Nureyev, based on the line from the Sonnet. The choreography was elaborate and imaginative and at one point Kenneth invented a brilliant movement in which the woman was thrown in the air, executed a double turn and was then caught in her partner's arms, a piece of virtuosity that has since been extensively copied. The success of this trio owed much, of course, to the splendid dancing and strong stage personalities of the three executants.

That the ballet was, however, a disappointment – not least to Kenneth – cannot be denied although one cannot help remarking that it contained such good things that it was a pity the idea was never reworked to a new score. But if *Images of Love* was not the Shakespearean success that had been hoped it was quickly followed by a tremendous triumph, Kenneth's first full-length work and, appropriately enough, directly based on Shakespeare's greatest love story.

13

A major triumph

Ever since he had seen the Bolshoi Ballet's staging of Lavrovsky's *Romeo and Juliet* with which the company began its first visit to London in 1956 Kenneth had been attracted by Prokoviev's magnificent score for the ballet. And in 1963, when he had been in Stuttgart, he had seen and admired the way that Cranko had scaled his production to the limited resources of the young company. It was no wonder, then, that when he was asked to provide a *pas de deux* for a television programme for a Canadian company the music for the balcony scene from *Romeo and Juliet* was his choice.

The *pas de deux* was mounted on Lynn Seymour (Canadian born) and Christopher Gable and, with these beautifully matched young dancers giving a rapturous interpretation of the most passionately lyrical choreography that Kenneth had yet devised, it was an immediate success. It may have been this brilliant fragment that provided Ashton with the impetus to commission Kenneth to choreograph the whole work; at any rate the decision to do so concluded nearly two years of speculation about the Royal Ballet's own production.

Following the Bolshoi Ballet's Covent Garden season in 1963 there had been a proposal that Lavrovsky should mount *Romeo and Juliet* for the Royal Ballet and Ashton should produce his *La Fille mal gardée* for the Bolshoi. Difficulties arose, however, mainly because of Lavrovsky's commitments which would not permit him to come to Britain for a year or two. There was talk, also, of the possibility of Ashton reviving his own version, produced for the Royal Danish Ballet in 1955, but whether Ashton was too busy with his administrative duties as Director of the Royal Ballet, or whether he felt that his production would seem too lightweight after the sumptuous Russian version has never been definitely explained; whatever the reason, it was Kenneth who was entrusted with the long-awaited British version.

Kenneth, of course, was fully aware of the responsibility that had been settled upon him and just what a tremendous challenge it was. He read and reread Shakespeare's play, ready to put into the ballet those things that could be expressed in dance, although the score itself presented a structure and shape which allowed little deviation in concept from what had been done by other companies. He was puzzled by the comparatively small amount of music provided for Romeo, and so he 'stole' some sections, reassigning a few numbers and taking one passage from the last act intended for Juliet's friends in order to make a solo for Romeo in the ballroom scene of the first act.

He began work on the ballet in September 1964; the first night was scheduled for five months later. Every day he listened to the Bolshoi recording of the score so that every bar of the music should be familiar to him and had long discussions with Seymour and Gable about the psychological motivations of the two main characters and what it was feasible to express through the classical vocabulary.

At the centre of Kenneth's conception of the ballet was his conviction that it is Juliet who is the leading character of the play and the mainspring of the action. In this he was following Shakespeare himself who gave to Juliet a wilfulness, a determination and an independent spirit quite out of keeping with the essentially subordinate position of women in Renaissance Europe. It is Juliet who arranges the meeting – and marriage – at Friar Laurence's cell; it is Juliet who dares to defy her parents' wish that she should marry Paris; it is Juliet who tries to delay Romeo's departure after he has been banished – and, when that happens, it is Juliet who must then 'carry' the final scenes of both play and ballet.

Kenneth, however, did not wish Romeo to be a mere cypher in the ballet, a cardboard cavalier as in full-length classical works; his character undergoes a transcendental change from aristocratic play-

MacMillan's first full-length ballet, *Romeo and Juliet*, was created upon Lynn Seymour and Christopher Gable but, on the insistence of American entrepreneur Sol Hurok, the first performance was given by Margot Fonteyn and Rudolf Nureyev. *Above left*: Anthony Dowell with Natalia Makarova in the Balcony *pas de deux*. *Above right*: Merle Park with Mikhail Baryshnikov in the Ballroom *pas de deux*. (Both photographs: *Anthony Crickmay*.) *Below*: The first act setting. *Romeo and Juliet* is also in the repertories of the Royal Swedish Ballet and American Ballet Theatre. (From the collection of *Nicholas Georgiadis*.)

boy to impassioned lover, from the brawling companion of Mercutio and Benvolio, mawkishly proclaiming his love for Rosaline, to the maturing man seared by genuine emotion – 'He jests at scars that never felt a wound.'

To find the basic truth for each step, each movement, Kenneth applied his usual creative procedure which was to define exactly what it was the characters were trying to express, what the scene was intended to convey; when that had been done he strove to find – or invent – a step that would best convey that particular meaning or emotion. As a matter of fact this was the first time he ever used the *entrechat* which, until then, he had considered a classroom cliché.

With the balcony *pas de deux* already in existence Kenneth continued his usual custom of beginning with the (other) difficult double work, the ballroom *pas de deux*, the bedroom *pas de deux* and the final *pas de deux* in the crypt when Romeo tries to instil life into the seemingly dead Juliet.

Each one of these duets was, of course, different in mood, feeling and atmosphere. The ballroom is the first meeting and the first time that the lovers are alone, their awareness of each other a breathless extension of that 'love at first sight' meeting in the crowded ballroom minutes before. Those tentative moments are interrupted, first by the Nurse wondering why Juliet is not joining in the feasting and festivities; then by her parents accompanied by Paris. Finally Romeo and Juliet are left to engage in their first tender dance together, interrupted for the third time by the suspicious Tybalt.

The balcony *pas de deux* works as an extension of this scene, the ecstasy of young love when they both dance for each other, Juliet rapturous, Romeo showing off a bit, displaying the energy released by his new discovery, culminating in their first kiss and Juliet's delirious run back up the steep flight of steps leading to her balcony while Romeo extends his hand towards her and the curtain falls. This duet, created, as it were, in a vacuum, is perfectly integrated into the elaborate fabric of the ballet and makes a superb climax to the first act.

The bedroom *pas de deux* is an amplified yet subtly altered version of the balcony scene, the expression of 'Parting in such sweet sorrow.' Although there are moments that mirror the abandon of the previous duet the choreography is more intense – reflecting, especially, Juliet's anguish at the parting. This time it is not a lovers' languishing farewell but Romeo's banishment and the uncertainty of the future that affects them, and Kenneth portrayed this in the more extreme angles of Juliet's arabesques, in the ways that she is lifted and held as well as in the more explicit moment when she covers Romeo with frenzied kisses. He stops her with one final, strong embrace, gathers up his cloak and disappears over the window balustrade.

The *pas de deux* (if it can be called that) in the crypt is one in which Romeo desperately, almost ragingly, tries to infuse the apparently dead Juliet with life, holding her in some of the same lifts from previous scenes while her inert body droops and dangles in hideous, ungainly positions, culminating in the moment when he drags her across the floor by one arm. During the rehearsal period when Kenneth was creating this scene he made the point to Seymour and Gable that it had to be ugly; death is ugly, brutal, undifferentiating, and making pretty choreographic patterns in that situation would be all wrong.

Perhaps the biggest, most innovative breakthrough that Kenneth achieved in creating the ballet was to leave those scenes which were carried more by mime than dancing open to the individual interpretation of each dancer (within certain guidelines, of course) especially in the role of Juliet. Where it shows – and matters – most is in the third act when Lord and Lady Capulet are insisting that Juliet marry Paris and, subsequently, when she is left alone. This culminates in Kenneth's famous, and daring, decision to let Juliet, in despair and not knowing to whom to turn, just sit on the bed and do *nothing*. The music swells to a climax, the love theme is played *sforzando* and Juliet just sits there for what seems like an eternity of indecision until, snatching up her flimsy wrap, she circles the stage before running off to Friar Laurence. Most choreographers, given that thrilling music, would have devised a solo for Juliet, trying to convey her desperate loneliness; nothing, however, can match the dramatic impact of that small, solitary, immobile figure and the flying exit that follows.

When all the big *pas de deux* with Romeo were set, Kenneth worked on the two contrasting ones with Paris, the first expressing the shy curiosity of a young girl introduced to the man selected to be her husband, the second, deliberately awkward and strained, revealing her revulsion. There then followed dances for the female soloists – Juliet's friends; the three harlots; then the family scenes with the Capulets and the Nurse, followed by the male solos. With the dances completed for principals and soloists, Kenneth began the elaborate and detailed work involved with the big crowd scenes, using the full corps de ballet plus thirty-two extras. This was the first time that Kenneth had had to organise real crowd scenes, made more complicated by street brawls and sword-play. He remembers that he was very anxious in case the moves he organised should look confused and confusing, or seem boring; consequently he 'cut the score to ribbons' and then, finding that he had been too savage, had to put most of it back again.

To assist him in organising the actual sword-fights he called in the famous Shakespearean producer John Barton. The fights that Barton devised proved over-elaborate in relation to the score and subsequently had to be simplified by Kenneth so that certain actions could be synchronised with the distinctly accented music.

Georgiadis has remarked that his designs were produced 'in a hurry' which emphasises that this vast undertaking – the most elaborate production that the Royal Ballet had yet attempted – was, as is so often the case, mounted against the calender if not the clock.

Despite all the main creative work having been built upon Seymour and Gable, the first – gala – performance was awarded to Fonteyn and Nureyev, which occasioned a certain amount of bitterness. The decision really came about because the impresario Sol Hurok, who had always been responsible for presenting the Royal Ballet in America, insisted that Fonteyn and Nureyev should open the first night in New York and that they must also dance the world premiere in London – presumably because the publicity surrounding the two superstars would excite popular interest and help promotion in the U.S. The Covent Garden management acquiesced. Seymour and Gable were upset – Seymour even more so to discover that she was down as the *fifth* cast after Merle Park and Donald MacLeary, Antoinette Sibley and Anthony Dowell, and Annette Page also paired with MacLeary. Kenneth, too, was deeply distressed at the disappointment of the two young dancers with whom he had spent so many hours working out the ballet, but although he appealed to the management they accepted Hurok's *diktat*. Kenneth could do little about casting, either; Ashton was the Director of the company and made the decisions. As it happened, because of illness and injury, Seymour and Gable danced the second performance.

The first performance of *Romeo and Juliet* was on February 2, 1965 at the Royal Opera House and by any standards it was a tremendous triumph, receiving a record forty-three curtain calls. All the reviews were good, ranging from lavish paeans of praise in most of the national newspapers to more detailed criticism in the dance magazines. There were varying opinions, of course, about the performances by the leading couples but the general consensus was that here was a major ballet that offered leading roles open to widely differing interpretations. It was also agreed that Kenneth's version could stand proudly alongside the Bolshoi one and that the choreography was far more inventive. One item that the critics missed was the 'Cushion Dance' from the ballroom scene. One critic went so far as to write that it was a 'thing of immortal beauty which generation after

84

generation will revere and worship'. Kenneth, however, had deliberately changed that dance. Not that he did not admire Lavrovsky's
invention but he thought it wholly wrong within the context of the
period – wrong to show the men, in that sternly patriarchal and
macho society, in roles that depicted them subservient to women;
accordingly his dance to the relevant music reverses the role-playing:
it is the women who defer to the men.

Georgiadis's designs were unanimously praised for their evocation
of Renaissance grandeur as well as the practicality with which the
sets could be arranged for different scenes. One critic disapproved of
the lighting, saying that he missed the fierce sunlight of Italy,
although the market scenes are in fact played in bright 'sunlight'. All
in all, however, it was agreed that Kenneth's first full-length ballet
was a major achievement that would serve the company for many
years. And so it has proved. *Romeo and Juliet* has remained constantly
in the repertoire, its popularity with audiences rivalling that of *Swan
Lake* and *The Sleeping Beauty* and its choreography a continuing
challenge not only to the company's principals but also to famous
dancers from all over the world.

With *Romeo and Juliet* Kenneth had reached a creative peak, yet
that same year was to see him produce, in his very next work, a
masterpiece, while his career was to take an entirely different
direction.

14

'A masterpiece' – but 'parting is such sweet sorrow'

The effort of producing *Romeo and Juliet* left Kenneth exhausted and
the success that it achieved justified him in taking it easy for a month
or two. In the early summer of 1965 he and Georgiadis decided it
would be a pleasant idea to attend the arts festival in Spoleto, Italy,
where Cranko's Stuttgart Ballet was appearing. During the festival
season Cranko suggested to Kenneth that he might like to do a new
ballet for the company.

For several years Kenneth had nurtured the idea of creating a
ballet to Mahler's great symphonic song cycle *Song of the Earth* (*Das
Lied von der Erde*). He had put this proposal to the Board of Directors

at the Royal Opera House who had turned it down on the grounds that it was 'a musical masterpiece which shouldn't be touched'. Kenneth was well aware that it was a masterpiece which was one of the reasons why he was so attracted to the work. Over the years other masterpieces had been used – with varying degrees of success – by other choreographers, from Léonid Massine's choice of Beethoven's Seventh Symphony to Balanchine's use of Mozart. There are, indeed, many instances of great 'absolute' music being used as the basis for ballets, provoking heated debates between choreographers, critics, composers, musicologists, about the aesthetic integrity of doing so. The point is that simply because they *are* great masterpieces will withstand any amount of use, even misuse; Beethoven's Ninth Symphony is no less an Olympian achievement because Isadora Duncan danced to it and Shakespeare's *Romeo and Juliet* still stands as a great tragic play despite being transformed into orchestral music, operas, ballets and films. Moreover, some years before, Antony Tudor had demonstrated that it was possible to make a fine, deeply serious ballet from Mahler's intensely felt song cycle *Kindertotenlieder*. Finally, it might be observed that, to be pedantic, Mahler himself had taken (a German translation of) Chinese poems which purists would say were perfect and absolute in themselves and needed no music as elaboration. But if Mahler had heeded that sort of argument we would have been bereft of a musical masterpiece.

But the Board of Directors, then under the Chairmanship of Lord Harewood, was adamant: Mahler's *Song of the Earth* was sacrosanct and Kenneth was not to be allowed to make it into a work for the Royal Ballet. So when Cranko approached Kenneth for a new ballet and he suggested it Cranko jumped at the chance.

After the festival at Spoleto ended Kenneth travelled on to Positano in company with Georgina Parkinson and Donald MacLeary for a more relaxed holiday, but during that time his thoughts about the approach to *Song of the Earth* were maturing. He considers now that the Royal Ballet's rejection of his idea was probably a blessing in disguise in that the extra years of experience he gained were invaluable when he at last came to create the ballet.

Kenneth began work in Stuttgart in the early autumn and stayed there for three months. It was a period of intensely hard work but a happy one: he was engaged in creating something dear to his heart, he was working alongside his friend and colleague, Cranko, and he was extending the close rapport he had established with the company while producing previous ballets for it.

The Song of the Earth, subtitled *Symphony for Tenor and Alto Voices and Orchestra* (in concert performance there is often a difference in the disposition of the voices, i.e. the alto voice is sometimes female,

86

sometimes male), is divided into six songs, of which the last, *The Farewell*, is by far the longest, occupying almost half the work. The score has been said to represent Mahler's own personal farewell to life (he knew at the time of its composition that he had an incurable heart condition) although he was to go on and compose a further major work, the Ninth Symphony, and the essentials of a Tenth. The songs represent a valedictory leave-taking of all things beautiful in the world, sad but not bitter, resignation in the face of the inevitability of death and a celebration of the earth's renewal of itself.

Kenneth decided that he could not attempt a literal interpretation of the Chinese poems, freely translated into German by Hans Bethge; instead he relied on the mood evoked for each one by the score, taking a phrase of the music for the impetus behind the movement, although, now and again, a very explicit reference in the text does instigate a corresponding choreographic image. More importantly, he created three symbolic figures: the Man, the Woman, and the Messenger of Death. This last figure appears in almost every song, every scene, sometimes supportive, occasionally menacing, finally effecting a heart-easing reunion of the Man and the Woman in the last moments of the ballet. It is worth making the point that the figure of Death – or, rather, Death's Messenger – is the first personification of the idea of death, a concern – if not obsession – with the ultimate fate of us all that began to show itself in Kenneth's works more and more frequently, taking its place alongside the figure of the outsider that had so often recurred in previous ballets. Indeed, there would be times when Kenneth naturally fused the two into one.

The choreography of the first song, *Drinking Song of Earth's Misery*, uses the Messenger of Death, the Man and four other males. The words emphasise the transience of life, each stanza ending with the line Life is dark, so is Death, and the sorrow of such knowledge is drowned in golden wine. The music is fierce, defiant, opening the whole work with the main theme blared out on the brass before the ringing entry of the tenor. Kenneth paralleled that musical statement with a soaring entry for the Man followed immediately by his omnipresent alter ego, the Messenger of Death. The whole vigorous sequence closes with the Man held high by the other males then falling, as into a grave, on the last short, savage chord.

The second song, *Autumn Solitude*, is for the female voice and, as the title implies, is sadly contemplative. Kenneth gave the main emphasis of this melancholy sequence to the Woman, revealing in her movements an aching loneliness, a longing for a loving companion. Other dancers, three women and four men, are briefly involved, then the Woman is left alone to be consoled by the solicitous Messenger.

The third song, *Of Youth*, is happier: the text tells of a white

During the 1960s MacMillan had wanted to create a ballet to Mahler's symphonic song-cycle *Song of the Earth*, but the Royal Opera House Board of Directors rejected his suggestion on the ground that the score was sacrosanct. At the invitation of John Cranko, Director of the Stuttgart Ballet, MacMillan created the work for that company; it was immediately hailed as a masterpiece. *Song of the Earth* entered the Royal Ballet repertory six months later. *Above*: Marcia Haydée (guest artist from Stuttgart) as The Woman (the role she created), with Wayne Eagling as The Messenger of Death. On the left: Jennifer Penney and Deidre Eyden. *Below*: Anthony Dowell as The Messenger of Death, Monica Mason as The Woman and Donald MacLeary as The Man, in the moving final moments when all the three seem to fly into a serene eternity as the alto-soprano sings "... forever ... forever ... forever ..." (*Leslie E. Spatt.*)

porcelain pavilion reflected in the still waters of a pool. Young people disport themselves carelessly, four women with four men, with slight hints of *chinoiserie* in their attitudes and movements. A fifth woman – the second female lead – is manipulated by the men, as if on a swing, until she finally lands in the arms of the Messenger, who carries her off while the other dancers adopt upside-down positions – an image of the pool's inverted reflections.

The fourth song, *Of Beauty*, is even more idyllic. In the poem young girls pick flowers in the sunshine by the river bank. Young men ride by on horseback; there is a flirtatious encounter until one of the horses shies and rushes off, followed by the others. The girls look yearningly after them. Kenneth used seven men and seven women for this sequence, giving the leading man movements that suggested a horse pawing the ground. The third leading female has a significant solo; at the conclusion the seven couples pair off in the fading light.

The fifth song, *The Drunkard in Spring*, tells of a wine drinker ignoring the birds' heralding of the coming of spring, preferring to find his happiness in a drunken stupor. Kenneth used a trio of males, one of whom is the Messenger. Their movements portray a tipsy imbalance, grasping at illusions and fantasies, non-existant female partners until one of them, making a reeling exit, is confronted by Death's emissary.

The final song, *The Farewell*, is almost a ballet in itself, much of it an elaborate *pas de deux/trois* for the Man, the Woman and the Messenger of Death. It is full of poetic images, a loving partnership separated by death, of happiness overtaken by sorrow which, in turn, is dispelled by celestial reunion; the rebirth of the earth is symbolised by the meeting of souls in eternity. It was this part of the score that was the most challenging and Kenneth found in it what proved to be his most sublime inspiration up until that time.

Naturally, being the hardest part of the ballet, it was that final *pas de deux/trois* with which he began. The long *pas de deux* between the Man and the Woman becomes a *pas de trois* when the Messenger of Death intervenes; eventually he takes the Man away leaving the Woman alone and sorrowing. There follows a long, physically exhausting solo (when Kenneth first intimated what he wanted to Marcia Haydée who was cast as the Woman she almost fainted at the thought) in which Kenneth made marvellously expressive use of long, sustained *bourrées* (the small, travelling steps a ballerina makes on *pointe* giving the impression of gliding or floating over the ground). Throughout the long last song the full company of sixteen other dancers are used in telling support but it is the three principals who are alone on stage for the marvellous final moments. The Messenger of Death returns with the Man, now wearing a similar white mask and they join the Woman. As the alto soprano sings the final words of *The Farewell*

> Everywhere the dear earth
> Blossoms in the spring and grows green
> Again. Everywhere and forever
> The distance looks bright and blue!
> Forever . . . Forever . . . Forever . . .

the three figures move slowly downstage towards the audience, rising slowly on *demi-pointe*, their arms gently undulating as if flying into a serene eternity. It is a magical, mysterious, moving finale to a great work.

Georgiadis's setting was stripped down to a bare, blue-painted backcloth. The dancers' costumes began as fairly elaborate designs with floating draperies but at the dress rehearsal these, too, were simplified into tee-shirt type tops and plain tights for the men and simple tunics for the women in subtle shades of bluey-green and purple, except, of course, for the Messenger who was in black. Kenneth and Georgiadis rightly thought that the sumptuous score and complex choreography needed no further elaboration.

The first performance of *The Song of the Earth* was given at the Würtemburg State Theatre, Stuttgart, on November 7, 1965, with Marcia Haydée and Ray Barra as the Woman and the Man and Egon Madsen as the Messenger of Death. The work was given a rapturous reception by the audience and the German critics immediately pronounced it a masterpiece, thus vindicating Kenneth's faith in his abilities to create something of balletic value from the score as well as Cranko's courage and perception in providing the opportunity to do it.

*

While he had been busy in Stuttgart creating *Song of the Earth*, Kenneth was approached by the Intendant of the Berlin Opera House, Gustav Rudolf Selner, with an offer that was to prove another important landmark in Kenneth's career: he was invited to become co-Director of the Berlin Opera Ballet with John Cranko. But after the premiere of the ballet, Selner intimated to Kenneth that they wished to drop the suggestion of co-directorship in favour of Kenneth directing the company alone. Kenneth found the situation somewhat embarrassing, but Cranko seemed unconcerned – he was not only directing the Stuttgart Ballet but was also responsible for the Munich company as well – and talks were progressing about his also having artistic control of Frankfurt. Taking on part responsibility for Berlin would have stretched his administrative and creative capabilities to the utmost and beyond. He was quite happy, therefore, for Kenneth to take over Berlin by himself.

This, then, was the offer – and the problem – that Kenneth took back with him to London. During the early part of 1966 he talked with friends and colleagues about whether or not to tear up his roots at the Royal Ballet and accept the Berlin proposal. What may have clinched the matter was Ashton's advice, which was to take advantage of the opportunity to direct a company. Accordingly, Kenneth accepted and it was arranged that he should take up his position as Director of the Berlin Opera Ballet in June of that year, with the previous Director, Gerdt Reinholm, happy to continue as Kenneth's administrative assistant.

Meanwhile, the tremendous success of *Song of the Earth* in Stuttgart was not lost upon the Board of Directors at the Royal Opera House and Ashton commissioned Kenneth to produce the ballet at Covent Garden.

For the Royal Ballet the chosen colours for the setting and costumes were even more severe. The backcloth was a kind of dark graphite vaguely banded with greyish-beige; much the same shades were chosen for the costumes of the supporting cast, with the Woman in white, the Man in grey and the Messenger in black.

The first performance of *Song of the Earth* by the Royal Ballet took place at the Royal Opera House on May 19, 1966. Marcia Haydée came from Stuttgart as guest artist to recreate the role of the Woman, Donald MacLeary was the Man and Anthony Dowell was the Messenger of Death. The ballet was, if anything, even more of a success than at Stuttgart: critic after critic called it a masterpiece, considering it Kenneth's greatest work to date, and there could hardly have been a more fitting ballet with which to conclude his twenty years association with the company.

For Kenneth, of course, it was an emotional occasion: a personal triumph tempered with a heartfelt wrench at leaving the company with which his whole adult life, his career to date, had been spent. It also meant severence from a large number of friends and colleagues to whom he had become even more positive in his commitment than his own family. The first Royal Ballet performance of *Song of the Earth* was succinctly summed up by the ballet critic of the *Sunday Times* who concluded his enthusiastic review with the words: 'Goodbye Kenneth MacMillan and thanks a million. Parting is such sweet sorrow.'

15

Berlin beginnings – Expressionism and a brilliant *Beauty*

Before Kenneth could start thinking about the aesthetic aspects of his new post, what policy decisions he would need to make, what administrative difficulties he might face, there were more practical, domestic concerns to be seen to: packing up his effects in London, finding somewhere to live in Berlin.

The move was bound up with artistic decisions. Kenneth approached several friends and colleagues with the suggestion that they might accompany him. Lynn Seymour, of course, was the first person he asked and she was happy to accept the position of his leading ballerina. Vergie Derman also agreed to leave the Royal Ballet for Berlin, as did Ashley Lawrence who accepted the post of Musical Director and Conductor. Ray Barra, one of the leading dancers of the Stuttgart Ballet who had suffered a serious injury which had affected his dancing, was appointed as Ballet Master; he also undertook to find suitable accommodation for Kenneth and the other British emigrés.

For Kenneth, leaving London was not a problem. He had never been a 'home-maker' and he had very little in the way of personal belongings to pack up. Ray Barra found a huge, rambling apartment in the Reichsstrasse in Berlin which could accommodate Kenneth and his small entourage so that they scarcely encountered each other. They arrived in August and Kenneth immediately set about the task of preparing for the first night, scheduled for November.

Despite the promises Kenneth had received about the number of performances the ballet company would be given, he soon discovered that it would be restricted to a mere three per month and was very much a second string to the opera company. In Stuttgart, Cranko had had a continual fight for more ballet performances in the face of an established opera company, but Kenneth's task in Berlin was even more difficult: he was working under the shadow of a much greater opera company, long established as one of the major operatic forces in the world, with a history and reputation as great as that of Vienna, Milan or Paris. Not only was Kenneth severely restricted in terms of the number of performances but also financially: his very limited budget meant that most of his ballets would have to be produced on the proverbial shoestring.

Unlike the Royal Ballet, the Berlin company contained no basic

Concerto was one of the first works that MacMillan created when he was Director of the Berlin Opera Ballet. Set to the Piano Concerto No. 2 by Shostakovich, the beautiful lyrical *pas de deux* to the slow movement was inspired by watching Lynn Seymour warming up in class. The male dancer's arms are used as the studio *barre* for the ballerina to balance upon. The photograph is of Alfreda Thorogood and Kerrison Cooke in the production by Sadler's Wells Royal Ballet. (*Anthony Crickmay.*)

classical repertoire, but was wildly eclectic without any balance. Kenneth's first task after acquainting himself with the dancers and their technical standards, was to devise a programme for the first night which would not only initiate a sense of style and corporate identity but please the dancers by getting them all on stage.

The programme that he devised consisted of *The Invitation* as a dramatic centrepiece flanked by two new abstract works, one danced to Ravel's *Valses Nobles et Sentimentales* and the other to Shostako-vich's Second Piano Concerto, which he entitled, simply, *Concerto* (similar to the manner in which his previous use of a Shostakovich score had been called *Symphony*). The inspiration for the serenely lyrical *pas de deux* in the slow movement of *Concerto* came while Kenneth was conducting a rehearsal: his attention was continually distracted by Seymour 'warming up' at the *barre* in the background. Her poses, repeated first on one side, then on the other, gave Kenneth the idea of using the male partner as a moveable *barre*, his arms sometimes outstretched for his ballerina to balance upon, at other times lifting her or gently changing her position. This beautiful slow movement was enclosed by the opening allegro, with two other leading principles supported by a further three couples, while the final movement introduced another female soloist and an extended corps de ballet.

The third ballet in the triple bill initially used Ravel's *Mother Goose Suite* but Kenneth, intending to make an abstract work, kept getting involved with the obvious narrative implications of the score. Accordingly he changed the music to Ravel's *Valses Nobles et Sentimentales* which, like *Concerto*, had a simple decor and costumes by Jurgen Rose whose work for Stuttgart Ballet Kenneth had found attractive. The change of Ravel score, however, meant that time was running short and the ballet was put together in a hurry. Kenneth says now that *Valses* was 'an awful ballet, created in panic'.

The opening programme, however, given on November 3, 1966, was a success and Kenneth's appointment as Director of the company got off to a good beginning.

Sir David Webster, at that time General Administrator of the Royal Opera House, flew out to Berlin to be present at Kenneth's first night. After the performance he offered Kenneth the Directorship of the Royal Ballet three years hence when Sir Frederick Ashton was due to retire.

Kenneth was overwhelmed. Of course it was a tremendous challenge but, at the same time, an offer he couldn't refuse. It was also a logical appointment: after Dame Ninette, the founder of the company, and Sir Frederick, her founder-choreographer, who better than Kenneth, British born and a total product of the Royal Ballet and a choreographer of international reputation? Moreover, his appointment as Director of the Berlin Opera Ballet would be ideal experience in running a large classical company, in building and maintaining a repertoire, in handling a hundred demanding egos and temperaments and in dealing with the innumerable problems of day-to-day administration. Of course, Sir David's offer was confidential but for Kenneth, already beginning to feel the strain of running a company in an alien environment, to return to the Royal Ballet as its Director provided an ultimate goal, a pinnacle of attainment that he could look forward to in the not-too-distant future.

*

Meanwhile, Kenneth's initial success in Berlin was sustained by further programmes that continued to please the local audiences and critics. Although there was virtually no tradition of classical ballet in modern Germany and German audiences seemed indifferent to it, Kenneth – imbued with the Royal Ballet tradition that a classical company worthy of the name should found its repertoire on carefully considered productions of the classics – was intent upon a policy of doing just that. But any consideration of producing a major work such as *The Sleeping Beauty* or *Swan Lake* was dependent on developing the company to standards that were sufficiently high to cope with the technical demands of such works. A fine corps de ballet was an essential requisite, of course, but the ability to produce a second cast of soloists in case of illness or injury was also of major importance. Yet, despite the manifold problems of presenting a major classic with the material he had at his disposal and the circumstances under which the company had to operate, Kenneth went ahead with plans to produce *The Sleeping Beauty* on a really grand scale.

While that was in preparation, however, Kenneth continued to 'mix and match' part of the existing one-act repertory that he had inherited with his own works. He dropped several ballets that he thought were poor but kept Serge Lifar's *Suite en Blanc*, a large-scale, abstract company display-piece composed with a certain Gallic chic, and a very dramatic interpretation of *Rashomon* by Tatiana Gsovsky, wife of Victor Gsovsky, a choreographer-teacher-balletmaster who, born in St. Petersburg, had worked extensively throughout Europe since the 1920s.

Kenneth brought into the repertoire Cranko's very idiosyncratic version of Stravinsky's *Firebird* and George Balanchine's *Ballet Imperial*. This work, based on Tchaikovsky's Second Piano Concerto, was originally created for American Ballet Caravan in 1941 and was in several major repertories including, of course,

Balanchine's own New York City Ballet and the Royal Ballet – indeed, Kenneth had had one of his major successes as a dancer in this work. It was Balanchine's own homage to his classical training in St. Petersburg and to Marius Petipa, the 'Grand Master' of the classical style brought to its height while Petipa was choreographer/balletmaster to the Czar's Imperial Theatres from 1862 to 1910. If Lifar's *Suite en Blanc* was a contemporary distillation of the great classical heritage of the Paris Opera Ballet, then Balanchine's *Ballet Imperial* (later retitled, simply, *Piano Concerto No. 2*) was its Russian counterpart.

No one was more surprised, therefore, than Kenneth when, at its Berlin premiere, *Ballet Imperial* was subjected to boos, jeers, and howls of laughter during the performance. The luckless solo pianist, taking his curtain call, was mistaken for Balanchine and was the recipient of a veritable storm of abuse, catcalls, whistles and slow handclaps. All of which was an indication of the tastes (or lack of them) for which Kenneth was catering. Undaunted, however, Kenneth went ahead with his plans to produce *The Sleeping Beauty*, confident in the belief that, whatever audiences might think or prefer, the major classics must be the cornerstone of a classical company's repertoire.

The designer that Kenneth chose for *The Sleeping Beauty* was Barry Kay. Kenneth had much admired Kay's magnificent setting of the third act of Petipa's *Raymonda*, produced for the Royal Ballet by Nureyev. Its white and gold Romanesque grandeur was the sort of sumptuous splendour that Kenneth had in mind for his production of *Beauty*; he not only wanted to excite the Berliners with real ballet spectacle but was also of the opinion that if this work, the pinnacle of classicism, was to be done at all it should be done in a manner worthy of Czar Nicholas II's Imperial Theatres where it was first presented.

Barry Kay joined Kenneth in the big Berlin apartment and they began long discussions about the style, manner and period in which *Beauty* should be done. The final decision was that the ballet should reflect its Russian origin, the stage designs being what might be called 'Byzantine baroque'; the *Prologue* and first two acts should be set in the late eighteenth century, the period of Catherine the Great, so that the Court's awakening after its one hundred years sleep should coincide with the year in which Tchaikovsky and Petipa's masterpiece was first produced, 1890, which was a nice historical conceit. It was also decided that the *Vision Scene* and the *Panorama* should be set in winter, a departure from the usual arboreal luxuriance of most productions and carrying through the predominence of white in the decor.

Kay constructed a model which was shown to the Intendant of the

MacMillan's Berlin production of *The Sleeping Beauty*, with designs by Barry Kay.
Above: Kay's model for the Prologue and Wedding;
middle: the actual set. The solo dancer is Vergie Derman.
(From the *Barry Kay Archive* by permission of Michael Werner.)
Below: Photograph of the model of the set for *Swan Lake* from the collection of
Nicholas Georgiadis.

Berlin Opera, Gustav Rudolf Selner. He was obviously taken aback by the sumptuousness and scale of the production and immediately proposed that it should be of more modest proportions. But Kenneth was adamant: *The Sleeping Beauty*, of all ballets, had to be produced as opulently as possible and he was anxious for his German audiences to see just how magnificent classical ballet could be. His argument prevailed and upwards of a dozen dates were set aside for technical rehearsals. It soon became apparent, however, that the time available before the announced first night was too short in which to prepare and rehearse the company properly; the opening was accordingly postponed. That produced a new problem: the original date was still scheduled as a ballet programme and audiences would be expecting something new. However, because so much money was being spent on *The Sleeping Beauty* there was nothing to spare for any other new production. Whatever Kenneth devised would have to be done for next to nothing.

Kenneth had been reading the story of Anna Andersen, the woman who, living in a Berlin clinic, believed and insisted that she was the Grand Duchess Anastasia, sole survivor (she claimed) of the massacre of the Russian Royal Family by the Bolsheviks in a cellar in Ekaterinburg in 1917. Whether or not Anastasia had indeed escaped the savage fate of the other Romanovs, Kenneth was moved and intrigued by the predicament of the woman in the clinic: another outsider, clinging to her beliefs and convictions in the face of rejection by the rest of society. This gave Kenneth the theme of his new ballet.

It was conceived in Expressionist form: memories and events in a succession of scenes recollected, as it were, in Anastasia's mind as she lay confined in the bleak world of the clinic. This format was ideal in both artistic and practical terms: it allowed the audience to glimpse the historical elements – the carefree childhood, the horrendous mass-murder, the wild escape, the ultimate psychological and social predicament – without the need for elaborate settings.

Although there were to be no settings as such, Kenneth wanted to use film projections as part of the Expressionist technique: Anastasia herself would be shown flickering reminders of the past as part of her therapy and these, in turn, would generate the stage action. Accordingly, Barry Kay devised two curving screens suspended from above, upon which were projected the film clips to Anastasia and the audience.

Costumes for the various characters – the clinic staff, members of society who came to verify Anna Andersen's claim, her peasant husband, Russian soldiers – were almost all from the Berlin Opera wardrobe. The one luxury with which the director and designer were able to indulge themselves was the twelve technical rehearsals that had originally been scheduled for *The Sleeping Beauty*. This was fortuitous because, although the staging of the ballet was done in the simplest manner, the projections and lighting needed to be meticulously worked out to achieve the full effect.

The character of Anna Andersen was, of course, a 'natural' for the dramatic talents of Seymour upon whom the main choreographic conception was built – although there was a big central *pas de deux* for Anastasia and her peasant husband which demanded strong partnering. Kenneth asked Ashley Lawrence if he could find some suitably dramatic music for the work, and the very next day Lawrence produced the score of Bohuslav Martinu's *Fantaisies Symphoniques* (his sixth symphony) which, with its sinister trumpet calls, insistent rhythms, dark sonorities and haunting melodic themes proved almost as ideal for the subject as a commissioned score. In addition Kenneth arranged for the addition of some introductory recorded sounds from the Studio for Electronic Music attached to the Berlin Technical University. The film clips were a selection taken from a documentary film, *From Czar to Stalin*, by Aero Film Productions.

A month before the opening night of *Anastasia* (as the ballet had been entitled) *Concerto* entered the repertoire of both the Royal Ballet Touring Company (as it was then known) on May 26, 1967, and American Ballet Theatre, on May 18, 1967; it proved a success in both instances and the work has been regularly revived by both companies ever since. Sir David Webster had told John Field (then Director of the Royal Ballet Touring Company) about it and Kenneth had sent Vergie Derman to England to teach it to the dancers. Lucia Chase travelled to Berlin from America to see it and Ray Barra taught it to the American Ballet Theatre cast. The ballet also entered the repertoire of the Royal Swedish Ballet on February 24, 1969, and the Stuttgart Ballet on December 22, 1973.

Rehearsals proceeded well with *Anastasia* until, not long before the first night, Seymour was stricken with a sudden thrombosis in her arm. From the doctor's prognosis it seemed highly unlikely that she would be well enough to dance at the opening – or, indeed, for the rest of that season – so the opening had to be postponed. Kenneth sent an urgent request to the Royal Ballet for Georgina Parkinson to be given leave of absence to learn the role. This was granted and Parkinson hurried to Berlin, joining Kenneth and the several other occupants in the Reichstrasse apartment which, despite its size, was now becoming rather crowded. (Kenneth paid Parkinson's air fare himself as the Berlin authorities refused to do so.)

Parkinson learnt and rehearsed the role of Anastasia very quickly but, against all expectation, Seymour was sufficiently recovered to dance the role on the postponed opening night, June 25, 1967. *Anastasia* was an immediate and enormous success, its dramatic content and Expressionist style much to the taste of the Berlin audiences and critics. Seymour, too, achieved another great personal triumph for, of course, it was her role and her performance of it that completely dominated the ballet. Later in the same season Marcia Haydée, as guest artist from the Stuttgart Ballet, also had a tremendous success in the part. Sadly, after all her hard work, Parkinson did not get to perform as Anastasia although, as some compensation, Kenneth produced *Solitaire* for her in the same programme, danced in practice clothes without scenery.

With *Anastasia* successfully bridging the gap the production of *The Sleeping Beauty* proceeded without further crises – apart from those that are always attendant upon large productions. The first perform-ance was given on October 8, 1967. It was well received by the critics and Barry Kay's superb sets and costumes were singled out for almost unanimous praise. Choreographically, the *Prologue* and Act I were very like the Royal Ballet (Oliver Messel-designed) version that was still current after more than twenty years and in which Kenneth had danced, except that in the Berlin production the Court women were dressed in bustled skirts and the men in glittering military uniforms. The fairies, according to one critic, were like 'Fabergé confections, artificial and remote from humans'. Kenneth choreographed new dances for the winter hunting scene, and the *Panorama*, after the *Vision Scene*, utilised the huge revolving stage: 'As the panorama begins the stage revolves bearing the staircase section' which 'divides into two and a great canopied bed with Aurora slides into view'. For the last act, with its setting reminiscent of the old Kremlin Palace in cream and gold, Kenneth created new choreogra-phy for a spectacular mazurka for thirty dancers. The Berlin audi-ences were excited by the sheer spectacle but remained indifferent to Petipa's glorious choreography; they did not want fairy tales, they preferred real-life characters like Anastasia.

Undaunted, however, and still believing that a company based on the classical technique should have the major classics in its reper-toire, Kenneth went ahead with his plans to produce *Swan Lake* in a further two years time. Meantime, limited by his budget, he con-tinued to create the sort of dramatic one-act ballets that his German audiences demanded.

*

With the long sojourn in Berlin of Barry Kay and the sudden arrival of Georgina Parkinson, the domestic problems of the Reichstrasse apartment – catering, apportioning of telephone bills and what Kenneth calls 'bedroom arrangements' – became acute. Kenneth decided that it was time he found other accommodation for himself. This he did, in a gloomy apartment by a canal, and although it had practical advantages the resulting solitariness was, for someone as introspective as Kenneth, psychologically not so good. Loneliness and boredom with his own company were insufferable, he needed the conviviality of friends and colleagues. It did not help, either, that he spoke little or no German so that even a chat with the concierge or postman or local shopkeepers was not possible. Unlike Cranko – whose foreseeable future was to continue in Germany and who, with his South African background and knowledge of Afrikaans had found little difficulty in learning the language – Kenneth knew that he was to return to Britain after three years; learning German would be a waste of time. As a consequence of his isolation Kenneth took to drinking. The habit was all the more insidious because he never felt, or appeared, drunk, was never slurred in his speech, never unsteady in his deportment, never absent from work, still able to attend to his many administrative duties and still able to choreograph as effectively as ever, so that his growing dependence upon alcohol was not apparent to his colleagues. If he drank at dinner with friends, or at a reception or a party, then he was doing no more than everyone else; what they did not know was that he had been drinking steadily all through the day.

16

Goodbye to Berlin – and to alcohol

In his canal-side apartment Kenneth planned two more one-act ballets for his Berlin company as well as a production of *Swan Lake* – despite the apathetic audience reaction to *The Sleeping Beauty*. It was in Berlin, too, that he read an article about Isadora Duncan, who had had some of her greatest successes in that grim Prussian city where she established the first of her many schools of dance. Kenneth pondered the idea of a ballet based on Duncan's life but the more he thought about it the more he was aware that the resources available to him were insufficient to realise the subject on the scale that it demanded. It was to be another decade and a half before the project reached fruition.

His next work was, in fact, *Olympiad*, a semi-abstract work based on sports and athletics danced to Stravinsky's *Symphony in Three Movements*. In the first movement Kenneth displayed seven male dancers in choreography based on gymnastics; the second movement was a mixed doubles tennis match – with a leading role for Seymour – and the third movement was a 'mini-marathon' for the ten dancers.

Olympiad, which had its premiere on March 11, 1968, was another shoestring ballet – Kenneth himself designed the costumes copied from athletic clothes – and something of a pot-boiler, too. Kenneth now says that half way through creating the work he 'had not understood the aims of the music'. If he was under any misapprehension about its 'aims', he can be forgiven for thinking that its aggressively rhythmic first and third movements suggested sportive struggle: just before Stravinsky composed the work – in the early forties, soon after America had entered the Second World War – he had been engaged on an abortive plan to rescore *The Rite of Spring* which doubtless influenced the fierce nature of the outer movements of the symphony. At any rate, Kenneth devised several inventive and amusing choreographic ideas and the ballet fulfilled its function of providing a new work for the season with the minimum of expenditure. It was quite well received.

Kenneth's next work was a commission from Cranko for whom he produced a one-act ballet, *The Sphinx*. This came about in a rather odd way. Cranko had a recording of two works by Darius Milhaud: on one side was the suite from *Salade*, on the other was the *Small Suites for Orchestra*, and he proposed to choreograph a work to each score using casts of three women and one man for one and three men and one woman for the other, commissioning Elisabeth Dalton to do the designs for both. In the event he found he had neither the time nor the inclination to do the *Sphinx* ballet (the music had apparently suggested the theme) so he asked Kenneth to take it over.

Visiting Berlin in order to talk to Kenneth about the designs for *The Sphinx*, Elisabeth Dalton found accommodation in a weird household run by a flamboyant Frau – more of a Madame, actually – and her ever-present Arabian lover. Kenneth was so taken with the *bizarrerie* of it all, reminiscent of something from an Isherwood novel, that he relinquished his gloomy canal-side apartment to take up residence in the more stimulating *ménage* close to the Kurfurstendamm. Kenneth and Elisabeth would amuse themselves of an evening, sitting on a seat in that famous thoroughfare, watching the parade of prostitutes and trying to guess their sex – a polite 'good evening' would often produce a surprisingly deep and guttural response! There was a grotesque finale at the Madame's household when the Arabian, trying to climb into somebody's bedroom window, fell four floors to his death.

The theme of *The Sphinx* was the familiar one of the Theban monster – an animal with a woman's head – who asked travellers: what is it that goes upon two legs in the morning, three legs in the afternoon and four legs in the evening? Those who could not solve the riddle were killed. Marcia Haydée was cast in the title role, with Heinz Clauss, Richard Cragun and Egon Madsen as her three victims, each of whom was given a solo variation. During the ballet Haydée presented the riddle by holding up two, three and four fingers while dancing on *pointe* and Kenneth devised a theatrically effective shock ending in which the Sphinx decapitated the three men using her legs in scissor-fashion. The work, which was first performed in Stuttgart on June 1, 1968, was no masterpiece, but it served its purpose well enough and provided the sort of seasonal novelty that Cranko required and the dramatic hokum that German audiences enjoyed. One critic described it as 'the strangest, most distant, least MacMillan-like' of all his ballets, producing 'an icy, razor-sharp thrill which one watches with an awed chilliness'.

*

During the first week of November, 1968, the Berlin Opera was on tour (the first time the opera had been away during Kenneth's period of residence) and the ballet company was therefore awarded the luxury of a week of performances all to itself. It so happened, however, that at this time Kenneth's leading ballerina, Seymour, for whom he would have produced a new work, had recently been delivered of twin boys and was on leave of absence. Accordingly, the new ballet (the last one-act work that Kenneth created for the Berlin company) was devised around the talents of Frank Frey, a German dancer recruited from the Zurich company whose strong dramatic presence and sensational jump had already established him as something of a box-office attraction for the Berlin ballet fans.

This time the theme was not one from classical antiquity but a biblical one, the story of Cain and Abel which was also the title of the work. The role of the fratricide, Cain, completely overshadowed the supporting parts of Daniel Job as Abel, Rudolf Holz as Adam, Dorothea Binner as Eve and Gerhard Bohner as the Serpent. Barry Kay's setting had moving metallic walls and was dominated by a large triangular eye – the all-seeing eye of God – looking down upon the action. The chosen music was an amalgamation by Ashley Lawrence of Andrzej Panufnik's *Sinfonia Sacra* and *Tragic Overture*. The work received its premiere on November 1, 1968. Once again the somewhat melodramatic subject matter appealed to the German audience and, considered purely as a vehicle for the raw, virile talent of Frey, the ballet was a success. It was proposed to produce *Cain and Abel* for the Royal Ballet at Covent Garden but in the event the casting of Cain proved difficult and *Olympiad* was substituted instead. The casting of that ballet was none too succcessful, either – the Royal Ballet's males at that time were insufficiently athletic – and the work, which received its first London performance on February 21, 1969, was not retained in the repertoire for very long.

To make that Berlin all-ballet week into something of a gala occasion, as well as premiering *Cain and Abel*, Kenneth invited Yvette Chauviré and Flemming Flindt, Margot Fonteyn and Rudolf Nureyev, as guest stars in Antony Tudor's production of *Giselle*, the Stuttgart cast for *The Sphinx*, and Marcia Haydée taking the title role of *Anastasia* as well, so with the opera away Kenneth made sure that the ballet audiences were treated to a feast of dance.

*

Despite all this activity, however, Kenneth's main preoccupation at this time was with his production of *Swan Lake* which was to be, appropriately enough, his swan song in Berlin. His designer was Georgiadis, and he and Kenneth had long conversations about the conception of the ballet. Bearing in mind the Berliners' indifference to classical choreography as such, Kenneth wanted to make *Swan Lake* as dramatically exciting as possible. Accordingly he devised a 'framing scenario' which presented the fairy story of the enchanted Swan Queen more or less as 'Siegfried's dream'. This enlarged Siegfried's role somewhat and made him more of a human character rather than just a fairy-tale prince.

At the end of the first act celebrations of Siegfried's coming-of-age, during which Siegfried's father appeared as a shadowy, sinister figure, Siegfried fell asleep. The second, third and fourth acts were presented more or less in the traditional manner, with the *eminence grise* of the father-figure revealed as the evil sorcerer, Rothbart. At the end of the fourth act there was a short epilogue in which Benno, the Prince's friend, found him asleep in the same position as at the close of Act 1.

Kenneth was anxious to get away from the usual vaguely Gothic setting and the period that he suggested to Georgiadis was the Napoleonic First Empire with lots of highly decorative military uniforms, swirling capes and cocked hats. The scenery made use of painted backcloths and was far more manageable than the sumptuous *Sleeping Beauty* with its elaborately built set-pieces.

Not long before the premiere of *Swan Lake* Kenneth was the recipient of shattering news: his sister Jean, travelling to visit

104

relatives over the Easter weekend, had been killed in a horrendous motor accident. Kenneth's younger sister Betty telephoned Georgina Parkinson in London who managed to contact Ray Barra in Berlin who broke the news to Kenneth who was ill in bed with influenza. Kenneth had often tried to dissuade Jean from driving because of her acute deafness but it would seem that her affliction was not to blame for the accident: she was overtaking a truck which had suddenly pulled out, forcing her into the path of an oncoming car. Because of his illness and the pressing preoccupation with the final rehearsals of *Swan Lake* Kenneth was unable to attend Jean's funeral which saddled him with guilt feelings for a long time and inevitably cast a cloud over his last days in Berlin.

With Seymour in the dual role of Odette-Odile and Frey as Prince Siegfried Kenneth's production of *Swan Lake* had its premiere on May 14, 1969. With two such strongly dramatic exponents in the leading roles, Georgiadis's beautiful settings and costumes and the Freudian overtones in the story, the production was a tremendous success with the German audiences and critics and it has remained in the repertoire until the time of writing. Certainly as his last production for the Berlin Opera Ballet this version of *Swan Lake* provided a fine finale for Kenneth who, in less than three years, had given the company two splendid classical works, two very fine one act works in *Concerto* and *Anastasia*, plus several other useful pieces, and had shaped the company itself into an ensemble of considerable significance.

For Kenneth the 'Berlin experience' had been an interesting and instructive one. As several people had prophesied he had learnt a lot about running a company, both in the day-to-day administration and the long-term planning of artistic policy. It had been a far from ideal situation, however – the subservience to the opera, the limited budgets (the productions of *The Sleeping Beauty* and *Swan Lake* could be accounted personal triumphs not only in the artistic sense but also in demanding, and getting, the necessary sums of money for such large projects) had imposed the sort of restrictions that any director would find irksome.

In personal terms Kenneth had not enjoyed his Berlin sojourn. Once again he had played his own 'outsider' role, an alien in an alien environment which had contributed towards – indeed caused – his finding solace in alcohol. Considering that, from the company's very first performance under Kenneth's direction, he had known that he would be leaving to take over the even more demanding direction of the Royal Ballet three years hence, his wholehearted commitment to the Berlin Opera Ballet and its development as a major classical company was remarkable.

*

With *Swan Lake* successfully produced and his contract with Berlin concluded, Kenneth travelled down to Munich to see three new ballets that Cranko had produced for that company. During his stay in the city he had arranged to go on a day's excursion to the nearby mountains with Cranko, Elisabeth Dalton (who had designed one of the Cranko ballets) and Frank Frey who, as a native of the area, had appointed himself their guide. On the morning of the proposed trip Kenneth remembers getting up in his hotel room and going into the bathroom and turning on the bath taps; at that moment he was suddenly stricken with some sort of severe spasm and fainted. Elizabeth Dalton called for him and getting no answer at the reception desk went up to his room. Luckily the door was unlocked; she entered and found Kenneth collapsed on the bathroom floor, the water overflowing. Kenneth regained consciousness but was afflicted with a form of paralysis. After a great struggle, Dalton managed to get Kenneth out of the bathroom and on to the bed. She telephoned Cranko and then set about mopping up the water. By the time Cranko and Frey arrived Kenneth had recovered his faculties and mobility and insisted that he was perfectly all right. He flatly refused to see a doctor. He was due to change hotels that morning and when that had been accomplished Dalton, Cranko and Frey concocted a scheme to get Kenneth to a physician. They pretended that, before starting out on their mountain excursion, they wanted Kenneth to see a marvellous new dance school that had just opened in the city. It was, of course, a rather feeble ruse and on arriving at the house Kenneth's suspicions were immediately aroused but, since he was there, he agreed to see the physician. It turned out that the man was actually a homeopathic practitioner and he recommended Kenneth to attend a very modern Munich clinic. Kenneth was admitted for a number of days for observation and tests. The doctors told him that he had suffered a severe vascular spasm – not a stroke as Cranko and Dalton had feared – brought on by over-work and exacerbated by his drinking.

Meanwhile, the Royal Opera House management had been informed and they were naturally most perturbed, suspecting that Kenneth was perhaps more ill than they had been told. They were prepared to send a car to Munich to collect him but Dalton reassured them that Kenneth was sufficiently strong to make the journey by train. On Kenneth's arrival in London, however, John Tooley (who was taking over as General Administrator of the Royal Opera House on the resignation of Sir David Webster) insisted that he should have further tests by British doctors. Accordingly, Kenneth was admitted to the Charing Cross Hospital (then still situated at Charing Cross) for ten days. The specialists' conclusions were similar to those of the

German doctors: that Kenneth had suffered a severe vascular spasm as the result of overwork, aggravated by drinking. The doctors advised him that his heavy consumption of alcohol – not a 'drink problem' in the usual sense – was a serious threat to his health and Kenneth, with characteristic strength of purpose, gave up drink there and then, as simply as that. There was no recourse to Alcoholics Anonymous, no gradual cutting down with the help and encouragement of friends or therapeutic groups. He just stopped drinking anything alcoholic. He has not had a drink since – even refusing trifle with a dash of sherry. The doctors also told him that his chain-smoking was severely harmful; he could not face giving up drinking and smoking at the same time, however, and his final abandonment of cigarettes came a little later.

Released from hospital and restored to active health, Kenneth stayed with Georgina Parkinson and her husband and began looking for a new home for himself which he finally found in a Victorian terrace in Battersea.

*

In the autumn of 1969 John Tooley received a formal request from the Intendant of the Royal Opera House, Stockholm, on behalf of Erik Bruhn, the great Danish *premier danseur* who was at that time Artistic Director of the Royal Swedish Ballet, to mount Kenneth's production of *Romeo and Juliet*. As Kenneth was very busy with his preparations for taking over the directorship of the Royal Ballet a year hence, it was arranged that the Royal Ballet choreologist, Faith Worth, together with Georgina Parkinson, would initially teach the Swedish company the ballet, with Desmond Doyle (the original Tybalt) to direct the elaborate fight sequences; Kenneth was to supervise the final rehearsals.

On arrival in Stockholm Kenneth was impressed with the company, especially the men, and enjoyed working with them very much. He established a particularly strong rapport with the Intendant, Goran Gentele, whom he found a most charming and cultured man. The Swedish premiere of *Romeo and Juliet* took place on December 5, 1969, with Georgina Parkinson and Jonas Kage in the title roles. The ballet received great acclaim. It has remained as one of the major works in the company's repertoire ever since. As a tragic postscript, Gentele, who had been appointed as the new Director of the Metropolitan Opera, New York, was killed in a car crash while on holiday in Sardinia, and Kenneth was deeply saddened by this loss of his new-found friend.

Early in 1970 Kenneth was asked by Cranko to create a new ballet for the Stuttgart company. It was a commission which, from the beginning, seemed fated to cause controversy. Naturally, when thinking of a theme for the new work, Kenneth had in mind the talents and abilities of Stuttgart's prima ballerina, Marcia Haydée, who had developed into one of the world's leading dramatic dancers. He selected as his source material Strindberg's powerful play *Miss Julie*, the story of an arrogant aristocrat who wrecks her life because of a physical passion for Jean, the household's valet. The narrative had a double theme of antipathy: the war between the sexes and the class struggle.

Kenneth was anxious to cast Frank Frey as Jean – he felt it was important to match the female role with an equally strong male protagonist – but Cranko's opposition to this idea was the first of several problems that beset the ballet. Cranko thought that the Stuttgart company could provide a suitable dancer for the role of Jean; Kenneth was of the opinion that none of them could match the dramatic presence of Frey. It was Kenneth's ballet and he wanted to cast it as he saw fit. He makes the point that he had several times accommodated Stuttgart dancers as guest artists in Berlin: when he wanted a Berlin dancer not just as a guest artist but to dance a role specially created for him, Cranko should have gracefully acquiesced. Eventually he did and Frey danced the role.

Kenneth had chosen Barry Kay to design the ballet. Kay created an interlocking set representing a large kitchen where – as in the play – the climactic seduction scene takes place. When, not long before the scheduled first performance, he went to see the scenery being built in the Stuttgart Opera/Ballet workshops, he was dismayed to find that it had been so badly made that assembly of the interlocking parts was difficult. When Kay reported this to Cranko, he merely shrugged and said that there was nothing that he could do – the opera took priority over everything. Both Kenneth and Kay well knew that if it had been Cranko's own ballet he would have kicked up an enormous fuss – probably making one of his regular threats to resign if it was not changed.

Just before the dress rehearsal Kenneth found Cranko in the theatre wardrobe making a radical alteration to Marcia Haydée's costume for the key seduction scene – indeed, he altered the costume completely. Kenneth, again following the play, had Haydée entering Jean's domain, the kitchen, in her riding habit. Cranko felt that outdoor clothes were wrong for a seduction scene (an odd opinion for such a sophisticate) and substituted a nightdress. Kenneth thought that no lady in Miss Julie's social position – whatever degree of sexual desire possessed her – would dream of entering that part of the house in her nightdress. But in any case, whatever the probabilities, Cranko's interference in another man's ballet, done without reference to him, was totally unwarranted. It was curiously perverse, unprofessional behaviour and inevitably it led to an estrangement.

Barry Kay was so upset about the way his sets had been made and his complaints ignored that he told a friendly member of the local press that he wished to be disassociated from the production. (He did not, as has subsequently been written, 'call a press conference'.) Kenneth felt that Cranko had taken it upon himself to supervise the production of the ballet and so he and Kay both left Stuttgart for London before the first night.

Miss Julie had its first performance on March 8, 1970, and was given a mixed reception. British critics were present. One wrote that 'MacMillan has used every ounce of his skill to explore the deepest recesses of human desire in movement that is unforgettably eloquent.' Another disliked the ballet so much that he wrote, bluntly, 'I earnestly hope never to see it again.'

Both Haydée and Frey received praise for their performances but Haydée was unhappy with the ballet (her loyalty to Cranko, her beloved company director, and her loyalty to Kenneth, who had furnished her with a number of fine roles, not least in his masterpiece *Song of the Earth*, was an unbearable emotional division). The ballet was soon dropped from the repertoire.

17

Director of the Royal – a difficult start

Long before Kenneth took up his appointment as Director of the Royal Ballet the Board of Directors had determined upon a radical reorganisation of the two Royal Ballet companies, the main one based at the Royal Opera House and the touring one (the old Sadler's Wells Theatre Ballet), under the direction of John Field, spending most of its time in the provinces. For both financial and artistic reasons, it was decided to dissolve the touring company and reform it as a group of twenty-two soloists without a corps de ballet. Full-length classics like *Swan Lake* (the two Royal Ballet companies had two separate, dissimilar productions at that time) would be dropped, and a repertoire composed of well-tried one-act ballets (such as *The Rake's Progress*, *Checkmate* and *Pineapple Poll*) would be supplemented by new, even experimental, works that would give creative opportunities to young choreographers without the risk of an expensive, well-publicised flop at Covent Garden. The company would occasionally be reinforced by leading soloists and principals from the Royal Opera House – thus, in part, answering a constant complaint that audiences in the regions, while contributing to the support of the London company as tax-payers via the Arts Council, were denied opportunities to see the Covent Garden 'stars'. (The Royal Ballet has always professed not to operate the star system but, of course, certain dancers attain a status, popularity and box-office attraction that others do not; in the past the partnerships of Margot Fonteyn and Rudolf Nureyev, Antoinette Sibley and Anthony Dowell, were cases in point.)

This, then, was the plan that Kenneth inherited when he took over as Director of the Royal Ballet at the beginning of the autumn season in 1970. It was a plan that was beset with inherent faults and fraught with other complications.

Ever since Kenneth had been approached by Sir David Webster in Berlin in 1967 he had understood that his appointment, as with his predecessor Ashton, would be as Administrative and Artistic Director. Some months before his actual assumption of the position he was asked by John Tooley if he would accept John Field as his co-Administrative Director when the Royal Ballet touring company was disbanded. Kenneth readily agreed – he would naturally be happy with any arrangement that lightened the administrative load because he would not only be concerned with the artistic policies for both companies but would be choreographing for them as well.

Not long before the opening of the 1970 season he saw the 'throw-away' leaflet advertising the forthcoming programmes; on the cover John Field's name was printed above Kenneth's and both men were accorded the simple, undifferentiated title of 'Director'. Kenneth sought immediate clarification, insisting that decisions about artistic policy should be his alone. It transpired that Field had understood that they would both be sharing the position of Artistic Director. It was an unfortunate misconception for both men and, clearly, an untenable situation. Field resigned in December of that year. To replace him, Peter Wright, who had taken over as Director of the New Group (as the re-formed touring section was called) was brought in to assist Kenneth with the administration of both companies as Associate Director.

One of Kenneth's earliest tasks was the unhappy one of having to dismiss those dancers who were considered superfluous to the needs of the re-formed companies; the demise of the touring company had left the consequent 'pool' of artists top-heavy with soloists. Excellent dancers who had served several years with either company were told they were redundant and Kenneth was, perforce, seen not so much as a new broom as a butcher, which did little for company morale. Despite this wielding of the axe, there still remained a disproportionate number of soloists and principals for whom it was impossible to find roles in the initial programmes of the season; some dancers had nothing of importance to do for three months which, again, was a demoralising situation for those involved – or, rather, *not* involved – for which Kenneth was not directly responsible but for which he was criticised both inside and outside the company.

Kenneth's most immediate preoccupation, however, was in devising an interesting repertoire that would exploit the talents of the newly constructed companies. For the Covent Garden company he was anxious to acquire Jerome Robbins's *Dances at a Gathering*. This work, a suite of dances in varying moods to piano music by Chopin, had been given its premiere by the New York City Ballet the previous year. It had been an immediate popular and critical success – indeed, it was proclaimed a masterpiece by many. Kenneth had not seen it himself but Peter Wright was one of those who had and he supported the general consensus that it was a very beautiful ballet indeed. Quite apart from its intrinsic quality, it was a work that was particularly suitable for the regrouped company at Covent Garden providing, as it did, splendid roles for no less than ten top line dancers. But in any case, Kenneth had long felt that the lack of any Robbins ballet in the Royal Ballet repertoire was a serious omission and so for some months he had pressed Robbins to produce the new work for the Royal Ballet, writing letters, telephoning and sending telegrams. So importunate did he become that Robbins finally sent a telegrammatic reply that said, simply, *Relax!*

Kenneth's persistance paid off and *Dances at a Gathering* opened at the Royal Opera House on October 17, 1970, with a cast that included Rudolf Nureyev, Anthony Dowell, David Wall, Michael Coleman, Lynn Seymour, Antoinette Sibley, and Monica Mason and to the same sort of acclaim from audiences and critics that it had received in New York. (It is worth noting that after Kenneth had resigned as Director of the Royal Ballet *Dances at a Gathering* was allowed to fall into desuetude; after nearly a decade, despite promises by the management that it would be restored, this fine work was still not in the repertoire.)

But if Kenneth's *coup* in obtaining the Robbins ballet had initiated his first season with a resounding success there still remained a number of problems that needed to be resolved. For example, the amalgamation of the two companies meant that, for a time, there was no semblance of a unified style in the corps de ballet. A ballet-master, through his individual methods of working and teaching, imposes his own imprint upon a corps; the two groups from the Royal Ballet

Checkpoint was the first ballet MacMillan created for the newly-formed, short-lived Royal Ballet New Group (now Sadler's Wells Royal Ballet), after he had become Director of the Royal Ballet in 1970. Loosely based on the all-seeing eye of the Big Brother theme of George Orwell's novel, *1984*, the ballet was notable for an extraordinary *pas de deux* which took place high above the stage on the vertical surface of the backcloth, made from elasticised material; unseen hands held the dancers in place. *Above*: The intrepid principals, Svetlana Beriosova and Donald MacLeary, during their vertiginous duet. Note Elisabeth Dalton's setting with its monitoring camera. (*Zoe Dominic.*) The ballet proved too technically elaborate for practical touring and was dropped from the repertoire. *Opposite*: Costume designs for Beriosova and MacLeary. (By kind permission of Elisabeth Dalton.)

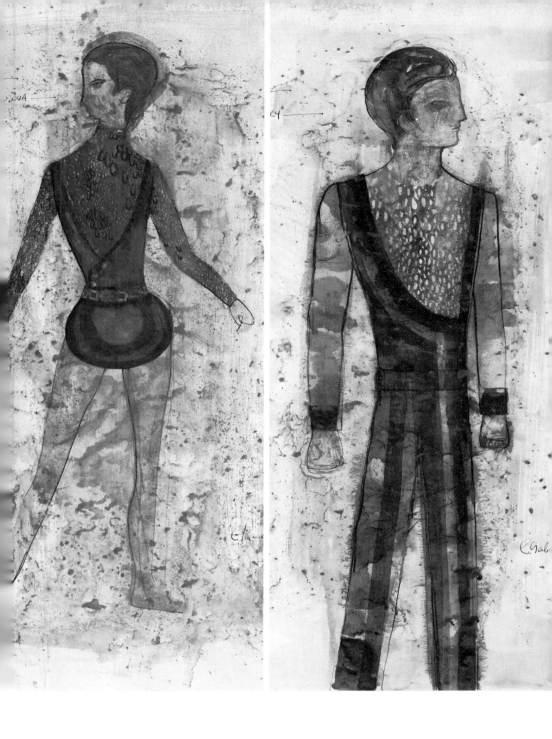

companies were consequently quite disparate and so, until there was a corporate identity, Kenneth did not include any of the big classic works in the immediate repertory and for this he was the recipient of much carping criticism. It is safe to conclude, however, that if *Swan Lake* or *The Sleeping Beauty* had been produced without a well-drilled corps there would have been an even greater barrage of complaints. As it was there was no full-length work produced for the Christmas season that year and to aggravate matters Ashton, who might have been able to supervise his productions of *Cinderella* or *La Fille mal gardée* for the holiday period, was heavily involved with the making of the film *Stories from Beatrix Potter*.

To instigate the revised repertory for the New Group, Kenneth commissioned a ballet from Glen Tetley who, following his choreography for, and subsequent direction of, the very *avant garde* Nederlands Dans Theater, as well as the several works he had created for Ballet Rambert (re-formed as a modern dance company in 1969), had become one of the most successful and sought-after choreographers in the world. Tetley created *Field Figures* for the New Group: its Stockhausen score, strange (but beautiful) decor of hanging tubes by Nadine Baylis and very unclassical choreography with much on-the-floor work was, indeed, a radical departure for the Royal Ballet. It was given its premiere at Nottingham on November 9, 1970, in a triple bill that included Balanchine's *Apollo* and Ashton's *Symphonic Variations*.

For the Covent Garden company Kenneth had intended to expand his one-act *Anastasia* into a full-length work, partly designed to show off the splendid in-depth strength of the company, but the need to give priority of casting and rehearsal time to the two guest choreographers, as well as sorting out the many teething troubles attendant upon the two amalgamated companies, meant that the three-act version of *Anastasia* had to be postponed.

*

Kenneth's own first contribution to the repertory of the New Group was something of a disaster. He took as his narrative idea the 'Big Brother' theme of George Orwell's novel *1984* and, of course, he had had first-hand experience of the divisive Berlin Wall with its searchlights, machine-gun towers and notorious Checkpoint Charlie – a name reflected in the title of the new ballet, *Checkpoint*.

Elisabeth Dalton was commissioned to do the designs and her stark setting included a huge battery of lights and a number of monitoring cameras and TV screens from which the faces of the 'Thought Police' constantly menaced the two lovers, the leading protagonists of the stage action. The backcloth of the set was made from stretch material upon which Kenneth devised an ingenious and astonishing *pas de deux* performed several feet up, like climbers on a rock-face, in which precarious position the lovers were free from surveillance. Their vertiginous movements were supported by unseen hands behind them, feeling for them and holding them through the elastic material. The music was by Roberto Gerhard, the Sixth Little Symphony.

On the first night in Manchester, November 27, 1970, the film material for use on the monitoring screens was accidentally dropped from the flies and the curtain had to be held for nearly an hour while the whole length of the film was laboriously rewound. Despite the undoubted drama of the theme and the dexterity (and courage!) with which Svetlana Beriosova and Donald MacLeary as the illicit lovers performed their levitational duet, the ballet proved prohibitively complicated to stage and was soon dropped from the repertory.

Throughout 1971 it became increasingly apparent that regional audiences did not like modern experimental ballets. To include even one in a programme of old favourites went directly against the accumulated experience of more than twenty-five years of touring: provincial audiences were – still are – ultra-conservative; they prefer full-length classics and if they do respond to mixed bills they have to be long-established favourites such as *Les Sylphides*, *Boutique Fantasque* and *Les Patineurs*. Almost any new work is suspect and liable to result in a drop in bookings. Works as radical as *Field Figures* lead to an instant decline in box-office takings. The result of all this was that it was not long before the New Group (that title, too, was soon to be dropped) was expanded to thirty-four dancers and, under the adroit direction of Peter Wright with John Auld later brought in as Assistant Director, the repertory began a protracted return to popular ballets.

New works continued to be introduced, of course, but they were far less radical, much more calculated to appeal to conformist taste. In this vein, Kenneth commissioned a young American choreographer, Joe Layton, who had had considerable success on the American musical stage, to create a work for the company and he produced *The Grand Tour*. Danced to an arrangement of Noel Coward's music the ballet depicted stage and screen celebrities of the 'twenties and 'thirties against an attractive Art Deco shipboard setting.

Two of Kenneth's own works were brought into the New Group repertory that same year, the abstract *Diversions* and the dramatic *Las Hermanas* in which Lynn Seymour made 'guest' appearances and which was produced in the summer season at Sadler's Wells Theatre when the company returned there after an absence of fourteen years.

Another American choreographer whose works Kenneth was responsible for introducing into the New Group repertory was Herbert Ross (who had married Nora Kaye). At Wimbledon on October 12, 1971, the company presented his darkly dramatic *Caprichos*, based on Goya's commentaries on his Caprichos engravings, followed a week later by his even more arresting – and more successful – *The Maids*, a balletic version of Jean Genet's bizarre play of the same title, an extended, violent duet for two men, resulting in the erotic murder of one of them. With Nicholas Johnson and Kerrison Cooke in the leading roles the work was something of a *tour de force* and remained in the repertory for several seasons.

*

During the spring and summer of 1971 Kenneth had at last been able to work on his new version of *Anastasia* for the Royal Ballet at Covent Garden, expanding it by two acts preceding the one created in Berlin. His twofold intention was to show something of the historical background and circumstances that had led to Anna Andersen's incarceration in the clinic, and to present a new three-act work which would display the magnificent strength of the Covent Garden company, providing the many soloists and principals with new roles. (Nothing pleases dancers so much, of course, as having parts created specially for them and having something new to do – so much of their work involving endless repetition of the regular repertory.)

In the new narrative additions, the first act revealed Anastasia as a pubescent young woman surrounded by her family, and the second dealt with court intrigues and the 1917 revolution, for which a friend suggested using Tchaikovsky's First and Third Symphonies. The opening scenes depicted the Czar and his family, accompanied by the sinister monk Rasputin and young naval officers, enjoying themselves at an informal picnic; at the end of the act a messenger brought a telegram announcing the declaration of war between Germany, France and Great Britain. The young officers were blessed by Rasputin, formed up and marched off to mobilisation.

The second act was set in 1917. A ball was in progress for Anastasia's coming out and she observed the covert relationships beneath the surface of the court formalities: her mother's fascination with Rasputin, her father's association with his ex-mistress, the prima ballerina Mathilde Kchessinska who, as part of the court entertainment, danced a brilliant *pas de deux* with her partner. At the end of the act revolutionaries burst into the palace and the Royal Family were marched away under armed guard.

The last act was the original impressionistic *Anastasia* danced to the Martinu score, the only minor alteration being that the final *coup de theatre* of the bed encircling the stage was achieved with an electronically controlled bed in the absence of a stage revolve.

Barry Kay designed two beautiful new settings: the first-act was set in birch-woods with the vortex-shaped panels which, in the last act, served as screens for the film projections, representing stylised foliage. The second act ballroom was a metallic structure not unlike the skeletal framework of a dirigible. In that scene the ladies of the Court, including the Czarina and her daughters, were dressed in shades of pale blue, aquamarine and turquoise with silver and diamante trimmings, a shimmering foil for the darker shades of the officers' uniforms. Kchessinska and her partner were dressed in the elaborate ballet costumes of the period, carried out in black and silver. The glittering assembly of the Court contrasted with the grim, slogan-scrawled drop-curtain for the brief scenes of the revolutionaries' gatherings.

Choreographic highlights of the first act included an amusing first entrance for the young Anastasia on roller-skates; brilliant solo variations for the young officers; a lovely and touching duet for the Czarina and Anastasia and a dramatic incident when the haemophiliac young Czarevitch fell over and was encouraged to take faltering steps again by the mesmeric Rasputin. The second act included splendid ensembles for the Court – mostly grand polonaises, a sympathetic solo for Anastasia and the dazzling and difficult *pas de deux* for Kchessinska and her partner.

The first performance of the full-length *Anastasia* took place at the Royal Opera House on July 22, 1971, with Lynn Seymour in the title role, Svetlana Beriosova as the Czarina Alexandra, Derek Rencher as the Czar Nicholas II, Adrian Grater as Rasputin, Vergie Derman, Jennifer Penney and Lesley Collier as Anastasia's sisters, Anthony Dowell, David Wall and Michael Coleman as naval officers, Antoinette Sibley and Anthony Dowell as Kchessinska and her partner and David Adams as Anastasia's husband. The critical reception was, in the main, unfavourable, ranging from the completely dismissive to a general cavilling about this, that or the other historical detail, the choreographic conception, the choice of music and even whether or not Kenneth believed Anna Andersen's claim.

The critic of the *Dancing Times* felt that the ballet lacked any story-line: 'It is neither straightforward narrative nor a remembrance of things past,' but 'drastic cutting would save something very beautiful'. *The Times* critic disliked practically everything about the ballet and thought that the choreography was an 'insipid copy' of Ashton's *Enigma Variations* and Grigorovitch's *Spartacus* for the Bolshoi Ballet (a strange mixture indeed!) But the critic of the *Financial Times* gave the ballet a rave review, holding the opinion that 'it is one of those rare and precious works of art in which a major creator consolidates all that he has done before and on this firm foundation goes on to build something new, larger and stranger and more exciting than anything he has done before'.

The *Guardian* critic thought the expansion of the original one-act work into a full-length one was 'little short of disastrous, there being really no dramatic or narrative link between the final act and what precedes it'. The *Telegraph* critic was of a similar opinion, writing that 'the first two acts were dull and repetitious'.

The *Observer* critic thought that 'the structure of the ballet is very awkward' but that 'MacMillan has brought off several major feats. He has provided an evening packed with classical dancing which is always distinguished and inventive in that quiet way which rewards repeated viewings.' The *Sunday Telegraph* critic called the ballet 'an honourable failure, displaying everywhere MacMillan's undoubted talent', and concluded that 'the encouraging thing about *Anastasia* is the feeling that in spite of all his faults it is a definite advance in MacMillan's progress towards his next achievement.'

The general consensus was that the ballet was flawed by the structure imposed upon it by the two Tchaikovsky symphonies, that the first two acts were full of padding – albeit including some beautiful and brilliant choreography – and that it was, overall, a disappointment.

Seymour received universal praise for her performance and the supporting cast were all accorded generous accolades. Barry Kay's sets and costumes, too, were enthusiastically praised – with the exception of *The Times* critic who thought that 'the whole ballet is tastelessly Ruritanian in concept'.

Although audiences seemed to enjoy the work and applauded every performance enthusiastically, Kenneth was very despondent about the critical barrage the ballet suffered as, indeed, were the entire company. One senior principal wrote to the Editor of *The Times*, very upset that that paper's reviewer had written 'Svetlana Beriosova as the Tsarina does her dutiful, understanding wife act once more.' (He was referring to Beriosova's role as Elgar's wife in *Enigma Variations*.) But, for Kenneth, the poor reviews cut much deeper; it had been a difficult year coping with the administrative trials attendant upon the radical changes in the companies' reformation and taking the brunt of the criticism for their redeployment. He had put much time, thought, care and creative energy into *Anastasia* and was taken aback by the ferocity with which it was attacked by some of the critics. Gone were the days when they looked upon him as the brilliant, natural successor to Ashton; now they appeared to vilify everything he attempted to do. The growing attacks upon him – both overt and covert – produced in Kenneth a deep depression, so much so that it threatened to overwhelm his ability to function, both as Director of the company and as a private person. A friend advised him that now was the time to try psychoanalysis. Years before he had remarked to an interviewer that, when he was rich, he would undertake analysis, more out of curiosity than anything else, a feeling that a deeper understanding of his psyche might, perhaps, provide an insight into what motivated his ideas as a choreographer, such as his predeliction for the 'outsider' character and his preoccupation with death. Kenneth was far from rich, but the need for analysis was now of a more practical nature: it would help to re-establish his emotional equilibrium and put the attacks upon him into a proper perspective.

Kenneth's psychoanalysis was to last three years – there is no quick way with such a course.

18

'She likes you, too'

At a time of deep despondency, when a bright, challenging future seemed suddenly bleak, something happened that changed Kenneth's life, gave him new incentives, reinvigorated his work – even altered his personality: he met the woman who was to be his wife.

Deborah Williams was born in Australia. Slim and elegant, she had trained as an artist and been a fashion model before setting out on world-wide travels – Mexico, the United States, Morocco, Greece, Britain – in an attempt to forget an early and unhappy marriage and an equally unhappy subsequent *affaire*. In London she had run out of money and, loathe to go home, worked as a waitress and then as a nanny. She met Kenneth through a mutual friend, Geoffrey Solomons, who had got up a party of four to see a film, Clint Eastwood in *Play Misty For Me*.

After the film, Kenneth went back to his house in Battersea. Deborah went home with Geoffrey and his flat-mate; they were sitting talking when the phone rang. Geoffrey picked it up and, guessing that it would be Kenneth, said without preamble, 'She likes you, too!' There had, indeed, been an instant rapport between them which, within a few weeks, had burgeoned into a close relationship.

It came, providentially, at a time when Kenneth was most in need of friendship, support and love. Without it, it is doubtful if he would have been able to surmount the trials that lay ahead for he was finding that directing the two companies was a heavy burden indeed.

At the Royal Ballet Benevolent Fund Gala on December 14, 1971, Kenneth introduced another Robbins ballet into the repertoire, this time the short *Afternoon of a Faun*. Taking the Debussy score used by Nijinsky in 1912, Robbins changed the theme from a stylised erotic encounter between a faun and some nymphs in an Arcadian setting, to one of boy-meets-girl in a dance studio. It is a charming, delicate work (originally created for the New York City Ballet in 1953) and, danced by Antoinette Sibley and Anthony Dowell, it was an immediate success; it has been regularly revived ever since. In the same programme Ashton created a lyrical *pas de deux* to Massenet's *Meditation* from *Thais*.

A month later Kenneth produced a new one-act ballet of his own for the Covent Garden company, *Triad*. The theme was one of emotional betrayal – the filial relationship of two young brothers sundered by the intrusion of a woman. It was an idea that had its genesis in Kenneth's memories of having to keep watch while his elder brother engaged in amorous dalliance with girls under the pier at Gt. Yarmouth – another return, though muted, to the outsider.

The chosen score was Prokoviev's youthful, lyrical, bitter-sweet First Violin Concerto which, Kenneth felt, fitted the mood of the ballet most effectively. The sets and costumes were by Peter Unsworth, a designer whose work for Geoffrey Cauley Kenneth had admired. (Cauley was a member of the old Touring Company and Kenneth had 'inherited' promises given to him and other company members to be allowed to produce works for the New Group, after tryouts with the Choreographic Group; none proved very successful.) Unsworth created a gauzy, silvery-blue arboreal setting and dressed the dancers in leotards decorated with veined patterns; the effect was to make them seem like woodland creatures.

The ballet began with Anthony Dowell, as the Boy lying prone, and Wayne Eagling (in his first major role) as his brother, sitting close by. A brief duet established their sibling relationship. Antoinette Sibley, as the Girl, glimpsed through the gauze with three male companions, entered and, after provoking the attentions of both males, settled for the older one while the younger revealed increasing disturbance at his exclusion. When the Girl made an exit the younger brother was briefly consoled by the elder who then callously turned him over for some rough treatment by the Girl's three companions. The Girl returned for an erotic *pas de deux* with the elder brother and the ballet ended with them entwined on the floor while the younger brother brooded over them.

The choreography was both lyrical and brilliant, with many daring acrobatic lifts and throws, including the sequence of the younger brother maltreated by the companions. The trio of relationships were expressed through the intricate, spiralling movements – very much dictated by the music – and were far less explicitly mimed than in many of Kenneth's previous ballets. On the first night the audience gave the work a warmly enthusiastic reception.

The critics, too, with one or two exceptions, were complimentary, commenting on the inventiveness of the choreography and the subtle affinities it had with the score. Some, however, confessed to be nonplussed about the relationships, thinking that they should have been made more explicit, and one critic went so far as to suggest that, despite the programme's description of the two males as brothers, it was really a homosexual association. All three principals received excellent notices for their interpretations and the brilliance with which they coped with the virtuoso demands of the choreography.

The critic of the *Dancing Times* thought that Prokoviev's music was 'wonderfully explored by the choreographer', and that the ballet gave 'three such potentially superb roles to the principal dancers'. The *Observer* critic wrote, 'What is evident already is the abundance of dancing and the rich invention of new steps and manoeuvres,' although he went on to say, 'There is little of MacMillan's usual telling command of expressive movement and perhaps as a result the emotion is so faint as to be almost non-existent.'

The *Sunday Times* reviewer said, 'MacMillan has always had a lyrical gift for the invention of *pas de deux*, and this extended *pas de trois*, with Cain and Abel overtones, showed him at the height of his powers.' The *Sunday Telegraph* critic wrote, 'MacMillan seems, after flirting with abtract movement, to be returning to what he does best, creating striking imagery and dramatic tension to express character and feeling; but he returns with all his abstract vocabulary to enrich everything he does.'

Yet, despite the generally favourable reception accorded to *Triad*, it was not, to quote the *Sunday Telegraph* critic again, 'an immediate, overwhelming success that silences every hostile voice'. And hostile voices there were, not only in the press but backstage, too, where some dancers in the company began to agitate for Kenneth's resignation as Director – although, at that time, Kenneth was unaware of it. (Within a few years those same dancers were to be some of Kenneth's most ardent supporters.)

*

On February 15, less than a month after the premiere of *Triad*, Kenneth introduced another new work to the repertoire, this time a vehicle specially created for Margot Fonteyn in Stuttgart two years earlier, Cranko's *Poème de l'Extase*. Danced to Scriabin's orchestral tone poem of the same title, it depicted an ageing beauty, called *The Diva* in the programme, who, courted by a young man (Michael Coleman), dreamed of former lovers (David Drew, Desmond Kelly, Carl Myers, Peter O'Brien and David Wall). The choreography was notable for the way in which Fonteyn was lifted and thrown about in the Bolshoi manner without much opportunity to display her own brand of classicism. It had a spectacular set by Jurgen Rose in the Viennese *Jugendstil* manner after Gustav Klimt. The ballet was not much liked. More important than the work itself, perhaps, was the fact that the first night was the occasion for a *rapprochement* between Kenneth and Cranko after the unfortunate incident over *Miss Julie* – their friendship was far too firmly based and long-standing for it to be permanently affected by such a *contretemps*.

It is worth pointing out that at this stage in Kenneth's directorship of the company he was faced with finding roles for no less than eleven principal ballerinas. In addition, despite the almost weekly rumour of a definite 'last appearance', Margot Fonteyn, then fifty-three, was appearing regularly with the company as a guest, a great dancer still possessed of considerable artistry and a potent box-office draw. At that time, and subsequently, Kenneth was criticised for not giving more opportunities to younger members of the company, but his detractors conveniently ignored the fact that he was saddled with the need to provide roles for an unprecedented number of principals. This was a result not only of the amalgamation of the two companies but also of a generation overlap – a number of dancers had reached full maturity but were still some years away from retirement, while others were approaching the *apogée* of their careers. The situation was complicated not only by a plethora of artists clamoring for exposure but also by the perennial restrictions placed on the number of Royal Ballet performances by sharing the theatre with the Royal Opera. As it was, in that spring season of 1972, the Royal Ballet at Covent Garden presented an exceptional variety of programmes with no less than eighteen different productions in less than twelve weeks.

Meanwhile the touring company was also concentrating on new productions and during the February season at Sadler's Wells Theatre they presented a new work by Joe Layton, *OW*, which took its theme from the trial of Oscar Wilde and his *Ballad of Reading Gaol*. There was almost an element of burlesque in the ballet, with Wilde (Michael Somes, no less!) floridly dressed in green velvet, leaping about the stage capturing young men with a butterfly net while, on a sound track, John Geilgud's magisterial voice recited Wilde's poem. Audiences and critics did not like the pantomimic, flippant approach to a celebrated personal tragedy and the work was soon dropped. In retrospect it might have been a subject for Kenneth himself to have tackled rather more seriously.

*

During the first weeks of their friendship Kenneth had taken Deborah to *Triad*, the first ballet of his that she ever saw. At that time both Royal Ballet companies were preparing for trips abroad, the Covent Garden company to New York and the touring company to Portugal, for which season Kenneth was to provide a new work. He planned to join the Covent Garden company in New York towards the end of its visit. He was anxious that Deborah should accompany him to America but Deborah was reluctant, mainly because she thought it might upset her parents. She felt that they would worry about her, knowing that her previous experience with men had been unfortunate, yet here she was preparing to go off to the U.S. with a man whom she had known only a short while and whom they had never met. In fact, Deborah's qualms led, indirectly, to Kenneth suggesting marriage: his oblique proposal was made not to Deborah but to her mother! 'Let me speak to her,' Kenneth insisted, so they telephoned Deborah's parents in Australia and, during the conversation, Kenneth announced, somewhat formally, 'My intentions towards Deborah are perfectly honorable.' Whatever his intentions, however, the 'law's delay' was an obstacle to an early marriage, because Deborah had first to file for divorce. But Deborah now knew that Kenneth was set upon a permanent relationship. She agreed to accompany him to New York.

While the Covent Garden company flew to New York Kenneth was busy working on his new ballet for the touring company. Called *Ballade*, after the Ballade for Piano and Orchestra by Fauré, to which the work was set, it was an essentially simple piece, the decor just a table and chairs painted white, the choreography an extended *pas de cirque* for a girl and four boys, the theme, slight as it was, suggested by Kenneth's first meeting with Deborah. It was not intended as a major work but a shoe-string, pot-boiling ballet such as Kenneth had had to produce in Berlin, a *bonne bouche* for the company's trip to Portugal. The work was given its first performance on May 19, 1972, with Vyvyan Lorrayne as the Girl and Kerrison Cooke, Paul Clarke, Nicholas Johnson and Stephen Jefferies as the supporting men. In that same season in Lisbon the touring company also performed *Triad* with Marilyn Trounson, Paul Clarke and Nicholas Johnson as the titular trio.

Because of his intense dislike of flying Kenneth and Deborah sailed for New York on the *Q.E. II*. The season had opened, inauspiciously, with a gala programme that included various bits and pieces that had not pleased the critics, including Kenneth's trifle, *Side-Show*, a burlesque *pas de deux* for a circus strong-man and a ballerina that had been given its first performance by the (then) New Group in Liverpool. The fact that it was performed in New York by two such high-powered artists as Lynn Seymour and Rudolf Nureyev probably led the audience to expect some dazzling pyrotechnic display rather than knockabout comedy. Neither *Triad* nor *Poème de l'Extase* (which had already been shown by the Stuttgart Ballet) were well received and when Kenneth took a curtain call after *Anastasia* he was booed by a certain faction in the audience. For some reason it was thought that Ashton's retirement had been 'engineered' and Kenneth was looked upon almost as a usurper. He realised, afterwards, that it had been a psychological mistake not to have been present at the company's first night, or to have been available for press conferences when any misconceptions about his succession to Ashton might have been cleared up. But a number of critics and New York fans of the Royal Ballet felt that Kenneth's absence was, at worst, an insult, at best a demonstration of indifference – which was not the case at all. First, Kenneth, naturally, had the good name and reputation of the company very much at heart; secondly, ever since the Royal Ballet's first appearance in New York in 1949, when Kenneth was a dancer with the company, he had enjoyed his visits to that city. But Kenneth and Deborah were subjected to a lot of unpleasant harassment by disaffected fans of the company. One large lady followed them in the street making vomiting noises; a man threatened Kenneth with physical violence unless he put back a certain variation in *The Sleeping Beauty*. In vain Kenneth explained that the production was by Peter Wright and that the matter was entirely his decision; the man still made dire threats whenever Kenneth emerged from the stage door.

*

Back in London for the summer season, the Royal Ballet's programmes offered much to interest the balletomane. On June 20 Natalia Makarova made her debut at the Royal Opera House in *Giselle* partnered by Anthony Dowell, and in *Swan Lake* partnered by Donald MacLeary. They were the first of many performances she was to give over the next few years when, like Nureyev, she became a 'permanent guest artist'. Just over a month later, on July 26, Glen

Tetley presented another major modern work, *Laborintus*, in which a small cast of three couples were led by Lynn Seymour and Rudolf Nureyev. Inspired partly by a drawing by Pollaiuolo and partly by Dante's *Inferno*, the ballet, which combined classical technique with the *plastique* of modern dance, had a score by Luciano Berio and a mysterious but dramatic decor by Ruben Ter-Arutunian. It was, for its time, a very *avant-garde* work and consequently was not popular, but no one could complain that, while maintaining the classics and its own regular repertory, the Royal Ballet was not making an effort to keep abreast of the latest developments in dance.

Nevertheless complaints there were, not so much about the company as Kenneth's direction of it. In its issue of July 14, 1972, the *New Statesman and Nation* published a long attack by its dance critic, headed *What's Happened to MacMillan?* Beginning with a dismissive review of *Ballade* it went on to state a) that Kenneth had not produced a real success since *Concerto* in 1966; b) that New Yorkers had been insulted and the company abandoned by Kenneth's late arrival in the season; c) that the proposed works to be added to the repertoire (by Robbins and Balanchine) would scarcely help to provide a suitable repertoire for the next New York visit; d) that the company's own promising choreographers, such as David Drew and Geoffrey Cauley, should receive more encouragement; e) that Kenneth had an apparent reluctance to engage guest stars; f) that illnesses and accidents which had occasioned some programme alterations were brought about by psychosomatic causes; g) that it would be a good thing if Kenneth were replaced by Nureyev, or Fonteyn, or Field, or Cranko.

Leaving aside artistic judgements, such charges were, in the main, based on misconceptions. Kenneth was not responsible for some of the administrative decisions that accompanied his Directorship of the Royal Ballet; additions to the Royal Ballet's repertoire were not decided upon the basis of whether or not they might be suitable for New York; both Nureyev and Makarova had been engaged as guest artists; all companies are, from time to time, decimated by illness and accident; neither Kenneth nor the management were trying to 'revolutionise' the company's image; and neither David Drew nor Geoffrey Cauley had shown the sort of choreographic talent in their ballets (*From Waking Sleep* and *St. Thomas' Wake* by Drew and *Symphonie Pastorale* and *Ante Room* by Cauley) that warranted much encouragement.

Kenneth was naturally upset but he was reassured by the management which reiterated its fullest support for his directorial policies. The attacks continued, however, and seemed at times to be like a concerted campaign, so much so that the Editor of the *Dancing*

Times, in the issue for December, 1972, felt constrained to write: "MacMillan . . . has been subjected for nearly two years now to a new and very pernicious kind of "criticism" – from both sides of the Atlantic. This is neither outspoken condemnation nor reasoned arguing. It is snide, personal and usually couched in such short, stinging phrases that it will cause the greatest possible hurt to the victim. I find it irresponsible and very short-sighted. It is one thing to criticise the Director of the Royal Ballet – and the direction has come in for anti-Establishment blastings for all its successful life. It is quite another thing to slaughter a creative artist. If MacMillan's zest for creative choreography is killed who, in heaven's name, have we got left?'

*

For the touring company's autumn season Kenneth produced another new ballet, *Poltroon*. He had been reading a book, *Pierrot* by Kay Dick, which was both a history and an analysis of *commedia dell'arte* characters – Pierrot, Harlequin, Pantaloon, Columbine, Brighella and co. These street-theatre figures from the Renaissance have probably provided the inspiration, if not the substance, for more ballets than any other fantasticks from folk-lore, from Fokine's *Carnaval* to Tetley's *Pierrot Lunaire*. Kenneth had the clever idea of twisting the stylised characters, and the centuries of symbolism attached to them, to show the bitter reverse of the sentimentalised encrustations they had acquired. In particular, Pierrot, the eternally put-upon innocent, became the vicious poltroon of the title, a worm who finally turned and, backstage, slayed his tormentors. (Kenneth revenging himself upon the critics?) Harlequin was also de-romanticised and Columbine revealed as a harlot.

The music for the ballet was an existing score by Rudolf Maros, a little-known Hungarian composer who had, in fact, written a number of ballet scores. It was suggested by Ashley Lawrence. The ingenious set, which reversed to show the on-stage slapstick and the back-stage slaughter, was by Thomas O'Neil. The work, which received its premiere on October 12, 1972, was not popular, either with the critics or audiences, who may have been upset by this irreverent unmasking of a familiar troupe of entertainers.

For the autumn season at Covent Garden Kenneth revised *Swan Lake*; previous alterations, in effect, had practically restored the old Touring Company Sergeyev-based version of the ballet. Kenneth reverted to the original Ivanov choreography of Act IV and moved Ashton's brilliant *pas de quatre*, created for the 1963 production, to a more appropriate place in the ballroom scene of Act III. He also retained Nureyev's melancholy solo for Prince Siegfried in Act I.

This production was well received and much preferred to the earlier revised version.

For the Benevolent Fund Gala in November Kenneth acquired another major Robbins work, *Requiem Canticles*, created the previous June for the New York City Ballet's Stravinsky Festival. Less obviously attractive than *Dances at a Gathering*, its nine episodes for a large cast set to an elaborate score for singers and orchestra, proved unpopular with audiences and the work was soon dropped, which was a pity: works which receive initial antipathy often grow to be appreciated by repitition – as Kenneth was to prove, subsequently, with several of his own ballets. For the same gala Ashton produced his felicitous *pas de deux*, *The Walk to the Paradise Garden*, the first work he had contributed to the repertoire since Kenneth became Director.

1972 had been a year of stress for Kenneth, but it ended on a happy personal note. Late in the autumn Deborah had contracted a very bad dose of influenza, so bad, in fact, that she was taken to hospital. During her stay there the doctors carried out a pregnancy test which they pronounced positive. Deborah was apprehensive, thinking that an unplanned pregnancy might have a deleterious effect on her friendship with Kenneth, who, although he had implied a readiness for marriage, might not yet wish to contemplate parenthood. The very opposite proved to be the case: when the doctors' prognosis actually proved wrong Kenneth was terribly disappointed and suggested that it would be a good idea if they did have a baby. Just before Christmas Deborah was able to announce that a further pregnancy test had proved positively positive; they were both absolutely delighted and to mark the occasion Kenneth presented Deborah with a shi'-zu puppy.

19

Death of a friend, birth of a baby, creation of *Manon*

The 1973 season at Covent Garden began with a glittering gala, *Fanfare for Europe*, to commemorate Britain's entry into the European Economic Community. Kenneth produced a lyrical *pas de deux*, *Pavane*, for Antoinette Sibley and Anthony Dowell, to music by Fauré. At this time he was also engaged on a new production of *The*

Sleeping Beauty to replace the Tennysonian-Medieval one by Peter Wright which had never found much favour. The new production was to be paid for by The American Friends of Covent Garden and it was also to be included in the repertoire of the Royal Ballet's forthcoming first trip to Brazil. The essential 'portability' of the ballet for this tour precluded Kenneth from producing anything like his brilliant version of the ballet for the Berlin company with its large 'built' sets by Barry Kay; everything for the new version had to be painted on easily portable cloths.

Kenneth made the initial mistake of agreeing to use a designer whose work he had not seen but who had been employed by the Covent Garden management for the Royal Opera with some success. When Kenneth saw the designs for *The Sleeping Beauty* he was appalled – 'Everything in Day-Glo colours and covered in scrambled egg,' he said. Hastily, with time running out, he approached Peter Farmer to do a quick re-design job.

Kenneth made some minor alterations to the traditional choreography – more to do with the presentation of the characters than the actual steps. Taking his cue from the title of the Lilac Fairy, he also named the other supporting fairies in the *Prologue* after flowers, instead of the largely meaningless traditional titles such as the Fairy of the Woodland Glades, the Fairy of the Enchanted Garden etc. In the Act III wedding scene the variations for Florestan and his Sisters were simplified into solo variations for what were called Jewel Fairies, and Kenneth also devised a brilliant new solo for a new character, Hop O' My Thumb, for the Royal Ballet's diminutive virtuoso dancer, Wayne Sleep.

Most of the critics disliked the production, particularly Peter Farmer's decor (naturally they were unaware of the fraught circumstances under which the work had been done) and his accentuation of colour-tones, particularly the blues – from indigo to aquamarine – for the *Prologue* and the russety reds and oranges for Act I. The one undoubted success was the Awakening: Aurora was discovered asleep in a large salon with shafts of moonlight shining through tall windows and gauzy curtains billowing in a soft breeze. It looked ravishingly romantic although it was, perhaps, more reminiscent of Hollywood than sixteenth/seventeenth century France.

In early February Kenneth introduced an all-Balanchine triple bill which, at one stroke – or, rather, one programme – doubled the number of Balanchine ballets in the company's repertoire. The works covered a wide period of Balanchine's creative canon: *The Prodigal Son*, a retelling of the Biblical story and one of the last works produced by Diaghilev's *Ballets Russes*, dating from 1929; *The Four Temperaments*, created in 1948, based on Hindemith's score which

Balanchine himself described as 'a Dance Ballet without plot', but which nevertheless reflected the moods, or 'humours' that had inspired the music – melancholic, sanguinic, cholaric and phlegmatic; and *Agon*, choreographed in 1956 to the same score that Kenneth himself had used a year later, totally plotless, Balanchine at his most austerely inventive.

Nureyev made a considerable dramatic impact in the title role of *The Prodigal Son*, but the other two ballets, with their highly idiosyncratic choreography, presented the Royal Ballet dancers with certain problems made all the more complicated by the fact that all three ballets were rehearsed in the same tightly-scheduled period. Nevertheless, under the circumstances, the dancers gave an excellent account of themselves – and the works – even though they may have seemed less razor-sharp than the artists of the New York City Ballet. Yet it was not a popular programme despite the fulsome praise lavished by critics on anything created by Balanchine. *The Prodigal Son* and *The Four Temperaments* were transferred to the repertoire of the touring company where the dancers were given time to familiarise themselves with the Balanchine style (*The Prodigal Son* has been fitfully revived at Covent Garden from time to time) but *Agon*, one of Balanchine's most important and innovative works, was soon dropped before the cast had had time to 'play themselves in'.

The Covent Garden company began its strenuous three-week tour of Brazil at the beginning of April. Kenneth travelled with his dancers but Deborah, who was experiencing some troublesome prenatal symptoms, stayed in the house in Battersea. Already they had the feeling that, when the baby was born, the little terrace villa would be too small for them and would necessitate moving to something larger.

The tour of Brazil was a tremendous success and when the company returned to London it opened a four-week season not at Covent Garden but the Coliseum with a wide-ranging repertoire that included *Anastasia* and *Romeo and Juliet*. The Royal Opera House may have greater elegance and atmosphere than the Coliseum but the latter theatre has infinitely better sight-lines and audiences were pleased to gain what amounted to a close-up view of the company and its works.

Back at Covent Garden, guest artists Makarova and Nureyev appeared together for the first time (anywhere), first in *The Sleeping Beauty*, and then, much more notably, in *Romeo and Juliet*. In that same season David Blair, who had been the first Mercutio, gave his farewell performance, as Colas in *La Fille mal gardée*, and then, the following day, June 26, 1973, came the distressing news that John Cranko had died in a plane, returning with the Stuttgart Ballet from a tour of the United States. Peter Wright telephoned the news to Kenneth who was in rehearsal. Naturally, he was deeply upset at the loss of his friend and colleague and at such an early age – especially as Cranko was not suffering from any serious illness and his death was brought about by one of those rare mischances (he choked on his own vomit after taking a mild sedative on the plane).

At that time Kenneth was extremely busy producing a new, enlarged version of *The Seven Deadly Sins* for the Covent Garden company so any thought of attending Cranko's funeral in Stuttgart was out of the question. (Subsequently he contributed a commemorative article to a paperback tribute to Cranko edited by Johannes Kilian.)

Although Ian Spurling's decor for the Brecht-Weill ballet was basically the same as he had designed for the small Western Theatre Ballet version in 1961, Kenneth completely revised the choreography for the larger number of dancers he was able to employ with the Royal Ballet. The dancing role of the leading character of Anna was given to Jennifer Penney, the first major role that Kenneth had created for her, and he was delighted with her responsiveness. For the singing half of the role Kenneth approached Georgia Brown whose strong, warm voice he had admired in the musical *Oliver!* Georgia Brown was most pleased to be asked to appear at Covent Garden and Kenneth enjoyed working with her immensely.

The critics, as so often, were very divided in their opinions when *The Seven Deadly Sins* received its Royal Opera House premiere on July 19, 1973. There were one or two who felt that Georgia Brown was wrongly cast as the singing Anna: the music critic of the *Financial Times* wrote a long piece about how the 'musical direction' of Covent Garden had failed to study Weill's original scoring, and did not like the fact that Miss Brown had to sing the songs (originally composed for Lotte Lenya's 'light, clear, soprano') 'transposed down a full fourth'. But most critics liked Georgia Brown's interpretation as they did Jennifer Penney's reading of the fresh, innocent, impulsive side of the Anna character. Several reviewers thought the choreography rather 'uninspired'. But, again, others very much enjoyed the tap-dancing roles for Vergie Derman and Christopher Carr; Michael Coleman's amusingly adroit dancing as a waiter holding a huge gateau at the same time as he was partnering Penney; and Lynn Seymour's scene as a sleazy burlesque queen waggling tassels on her bosom and bottom.

The episodic nature of Brecht's scenario occasioned some rather interruptive blackouts and scene-changes after each sequence and, although they were speeded up after the first night, each hiatus, however short, tended to spoil the flow and slacken the pace of the ballet. But audiences enjoyed it and Weill's music and the burlesque style made a welcome change in a repertoire that was, perhaps rather overloaded with serious works.

As opposed to the *Financial Times* music critic, *The Times* ballet reviewer thought that 'it was the musical aspect of the performance to which one can give unqualified praise'. He thought the choreography for the dancing Anna seemed 'to be based on an experiment in finding how many difficult and ungainly ways there are in lifting a girl up'. The critic of the *Observer* wrote, 'MacMillan has created a fascinating concoction – lovingly light-hearted about the rather naif "message", inventive, original and marvellously original in texture.' The *Sunday Telegraph*'s reviewer, after itemising the faults that he thought were 'imposed by the form of the piece', concluded that 'the final account is comfortably in credit. A fun spectacle, some gorgeous dancing, attractive music well sung and suitably moralised and satirised – definitely a slick concoction.' Which seemed to sum up the audience's reaction pretty accurately.

While Kenneth was working on *The Seven Deadly Sins*, he was also planning a new full-length ballet that, like *Romeo and Juliet* and *Anastasia*, would provide the company with another chance to show its strength in depth. Some years before he had seen a French modern-dress film version of the Abbé Prevost's eighteenth century novel of *Manon Lescaut* and this had set him to reading the original book. From the semi-autobiographical picaresque novel (one of several volumes issued under the generic title *Mémoires d'un Homme de Qualité*) describing the somewhat reptitious adventures of the amoral heroine, he extrapolated a sufficient number of key scenes for the ballet scenario.

Less than a month after the premiere of *Seven Deadly Sins*, on August 16, 1973, Deborah had her baby at the West London Hospital. Kenneth was with Deborah until moments before the actual birth, when he felt he would be in the way. He says that next day he suffered from sympathetic pains from the delivery, his joints stiff and aching as if he had done an exhausting class! The baby was a girl, named Charlotte, derived from Karl, the name of a close friend of Kenneth's and the baby's godfather.

The autumn season at Covent Garden began with yet another ballet by Jerome Robbins, a pendant to *Dances at a Gathering*, *In the Night*. Also danced to piano pieces by Chopin, it was shorter and slighter than the former work, essentially three *pas de deux* with a finale for all six dancers. Although of less importance than *Dances at a Gathering*, it was very popular although, for some unaccountable reason, also allowed to fall out of the repertoire.

*

Anastasia was first produced as a one-act Expressionist work for the Berlin Opera Ballet in 1967. In 1971 MacMillan expanded it into a three-act work for the Royal Ballet to demonstrate the company's great strength in depth. *Below*: Barry Kay's lovely setting for the first act in which Czar Nicholas II and his family enjoy an informal day in the country. The spiral motif was ingeniously incorporated in all three acts, finally used as a screen upon which were projected films of the young Czarina Anastasia. (*Michael Werner*, photograph from the Barry Kay Archives.) *Right*: Lynn Seymour in the last act as Anna Anderson recalling her memories in a Berlin clinic. (*Anthony Crickmay*.) The one act version of the ballet is also in the repertory of American Ballet Theatre.

Manon was the first, complete, full-length ballet that Kenneth had created while being, at the same time, involved in the multitudinous tasks of running a large company. (Peter Wright had, by then, more or less completely taken over the direction of the touring company but, even so, it was necessary for him to liaise closely with Kenneth, to discuss the day-to-day plans for both companies, their repertoires and the dispositions of the dancers.)

When Kenneth came to enlarge *Anastasia*, one third of it had already been set and the two Tchaikovsky symphonic scores for the additional acts were complete in themselves, but the music for *Manon* had to be assembled piecemeal for each scene – Kenneth still being very wary of a commissioned score.

Massenet had created his operatic version of the story in 1884 and, with Leighton Lucas as his musical adviser, Kenneth had settled upon using music by Massenet – but not from the opera. Instead, they sifted through literally scores of scores, of oratorios, orchestral works, songs and other Massenet operas. Hilda Gaunt and Leighton Lucas played them on the piano to Kenneth who then selected those pieces that he felt were right for his choreographic needs and the scenario that he had developed. When the music had finally been chosen, Leighton Lucas began work orchestrating it.

As had become his custom, Kenneth began work on the ballet with the four big *pas de deux* for the lovers which are the core of the choreography. The first one records their instant attraction for each other at their initial encounter; the second follows almost at once, the opening of the second scene of the first act in Des Grieux's squalid apartment, and celebrates their rapturous physical infatuation. The third comes at the end of the second act, when Manon has left Monsieur G.M., her 'protector', and returned to Des Grieux; and the fourth is the climax and conclusion of the ballet when Manon dies in Des Grieux's arms in the swamps of Louisiana. Each *pas de deux*, therefore, registers a different aspect of their relationship throughout their fluctuating fortunes and Kenneth reached new heights of inventiveness in these big scenes.

There were also several solos to construct, most notably for the role of Lescaut, Manon's pimping brother. One day, while rehearsing Lescaut's big variation in the second act 'hotel' (i.e. brothel) scene, Kenneth said to David Wall, upon whom the character was created, 'Why don't you do it as if you were drunk?' Whereupon Kenneth proceeded to reset the solo as an inebriated one – including a succeeding *pas de deux* for Lescaut and his mistress who also had a big solo. There were solos and ensembles for various supporting characters, including a group of beggars in Act I and a trio of gentlemen in Act II, a long set-piece for Manon supported, lifted and manipulated by a group of admirers also in Act II, a *pas de deux* for the Jailer and his mistress at the beginning of Act III, and a duet – hardly a *pas de deux* but nevertheless a very acrobatic physical encounter – for the Jailer and Manon in the penultimate scene of the ballet. There were two big crowd scenes, the opening scene of the ballet and the New Orleans dockside in the last act, and elaborate background vignettes for the card-playing scene of the second act. As with *Romeo and Juliet* and *Anastasia*, this was dance conceived on the scale of grand opera, with the corps de ballet used as a large number of individual characters, not *en masse*, as in classical ballet. Quite apart from the creative work involved, the sheer logistics of scheduling and integrating rehearsals with classes, and the rehearsal and performance of the current repertoire, was an immensely complex business.

To complicate matters still further, Antoinette Sibley, the first cast for Manon, fell prey to a protracted illness after the completion of the first act *pas de deux* and the rest of the role was created on Jennifer Penney.

At the end of December, in the midst of choreographing and rehearsing the new ballet, Kenneth went to Stuttgart to supervise the final rehearsals of *Concerto* which the company was taking into its repertoire; the initial teaching had been done by the Royal Ballet's choreologist, Monica Parker. *Concerto* was premiered at Stuttgart on December 22, 1973, with Marcia Haydée, Joyce Cuoco, Egon Madsen and Heinz Clauss leading the cast, and was well received – German critics were, after all, familiar with the work from the Berlin repertoire and Stuttgart audiences applauded it too. For Kenneth, even more important than the reception given to the ballet, was his renewal of contact with the Stuttgart company which had just appointed as its Director Glen Tetley who was responsible for taking *Concerto* into the repertoire.

The designs for *Manon* had been entrusted to Georgiadis. With the scenes moving from a town square to a squalid apartment to the flyblown grandeur of a brothel to a New Orleans dockside to the Jailer's quarters and finally the Louisiana swamps, Kenneth was particularly anxious to avoid, as far as possible, slow (and sometimes noisy) scene changes that could be disruptive of pace and atmosphere. To facilitate changes in the early scenes Georgiadis used reversible, revolving 'flats' and provided a permanent background setting of filthy rags (symbolic of the poverty and destitution that haunts Manon throughout the story) visible in varying degrees in every scene and finally constituting the only decor for Manon's death.

The costumes, particularly in the second act, provided Georgiadis with an opportunity to show the outward sumptuousness and extravagance of the period. (While designing the ballet Georgiadis says that he studied the social history of the epoch and discovered that France was going through a period of galloping inflation and that he was 'stimulated' by the analogy with Britain in the early seventies.) The dresses of the courtesans and 'actresses' frequenting Madame's 'Hotel Particulier' are richly decorated and lavishly trimmed with fur while, for the men, the silks, satins, brocades and lace ruffles reflect one of the most foppishly elegant fashion eras of all time.

Manon received its first performance at Covent Garden on March 7, 1974 at a gala attended by H.M. Queen Elizabeth the Queen Mother. The rather grand, self-important audience was moved to give the ballet a rapturous reception but the critics, as ever, were divided in their opinions. *The Times* critic wrote that 'inside the three sprawling acts' of the ballet 'there seems to be a presentable one-act work struggling to be born', and that 'the production is far longer than either its dramatic content or its dance interest will justify.' Yet he went on to say, 'On the credit side of *Manon* are three big roles and some of the best designs that the Royal Ballet can boast.' The critic of the *Financial Times* thought that 'the first thing to note is the effortless distinction that marks every aspect (but one) of its creation: the choreography, the dancing, the production, . . . everything, in fact except the score. Above all it is a feast of wonderful choreography, packed with *pas de deux, pas d'action, pas de trois*, and solos that delight the eye and will certainly reward repeated observation, and generations of interpreters.'

The *Guardian* reviewer wrote, 'MacMillan, for all his faults, is one of the very few choreographers today who can write a big spectacle ballet for an opera house company that is developed entirely in the classical idiom and is done entirely through dancing.' The writer went on to say 'There is so much beautiful dancing in *Manon* that it seems cruel to complain that there is too much. The ballet is too long but is eminently cuttable. . . . The choreography for Manon and Des Grieux is exquisite throughout and marvellously inventive.'

The *Observer*'s critic thought that 'most of the *pas de deux* would look good out of context', and that 'there are some excellent solos, especially in Act II and an acrobatic arrangement for Manon and her admirers which could bring the house down.' The *Sunday Telegraph* critic observed that 'the ballet's form is like the music, remarkably operatic. It depends on a number of set-piece *pas de deux*, alternating between a crowded stage packed with lively action, and the couple alone in a great shadowed space, dancing out their love and their tragedy, locked in a drama so intense the outside world seems to fade to nothing.'

Protecter
act I scen.

114

Manon was MacMillan's third full-length ballet. Freely adapted from the eighteenth century novel by the Abbé Prevost, it is a romantic drama that provides a splendid trio of leading roles with numerous parts for a large supporting cast. Somewhat indifferently received by the critics, it has always been a success with audiences, rivalling *Romeo and Juliet* in popularity and, like the earlier ballet, it has been danced by a large number of Royal Ballet principals as well as guest artists. *Above*: Antoinette Sibley and Anthony Dowell who originated the roles of Manon and her lover Des Grieux at the height of their famous partnership. (*Anthony Crickmay*.) *Above left*: costume designs for an Actress and a Gentleman Protector by Nicholas Georgiadis. *Below left*: Georgiadis's model for the set of Act One. (From the collection of *Nicholas Georgiadis*.) Manon is also in the repertory of the Royal Swedish Ballet.

The *Sunday Times* reviewer pointed out that 'one advantage of the three act ballet is that it makes possible the creation of roles which artists can really get their teeth into. In his *Manon* . . . MacMillan has provided wonderful parts for Antoinette Sibley, Anthony Dowell and David Wall, and the two men have never done anything better', and concluded that 'there is some original and striking choreography, particularly in the several *pas de deux*.'

Almost all the reviews gave glowing praise to the three leading dancers and the many soloists, although the lady critic of the *Morning Star* attacked Kenneth for 'an appalling waste of lovely Antoinette Sibley who, as Manon, is reduced to a nasty little diamond-digger'. She went on, 'You do not have to be a militant feminist to resent MacMillan's repeated representation of the female sex as deceiver and destroyer of the male. It is an obsessional view of human relations which makes all women monsters and all men willing victims. From such a viewpoint drama is impossible. There is no conflict, only violence; no feeling only lust.'

Nearly all the critics expressed dissatisfaction with the music, and Leighton Lucas's scoring. *The Times* critic thought that it 'lacked unity' and 'musical interest'. The *Financial Times* critic referred to it as 'weak', while the *Guardian* reviewer complained that 'by the end of the evening you do get awfully tired of Massenet'. The *Sunday Times* critic remarked that the 'hotch-potch' of (Massenet) bits and pieces' was 'conventionally orchestrated', and the *Observer* critic said that there was 'a lack of rhythmic drive in the score'. Once again Georgiadis gained universal praise for his sets. The *Financial Times* review referred to Georgiadis's 'splendid but never gaudy decor', and the *Guardian* said, 'the scenery and costumes . . . are ravishing and practical and perfectly suggest the period.' The *Observer* critic (also an art critic) wrote of 'the rich and beautiful costumes and ingenious settings' while the *Sunday Times* critic also referred to the ingenuity of the sets.

Soon after the premiere Kenneth made minor cuts in the ballet, mainly in the deletion of the *pas de deux* for the Jailer and his mistress at the beginning of Act III. These excisions were more for practical reasons (if the performance runs over three hours, including intervals, the orchestra gets paid overtime) rather than the aesthetic ones urged upon Kenneth by the critics.

Looking back over more than a decade one cannot help feeling that, whatever structural flaws *Manon* might have, the critics were exceptionally carping, cavilling over minor details and ignoring a cornucopia of marvellously inventive choreography which has provided successive casts with brilliant opportunities to display their dancing and dramatic talents. Even the much-maligned score has become a favourite and there have been many requests for a record to be made of it. *Manon* has been regularly revived over the years and has grown to be as big a box-office success and crowd-puller as *Romeo and Juliet*.

20

A popular success and an honour bestowed

Early in 1974 Deborah had heard that her *decree nisi* had been granted and so, two weeks after the premiere of *Manon*, on March 22, Kenneth and Deborah were married, quietly, with Peter Wright as best man and a few friends in attendance, at Chelsea Registry Office.

While Kenneth had been busy with the production of *Manon* Deborah had been equally busy house-hunting. At about the same time as Kenneth had bought his small Battersea house, he had also acquired a large basement flat in Brighton as a weekend retreat and the intention, now, was to sell both homes for a larger house in London. Kenneth is a non-driver; his London home had to be within reach by taxi, bus or underground of both the Royal Ballet rehearsal studios at Baron's Court, Hammersmith (in the building shared with the Royal Ballet Upper School), and the Royal Opera House, Covent Garden. Brighton, of course, was a mere hour away from London with frequent train services. While the new house had to have the same accessibility, Kenneth was anxious to remain in South London, an area he had grown to like very much and where a number of his Royal Ballet friends and colleagues also lived.

Deborah visited dozens of houses suggested by the agents until, finally, she was attracted by a large Edwardian villa in a quiet residential street not far from Wandsworth Common. She took Kenneth to look at it and he liked it too; they decided to buy it. The house was in a fairly delapidated condition but Deborah, with her artistic training, found the necessary redecoration a stimulating challenge and Kenneth, perpetually busy with the Royal Ballet, was content to leave everything, including the organisation of the move, to her.

In May of that year the Royal Ballet undertook another visit to the United States, with three weeks in New York and two in Washington, D.C. This time Kenneth flew with the company and took Deborah and baby Charlotte – only nine months old – with him. It was the first time that the Royal Ballet had visited America without its *prima ballerina assoluta*, Margot Fonteyn, and the first time that the company had not been presented by the impresario Sol Hurok – although the company was under the aegis of the Hurok Organisation. Nureyev was appearing as guest artist in a repertoire that included Kenneth's revival of *Swan Lake* and the American premiere of *Manon*.

The New York critics were more favourable towards *Swan Lake* than the London ones had been but, in general, were less enthusiastic about *Manon*. One celebrated Broadway reviewer (the same one who, eighteen years before, had called Kenneth a 'choreographic genius') went on radio and television telling audiences not to see it. On the Labor Day matinée of *Manon*, when New York was half empty anyway, the attendance at the Metropolitan Opera House was poor. Consequently the management proposed substituting *Swan Lake* with Nureyev (a sure-fire box-office attraction anywhere in the world) for the remainder of the *Manon* programmes. At that Kenneth dug in his heels: if they did so, he said, the company would be on the next plane home. *Manon* was given its advertised performances, the theatre was full for each one and the audiences were vociferously appreciative.

Only a week after its return from America the company began a new summer season at the Royal Opera House, with both Makarova and Nureyev appearing (separately) as guest artists. The London season ended with a gala for Lord Drogheda, who was retiring as Chairman of the Royal Opera House Board, for which Kenneth created a *pas de deux* to music by Stravinsky for Makarova and MacLeary. It had no title. Kenneth says, now, that 'it wasn't very good', so that may be why he never bothered to give it a name.

The company ended the summer by giving a season at Plymouth, for the first time, in the large circus tent colloquially known as the 'Big Top'. It proved a great success, paving the way for its extensive use at other locations in the regions where there was no theatre suitable for either of the Royal Ballet companies.

During the latter part of the Royal Ballet's American tour, in Washington, Kenneth had begun to feel an intense pain in his right foot which became more and more excruciating. Back in London, he sought medical advice and an X-ray revealed a spur of bone that was causing the pain; the doctors said it had to be surgically removed. During the summer holidays he went to the (new) Charing Cross Hospital (now situated in Hammersmith) and had his foot operated upon. While he was in hospital there was a strike by catering staff, and Kenneth remembers 'living on lettuce and salad cream' for which he now has an addiction.

A tremendous hit with audiences – though some critics were purse-lipped about its 'vulgarity' – *Elite Syncopations*, danced to ragtime music by Scott Joplin and others, was planned some time before the film *The Sting* made those scores popular. The photograph is of Michael Coleman, one of the original cast, in his bravura solo. (*Anthony Crickmay.*)

The operation was moderately successful (the foot was to go on giving trouble for a considerable time) but for weeks afterwards he was in pain, unable to wear shoes and hobbling about with a stick. During this time he was busy planning a new one-act work with which to open the autumn/winter season. More than a year previously Austin Bennett, at that time married to Monica Mason, had drawn Kenneth's attention to the attractive qualities of ragtime music, and suggested it as the basis of a ballet. Kenneth was then heavily involved in planning and producing *Manon*, but during the interim the film *The Sting*, utilising a ragtime score, had been released and been an enormous success, including the music which was incessantly played on every radio programme and juke-box. There had also been a couple of dance works using ragtime which had thus pre-empted Kenneth's intention of using such music. Even so he decided to go ahead with his ballet, although he knew he would probably be accused of merely following a popular trend.

The ragtime scores that Kenneth selected consisted of five numbers by Scott Joplin (excluding the popular one from *The Sting*), two by Joseph F. Lamb, and one each by Paul Pratt, James Scott, Max Nurath, Donald Ashwander and Robert Hampton – twelve in all.

As his designer, Kenneth returned to Ian Spurling whose colourful adaptation of the art-deco style for *Seven Deadly Sins* had been much praised. For the new ballet, which took its title *Elite Syncopations* from one of the Joplin rags, Spurling produced leotard costumes decorated in a riotous fantasy of liquorice all-sorts colours, buttoned and bowed, starred and arrowed, spotted and striped. Kenneth had decided to dispense with any set and to use the large Covent Garden stage opened up with whatever scenery was stacked there to create the ambience of a louche dance hall somewhere on the Mississippi Delta where the music originated. The twelve-piece band, plus pianist/conductor, was situated on stage and there were two rows of simple bentwood chairs for the use of those dancers not actually performing in any given number – the 'sitters-out' of any dance-hall.

The twelve rags were used for ensembles, solos and various duets ranging from slapstick humour for Vergie Derman as the tall girl with Wayne Sleep as the short man, to a shy duet for Jennifer Penney and David Wall, to one of showy brilliance for Merle Park and Donald MacLeary. There were also solos for Monica Mason as a burlesque queen and Michael Coleman as a macho dance-hall dandy.

For all its rumbustious humour the ballet demanded considerable classical virtuosity from all the principals who found it great fun to perform, enjoying the rare opportunity to let their hair down and give fairly free rein to their comic talents.

The ballet was given on the opening night of the season, October 7, 1974, in a triple bill with *Scènes de Ballet* and *Song of the Earth* and was a tremendous success with the audience – it was a long time since the Royal Opera House had resounded with belly laughs.

A few of the critics welcomed the ballet although, as Kenneth had anticipated, they nearly all assumed that he had been inspired to do it because of the popularity of *The Sting* and, while praising it, thought that it was essentially a transient work, a seasonal joke that would not remain long in the repertoire. Most critics, however, were rather prissily purse-lipped about the work. 'MacMillan has successfully avoided good taste; but what he has arrived at is a kind of salon vulgarity,' wrote the *Observer* critic. 'There is no denying that this extravaganza was rapturously received, largely, I suspect, for the element of surprise – surprise at the riot of colour, at the grotesqueries, at so many noble dancers poking their bottoms out,' sniffed the *Sunday Times* critic. Writing in the European edition of the *Herald Tribune*, the critic who had attacked Kenneth in the columns of the *New Statesman* a couple of years before, said: '*Elite Syncopations* is amusing in places – mildly or uproariously depending on one's sense of humour. Some of the jokes are crude, most of them are obvious, and there is very little choreographic invention. While it certainly entertained the majority of the first-night audience I doubt if it will bear much repetition.' *The Times* critic thought 'the total effect is of a fifth-rate cabaret', and went on to compare Kenneth's choreography unfavourably with the work of a little-known choreographer, Alfonso Catá whose Frankfurt Ballet had presented a rather more seriously intentioned work at Birmingham a month before. But for all the critics' disdain of 'school-boy humour' and 'vulgarity' and their predictions of an early demise, *Elite Syncopations* has remained perennially popular, affording many different casts an opportunity to display their comic talents in dancing that demands considerable bravura. The work was soon taken into the repertoire of the Royal Ballet touring company, where it is frequently revived, and later acquired by the National Ballet of Canada.

At the end of January, 1975, Kenneth introduced the first work by Hans van Manen into the repertoire of the Covent Garden Royal Ballet. A number of van Manen's works had already been produced by the Royal Ballet touring company with considerable success, and the completely new *Four Schumann Pieces*, danced to Schumann's A major quartet, was conceived by the choreographer as a vehicle for Anthony Dowell, the finest *danseur noble* that the Royal Ballet had, to date, developed.

Less than two months later, at a Royal Ballet Benevolent Fund gala, Kenneth introduced yet another – the fifth – Robbins work to the Covent Garden repertoire. This time it was a very funny comedy ballet, *The Concert*, a series of short scenes depicting the reactions of a group of people listening to a Chopin recital. The jokes ranged from wild slapstick, stage-hands arranging dancers like dummies in grotesque positions, to a music-hall sketch of a woman trying on hats, to a tongue-in-cheek spoof of corps de ballet girls getting their timing all wrong. Good comic ballets are a rarity and this short work, originally created for New York City Ballet in 1956, was an immediate success with London audiences and has been regularly revived.

The following evening, March 5, 1975, Kenneth produced another new work of his own, *The Four Seasons*. Once again the music, the ballet divertissement from Verdi's *Sicilian Vespers*, plus additions, had been suggested to him, this time by the music critic Andrew Porter. Kenneth liked the score, and the simple theme of the seasons, while somewhat commonplace, provided him with the opportunity to create for the company the kind of work that it lacked, a big display piece, using a large cast with corps de ballet, soloists and principals.

Kenneth chose Peter Rice as the designer. He produced a rather elaborate facade of what looked like an alpine inn of several storeys, given the name *Le Quattro Stagione*. The costumes, with one or two exceptions, were in stage-peasant style, with much use of checks and stripes, predominantly pink, blue, green and brown.

In addition to the *Sicilian Vespers* music, Kenneth had added five numbers from Verdi's *I Lombardi* and one from the *Don Carlos* ballet suite as a prologue, and two further numbers from *I Lombardi* for additional male variations.

The ballet began with a number of ensemble dances; Kenneth was anxious to show off the prowess of the corps de ballet which, only two months before, had been given the *Evening Standard* (as it then was) Ballet Award for the outstanding contribution to dance for 1974. After the opening ensembles with their elaborate footwork, the lights dimmed and the first of the seasonal variations, *Winter*, began. This was a *pas de trois* for Donald MacLeary, dressed in a scarlet and white hussar uniform, with Vergie Derman and Marguerite Porter, also is scarlet and white, as two *vivandieres*, with subsequent solos for each artist.

Spring was a *pas de quatre* for Lesley Collier supported by Wayne Eagling, David Ashmole and Michael Coleman; it was especially notable for one sequence which used a highly inventive lift in which the three men encircled Collier's waist, clasped each other's wrists and bore her across the stage. *Summer* was a languorous *pas de deux* for David Wall and Monica Mason, and *Autumn* another *pas de trois*, this time for Jennifer Penney, Anthony Dowell and Wayne Sleep in which Kenneth fully exploited the tremendous technical virtuosity of all three dancers.

At its premiere at Covent Garden *The Four Seasons* was moderately successful. Audiences enjoyed seeing a large roster of the company's principals showing off their paces, but critics gave the ballet a rather lukewarm reception. Most of them disliked the set, finding it fussy (several were disapproving in that it seemed, as one critic delicately put it, 'a house of assignation', while another referred to it, bluntly, as 'a brothel'), and found the opening sequence too long (Kenneth subsequently shortened it somewhat) and the *Winter* section rather weak.

The critic of the *Financial Times* liked the ballet: 'MacMillan has produced a firework display of steps that set out – and succeed most handsomely – to tax, inspire and show off his company, a virtuoso ensemble that frames virtuoso principals.' He went on to say, 'The seasons are an excuse for a cascade of solos, duets and pas for various numbers that are the most sheerly inventive choreography MacMillan has given us in the classical idiom.'

The *Sunday Telegraph* reviewer was also enthusiastic: 'Each dance is inventive in itself, adds to the variety of the whole piece and above all shows off the Royal Ballet at its superb best.' He concluded 'the piece is an undoubted triumph, all enjoyment from beginning to end.' *The Times* critic found 'the level of inspiration uneven', and thought, for some reason that he failed to make explicit, that Kenneth had been 'borrowing an idea from Ashton and Cranko'. The *Morning Star* reviewer – who seemed to loathe everything Kenneth did – found the ballet to be 'a lavish bore' adding 'when the choreography ceases to be conventional and repetitive it becomes embarrassingly undanceable' – whatever that may have meant.

*

Just over a month later the Royal Ballet took off for its first visit to Japan, after a three-day stop-over in South Korea. Kenneth flew with the company but Deborah travelled with Charlotte to see her parents in Australia, her first visit home since her meeting with Kenneth.

The Royal Ballet's Far Eastern tour was a great success and for Kenneth highly stimulating – what he refers to as 'a culture shock'. His impressions of Japan, its traditional forms of theatre, the Noh plays, Bunraku puppets and martial arts contests were to be the inspiration for his next work.

On its return from Japan the company was to have had a six weeks season at the Coliseum but because of a last minute pay dispute with

Kenneth with his wife, Deborah, pictured in the first house they chose together, near Wandsworth Common, South London.

Kenneth on the day he received an honorary degree – *Honoris Causa* – from the University of Edinburgh.

Deborah and Kenneth's baby, Charlotte, was born on 16 August 1975. This photograph was taken when she was a few days old.

the stage staff the season was cancelled. As a result both Royal Ballet companies embarked upon a hastily assembled season in the 'Big Top' which was set up in Battersea Park. It was not as financially rewarding as the Coliseum season would have been, but artistically it was a resounding success, not least because the jolly circus atmosphere of the tent attracted a large new audience who probably would not have considered seeing the company in its Covent Garden home. The repertoire included *Romeo and Juliet* and – a tremendous popular hit – *Elite Syncopations*, the B.B.C. taking this opportunity to record the latter ballet in which Makarova made her debut.

Just after the opening of the autumn season at Covent Garden Kenneth travelled up to Scotland to have bestowed upon him an honorary degree – *Honoris Causa* – by the University of Edinburgh. Part of the long citation read: 'It would be idle to pretend to originality in summing up, against this backdrop of achievement, the remarkable qualities which have made MacMillan a great choreographer. Commentators and critics have been unanimous in attributing to him a driving dedication, a sure sense of theatrical drama, an uncommon response to music, a flow of lyrical invention which never seems contrived, a mastery of form and a quite extraordinary ability to convey in dance images that cannot be verbalised. Mindful of tradition, he remains a man very much of his time, carrying conviction in all he does: "a romantic choreographer, but one with a cutting edge – a classicist of the age of anxiety."' It was pleasantly appropriate that Kenneth, born in Scotland, should have received the first of his several accolades from this Scottish seat of learning and. as an equally appropriate arabesque to the occasion, the citation was read by Professor Iain MacGibbon, Professor of International Law at the University and father of Ross MacGibbon, a Royal Ballet dancer who had joined the company from the Royal Ballet School two years earlier.

Back at the Royal Opera House Kenneth revived *Symphony* with new. rather less overwhelming, designs by Yolanda Sonnabend, and which provided a fine vehicle for Lynn Seymour's highly expressive powers even though it was a plotless work. Natalia Makarova also made a tremendously successful appearance in *Manon* but both these great ballerinas were somewhat overshadowed that season by the London debut of Mikhail Baryshnikov in *Romeo and Juliet*. He illumined the eponymous role not only with his amazing technical virtuosity but also with a special youthful brio that made his interpretation particularly memorable. He partnered Merle Park as Juliet and both dancers were also paired in *Swan Lake* with great success.

The music for Kenneth's new ballet, which received its premiere at the Royal Opera House on December 11, 1975, presented something of a problem, the choice being between genuine Japanese musical accompaniment – flutes, stringed instruments, bells and gongs – which would inevitably incur attendant problems of finding a composer and musicians, or some form of pastiche which always tends to sound phoney. The Royal Ballet conductor/pianist Anthony Twiner suggested Bartók's Sonata for Two Pianos and Percussion which, although it has no connection with the orient, has an emphasis on strange sonorities, a fierce rhythmic drive and an idiomatic use of percussive intruments, some of them rather esoteric, which made it ideal for Kenneth's purposes.

The choreography for the first movement was based on kung-fu, a highly acrobatic contest between two very lithe male dancers, Wayne Eagling and Stephen Beagley, as neophytes, referred by a Grand-Master, David Drew. In the slow central movement Kenneth used Vergie Derman and David Wall as two life-sized Bunraku puppets, elaborately manipulated by two groups of puppeteers in a formal mating 'dance'; when the 'naked' puppets were recaparisoned in their gorgeous robes and the puppeteers withdrew, they slowly collapsed in a heap. The last movement suggested a somewhat arcane oriental approach to childbirth with Lynn Seymour as a mother-to-be attended by Monica Mason as a midwife. The ballet was called *Rituals* and had a most beautiful decor by Yolanda Sonnabend, making use of typical Japanese materials – wood, paper, bamboo – with suggestions of origami and the delicate brush-strokes of black ink on aged parchment. The dancers' make-up was highly stylised with impenetrable white mask-faces. Costumes ranged from simple combat gear, reminiscent of kung-fu practitioners or Sumo wrestlers, for the opening sequence to elaborate, beautifully embroidered garments for the Bunraku puppets, to pretty, abbreviated figured-silk kimonos for the childbirth section.

Audiences, who had not experienced the 'culture shock' of a visit to Japan, seemed to find the ballet rather puzzling and remote. Most of the critics thought that the puppet sequence was the most successful and one or two were nonplussed by the childbirth scene.

The critic of the *Dancing Times* was possibly the most enthusiastic, writing: 'I know nothing of Japan and am no expert on Japanese dance or dance drama but MacMillan has succeeded in giving theatrical truth to his subject matter which, when it comes to translating a different art form to the ballet stage, is the most important achievement.' After a long, highly complimentary assessment of the ballet's three sequences the critic concluded, 'MacMillan has returned to the style of *Rite of Spring* (but more powerfully, these dancers no longer look like little ballet people) and,

148

greatest compliment, to the style of *Song of the Earth*. It is his very own choreographic language and I salute not only the achievement but the courage to make a ballet in which he believes and which stretches the Royal Ballet in a new, contemporary yet basically classical style.'

The *Financial Times* critic was almost equally enthusiastic: '. . . MacMillan shows an uncanny skill in fixing the flavour of Japanese theatre – and also one in which he has dared to superimpose oriental mannerisms upon a musical materpiece. Dared, and won. The percussive brilliance of the score, even its atmospheric nocturnal *lento*, have inspired dances both strange and beautiful.'

The Times critic remarked that '. . . what has to be said is that it (*Rituals*) marks a return to the confident experimentalism of his early works. Unfortunately, of its three sections, the first is not very original and the third not very successful. That leaves the second movement as the work's strangest advocate.' The *Guardian* critic gave guarded praise: 'Still, it is an obviously sincere and sensitive attempt by a major choreographer to convey to us his aesthetic emotional reaction to things (or some things) Japanese. He has done it with the help of Bartók's Sonata for two pianos and percussion, help not always apposite if only because, in the first movement particularly, it outlasts the choreographic inventiveness, but still not so incongruous as might have been feared; the choreographer is also helped – hugely – by Yolanda Sonnabend's designs and costumes.'

Almost without exception the designer received unqualified praise: 'She captures the ritual aspects as well as the beauty; inside her charming setting are some frightening veils and make-ups and how cleverly she adapts Japanese costume for dancing.' (*Dancing Times*.) 'The ballet ends exquisitely, with a tickle on the drums, a handclap, and the drawing of a bamboo and gauze curtain – which, with Yolanda Sonnabend's suspended hieroglyphic papyrus and some authentic costumes, is fine decoration.' (*Sunday Times*). 'Yolanda Sonnabend's designs provide a magnificent setting: a white-hung stage, partially tented above in ink-spattered fabric; dress that seems an essence of Japanese costume shapes and decoration; the dancers made up so that their features are largely unrecognisable under Kabuki striations, or impassively masklike.' (*Financial Times*).

If *Rituals* was one of those ballets inevitably destined not to be popular – and therefore not to last long in the repertoire – it had been an exercise well worth doing, full of exquisite things for those able to discern them, an interesting foray into an exotic style and an extension of the dancers' technical capabilities. It concluded a year – two years, in fact – that Kenneth could look back upon with a certain satisfaction: he had embarked upon a happy and successful marriage which had added inestimably to his personal and professional wellbeing; he had received his first accolade in recognition of his achievements; he had consolidated his Directorship of the Royal Ballet, in the face of some severe factional criticism, not only by his standing with the company which was now united behind him, and the public, but, in very practical terms, by creating one very successful full-length ballet and three one-act works, and introducing ballets by van Manen and Jerome Robbins to the repertoire. In concluding his review of *Rituals*, the critic of the *Glasgow Herald*, presumably fairly remote from the gossip, rumour, innuendo and generally hot-house atmosphere that affects all dance companies, wrote: 'The Royal Ballet seems to have hit peak form recently. Much of the credit must be given to its Director, Kenneth MacMillan.'

21

A nasty accident and a resignation

Throughout the five years that he had been directing the Royal Ballet Kenneth had been gently pressing Frederick Ashton to create something new for the company. Now, in the winter of 1975/6, Ashton was ready to work on a ballet that had been germinating in his mind for some years, a one-act adaptation of Turgenev's play *A Month in the Country*. With a score by Chopin arranged by John Lanchbery, and an elaborate decor by Julia Trevelyan Oman, the new ballet had its premiere on February 12, 1976 and was an immediate and immense success with a cast that included Lynn Seymour, Anthony Dowell, Derek Rencher, Wayne Sleep, Alexander Grant and Denise Nunn.

Early in April the Royal Ballet took off once more for a trip to America, a schedule of five weeks in New York, three in Washington D.C. and one in Philadelphia. This time Deborah did not go with Kenneth and the company but, with Charlotte, she joined her brother Simon who was at that time in France as part of a European tour.

The Royal Ballet season in New York opened very successfully with Natalia Makarova and Anthony Dowell in *Romeo and Juliet*. For some curious reason, two weeks before the season finished, Kenneth felt impelled to say goodbye to his friends Jerome Robbins and George Balanchine, whose own company, the New York City

Ballet, was also appearing at that time. Next day Kenneth received the alarming news that Deborah, Charlotte and Simon had met with a bad motor accident at St. Cloud, just south of Paris. They had started out on a trip to the Loire valley when the Mini in which they were travelling had been hit broadside on by a car at a crossing where, through an electrical fault, both sets of traffic lights were at green. After a hurried telephone consultation with John Tooley, General Administrator of the Royal Opera House in London, Kenneth caught the first plane to Paris.

Motor accidents had featured horribly in Kenneth's life – his own crash with John Cranko; the deaths of Matyas Seiber, Goran Gentele, and his beloved sister Jean – and throughout the flight Kenneth's anxiety about his wife and child was naturally extreme. For Deborah the experience had been equally terrible – quite apart from the accident itself. After the crash she and Charlotte had been put in separate hospitals; Deborah suffered concussion for two days but when she recovered full consciousness and asked about Charlotte she was told, 'Your little *boy* is quite all right,' which did nothing to reassure her. Deborah thinks that the confusion arose from her pronunciation of the word *fille*, not helped by the fact that she had suffered a cut lip. Simon, who had been sitting in the back of the car, escaped with cuts and bruises, but Charlotte had incurred facial injuries which the French doctors assured Kenneth and Deborah were basically superficial. But, when Kenneth, Deborah and Charlotte had flown back to London and Charlotte's dressings had been removed, it was found that she had sustained such a vicious blow on the forehead that the tissue had been torn apart and the bone was visible. Charlotte had to have immediate surgery by a plastic surgeon, first so that the wound would heal, secondly so that she should not be badly scarred for life.

*

On its return from America the Royal Ballet had three weeks at Covent Garden before going off on tour again to Plymouth to dance in the 'Big Top', which concluded the summer season. Kenneth, Deborah and Charlotte stayed on in the West Country for a couple of weeks of much-needed relaxation before Kenneth began work again on scheduling the autumn season. For the beginning of the new season Kenneth had arranged for the production of two works new to the repertoire, Glen Tetley's *Voluntaries*, and Hans van Manen's *Adagio Hammerklavier*.

Voluntaries had been created for the Stuttgart Ballet as a memorial to Cranko. A plotless work danced to Poulenc's highly theatrical Concerto for Organ, String Orchestra and Timpani, for a leading couple, a trio and a small corps, its opening and closing moments have the ballerina lifted in a crucifixion pose by the male dancer. It is a beautiful work, far less 'difficult' than Tetley's previous *Field Figures* and *Laborintus* and, premiered on November 18 with Lynn Seymour and David Wall as the leading couple, was highly successful with both audiences and critics. *Adagio Hammerklavier*, which received its first performance by the Royal Ballet only a few days later, on November 23, had been created by van Manen in 1973 for his own Dutch National Ballet, using six principals as three couples dancing to the slow movement of Beethoven's Hammerklavier Sonata, a taped recording played with extreme slowness and intense introspection by Christof von Eschenbach. A typical van Manen mixture of classicism and his own modern idiom, it was eloquently danced by Natalia Makarova and David Wall, Monica Mason and Wayne Eagling, Jennifer Penney and Mark Silver, but was never very popular and did not stay in the repertoire very long.

Only five days later came the premiere of an important new ballet by Kenneth – but not for the Royal Ballet: his plans for setting it on his own company once again ran into difficulties with the Royal Opera House Board of Directors. For some time he had wanted to create a work that would stand as his own tribute to the memory of John Cranko and his choice of music was Fauré's gentle, lyrical *Requiem*. But once again, as with *Song of the Earth*, the Board (to be precise, one particular member of the Board) objected to the score, feeling that the use of such music in a ballet would offend audiences' religious sensibilities. And so, once again, Kenneth offered the work to the Stuttgart Ballet which was, by then, directed by Marcia Haydée; she accepted instantly. Immediately after the opening of the Covent Garden season, therefore, Kenneth flew to Stuttgart, taking Deborah and Charlotte with him. Although working with the Stuttgart Ballet was inevitably full of poignant memories of the company under Cranko's direction, Kenneth's relationship with Marcia Haydée was a happy one – and, as it proved, fruitful as well. He created the new ballet in a mere three weeks, the choreographic inspiration flowing easily and fluently, although the rehearsal period was interrupted by the company's engagement in Madrid. Kenneth and family flew to Spain with the company – after an inauspicious beginning at Stuttgart airport. Just after the aircraft had taxied away from the terminal news came of a strike by Spanish air traffic controllers and the 'plane was held on the runway for *seven hours*. Because the aircraft was technically deemed to have begun its departure it was not allowed to return to the terminal; in order to escape from the hot, claustrophobic atmosphere of the cabin, passengers took it in turns to sit on the mobile steps – they were not allowed to set foot on the tarmac. It was an experience that did nothing to lessen Kenneth's intense dislike of flying.

In Madrid rehearsal facilities were extremely limited. Kenneth created the sixth movement of the work, the *Libera me* for the four leading males, in a tiny room in which half the floor had an unsuitable surface for dancing.

Requiem, which took its title from the score, is divided into seven sections and uses a leading couple supported by a trio of two men and a woman plus a large corps. It begins with the *Introit and Kyrie* in which the whole cast make an entrance together, shuffling forward with mouths agape and fists shaking in rage and misery at the deprivation of death. There follows the *Offertoire* for eight of the leading dancers, then the *Sanctus*, the most choreographically brilliant movement, for the principal ballerina and partner. That leads into a long, exceptionally beautiful solo, the *Pie Jesu*, for the ballerina, who emerges as something of an 'angel figure', made more distinct from the rest of the cast by different costuming. The *Agnus Die* uses the second ballerina with four supporting couples, the *Libera Me* is mainly for the four leading men and the final *In Paradisium* combines the whole cast.

Yolanda Sonnabend designed an all-white gauzy set, with three asymmetrically placed pillars soaring heavenwards. The costumes, except for the leading ballerina (Marcia Haydée, partnered by Reid Anderson) who wore a simple white shift, were silver-grey body-tights delicately dappled with individual patterning in blues, greens, purples and pinks. The lighting, by John B. Read, played an exceptionally important part in the production, including a moment in the last movement when the unoccupied centre of the stage becomes ablaze with white light, a manifestation of the Holy Spirit, *In Paradisium*.

Requiem was premiered in Stuttgart on November 28, 1976, and had what can only be described as an ecstatic reception from audience and critics – including some members of the British press who unhesitatingly called it Kenneth's best ballet for years.

*

On returning to London Kenneth was approached by the Olympic gold medal skater John Curry, who was producing his own balletically-conceived ice dance show, to choreograph a solo for him. Kenneth was pleased to oblige, intrigued by the technical possibilities – and limitations – of the medium. He chose a glittering trifle, Liszt's *Feux Follets* pianistic study, to show off Curry's technical bravura and extreme fluency as a skater. After the first night of the show on December 26, 1976, several people thought that Kenneth's contribution was among the best items in the programme. *The Times* critic wrote: 'The most successful serious items on the present programme are Norman Maen's *Afternoon of a Faun* and the solo *Feux Follet* created for Curry by Kenneth MacMillan. The latter reveals the seamless flow which is a speciality of the Curry style. Capricious changes of direction and multitudinous spins match the will-o'-the-wisp connotations of Liszt's piano solo.'

During Kenneth's stay in Stuttgart he had negotiated with Dieter Graefe, the Administrative Director of the Stuttgart Ballet, to acquire Cranko's full-length work *Onegin*, based on the Pushkin narrative poem and using an assembled score from various pieces of music by Tchaikovsky (although not from the opera) which Kenneth considered to be Cranko's finest ballet. All went well until the ballet was in rehearsal when it was discovered that certain gauze and net sections of the scenery could not be fireproofed sufficiently to satisfy the stringent British laws. (In Stuttgart there are firemen on duty backstage when the ballet is performed. Seven years later, when the work was produced by the London Festival Ballet, a chemical agent had been developed which was able to fireproof the scenery satisfactorily although, significantly, the designer, Jurgen Rose, would not allow his name to be credited on the programme as he was dissatisfied with the quality of the reproduction of the designs.)

Hastily it was decided to replace *Onegin* with another full-length Cranko work, *The Taming of the Shrew*. The ballet included some brilliant knockabout comedy *pas de deux* for the Stuttgart company's stars, Marcia Haydée and Richard Cragun, but the work itself is not in the same class as *Onegin*. The first performance of *The Taming of the Shrew* by the Royal Ballet was given at Covent Garden on February 16, 1977, with Haydée and Cragun appearing as guest stars. The leading roles were also danced by Merle Park, Lynn Seymour and Lesley Collier, with David Wall, Wayne Eagling and Stephen Jefferies. Later the work was also produced with considerable success by the Sadler's Wells Royal Ballet. (The company had adopted this much more satisfactory name in September, 1976, a title that distinguished it from the larger company at Covent Garden and which reunited it with the Islington Theatre which once more became its permanent London home.)

While in London to mount *The Taming of the Shrew*, Haydée and Cragun gave a memorable performance of *The Song of the Earth*, joined by another Stuttgart luminary, Egon Madsen, who danced the role of the Messenger of Death which he had created eleven years before. In March, 1977, Baryshnikov also returned to Covent Garden as a guest star, dancing in *Romeo and Juliet* and Ashton's *La Fille mal gardée*.

In that same month Kenneth introduced a new work by yet another guest choreographer. For some time several leading critics had been giving much praise to the ballets of John Neumeier, an American-born dancer who, having studied at the Royal Ballet School, appeared with the Stuttgart Ballet before becoming Director of the Frankfurt Ballet and then the Hamburg Ballet. For the Royal Ballet he produced *Fourth Symphony*, a ballet about childhood, to Mahler's fourth symphony which supposedly contained auto-biographical material relevant to Mahler's own early years. The ballet had its premiere on March 31, 1977, with a cast that included David Wall, Lynn Seymour, Wayne Eagling and Jennifer Penney. The choreographic treatment of the subject matter seemed obscure and diffuse, the ballet was poorly received, given only four performances and never revived.

During this time Kenneth was thinking about the subject of his own next full-length ballet. He had always admired Benjamin Britten's score for Cranko's first full-length ballet, *The Prince of the Pagodas*, although the work was choreographically uneven and saddled with an over-elaborate fairy-story scenario by Cranko which combined elements of *Beauty and the Beast*, *Cinderella* and *The Sleeping Beauty* as well as having superficial affinities with *King Lear*! Kenneth thought that with judicious cutting and new choreography it would make a fine neo-classical ballet to add to the regular classical repertoire. To this end he drafted a new, simplified scenario in collaboration with Ronald Crichton and arranged to go to Britten's home in Aldeburgh to discuss cuts in the score. By then, however, Britten was a very sick man and his doctors would only allow Kenneth a ten-minute interview which was obviously inadequate for his purposes. Reluctantly he had to abandon plans for a new *Prince of the Pagodas*.

As it happened his next work, slight though it was, was set to Britten's music. It was a short divertissement for a gala at the Royal Opera House celebrating H.M. the Queen's Silver Jubilee. It was basically a convoluted *pas de quatre* for Lynn Seymour as Queen Elizabeth I attended by three males, Michael Coleman, Wayne Eagling and Stephen Beagley, supported by four other males, and danced to music from Britten's opera *Gloriana*. The most memorable moment of the *pas de quatre* was when the imperious queen was turned upside down by her courtiers.

*

Deborah had given Kenneth a book about the collapse of the great royal families of Europe, the Romanovs of Russia, the Hohenzollerns of Prussia, the Wittelsbachs of Bavaria, the Habsburgs of Austro-

Hungary. Kenneth was intrigued by the story of Crown Prince Rudolf and how, in 1889, he had murdered his young mistress, Mary Vetsera, before committing suicide at the royal hunting lodge at Mayerling, not far from Vienna. What interested him most was how the ascertainable facts differed from the highly romanticised film versions of the story, particularly a French one starring Charles Boyer and Danielle Darrieux and a later Hollywood one with Omar Sharif and Catherine Deneuve. What emerged from the history book was not the lives of two people deeply in love, thwarted by political protocol, but a corrupt, depraved prince, a drug addict suffering from venereal disease, and a precocious, social-climbing young woman ready to sacrifice herself for a romantic chimera. Here were two human beings whose emotional development – despite the disparity in their ages – was tainted by the decadent, vicious milieu in which they lived – two ultra-outsiders driven to die together by the poisonous physical and psychological circumstances in which they were trapped: ideal MacMillan material. Kenneth immediately decided that that would be the theme of his next full-length work.

In May 1977 the Royal Ballet at Covent Garden undertook another visit to Bristol. *Romeo and Juliet* was included in the repertoire and, as Director of the company and choreographer of the ballet, Kenneth found himself sitting through several consecutive performances of the work; it was the catalyst that precipitated a decision that had been crystallising in his mind for some time: to resign as Director of the company. His administrative duties had become so onerous, had interfered with his creative powers so enervatingly, that he felt he could no longer give of his best in either capacity, as Artistic Director or company choreographer. To alleviate the double burden, John Hart (an ex-Royal Ballet dancer who had previously held the position of Assistant Director from 1963 until his resignation in 1970, after which he became Ballet Director at the International University of the Performing Arts at San Diego, California) had been brought in to assist Kenneth with the company administration, but he had resigned after a couple of seasons in order to concentrate on his Directorship at San Diego. Obviously, Kenneth's creative gifts were far more important than his administrative position and the simple solution was for him to resign as Director and concentrate on choreography.

The Royal Opera House Board of Directors were sympathetic to his dilemma and, accordingly, Kenneth's resignation as Director of the Royal Ballet was announced at a press conference at the Royal Opera House on June 13, 1977. To succeed him, the Board appointed Norman Morrice who, as co-Director with Dame Marie

Rambert, had been most successful in transforming Ballet Rambert from a classical to a modern dance company.

Kenneth had undertaken the Directorship of the Royal Ballet at a most difficult time when, as a result of decisions taken by the Board of Directors, the company was undergoing a major reorganisation of its resources and a redirection of its artistic policy. At the time of his take-over the company was top-heavy with soloists, and a number of its principals, particularly the ballerinas, were entering the final decade of their careers, making it difficult to promote younger dancers. Nevertheless he managed to find roles for them all, for front-line artists such as Deanne Bergsma, Svetlana Beriosova, Vergie Derman, Monica Mason, Merle Park, Georgina Parkinson, Jennifer Penney, Lynn Seymour, Antoinette Sibley, Michael Coleman, Anthony Dowell and Donald MacLeary, while giving opportunities to younger dancers such as Lesley Collier, Laura Connor, Wendy Ellis, Ann Jenner, Marguerite Porter, Rosalyn Whitten, David Ashmole, Wayne Eagling, Julian Hosking, Stephen Jefferies and Wayne Sleep. In addition he had invited such internationally renowned dancers as Marcia Haydée, Natalia Makarova, Mikhail Baryshnikov, Richard Cragun, Egon Madsen and Rudolf Nureyev (as well as the Royal Ballet's own *prima ballerina assoluta*, Margot Fonteyn) to appear in major works of the repertoire.

Between November 1970 and June 1977 Kenneth created five new one-act works and two full-length ballets for the Covent Garden company, as well as reviving several of his own works, supervising *Swan Lake* and producing a new version of *The Sleeping Beauty*. He also created three new one-act works for the Sadler's Wells Royal Ballet. He had persistently encouraged – not to say beseeched – Frederick Ashton to create something new and was rewarded with *A Month in the Country*, as well as revivals of such works as *Symphonic Variations* and *Scènes de Ballet*. He had introduced into the Covent Garden repertoire a considerable number of important ballets by foreign choreographers, particularly from America, including five from Jerome Robbins, three from George Balanchine and three from Glen Tetley. There had also been two works by John Cranko (including the full-length *The Taming of the Shrew*), two by Hans van Manen and one by John Neumeier. It was a record that equalled, if not surpassed, that of any similar period in the history of the company and one of which both Kenneth and the company could feel proud.

22

A hectic year – a succession of successes

Freed from the worries of directing the company Kenneth was able to concentrate all his creative energies on plans for his next full-length work for the Royal Ballet, *Mayerling*.

After reading about the Mayerling tragedy in *The Eagles Die* by G. R. Merrick, Kenneth followed up with more background reading and came to the conclusion that the material was so extensive, so chronologically complex and frequently contradictory, that distilling a scenario from it required the expertise of a professional writer. Moreover, he felt that because of his years of experience with the full-length classics he was too imbued with the set-piece formulae of works like *Swan Lake* and *The Sleeping Beauty*, and for the new ballet he wanted greater flexibility of staging with the minimum of pauses for scene-changing. Accordingly, Kenneth attempted to contact John Osborne, first because the two men had collaborated on Osborne's *The World of Paul Slickey*, secondly because Osborne had already written with great insight about that same period of Imperial Vienna in his play *A Patriot For Me*.

Some weeks went by and Kenneth was unable to communicate with Osborne; with time getting short, he began looking for an alternative writer. Deborah suggested Gillian Freeman who was a personal friend; both she and Kenneth had read Gillian's novel *The Alabaster Egg* which dealt, in part, with the downfall of King Ludwig II of Bavaria (who was the cousin, and confidante, of the Empress Elisabeth, mother of Crown Prince Rudolf). Kenneth telephoned Gillian late one evening and put his suggestion to her. Gillian – a great admirer of Kenneth's work – was excited by the idea and immediately agreed.

Gillian began reading the massive bibliography on the period in general and the tragedy in particular. What emerged most saliently from the many biographies, autobiographies, memoirs, monographs, official histories, private investigations and police reports was, first, the complex psychological make-up of Rudolf stemming, in part, from an unhappy childhood and a formal, remote relationship with his parents; his own rather depraved nature and behaviour, including an obsession with firearms; his political involvement with the separatist factions working for the independence of Hungary within the Habsburg empire. Secondly, the corruption and decadence of the Imperial Court; the enormous amount of police surveillance that ranged from minor servants through politicians and court officials to the Royal Family itself. And thirdly, the equally complex motivation of Rudolf's young mistress, Mary Vetsera who, at seventeen, had already been involved in a social scandal in Egypt.

Gillian found that to construct a comprehensive narrative suitable for the simplistic conventions of ballet, to provide a practical arrangement of *pas de deux*, solos and ensembles, to retain at the same time the main elements of the story with its plethora of characters and incident without substantially distorting or falsifying the recorded facts, was a difficult task indeed. She began by making a minimal list of characters – particularly the women in Rudolf's life – and those who were instrumental in producing or furthering the circumstances that precipitated the tragedy. The list included twenty-three named characters, a large number for an audience to assimilate, but then, as Gillian pointed out to Kenneth, there are an even greater number in *The Sleeping Beauty*. She then plotted the story in a first draft of master scenes which Kenneth broke down into suggested lengths with brief intimations of mood and atmosphere from which John Lanchbery was able to assemble the score.

Because, after the double shooting, there had been an immediate official cover-up by the Court authorities, Gillian decided upon a cyclic framework for the ballet, beginning and ending with the secret burial of Vetsera in the deserted cemetary at Heiligenkreutz – with the slight but important difference that in the prologue the audience does not know who is being buried; in the epilogue Vetsera's body, macabrely dressed as if going for a drive, is dragged from the carriage and bundled into the coffin.

The 'ballet proper' began with a court ball celebrating Rudolf's marriage to Princess Stephanie of Belgium, thereby allowing the introduction of nearly all the main characters. A subsequent scene revealed Rudolf's unhappy relationship with his mother, and the act ended with a violent scene between the married couple on their wedding night in which (a historic fact) Rudolf terrified Stephanie with a pistol that he kept in his room.

The second act commenced with another set-piece, showing Rudolf in a different milieu, one of the low taverns which he used to frequent, more or less incognito. This scene allowed for the introduction of his private cabman, Bratfisch, a trusted confidante in Rudolf's underworld escapades, as well as his favourite prostitute companion, Mitzi Caspah, who, unknown to Rudolf, was one of the ubiquitous police informers. The scene also provided an opportunity to show Rudolf relaxing with his officer friends who were pressing him to join the Separatist cause.

Other scenes in Act II depict Rudolf's first meeting with Vetsera

Macmillan's fourth full-length work, *Mayerling*, deals with the double suicide of Crown-Prince Rudolf of Austria-Hungary and his young mistress Mary Vetsera in a more factual, less sentimental way than the various film versions of the story. The ballet reveals Rudolf as a violent, degenerate character, obsessed with firearms, a lover of low-life, a diseased drug-addict. It presents a number of spectacular *pas de deux* for Rudolf and the women in his life, and the role of the Prince is an enormous challenge to the male dancer interpreting it. The decadence and corruption of the Imperial Viennese Court is a secondary theme and the grandeur of the period is brilliantly captured in Nicholas Georgiadis's beautiful costumes. *Opposite*: David Wall, upon whom the role of Rudolf was created, with Merle Park as the conniving Countess Larisch. *Above*: Wayne Eagling with Lesley Collier as Mary in their first encounter in the Prince's private apartments. (*Anthony Crickmay*.)

as a young woman (he had met her previously as a child), connived at by Countess Larisch, and a party to celebrate the Emperor's birthday which served to reveal other interesting relationships: the Empress with her English paramour, 'Bay' Middleton, and the Emperor with his 'friend', Katherina Schratt. Schratt was, in fact, an actress but Kenneth had the idea of making her a singer to entertain the Court. 'Operas often had ballet divertissements,' he said. 'Why shouldn't we have a big narrative ballet with a short vocal insertion?' The song, of course, was not just a gratuitous addition but provided a punctuation mark in a hectic work, a moment of repose when the several covert relationships beneath the surface of rigid formality were tellingly, but subtly exposed. Gillian also added a firework display which not only served as a distraction so that certain action could take place in the forground, but emphasised the pyrotechnic, explosive theme that ran through the ballet to its climax. To this end she also provided for 'Bay' Middleton, a constant practical joker in real life, to give Count Taafe, Rudolf's political enemy at Court, an explosive cigar but in practice it was found too difficult to time the explosion with the music; a different joke cigar was substituted. The act ended with a tempestuous meeting between Rudolf and Mary, another opportunity for a passionate *pas de deux* which indicated the lovers' psychological and temperamental rapport.

The last act, like the previous two, also began with a set-piece, a winter shoot at which Rudolf's gun went off by accident, just missing the Emperor and killing a servant, another historical incident which added to Rudolf's increasing depression and oppression. Physical and mental deterioration increased rapidly, hastening the ballet to its closing scenes of despair and death, this time two big *pas de deux* for the lovers before the murder and suicide. Kenneth solved the problems of how to depict the horrendous double shooting by having it take place behind a screen. Rudolf's falling figure knocked over the screen, revealing both bodies.

After considering a number of composers Lanchbery had decided that Liszt's music would be both close enough to the period and provide a suitably dramatic/romantic context for the narrative. In fact, while researching much of Liszt's prolific output, Lanchbery discovered a piece that the composer had written especially for the Empress and used it for the Empress's scene with Rudolf – a nice touch. The elaborate score drew upon such major works as the Faust Symphony and some of the tone poems as well as a large number of piano pieces, from the brilliant Transcendental Studies to the slight, melancholy Consolation No. 1. It proved a most effective and appropriate assemblage.

For the design of the ballet Kenneth turned yet again to

Georgiadis. To facilitate the quick and smooth transition from one scene to another he designed a simple gauze box-set, using minimal furnishings and props to dress each scene. Much of the period grandeur and formality came from the magnificent costumes, including many splendid military uniforms which were such a feature of Imperial Vienna. Georgiadis was particularly clever in designing the long, bustled dresses of the era in such a way as to permit maximum balletic movement, but it was fortunate that Mary had once turned up at Rudolf's private apartments almost naked under her all-enveloping coat! A decorative feature of the ballroom scene and the Empress's apartment were dummy uniformed guards and dressmaker's dummies symbolising the ever-watchful, eavesdropping officials and servants in the pay of the police.

Choreographically the ballet was an immense undertaking, from the several *pas de deux* for Rudolf and the women in his life to the many solos and big ensembles. The opening waltz, for example, looked as if the dancers were moving in the impromptu patterns of a ballroom but of course each couples' movements were meticulously worked out. The role of Rudolf had been intended for Anthony Dowell but unfortunately, before rehearsals began, he suffered an injury to his shoulder which demanded several months rest and therapy if he were to recover. Accordingly, the role was created upon another of the Royal Ballet's leading male principals, David Wall. It proved to be a tremendously taxing part, one of the longest – and, in a full-length ballet, probably the first – in which the leading part is for a man, and one which demanded a virtuoso technique, great stamina and partnering ability combined with a wide histrionic range. The ballet, in fact, provided a number of meaty parts as well as the opportunity for a number of important vignettes, from the scheming Countess Larisch to the remote, self-absorbed Empress, from the flirtatious Mitzi Caspah to the sympathetic Bratfisch. Because of Bratfisch's real-life reputation as a popular entertainer – he specialised in whistling and singing – Kenneth sent Graham Fletcher, first casting for the role, to a circus to learn some dexterous tricks with his top-hat which were incorporated into his solos.

Four days before the world premiere of *Mayerling*, *Elite Syncopations* entered the repertoire of the Sadler's Wells Royal Ballet, although Kenneth stipulated, at that time, that the work should not be performed in London. Regional audiences enjoyed its rumbustious humour just as much as Londoners had done – a nationwide awareness having been generated by a T.V. transmission.

Mayerling, which was dedicated to Frederick Ashton, received its first performance on February 14, 1978, at a Royal Gala in the presence of Queen Elizabeth the Queen Mother and was given a long standing ovation by the audience. The critics, too, gave the ballet a much greater welcome than they had accorded either *Anastasia* or *Manon* although, as always, there was a certain amount of nit-picking over so complex a theme.

The Times critic waxed unusually enthusiastic: 'Kenneth Mac-Millan's new three-act ballet lasts three hours or more and provides its protagonists with an outsize role which David Wall fills magnificently. Even if *Mayerling* had nothing else to commend it (and that is far from being the case) I would unhesitatingly commend you to see this performance.' And: 'The choreographic idiom for those duets shows MacMillan at his best. He has always been addicted to innovative, sometimes hazardous lifts and manoeuvres. This time, even the most far-fetched inventions are well worth the fetching. Daring throws and catches, swings right round Rudolf's neck, vertiginous falls to the ground all vividly express the increasingly hysterical mood . . . it is good to see MacMillan working so boldly once more. If he will be bold enough now to trim each act slightly and perhaps play down even further the less important characters, *Mayerling* will offer a mighty challenge to the casts who follow its admirable first interpreters.'

The *Financial Times* reviewer analysed the work with great insight and enthusiasm in a long article. '. . . *Mayerling* is a tense, searing ballet in which a tragic figure is seen in his very special and dramatically fascinating social setting, his motives and his psychology explored in dances of rare power, his destiny explained in terms of political, family and social pressures.' And: 'In the duets for Rudolf and Mary MacMillan is at his most persuasive as an erotic poet, exploring passion with images of extreme beauty – the final coupling at Mayerling marvellously combining lust and despair. As a setting for this core of *pas de deux* MacMillan has provided big set-pieces: a grand and magnificently organised set of waltzes at the Hofburg, a birthday party for Franz Josef and a boisterous tavern scene. At every moment in them the artists of the Royal Ballet are at their best . . . the ballet stands as a fascinating and innovative development, with MacMillan, Wall and the entire cast meriting every praise.'

Most of the reviews were in the same vein, with individual likes and dislikes discussed at length. Georgiadis's costumes were universally praised, but one or two critics wished he had designed heavier, more permanent sets for the Hofburg scenes. Some thought the assembled Liszt score absolutely right, others found it no more than serviceable (there are two distinct schools of thought about Liszt's music, anyway, although in latter years he has often been more appreciatively reassessed). Most critics thought that the ballet needed some careful cutting but, as the *Guardian* critic later wrote: 'I now think (after much vacillating) it needs the length to give a true picture of the characters and circumstances which govern its tragic shape. Easy, after one or two viewings, to say this or that scene must go. But patience and understanding bring rewards; every scene tells us something about Rudolf and the Court of Vienna in his time.'

But perhaps the most interesting and incisive review came not from a regular dance critic but Bryan Robertson, an art critic – an indication of how far Kenneth's breach in the barriers of ballet had penetrated. In a long article in the *Spectator* Robertson wrote: 'With dance it has taken Kenneth MacMillan's brilliant imagination as a choreographer to dissolve my distrust of narrative ballet, most particularly when it deals with historical themes, springing from fact or fantasy, dressed and decorated in period costumes and sets. The whole enterprise can so easily be a lifeless exercise in period taste, the theatrical *Grand Machine* equivalent of bad academic painting. But if Bacon, or even lighter weight Hockney, can revitalise and so extend the tradition of figurative art through their instinctively post-Freudian awareness, so can MacMillan, in ballet, with his powerful insights into character and situation.

'Most of MacMillan's ballets, descriptive or abstract, tackle themes of crisis and violence and the dramatic momentum of *Mayerling* springs from a chilly dissection of both these elements. The steely, clear-cut unfolding of the plot is due partly to Gillian Freeman's tight, unsentimental scenario: the double suicide of Crown Prince Rudolf of Austria–Hungary and the seventeen year old Mary Vetsera, their coldly passionate love affair, the unhappy political marriage of the Crown Prince, the oppressive court life with its hollow elegance and formality – the fast-moving scenario is exactly matched by the ferocious pace and energy of MacMillan's choreography. The action revolves around the startling progression of duets for the two principal dancers: abrasive, threatening, erotic and geared almost without respite to destruction. MacMillan projects the dark underside of romanticism: the ballet has domestic interludes of great charm but they're brief, the dominant mood is acrid, sour, and glitteringly dark.' The whole review was an exceptionally perceptive critique of Kenneth's intentions and achievement.

After the dress rehearsal Kenneth was well aware that the ballet was too long but it would have been disconcerting to the artists to start making cuts during the first few performances; excisions were planned for when the ballet was due to return to the repertoire in the autumn.

Throughout the rehearsal period of *Mayerling* a camera crew from

London Weekend Television, creating a programme for Melvyn Bragg's arts series, the South Bank Show, had been filming a documentary programme which included shots of the actual performance. The film, entitled *MacMillan's Mayerling*, directed by Derek Bailey, subsequently won the coveted Prix Italia prize in the musical section.

*

On April 28, 1978, a new production of *Solitaire*, redesigned by Barry Kay, entered the repertoire of the Sadler's Wells Royal Ballet and was given its first performance at the Sadler's Wells Theatre. The set was dominated by an immense, inflated irregularly-shaped balloon made of transparent, iridescent material upon which was painted the outline of a tree. The cast were dressed in fantasticated versions of pierrot and pierrette costumes with elaborate wigs, and the one prop (which in the original production had been a giant alpenhorn) became an outsize set of pan-pipes. It was all very elaborate and very beautiful but several critics thought that the designs overwhelmed the delicate, bitter-sweet mood of the work.

Exhausting as it had been creating and rehearsing *Mayerling*, Kenneth had little time to relax. He had been approached by Marcia Haydée to create a ballet around the specific talents of another outstanding Stuttgart dancer, Birgit Keil, and so, a few weeks after the premier of *Mayerling*, Kenneth, Deborah and Charlotte were once more in Stuttgart.

The new ballet was the outcome of Kenneth's reading on the subject of the Brontë family – although the work was not intended to be anything like a biographical interpretation of their lives, merely a launching pad for an idea. Kenneth (as his programme note subsequently stated) took 'a family set apart by landscape and circumstance' and proceeded to invent for them (his family differed from the Brontës in having one brother and five sisters) an enclosed, emotionally self-obsessed world in which they acted out a number of private psycho-sexual fantasies and games. One of the elements that Kenneth included in these games was masks, an idea borrowed from the Brontës whose clergyman father used to cover the siblings' heads with a cloth when they were confessing their sins – a pre-Freudian act that gave a chillingly bizarre effect to Kenneth's post-Freudian ballet.

As the work progressed – like his previous ballet for Stuttgart, *Requiem*, it was created in the short space of three weeks – Kenneth found that he was, in fact, concocting a murder story: one of the fantasy games of death becomes all too real. To the family of six

Kenneth added another, enigmatic, character called, simply, 'He', an impassive observer of the brother and sisters' strange relationships, representing their ideal romantic hero, who is himself a fantasy, unable to help when tragedy overtakes them.

The music that Kenneth used for this strange, compelling, frightening work were Schoenberg's Five Pieces for Orchestra, Opus 16; and Webern's Five Pieces for Orchestra, Opus 10 and Six Pieces for Orchestra, Opus 6, all of them scores that he had had 'at the back of his mind' for some years, waiting for a suitable balletic idea to emerge. *My Brother, My Sisters*, the title given to the new work, seemed right for those scores. Yolanda Sonnabend created an abstract decor which added considerably to the ballet's brooding, claustrophobic atmosphere.

My Brother, My Sisters had its premiere on May 21, 1978, and proved something of a sensation to its Stuttgart audience. The primary reason for the ballet, to provide a vehicle for Birgit Keil, was effectively realised: she received acclaim for her performance as the malevolent sister incestuously involved with her brother, the leader of the deadly games which get out of hand. But all the cast won praise, particularly Richard Cragun for whom Kenneth had created some amazing solos.

The day after the premiere of *My Brother, My Sisters* Kenneth and family flew from Stuttgart to Los Angeles to join the Royal Ballet which was embarking upon another American tour, its first visit to the West Coast in nine years, and including *Elite Syncopations* and *Mayerling* in its repertoire. The MacMillan family stayed with Kenneth's old friends Herbert Ross – who had become a most successful Hollywood film director – and his wife Nora Kaye in their large, beautiful Beverly Hills home. Charlotte immediately took to the luxury Hollywood life with its poolside parties, Malibu beach homes, Cadillac limousines and star-studded glamour.

Mayerling received its U.S. premiere on May 30, 1978, and proved a triumph with both critics and audience which included many Hollywood celebrities in the vast Shrine Auditorium in downtown L.A. although David Wall suffered an injury in rehearsal and had to be replaced by Stephen Jefferies at short notice.

Kenneth's short 'working holiday' in the Californian sunshine was soon over. Three days after the *Mayerling* premiere in L.A., the Stuttgart Ballet began a two week season at the London Coliseum and included Kenneth's *The Song of the Earth*, *Requiem* and the new *My Brother, My Sisters* – the first chance for most British critics to see Kenneth's latest ballets for the Stuttgart company. In fact, because several of the Stuttgart's programmes that season included new works by young, inexperienced choreographers, Kenneth's ballets dominated the repertoire, the only other major work being Cranko's rather crude version of *Carmen*.

Both *Requiem* and *My Brother, My Sisters* were given standing ovations – as was Kenneth himself. He rarely took curtain calls at the Royal Opera House and with these two new works at the Coliseum he was heartened to see with what enthusiasm he was personally received by the London audiences; it redeemed the several years of carping criticism and snide comments he had endured as Director of the Royal Ballet. Most of the critics, too, acclaimed the new ballets.

The *Financial Times* critic wrote: 'What MacMillan has done in his realisation of the score is to match at every point Fauré's refinement and subtlety of means: without bombast or hysteria or penitential wallowing he finds images and streams of movement that treat with deepest sincerity of the hopes and fears we know in the face of death. *Requiem* is a ballet that needs almost to stand by itself in a programme, so deep are the feelings it engenders, so powerful the performances it inspires from its admirable cast.'

The Times critic seemed to retreat a little from his initial enthusiasm written after the Stuttgart premiere: 'The strength of the work lies in its simplicity. There are moments of knotty invention, especially in the solo for Richard Cragun during the Offertorium, but mostly MacMillan has gone for the obvious effects in movements of sorrow, contrition and consolation.

'That is one of the traditional duties of religious art, to provide a picture the ordinary man or woman can understand. *Requiem* is recognisably a MacMillan ballet, but it seems a public, not a private expression of feelings, which is surprising from him.' To which one can only answer that a ballet is, of necessity, a public expression of feelings.

The *Guardian* critic thought: 'The setting, by Yolanda Sonnabend, and the lighting are shimmering and radiant but radiance only touches the choreography occasionally. Much of the group dances are reminiscent of movement MacMillan has used before in *Rite of Spring* and *Song of the Earth*. But when his imagination takes flight, as in the wonderful Pie Jesu solo for Marcia Haydée and in the great soaring lifts at the end, then the ballet becomes a deeply felt tribute to his friend and colleague, John Cranko.'

The *Sunday Times* reviewer said that *Requiem* 'is a work which perhaps does not reveal all its qualities at a single viewing. Its tone is restrained – emotion kept in check by understatement – and in that respect parallels a particular glory of the Fauré music. Parallels, but does it *match* that glory?

'We had passed the Introitus and Kyre, the Offertorium and

Sanctus – all impressive – and reached Pie Jesu before I found myself truly moved: this was by a gentle solo for the wonderful Marcia Haydée, dancing in a spot of white light with child-like innocence – a simple faith. At the close of the Agnus Die she is held inverted by a group of men to bless the recumbent Birgit Keil – one of the series of potent tableaux which carry much of the ballet's devotional weight, rather in the formalised manner of medieval painting.'

In a review which covered the whole Stuttgart season, the *Sunday Telegraph* critic paid fleeting tribute to *Requiem* when he said that the ballet 'is clearly a masterwork'.

My Brother, My Sisters inevitably had the critics with more crossed lines than usual, either immensely enthusiastic or loathing it – although most acknowledged it to be disturbingly original.

In a long review the *Financial Times* critic wrote: 'The text of the ballet is very complex, all the more so because MacMillan hides nothing, and – analyst once again to his characters – shows how ritual and reality become inseparable to the figures in case histories like these.

'Fascinating though the themes of *My Brother, My Sisters* are, the piece would be no more than a psychiatrist's toy were it not that MacMillan has evolved a language of extraordinary originality and excitement in which to explore the situation . . . I do not know if *My Brother, My Sisters* will become a "popular" ballet; but its combination of action on two narrative levels, in that what we see at first glance is doubled by another and even more uneasy "inner" narration, grips the mind, and demonstrates yet again MacMillan's mastery as a choreographer able to explore the convolutions of the human psyche in exciting movement.'

The *Daily Telegraph* critic found Kenneth's explorations of the human psyche rather too much: '*My Brother, My Sisters*, proved in total contrast to his magnificent and moving Fauré *Requiem* shown last week. It qualified as one of the most bizarre ballets to be staged recently by a major choreographer. Its oddity was entirely purposeful and controlled. Undoubtedly it fulfils its creator's intentions and it is perfectly interpreted by the dancers with a particularly haunting contribution from Birgit Keil; but it will prove unpalatable to many people.

'MacMillan has frequently sought out and translated into dance the dark and devious areas of human behaviour. This time he has turned to the fantasies of a family not only unbalanced in the ratio of five sisters to one brother but in mental and emotional development.

'The games they play, portrayed in strident and eccentric movement to a score chosen from Schoenberg and Webern, are macabre, incestuous and cruel. The action has a bitter effectiveness but

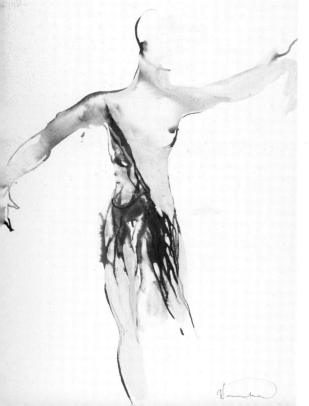

Before designing the costumes for *Requiem* Yolanda Sonnabend drew many
anatomical studies emphasising the muscular, vascular and nervous systems
which were the basis of the striations that appeared on the dancers' leotards.
Above: Bryony Brind on *pointe* with, seated, left, Ashley Page and, right, Wayne
Eagling. *Left*: Fiona Chadwick. *Below left*: The original costume design by
Sonnabend for Brind and, right, for three supporting males for the Royal Ballet
production for which the costume designs differed slightly from that of the
Stuttgart production. (*Leslie E. Spatt.*)

the characters are so lacking in humanity and so unremittingly abnormal that they forefeit any claim to pity or sympathy.'

A long review of the Stuttgart Ballet season in *Country Life* became an assessment of Kenneth's career, with particular emphasis on his most recent works, including *Mayerling*. Of *My Brother, My Sisters* the critic wrote: '. . . I see no flaw at all. It again is no nice ballet; the family relationships explored by it are mostly horrid. Yet what a marvel it is of taut, expressive dance – like those previous successes, *The Invitation* and *Las Hermanas* in being intensely dramatic but unlike them, and better, in transmuting the whole of its ugly theme into the elusive poetry of neo-classical movement. We say that ballet, like any other art, must, if it is to flourish, constantly seek to enlarge its frontiers. Here is an example, if ever there was one, of a balletic frontier enlarged. I would not have believed that dance – and especially classical dance – could have been the right art-form for such rum subject matter; MacMillan has changed my mind.'

'Bizarre', 'macabre', 'disturbing', whatever the critics thought no one could say that Kenneth, in his latest ballet, had not once again provided something that made the work of most other choreographers seem tame, effete and precious.

*

Within a few weeks of the Stuttgart season, Kenneth and family embarked on another long journey – literally half way round the world – to Australia via Canada. They stopped in Toronto to see the National Ballet of Canada and to discuss with its (then) Artistic Director, ex-Royal Ballet dancer Alexander Grant, plans for the company to take *Elite Syncopations* into its repertoire – which it subsequently did, with the same success that the ballet had had in Britain. Then Kenneth and family flew on to Australia where Kenneth saw the (then) Director of the Australian Ballet, Peggy van Praagh, to discuss the possibility of the company doing *Song of the Earth*. Those plans did not materialise but that visit to the great Australian continent allowed Kenneth to meet, for the first time, his in-laws in Sydney, and to enjoy a trip to Queensland with Deborah to have a look at her birthplace. It was a happy visit except, of course, it was undertaken during the Australian winter and the weather that year was particularly inclement.

Back in London Kenneth just had time to dash off a short little work for the Sadler's Wells Royal Ballet, given in a programme as a – somewhat belated – tribute to Dame Ninette de Valois's birthday, before leaving for a protracted stay in Paris.

The birthday piece, entitled *6.6.78*, the actual date of de Valois's birthday, consisted of little more than a long, rather acrobatic *pas de deux* for Marion Tait and Desmond Kelly as the Gemini twins of de Valois's birthday sign, with eleven other couples representing the remaining symbols of the zodiac. Ian Spurling designed some colourful costumes with elaborate zodiacal headresses and the music Kenneth chose was Samuel Barber's Capricorn Concerto. The ballet made some humorous references to poses used by de Valois in her own ballets but it was no more than a slight *piece d'occasion* and several critics, perhaps expecting something more serious from what had been billed as 'a new MacMillan work', were disappointed by it.

The invitation to go to Paris had come some months before from the (then) Director of the Paris Opera Ballet, Violette Verdy, who wished to produce an all-MacMillan programme – the first such invitation issued to a British choreographer from that distinguished and historic company. Kenneth, of course, was pleased and flattered, and planned to revive *The Four Seasons* with new decor by Barry Kay; to create an entirely new work, also designed by Kay; and to end the evening with *Song of the Earth*.

Kenneth arrived in Paris with Mrs John Auld (wife of the then Assistant Director of the Sadler's Wells Royal Ballet) as interpreter, and stayed at the Grand Hotel, just around the corner from the great, ornate opera house. Almost immediately Kenneth found himself enmeshed in the notorious back-stage political intrigues, the inter-departmental rivalries and personal feuds that have always been part and parcel of the Paris Opera. Since her original invitation to Kenneth, Violette Verdy's resignation as Director had been announced; as a consequence she no longer carried much authority with the dancers.

The huge roster of artists in the company is divided into a rigid hierarchy, each with its own jealously guarded rights and privileges. For example, when planning a move, Kenneth discovered that a mere *choryphée* was not permitted to cross in front of an *étoile*, whatever the choreographer's needs. Kenneth had chosen a brilliant young dancer, Patrick Dupond, to play the role of the Messenger of Death in *Song of the Earth* and this incensed a number of senior principals who felt that such a junior member of the company should not be given such an important part. But Kenneth was adamant and in the end Dupond danced the role.

There were antagonisms at every turn; not long before the dress rehearsal it was discovered that the props for *The Four Seasons* had been made so heavy that the dancers refused to handle them, an act that both Kenneth and Kay subsequently felt to have been deliberate sabotage. The dress rehearsal was fraught by another singular circumstance: several senior artists, without previous reference to either Violette Verdy or Kenneth, suddenly announced that they had undertaken to give a charity performance for Princess Grace in Monaco and that therefore they would be unable to attend the dress rehearsal. Kenneth was driven to summoning his lawyer and threatening to abandon the whole programme before the dancers involved agreed to be present. It was not a situation calculated to create a harmonious atmosphere and a further complication was that the (then) Intendant of the Paris Opera was involved in a dispute with stage staff who were pursuing a 'go slow' policy that affected scene changes to a considerable degree.

The Paris Opera's MacMillan triple bill had its first performance on November 23, 1978. Barry Kay's decor for *The Four Seasons* (a ballet which, in fact, he had never seen at Covent Garden) was conceived on a grand scale. Each Season was represented by a deity from classical antiquity: Diana represented Winter; Venus, Spring; Pan, Summer and Bacchus Autumn, and each of them was attended by a large retinue which allowed Kenneth to make use of the huge corps de ballet. Venus was of particular interest, being played *en travesti* by a celebrated Australian transvestite, David Williams, who was then resident in Paris. The figure of Bacchus, too, was somewhat startling, making his entrance astride a large priapic carriage.

Using the great height of the proscenium-opening, Kay had placed dummy figures of black angels on platforms amidst billowing inflatable clouds made of translucent material. The whole sumptuous setting and elaborate costumes were designed in the ornate Second Empire style – as is the opera house itself – and Kenneth and Barry Kay thought of it as a sophisticated decorative conceit as well as a homage to the *grand siècle* architecture. Unfortunately, the Parisian audience thought otherwise, taking it to be an elaborate British joke at the expense of a famous French period, and booed and hissed at each processional entry. Brilliant as Barry Kay's decor was, it must be admitted that it did rather swamp the ballet itself.

The new work, *Metaboles* (the title taken from the score by Henri Dutilleux that Kenneth had chosen) restored the audience's good temper. The theme (in the programme Kenneth quoted from Oscar Wilde's *Ballad of Reading Gaol*: 'For each man kills the thing he loves') suggested by the title of the score, refers to the process in which the digestion of food provides the energy for a living organism – a woman literally devoured by her lovers, similar to the *comedie noir* film *La Grand Bouffe*, although the ballet was in no way comically conceived. At any rate the idea seemed to appeal to the French prediliction for *grand cocottes* and *haute cuisine*! Kay had provided a clever set consisting of a central dining table and chairs behind which were a semi-circle of oval pier-glasses and a gigantic backcloth of an X-ray photograph. The woman, danced by Dominique Khalfouni, was

174

elegantly dressed in a gown the colour of raspberry sorbet; the men, led by Patrice Bart, were in evening dress.

Commenting on the '*soirée* MacMillan', the critic of the *Financial Times* who had travelled to Paris for the occasion, wrote: '. . . eating and eroticism are correlated. And as the audience discovered, *Metaboles* generated an obsessive emotional force. MacMillan uses an almost expressionistic manner at times, (the men mime-eating, with hands rising and falling like pistons over the table) and the neurotic-erotic mood becomes very tense. Khalfouni and Bart were both excellent. Khalfouni, a pallid victim enjoying her fate, gave her role a morbid sensuality as she was manhandled in a variety of acrobatic/passionate lifts; Bart's speed and impetuosity made the central male role as disqueting as that of the lunatic teacher in Flindt's *La Leçon*.'

Song of the Earth completely restored the evening and received a magnificent performance from Patrick Dupond as the Messenger of Death, Wilfride Piollet as the Woman and her real-life husband Jean Guizerix as the Man, of whom the *Financial Times* critic said: 'Guizerix is an artist of the rarest distinction, blessed with a powerful style and emotional intensity, ideally expressive, virile – one of the greatest dancers of our time. As the Man he gives the most potent account of this difficult role I have seen, serious, thrilling in dignity and in dynamic range. The balance with the Woman (taken by the gifted and sensitively restrained Wilfride Piollet) was excellently judged and I suspect that the last song gained much from the fact that these artists are man and wife.'

The Paris episode had been both challenging and not a little harassing, but above all it had been, for Kenneth, an instructive experience. It brought to a close a year in which Kenneth had had successes with three of the world's major ballet companies – the Royal Ballet, Stuttgart Ballet and the Paris Opera Ballet – and fully vindicated his decision to resign as Director of the Royal Ballet and concentrate on choreography.

But the Paris venture was not his last choreographic commission for the year: no sooner had he returned from Paris than he began choreographing several sequences for the Herbert Ross film *Nijinsky*, in which Kenneth had to simulate the highly idiosyncratic choreographic style of Diaghilev's great protégé. With hardly any references to go by, except a few faded photographs, Kenneth was amazingly successful in creating pastiche choreography for the original *Sacre du Printemps* and – the most obscure of all Nijinsky's ballets – *Jeux*. When the film was released the following year it was Kenneth's choreography – and Georgiadis's settings for the dance sequences – that were acclaimed as the unequivocal triumphs of the film. So ended an unprecedentedly hectic year, full of travel, full of creative impulse, one of the high water-marks of Kenneth's career.

23

From haute couture to psychiatric clinic

Despite 1978 having been one of Kenneth's busiest and most productive years he had also found time to set in motion plans for his next full-length ballet for Covent Garden, not scheduled until the spring of 1981. Late one evening, after the summer holidays, Kenneth spoke to Gillian Freeman on the telephone and asked her if she would once again write the scenario for the new big work. He told her that after much thought and deliberation he had decided to base the ballet on the life and career of Isadora Duncan – the idea that he had first had in Berlin in 1967. He knew that the Royal Ballet resources – unlike those of Berlin – were adequate to the task. In the interim, during 1975–76, Frederick Ashton, however, had composed a number of Brahms waltzes 'in the manner of Isadora Duncan' as solos for Lynn Seymour who had performed them at various galas in Hamburg, Los Angeles and London. Although they were choreographic miniatures, created as homage to an artist Ashton had seen and admired as a young man, it seemed to Kenneth that however different in scope and style his work might be, to use Duncan's life for a ballet would be like poaching another choreographer's material. Even so, as he thought about several other ideas for a full-length work, he kept coming back to the Isadora theme; after all, his ballet would be so different in concept to Ashton's small pieces that he felt Ashton would understand his reason for choosing the subject.

Gillian was delighted to be asked to collaborate with Kenneth once more and immediately began reading the various biographies, memoirs and monographs about Duncan's life, as well as Duncan's autobiography. In discussing with Gillian the way he wanted to do the ballet Kenneth made two stipulations: one was that it should be in two acts and the other was that the treatment should be 'impressionistic' – in the same style that he had used so successfully for the original one-act version of *Anastasia*. He also said he would like the opening scene to be set in a railway station. He felt that because Duncan's life had been one of such constant travel the station setting would immediately symbolise her endless arrivals and departures.

Duncan's life was so crammed with amazing events, so full of important characters and world-famous celebrities, so wide-ranging in its locations, so full of lurid melodrama and so interspersed with terrible tragedy, that finding a construction, telescoping the action, selecting the essential characters and yet retaining some fidelity to historical accuracy, presented enormous practical and aesthetic problems which, by comparison, made *Mayerling* seem like a simple, straightforward narrative. For the first draft Gillian took two points of reference: the birth of Isadora's first child, Deirdre, by Edward Gordon Craig, and Isadora's violent, accidental death, both events told in flashback. In Act I all the events would occur before the birth, while Act II would mainly concentrate on the later years, the two acts being motivated by birth and death. In her research Gillian noted three recurring themes. One, the sea. Isadora was born by it, frequently claimed to have found inspiration from it, conceived by it, gave birth by it, found one of her lovers by it, three times tried to drown herself in it and finally died by it. Two, children. Not only the three that Isadora bore (two were drowned, one died soon after childbirth) but the succession of young people whom she took into her various schools in Germany, France, Russia and America. Three, travel. Isadora was constantly on the move, not only the many tours she undertook (as did Pavlova at the same time) throughout her career but also the dozens of capricious, impulsive journeys she made because of chance encounters, love affairs and sheer restlessness. The first draft of the scenario was sent to Kenneth in September, 1978.

*

But Kenneth's contract as Principal Choreographer to the Royal Ballet stipulated not only that he should produce a full-length ballet for Covent Garden every two years but also one new one-act work each year for both Royal Ballet companies so on January 2, 1979 he began work on a new ballet scheduled for Covent Garden in March. The very next day he received the highest accolade available from the British ballet establishment, the Royal Academy of Dancing Queen Elizabeth II Coronation Award 'for services to British ballet'. It was presented on a bitterly cold winter's night at the rather unlikely venue of Kensington Town Hall.

The new ballet was set to Ravel's Piano Concerto in G Major which Kenneth had long found attractive with its brilliant outer movements, its long, beautiful adagio and its suggestions of jazz rhythms. Written in 1931 it was essentially reminiscent of that time when film stars and celebrities regularly crossed the Atlantic in luxury liners, when intrepid aviators made record-breaking flights, when the *jeunesse doré* of the post-Depression period arrayed themselves in extravagantly beautiful Paris fashions and when, despite the glamour and glitter of Paris, London and New York, there were sinister intimations of what was to happen in Mussolini's Rome and Hitler's Berlin. So, using Ravel's evocative piano concerto, Kenneth devised a ballet that reflected what one now looks back upon as a period of dazzling decadence, the final cocktail era that disappeared in the darkness of 1939.

Kenneth had been looking at fashion plates of the thirties, at the chic, svelte creations of Chanel and Paquin, Worth and Schiaparelli, and for a pastiche – if not a parody – of those styles he turned once again to Ian Spurling whose fantasticated designs for *Elite Syncopations* had been so clever. The music and the fashion plates together coalesced into the idea for the ballet.

The ballet begins with the ten couples of the supporting dancers dressed in an extravaganza of *sportif* clothes and discovered on stage in the exaggerated poses of mannequins. They begin moving in jerky, puppet-like animation until the leading quartet – two couples – enter through a door up-stage centre and begin a complex double-duet. The men are dressed in pale pink and orange satin plus-fours with large golfing caps; the women in one-piece bathing suits in deeper shades of the same colours. For the long central adagio the women's bathing caps become flying helmets with goggles, reminiscent of those worn by the aviatrix of the thirties – Amy Johnson, Jean Batten, Amelia Earheart. Each of them are attended by five men, lifted, twisted, inverted in attitudes of flight, a complex canon in which their convolutions occasionally, briefly, achieve synchronisation. For the last, rather hectic, movement the cast are in evening dress, the men in satin pastel-coloured tails, the women in floating chiffon.

Spurling's setting is a creamy-white room with the wings profiles of watching faces; the central door upstage looks on to a garden. Throughout the last movement darkness slowly descends over the garden view; on the last pianistic chord one of the leading women closes the door, shutting out the holocaust that is to come, freezing them all in attitudes of elegant frivolity. Kenneth wanted to call the ballet *L'Heure bleu*, the title of Guerlain's famous perfume of the period, but the executors of the Ravel estate rather stuffily would not agree to Ravel's music being associated with anything so superficial as scent. Eventually Gillian Freeman suggested *La Fin du jour* and that title was adopted.

With Merle Park and Wayne Eagling, Jennifer Penney and Julian Hosking as the leading quartet, the ballet had its premiere at Covent

a Fin du jour was created as the direct
result of MacMillan looking at
fashion plates of the 1930s. It is
light-hearted, with two leading
couples and ten supporting pairs
dressed in Ian Spurling's clever,
colourful parodies of *haute couture*. But
as the ballet progresses darkness falls.
Choreographically, it represents
MacMillan at his most convoluted
and inventive. *Right*: Jennifer Penney
and Wayne Eagling in the first
movement of the work, danced to
Ravel's Piano Concerto in G Major.
(*Anthony Crickmay*.)

Gloria was conceived as a serious
commemoration of that generation
destroyed in the First World War, a
war in which MacMillan's father had
suffered as a victim of poison gas. The
ballet, danced to Poulenc's *Gloria*
from the Catholic Mass which
provides an ironic counterpoint to the
mise en scene, depicts the soldiers, and
the women who loved them, as
ghostly figures emerging from a bleak
no-man's-land. It inspired
MacMillan to some of his most
lyrically lovely choreography. *Below*:
Jennifer Penney and Julian Hosking
in the *pas de deux* performed to the
soprano solo *Domine Deus*. (*Anthony
Crickmay*.)

Garden on March 15, 1979, and the audience loved it – relieved, perhaps, to find Kenneth in comparatively happy mood after the fierce, degenerate passions of *Mayerling*, the heartfelt seriousness of *Requiem* and the macabre mysteries of *My Brother, My Sisters*. Actually, on stage, the evening was partly overshadowed by a management dispute with stage staff, and the other two ballets which made up an all-MacMillan triple bill – a revival of *Diversions* which looked under-rehearsed and *Elite Syncopations* – were given within the new ballet's set and with somewhat rudimentary lighting.

At the end of the evening Princess Margaret went on stage to present Kenneth with the *Evening Standard* Award for the outstanding contribution to dance for 1978, the citation making particular reference to *Mayerling* as well as Kenneth's seven-year direction of the company. He had a standing ovation as well as showers of flowers from the gallery.

Most of the critics liked *La Fin du jour* although there were one or two who, having been adult themselves in the thirties, were unable to relate to Kenneth's vision of the period as they remembered it, ignoring the fact that it was not a piece of nostalgic indulgence but a distant look back from the viewpoint of impressions received.

The *Guardian* reviewer wrote: 'The ballet is a pastiche of fashion, not actual fashion like such Diaghilev novelties as *Le Train Bleu*, but it does get the period atmosphere of a carefree world when Elsa Maxwell gave parties and Gertrude Lawrence was the epitome of sophisticated elegance. There is a lovely freshness about the design and the dancing of a mostly very young cast.'

The *Financial Times* critic said: 'MacMillan's invention is prodigal: from the demotic of games, from the photographic images of periodicals of the time, he has wrought a language of remarkable beauty . . . I think *La Fin du jour* a ballet far richer than it first seems, richer even than the prodigious outpouring of choreography which so stimulates the eye, and so stimulates the dancers. The piece is magnificently performed by Merle Park and Jennifer Penney, Julian Hosking and Wayne Eagling. It may seem frivolous, quirky at moments. It certainly does not presume to impose any political attitudenising upon the refinement of the Ravel score. It makes its points by hints, quick suggestions, but it does so with consummate sensitivity. It is a requiem for the *douceur de vivre* of an era, and it is nostalgically grateful for the '30's wayward charm.'

On the other hand, one of the three critics who reviewed the ballet in the specialist magazine *Dance and Dancers* wrote: 'To pretend that a decade of economic, socio-political and military crisis, during which people struggled desperately to find a better way of shaping society, is represented by this farrago of sporting scenes and hectic nightlife does just not bear serious thought.' But then of course it is hard to believe that anyone would think that, seriously or otherwise.

In a long article in *Country Life*, examining Kenneth's choreographic style in some depth, the contributor wrote: 'This new, relatively short work proves, at first sight, to be a beauty. Its second movement is MacMillan at his very best, a marvel of elusive, allusive poetry expressed in a basically classical dance language which is very much his own.'

*

Soon after the ballet's first night Kenneth, Deborah and Charlotte went on holiday. The original intention was that they should go to Jugoslavia but as Barry Kay was going to Morocco it was decided that they should go too. The Moroccan holiday was to some extent spoilt by poor weather but at the same time Jugoslavia was shaken by a huge and devastating earthquake and although Kenneth and family would not have been at its epicentre they would certainly have been in the region.

One evening, soon after returning from holiday, Kenneth rang Gillian to say that from a number of contemporary composers he had been thinking of approaching Richard Rodney Bennett to write the music for the Isadora ballet, not realising that Richard was a personal friend of Gillian's. She was able to give Kenneth the composer's telephone number and after a short, preliminary conversation in which Richard expressed great interest in the project (he later told Gillian that he had long wanted to write the music for a MacMillan ballet) it was arranged that Gillian should accompany Richard to Kenneth's house for further exploratory talks over an informal dinner later that week. During that meeting both men (who share a somewhat similar introspective disposition) established an immediate rapport and by the end of the evening it had been decided that Richard would be writing the music for the new ballet. The only difficulty was that Richard was on the point of taking up residence in New York and any collaboration would have to be conducted, for the most part, over the transatlantic telephone. But before Richard left Britain Kenneth supplied him with a very detailed breakdown of the scenario indicating (just as Petipa had done for Tchaikovsky with *The Sleeping Beauty*) the exact time-lengths of music he wanted for each scene as well as the dramatic mood or character-emphasis it should generate.

Commissioning a score was a big step for Kenneth to take (it was the first commissioned full length ballet score at Covent Garden since Ashton commissioned the music for *Ondine* from Hans Werner Henze in 1958) but the demands of the ballet were so wide-ranging and yet so specific that it would have been impossible to assemble a suitable score from existing music as had been done for *Anastasia*, *Manon* and *Mayerling*. So Richard spent the winter of 1979/80 working on the music for *Isadora* as it had finally been decided to call the ballet. For a while Kenneth and Gillian had considered finding something less obvious, thinking it might be a good idea to get away from one-word titles; they wondered whether something taken from one of Duncan's own phrases, such as her last words before taking the fateful ride in the Bugatti: '*Je vais à la gloire!*' somewhat freely translated as *Off to Glory* might be suitable, but after some discussion it was decided that after all it *was* Isadora's story and, despite – or even because of – the extensive use of her name in written and filmed biographies it would be better to retain her name as the title. So *Isadora* it remained.

*

Soon after the meeting with Richard, Kenneth began working on a new one-act work for the Sadler's Wells Royal Ballet, to be given its premiere during the Edinburgh Festival. From the Royal Opera House he had been sent a batch of tapes of music by contemporary British composers among which was a score by Gordon Crosse which had been commissioned by the Hallé orchestra a year or two before and which Kenneth liked very much. He does not remember now whether the music suggested the Orpheus theme or whether it was just another aspect of the legend's many manifestations that was at the back of his mind already; at any rate, when he decided to use the Gordon Crosse score for the new ballet he began rehearsal with the vague idea of setting it to a modern interpretation of the classic myth.

Not for the first time the basic thematic idea underwent a considerable metamorphosis during the creative period. The Orphean figure became a young man who intrudes upon a group of psychiatric patients and is emotionally involved with one of them, a young woman – an idea which certainly has echoes of descending into some sort of underworld.

The ballet begins with the curtain taken up quickly while the audience is still applauding the entrance of the conductor into the orchestra pit. On stage a large group of dancers are dressed in a rag-bag assortment of clothes, like children dressing up as adults; they copy the audience's applause somewhat mockingly before breaking up into self-absorbed groups or solitary figures, as in a children's playground. It is some time before their actions and reactions reveal that they are not children but grown-ups pursuing childish fantasies. Centre-stage a young woman is obsessed with a handbag and the make-up it contains; she is comforted and protected by a woman who adopts the role of her mother. A young man enters the compound which is surrounded by a high wire-mesh fence and becomes involved with the young woman who, in the frenetic 'games' that ensue, has an epileptic fit. Another woman and a man act out the charade of a vicar and his wife performing funeral obsequies over the form of the young woman. The young man resents their interference and becomes violent; he is restrained by white-coated doctors, who have been observing the behaviour of the patients who take off their dressing-up clothes and put on drab institutional uniform and file out. The young man is left alone, a forlorn, strait-jacketed figure rhythmically banging his head against the wire fence. Consciously or not, it was yet another of Kenneth's 'outsider' figures (among a whole stageful of 'outsiders') and there may have been further unconscious associations with childhood memories, such as the woman acting as a surrogate mother. For the past two or three years, Kenneth himself had been undergoing psychoanalysis – although, of course, in a manner far removed from the brutal, institutional world that the ballet portrayed.

Yolanda Sonnabend designed a marvellously bleak and claustrophobic set which at first seemed an innocuous playground enclosure and then took on a more sinister ambience as the narrative progressed.

Playground, as the ballet was called, was first performed on August 29, 1979, in the 'Big Top' in Edinburgh in a particularly well-balanced all-MacMillan programme which began with *Concerto* and ended with *Elite Syncopations*, designed as a tribute to an eminent Scottish-born citizen. The new ballet was very well received by the audience and at a reception after the performance a psychiatrist came up to Kenneth and asked him how he had arrived at such an accurate observation of the behaviour of mentally disturbed people. Kenneth's instructions to the dancers had been, of course, purely imaginative.

When Kenneth had first conceived the idea of doing an Isadora ballet in Berlin, Lynn Seymour was his leading ballerina. She was still a principal with the Royal Ballet when, early in 1978, Kenneth finally decided to do it. But a few months later Seymour signed a two-year contract to become the Director of (and dance with) the Bavarian State Ballet in Munich. This was a shock to Kenneth because, obviously, it meant she would not be available during the whole of the period during which *Isadora* was being created. Yet, of the many dancers that Kenneth had worked with throughout his career, it was with Seymour that he had had the closest relationship and rapport, and she, of all people, knew how important it was for him to be in almost daily contact with the artist upon whom he was creating the principal role. But, equally obviously, the offer from Munich was an important one for Seymour and she had made her choice. Reluctantly – because Kenneth had always considered Seymour to be the perfect casting for Isadora – he decided that he would have to build the part upon the talents of another ballerina and he chose Merle Park.

In September Gillian sent Kenneth the second draft of the *Isadora* scenario which included some structural changes (Kenneth had agreed to have an opening scene with Isadora going into labour on the beach) and some 'voice-over' lines taken from Duncan's autobiography which helped to establish character and situation and cut down the need for extensive programme notes. In the same month Kenneth and family spent a short holiday with friends at their country house in Devonshire before returning to London for the Sadler's Wells Royal Ballet season and the London premiere of *Playground*. Several of the London critics had already seen the ballet in Edinburgh; both premieres stimulated a number of good reviews that considered the work to be a powerful addition to the company's repertoire.

The *Guardian* critic wrote: '*Playground* is anything but a pretty story but it is a mighty powerful piece of theatre . . . a wholly contemporary work but (one which) conforms to the Diaghilev ideal of collaboration between the arts.' Both Sonnabend's setting and the Gordon Crosse music received much praise as well as Kenneth's adroit use of the score. The music critic of the *Glasgow Herald* wrote: 'So perfectly does the music complement the choreography that, had one not been told otherwise, it would have been assumed that the composer wrote his score to the scenario.' The *Sunday Telegraph* reviewer was equally impressed by the way the choreography, music and design complemented each other: 'What matters and what makes the piece hauntingly and horribly effective, is that we are gripped and held imaginative prisoners from start to finish – not in a melodramatic, Grand Guignol way, although the ballet edges in that direction, but by MacMillan's sheer ability at combining music and movement effectively in the theatre. Yolanda Sonnabend's sets are exactly right, Gordon Crosse's music stimulating, but MacMillan's inventive brilliance is at the heart of the ballet's achievement. He has found unguessed-at qualities in his dancers, and they all, particularly Siobhan Stanley in a maternal role, are frighteningly effective.'

The *Financial Times* critic wrote: 'Kenneth MacMillan's new *Playground* for Sadler's Wells Royal Ballet finds the choreographer working at his most intense in studying the human psyche. The ballet is a disquieting piece making no concessions to conventional attitudes of airiness and bodies beautiful. Instead, it offers distress and violence of spirit; yet because it treats of a human condition without romanticising or fudging its subject, it also achieves a harsh, uncompromising beauty. The classic dance is taken a further step along a path of truthful precision in revealing depths of feeling and suffering. MacMillan's style owes something to the manner of his *My Brother, My Sisters*, but *Playground* is even darker in mood though warmed by a compassion for the human derelicts it studies. The reverberence of the characters and their relationships makes the piece far superior to any mere observation of madness. It is not shocking for the sake of sensationalism and it never sinks into the sentimentality of the film *One Flew Over the Cuckoo's Nest*.'

The success of *Playground* prompted Kenneth to consider creating a trilogy of works based on Gordon Crosse scores and linked by their titles: the other two ballets were to be called *Parade Ground* and *Common Ground* (a ballet with the latter title has since been created by Jennifer Jackson) but for various reasons – mainly through pressure of other work – the idea never came to fruition.

Charlotte was now six and attending a day school, the Lycée Français, in Kensington. Deborah, therefore, found that she had more time to spare and was anxious to resume work as an artist which, because of her travels round the world, her subsequent marriage and motherhood, she had allowed to lapse. For this purpose she needed a modest-sized studio but the house in Wandsworth was too small to provide such a facility. Kenneth and Deborah considered the possibility of carrying out structural alterations or building an extension but for various reasons such plans proved impracticable. They also explored the possibility of buying a holiday home in rural France as some friends and acquaintances had done, and Deborah paid a visit to the small town of Cadillac to view a property there, but the difficulties of commuting, and the time it would take, made that idea impracticable too. They therefore began house hunting in London again, looking for something larger, but as Kenneth was anxious to stay in the same area it was another year before they were to discover what they wanted.

On November 23, 1979, *Danses Concertantes* was revived by the Sadler's Wells Royal Ballet with new designs by Nicholas Georgiadis and given its first performance at the New Theatre, Cardiff. The London premiere took place during the company's spring season at Sadler's Wells Theatre. The new designs were a radical departure from the original: gone was the airy fantasy palace and in its place was a slightly sinister, somewhat claustrophobic ante-room in scarlet, black and mustard yellow. The delicate sphinx-decorated chairs were replaced with huge armchairs, draped in red material (actually moulded, giving a trompe l'oeuil effect). There were lots of shiny, plastic surfaces – including costume trimmings – and the women's dresses were above the knee which accounted for many people placing the ballet either in the twenties (the ante-room to a Berlin cabaret club?) or the sixties (the parlour of a brothel?). Critical opinion was divided about whether or not the designs were an improvement but most were agreed that the choreography was as clever and challenging as it had been in 1955.

As the year drew to a close Kenneth was suffering once more with a very painful foot, this time a bunion, which the doctors said needed surgery. In December he entered a private clinic in Hendon, at the same time as Merle Park who also underwent a foot operation. Both operations were successfully performed by the renowned Danish specialist, Professor Eivind Thomasen, who has treated many famous dancers, but Christmas came and the year ended with Kenneth once more hobbling about with the aid of a stick.

24

Gloria and *Isadora*

Early in the new year, 1980, Kenneth began thinking about his new one-act ballet for Covent Garden. Its theme was inspired by a television series based on Vera Brittan's autobiographical *Testament of Youth* which covered the years of the First World War and its immediate aftermath – the mass slaughter of a whole generation of young men and the blighted lives of the women, mothers, sisters, sweethearts, wives, left behind. Kenneth's own father was one of the millions who had suffered in the fields of France and Flanders and the T.V. plays, produced and acted with great sensitivity, brought home to Kenneth the horror and futility of it all.

The music he chose was a score that had been brought to his attention by Michael Somes, Poulenc's setting of the Gloria from the Catholic Mass. In the T.V. series – and, of course, from other sources – Kenneth had been moved by the way in which the thousands of young volunteers had marched off to their bloody fate imbued with national pride and patriotism, wooed with jingoistic songs about King and Country, and he thought Poulenc's joyous music celebrating the glory and omnipotence of God would make an ironic counterpoint to the ghastly reality of war. But Frederick Ashton had also expressed some interest in the score and so Kenneth waited until Ashton had decided that he would not be making use of it as a ballet.

In choosing a designer, Kenneth once more repeated the process of looking at the work of the young artists of the Slade School. When he arrived there, the theatre class was closed so he went into the sculpture section and was very taken with the work of a young graduate, Andy Klunder, whom he commissioned to design the ballet which was to be called, simply, *Gloria*, after the title of the score.

Kenneth wanted his dancers to appear from, as it were, the no-man's-land of the battlefields or, perhaps, from the unseen realms of death; their entrance, therefore, was devised from behind a slope, or ramp, so that they appeared over the top, both as soldiers emerging from the trenches and as spirits from their graves. The slope was surmounted by a simple, angled framework which, in an abstract way, gave the impression of the blasted landscape of the battlefield. The costumes Klunder designed were coarsely-textured one-piece leotards for the men, in khaki and field-grey, stained with what looked like patches of mud and blood, and they wore hats reminiscent of the British steel helmet of the period. The women were also in textured all-over costumes with floating, rag-like skirts and close-fitting skull-cap wigs-cum-hats. Their pale make-up and the silvery-grey of the costumes made them look like ghostly wraiths.

The score itself is divided into six sections, some fast, some slow, some elegiac, some exultant. Kenneth set the dances for a central trio, two men and a woman, used for *pas de trois* and *pas de deux* with the odd man – lover? husband? brother? – given some fierce solos. They are supported by a quartet, a woman with three men, and a corps de ballet. While the main dances occur the corps frequently stand, sit or lie on the slope in attitudes that range from soldiers on guard to exhausted relaxation after battle to the arbitrary placing of crumpled corpses.

The lovely soprano solo *Domine Deus* provides the main *pas de deux*, one of the most lyrical and graceful duets that Kenneth has ever created, while the *Domine Fili Unigenite* is an exuberant *pas de quatre* in which the three men throw the woman around with joyous abandon, finally flinging her off-stage where she is caught, unseen, in the wings. *The Miserere Nobis* is a *pas de trois* involving the sort of convoluted, sculptural lifts, holds and poses that Kenneth had been developing in his most recent choreography. The big male solo begins with the dancer erupting over the rim of the ramp as if blasted by an exploding shell and its generally angry movement includes an accusatory finger pointed at the audience. During the final, long

Amen the dancers slowly walk back over the slope, into the past, into their graves, leaving the solitary male dancer to peer down after them; then he stands upright, silhouetted on the rim, before dropping backwards into the abyss.

Gloria was given its first performance at Covent Garden on March 12, 1980, with Jennifer Penney, Wayne Eagling and Julian Hosking as the leading trio (Eagling also taking the big male solos) and Wendy Ellis, Antony Dowson, Ross MacGibbon and Ashley Page in the fast *pas de quatre*. The ballet received tumultuous applause from the audience (the fact that the programme requested no applause during the performance possibly added to the intensity with which the audience released its pent-up emotion) and, subsequently, glowing notices from the critics.

The critic of the *Financial Times* wrote: 'Death and the after-life has been an inspiration for Kenneth MacMillan's choreography since the early *Journey* which he made for American Ballet Theatre over twenty years ago. Two major works of his maturity *Das Lied von der Erde* (*Song of the Earth*) and *Requiem*, have shown how potent is the response which this theme excites in his choreography. Now, in a setting of the Poulenc *Gloria*, MacMillan returns to this same subject, to magnificent effect. . . . The ballet's progress is a contemplation of lost hopes, lost joys, lost selves. And as so often with MacMillan, the evocation of the past . . . is a matter of fixing feeling and attitudes rather than of a superficial naturalism. . . . Everywhere MacMillan finds dance imagery that matches both the gravity and the happier aspirations of his score, suggesting that his ghosts survey what was, and what might have been, with some dispassion.'

The Times critic found himself a little confused by 'the contrast between words and deeds', meaning the difference between the score and the subject-matter of the ballet, but went on to say: 'Altogether, this is the most imaginative and individual choreography Mac-Millan has made for the Royal Ballet for quite a time, matching in atmosphere and intensity his recent works for Stuttgart and Paris, although I fear some will find it resembles them also in being far from easy to comprehend.'

Most other critics found Kenneth's intention perfectly easy to comprehend, however. The *Sunday Times* critic said: '*Gloria* moves us through the simplicity, the starkness, the beauty of its choreography; through the music; through the conviction of the dancers, and through the economy and aptness of the designs.' He also thought: 'In performance the contrast (between score and theme) proves astonishingly successful.'

The Editor of the specialist magazine *Dancing Times* (the publication that had first revealed to Kenneth the idea, the possibility, of ballet as a career) referring to Kenneth's use of the score, wrote: 'The choice is at once surprising and obvious. MacMillan's intention, surely, was to provoke a profound emotional shock by depicting one of humanity's most awful acts of carnage against the section of the Mass which glorifies the God in which it believes. The choreography and the music are totally at one, even though the sentiments are so different, and I confess the shock tactics did worry me; difficult, though, not to be carried by it while experiencing the actual perform-ance, especially when the dancers were responding so marvellously to the choreographer's intent. There is no moment when you do not feel that the action is absolutely right, that the statements being made are vivid, sensitive, angry and utterly sincere.'

The reviewer in the specialist publication *Set to Music* got to the heart of the matter when he wrote: 'Kenneth MacMillan's *Gloria* makes visible the ache in the heart and the grief in the soul expressed by so many of the poets, novelists and composers who have been moved by compassion for the youth in the carnage of the Great War. His evocation of the pity and the waste and the loveliness of youth despatched by the generation above them to premature extinction is the more powerful for being set to Poulenc's boundlessly confident version of the Gloria. The faith-filled music, eloquent in its recog-nition of man's dependence on God, provides powerful counterpoint for the choreographer's stark portrayal of the pitifulness of human vulnerability. The grandeur of God and the blight man was born for.'

Several critics thought that *Gloria* was able to stand comparison with *Song of the Earth* and *Requiem*, and indeed these three great vocal scores seem to have inspired Kenneth to some of his most beautiful and enduring choreography.

In the same programme as *Gloria* was a revival of *The Four Seasons*. Kenneth had made large cuts in the prologue, using fewer dancers and setting a more classically-based introduction to the main dances. The set was dispensed with altogether and Deborah (using her unmarried name of Williams) had designed simple costumes with dappled designs appropriately coloured for each season. Re-designed with a minimum of expenditure the ballet used the greyish textured backcloth from *Concerto* which was really not very suitable and the performance it was given – as several critics commented – was lacklustre and looked under-rehearsed. This is a ballet which, it seems, has still not reached its full potential as a company display piece; it requires a properly co-ordinated setting and costumes, and a virtuoso cast rigorously rehearsed.

*

With the success of *Gloria* behind him Kenneth felt free to concentrate on *Isadora*, still one year away. One evening in March, just after the premiere of *Gloria*, Richard Rodney Bennett played to Kenneth the rehearsal tape he had made of the piano score of *Isadora*. So that Kenneth should have as much intimation as possible about the orchestration, Richard had arranged the score for two pianos which he played with Susan Bradshaw, and he accompanied this first listening session with a comprehensive – and frequently funny – explanation of the intended orchestration, pointing out links between major characters and themes, and motifs that appeared and reappeared in new guises at significant moments during the action. Kenneth was immensely pleased with the score and very impressed with the way that Richard had integrated pastiche elements – imitations of music by Liszt, Chopin, Brahms and others that Isadora had used – with his own compositional style. There was also some pastiche ragtime and jazz as well as what Richard called 'early skyscraper music' for those sections of the ballet set in late Edwardian times and the twenties.

When Kenneth had decided to do the ballet he thought it would be a gracious way of paying tribute to Ashton if he were to invite the Royal Ballet's founder-choreographer to create Isadora's own solos within the ballet. Ashton was interested in the idea and touched by the compliment but declined when he knew the solos would be performed to pastiche music and not the actual pieces that Isadora had used.

On April 29, 1980, *My Brother, My Sisters* was given its first performance by the Royal Ballet with Wayne Eagling as the Brother, Jennifer Penney as the first Sister, Lesley Collier as the second Sister, Sandra Conley as the third Sister, Genesia Rosato as the fourth Sister, Deidre Eyden as the fifth Sister and Julian Hosking as He. Comparisons with the Stuttgart Ballet performances were inevitable, and while Wayne Eagling was commended for the physical abandon with which he attacked the role of the Brother, practically no male dancer on earth could be expected to equal the gymnastic feats and the sense of emotional ferocity achieved by Richard Cragun upon whose amazing technical prowess the part was built. But both Jennifer Penney and Lesley Collier were praised for their interpretations of the malevolent sister and her victim, and the ballet itself acclaimed as an immensely powerful addition to the repertoire.

On May 15, 1980, Kenneth received the Krug Award for Excellence at a grand white-tie-and-tails reception at the Banqueting House, Whitehall. The Krug Awards were devised by the famous champagne firm and given for outstanding achievements in the fields of science, medicine, sport and the arts. The award itself was designed by Salvador Dali and executed in gold; standing five or six inches high it looked like a scallop shell supported on a rococo scroll. While it was pleasant to receive recognition (and notwithstanding the celebrated men who received the awards) it was difficult not to look upon the occasion as a sales promotion exercise.

During this period Deborah had once more been looking at a number of houses in South London without success. Then, in April, she saw a large Victorian house ideally situated on the edge of Wandsworth Common. It stood in its own grounds, had a large garden at the back and plenty of space on several floors. It seemed perfect for their purposes except that it was in a poor state of repair and would need a considerable amount of renovation and alteration. Kenneth saw it and immediately liked it; an offer was made and the house was bought in May although it was another four months before the MacMillans were able to move in.

*

In June Kenneth created his first choreography for *Isadora* beginning, as always, with the central, most difficult *pas de deux*, the passionate nine-minute duet between Isadora and her most important lover, the famous theatre designer Edward Gordon Craig. Kenneth had had several conversations with Ashton – who had seen Isadora in his youth – about her style of dancing, but he was aware that to try and recreate Isadora's own steps and movements would be a mistake. For one thing Isadora's presentation of her dances would, today, seem impossibly corny if not ludicrous – just as the eye-rolling, declamatory style of Edwardian acting now appears rather comic. For example, when dancing her interpretation of Tchaikovsky's *Marche Slave* Isadora rushed about the stage chopping off heads and drinking goblets of blood! Instead, Kenneth aimed at establishing an impression of her style, its freedom from any classical restraint or, for that matter, the disciplined technique of modern dance that was slowly being formulated by other great women pioneers such as Martha Graham. But one thing that Ashton said led to Kenneth making a major innovative change in the ballet: 'At her performances,' Ashton said, 'Isadora talked as much as she danced.' On thinking this over Kenneth had the idea of introducing a greater amount of speech into the scenario; not only did it have a historical basis but it would also serve a useful function in establishing the *mise en scène* and explaining the motivation.

Kenneth telephoned Gillian and told her what he wanted. Gillian was due to leave for Los Angeles in a couple of weeks so she hastily re-examined the bibliography she had originally used for research for further additions to the text. The basis for it seemed to be in

Isadora's autobiography *My Life* and Gillian transcribed several of the passages directly; for all their (sometimes) unconscious humour and aesthetic incomprehensibility (Isadora was rarely able to express her feelings about her art with any clarity) they did reveal the passionate, wayward involvement with people and her profession that was the essence of Isadora's character.

The summer arrived, the Royal Ballet season at Covent Garden ended and there was an enforced hiatus in the progress of the choreography. While in Edinburgh the previous year Peter Wright had introduced Kenneth and Deborah to friends of his who enthused over the beauty of the Western Isles of Scotland. And so, instead of travelling half way round the world to Australia or California, Kenneth and family spent three weeks among the scenic serenity of the Isle of Arran. It was a simple, unsophisticated holiday, although they were impressed by the production of a new play by a young playwright that was put on in a local hall.

As well as introducing more text into the *Isadora* story Kenneth had also decided to split the title role, revealing the character through dance and the spoken word, a dancer and an actress, rather as he had used Brecht's division of Anna in *The Seven Deadly Sins*. The actress he chose to complement Merle Park's role was Mary Miller, whose stage career he had followed with some interest (she had worked extensively in America and could therefore manage the accent) and who, like Kenneth, had studied classical dance with Phyllis Adams in Gt. Yarmouth; Kenneth intended that there would be one episode when the acting Isadora would also dance. Kenneth also suggested that Mary might like to enlarge her spoken role even further and draw upon a wider bibliography than Gillian had used. Mary found relevant passages in *Your Isadora* by Francis Steegmuller; *Isadora* by Sewell Stokes; *Isadora's Russian Years* by Schneider; *Isadora's Russian Days* by Irma Duncan and A. McDougall, and *The Real Isadora* by Victor Seroff.

In September, when Kenneth resumed choreographing *Isadora*, the move was made to the new house with the attendant domestic disruption that such an operation entails. All was chaos: builders, plumbers – with winter approaching Deborah had decided that the first thing that had to be done was the installation of central heating – carpenters, plasterers, electricians, gasmen, telephone engineers, were in constant attendance for months on end and there were times when Kenneth, Deborah and Charlotte, living in the basement kitchen and surrounded by constant disorder and mess, wondered when it would ever be finished. It took more than two years. Gradually, with Kenneth hurrying off early in the morning to choreograph *Isadora*, throughout that winter of 1980/81, the basic alterations to the house were completed and a few rooms made habitable.

A leaking roof had to be reslated, which was an expensive business. The original house had nine bedrooms but only one bathroom; the alterations reduced the number of bedrooms to five and increased the bathrooms to three. Deborah had her studio, Kenneth his T.V. room-cum-study and Charlotte her own room. Enterprisingly, Deborah had reclaimed a short staircase from the nurses' quarters of a local hospital that was being demolished and installed it as a practical and decorative connection between the kitchen and the large dining room. She also made a start on redesigning and restocking the large garden. It all involved an enormous amount of work (Deborah, with the help of a friend, had dismantled the hospital staircase herself, watched by a group of tramps and derelicts who were squatting in the desolate remains of the building) but the end result was rewarding and the three MacMillans now have a home they all love and where they have enough room to entertain their many friends, including visitors from overseas. Kenneth's original present of the shi'-zu puppy, Sydney, had subsequently been joined by two cats, George and Ziggy; Ziggy was run over soon after the move to the new house but was replaced by another feline, Flora, and then – because Charlotte wanted a dog of her own – Molly, a Springer spaniel.

The choreographic progress of *Isadora* was plagued by problems: Merle Park was subject to illness and injury and David Wall, first casting for Edward Gordon Craig, also suffered from a foot injury which necessitated surgery and lengthy therapy; apart from the initial *pas de deux*, much of the subsequent development of the character was built upon Julian Hosking, second casting for the role.

In November, 1980, Kenneth spent three weeks in Stockholm mounting a production of *Manon* for the Royal Swedish Ballet. (He had been preceded by Monica Parker who spent a month in Stockholm preparing the groundwork for *Manon*.) The ballet was given its first performance on November 22 and was a tremendous success. Later, when the company included the work on a tour of Russia, the Moscow audience was so thrilled and excited by the ballet that they invaded the stage after the final curtain.

In London Kenneth was also kept busy rehearsing various casts in other works of his that were performed that season: *Manon*, *Mayerling*, *My Brother, My Sisters*, and *Gloria*. On December 7, 1980, at a ceremony at the Café Royal, Kenneth received the S.W.E.T. (Society of West End Theatres) Award (renamed the Olivier Awards in 1984) for *Gloria* as the outstanding ballet of that year. On January 27, 1981, Jennifer Penney received the *Standard* Award for her perform-

Kenneth working on the choreography of *Isadora*, with Merle
Park as Isadora Duncan and Derek Rencher as her millionaire
lover, Paris Singer, in the scene where they learn that Isadora's
two children have been drowned in a bizarre accident. The
agonised *pas de deux* consists of a series of falls, the partners
alternately collapsing to the ground. In performance the
sequence moved the critic of the *Financial Times* to write:
'There ensues a duet . . . so intense in grief, so intimate, that it
seems intrusive on our part to watch.' (*Clive Boursnell.*)

ances in *Manon* and *Gloria* as the outstanding contribution to dance for 1980.

It was not until mid-January, 1981, that Kenneth was able to resume regular rehearsalf for *Isadora* and they were often conducted with the absence of one or more major characters who were busy rehearsing the current repertoire. The first complete rehearsal 'run through' of the ballet did not take place until February 22. At that time Kenneth knew that his sister Betty was seriously ill; she was, in fact, suffering from cancer and her physical condition deteriorated rapidly. During March and April Kenneth made several visits to her in a hospice in Gt. Yarmouth and the final weeks when *Isadora*, one of the most technically elaborate works ever to be produced at Covent Garden, was finally being pieced together, were particularly harassing for him. Betty died on April 9.

During the final days of rehearsal there were several changes to *Isadora*: most important was the discovery that the electric motor which moved the circular gauze curtain which played an important part in Barry Kay's design (Isadora invariably performed in front of blue curtains which travelled everywhere with her) made an unacceptable noise, and it was also too slow. The stage crew tried everything to rectify the faults without success and it was finally decided to have the curtain pulled manually by two dancers dressed as porters. The video film of Isadora's car (which ran backwards into the Seine and drowned her children) did not work well; it was replaced by the projection of a newspaper clipping showing the recovery of the wrecked car and a headline. There were detailed changes to costumes and the abandonment of some decorative props; there were also a few last-minute minor cuts in the score. Twenty minutes before curtain-up on the first-night Royal gala premiere on April 30, 1981, to celebrate the Royal Ballet's first fifty years, Barry Kay was still spraying costumes to gain the effect he wanted!

More than any other ballet that Kenneth had created, *Isadora* divided critical opinion. It was interesting to see how several people instantly became authorities on Isadora herself, her life, her loves, her style of dancing – although, of course, most of them had never seen her.

The Times critic wrote: 'It would be unfair to blame MacMillan for trivialising Isadora Duncan's life. She began that process when she wrote a lurid, often fictional autobiography, responding to a publisher's suggestion that the more sensational it was the better it would sell. MacMillan and his librettist, Gillian Freeman, have merely extended the process their subject began. What MacMillan must answer for is scrubbing out any trace of the greatness as an

Last minute discussions: Kenneth did not hear the full orchestral score for *Isadora* until a day or so before the first performance. *Above*: with Richard Rodney Bennett, the composer, and Barry Wordsworth, the conductor. (*Clive Boursnell*.)

Isadora is, to date, the most ambitious and the most technically elaborate ballet to be staged at the Royal Opera House. The photograph shows the final tableau when Isadora, danced by Merle Park, meets her bizarre death in the Bugatti. (*Catherine Ashmore*.)

artist that transfigured her banal adventures and philosophy. To make a ballet about a real dancer without giving an impression, as authentic as might be, of how she danced seems to me unforgiveable.'

The *Financial Times* reviewer found it more compelling: 'MacMillan's procedures are, as I have suggested, cinematic. Gillian Freeman's scenario, and her text selected from Duncan's writings and orations, guide the narrative from one cataclysm to the next. MacMillan uses every source open to him in the theatre, from limpid or urgent evocations of Duncan's dances to tormented and involuted duets, from big set-pieces – the rain-washed funeral of Duncan's children is a stunning scene – to actors in the auditorium vilifying Isadora on her last American tour. I can but salute MacMillan's daring, the dramatic playing of the entire cast, and hail in particular the beautiful, potent interpretations of Merle Park and Mary Miller, not two Isadoras but one, and absolutely compelling.'

The *Guardian* critic also liked Kenneth's evocation of Isadora's dancing: 'There is a touching gaucherie and youthfulness about her first recitals in London. After the deaths of her children there are beautiful mourning dances. And her pupils in Russia . . . show something of the kind of dance associated with Duncan.'

The *Sunday Times* critic also realised that Kenneth had set out to prove that the big, full-length ballet could utilise every theatrical device: 'Never before has British ballet seen or done anything like Kenneth MacMillan's *Isadora*. It is brave and it is audacious. It seems to me, after one exhausting viewing, that the doubling of the role, though dramatically convenient, dissipates the focus. Park dances MacMillan's choreography barefoot and beautifully – and MacMillan's achievement in suggesting the Duncan style of dance, in all its moods from grief to ecstasy, is magnificent.'

The *Sunday Telegraph* reviewer considered the ballet to be splendid theatre: 'He (MacMillan) attempts to convey not only what Isadora's dance might have been like but to tell the story of her life in terms of her own dance style. The results are altogether exhilarating. MacMillan knows his dancers and the ballet shows off a whole range of exciting talent. It is not only a fresh challenge for Merle Park herself, on stage for most of the evening, always convincing and making a quite different language very much her own, but also almost equally a challenge for the longish list of lovers. The high points of tragedy, the death of Isadora's children, the nightmare of her fears about them, the poignancy of the actual death, are handled with a dramatic bravura that shows MacMillan as a sure master of theatre. The moments of anguish and pathos were just as effective, too. Above all *Isadora* is *theatre*. It has to be seen.'

Critics were also divided about the success of Barry Kay's designs and Richard Rodney Bennett's score. '. . . the many highlights of Barry Kay's splendid scenic efffects, even if his costumes are occasionally questionable' (*The Times*). 'Barry Kay's sets are sparse, his clothes fabulous' (The *Guardian*). 'Barry Kay's decor, with its drab brick walls, enormous curtain-runner and wishy-washy curtains, were all lacking in the harmony and fantasy demanded by the theme' (The *Daily Telegraph*). 'Barry Kay's design, a permanent set with a huge curtain on a circular track to aid the swift "dissolves' of the action, assist this fluidity of presentation' (The *Financial Times*). 'Richard Rodney Bennett's score kept trying to imitate, without much success, the music of Isadora's period' (The *Daily Telegraph*). 'Bennett has written clever imitations of many styles for the heroine's dances: Brahms, Liszt, Chopin, even Joplin. But the pastiche manner spills over into other episodes too. His sea music, for instance, is like Henze with a dash of Britten. Consequently, although agreeable enough, the music never develops a character of its own' (*The Times*). 'Richard Rodney Bennett's theatrically vivid score encompasses both pastiche piano music for Duncan's solos and clearly personal writing for the main text of her life' (The *Financial Times*).

The most perceptive assessment of the ballet, and Kenneth's intentions, came from the review in *The Times Educational Supplement*: 'What astonishes me, in the outrage that has greeted this work, is that no one seems to recognise the strategic significance of what MacMillan is about. He is insisting that classical ballet can and should be used for contemporary dramatic purpose. This means junking many structural conventions to drag the established evening-length form, resisting, into the twenty-first century. Since 1965, *Romeo and Juliet*, *Anastasia*, *Manon*, *Mayerling* and *Isadora* have struggled to this end, *Isadora* most of all. The ballet's importance, therefore, far outweighs its faults.'

But the most cogent comment of all came from Robert Cohan, the distinguished director of the London Contemporary Dance Theatre. Talking to Kenneth after the premiere of *Isadora* he remarked that the ballet was in the wrong theatre: if it had been produced as a commercial venture in London's West End, he said, it would have run for years.

25

A lot of television

At the dress rehearsal of *Isadora* it had been apparent that the ballet
was too long and so, following the first season, Kenneth considered
how it could be cut – particularly in view of the company's forthcoming tour of the United States and Canada where *Isadora* was
scheduled to be given in New York, Toronto and Washington, D.C.
Initially, the only excision in the first act was Isadora's second solo
during the scene depicting her first performance in London, but later
in the year Kenneth also cut the whole of the opening scene set in
Liverpool Street station. In the longer second act there were several
cuts: the whole of the scene with Isadora and her pianist, André
Caplet, was cut. (This was a rather comic episode, based on fact of
course, but which served as a lighter moment among the many
melodramatic or tragic ones, in which Isadora's rich industrialist
lover, Paris Singer, found Isadora seducing her accompanist under
the grand piano.) A *pas de deux* with Singer, intended to reveal their
deteriorating relationship, was also heavily cut. One of two scenes
set in the St. Petersburg railway station was cut. Finally, the male
solos around Isadora's bed during the birth of her third child were
carefully pruned. In all, the running time of the ballet was reduced
by nearly twenty minutes. There was some difficulty in making the
music cuts because Richard Rodney Bennett was still living in New
York; the problem was overcome by Henry Roche, one of the
on-stage pianists in the production, carrying out the musical
alterations over the transatlantic telephone.

In May, 1981, Kenneth went to Manchester to take part in a
television film, something of an experiment devised by the film and
television director, Jack Gold, who wanted to film a choreographer
at work – the actual process of creating a ballet. Tanya Bruce
Lockhart, who had been associated with London Weekend Television's award-winning documentary about the making of *Mayerling*,
had suggested Kenneth. In order to make the act of creativity as
spontaneous as possible Kenneth was not permitted to choose the
music until the day rehearsals began, but he had been able to engage
two dancers with whom he had worked very successfully before,
Birgit Keil and Vladimir Klos, from the Stuttgart Ballet.

Of necessity the works were short but to provide a contrast
Kenneth chose the first movement of Chopin's Third Piano Sonata
and George Gershwin's Three Preludes, with Royal Ballet pianist

Philip Gammon as accompanist, both in rehearsal and the actual performance. The theme of the Chopin-based *pas de deux* was that of Orpheus, forbidden to look at his wife Eurydice, on pain of her return to Hades. (Kenneth was already concerned with the subject because he was due to choreograph Stravinsky's score for Orpheus the following year.) The Gershwin *pas de deux* was more abstract but even so it was an amorous – not to say sexy – encounter.

Jack Gold filmed Kenneth working with his dancers, often interrupting to ask the sort of questions that might occur to an uninitiated viewer puzzled by the conventions of ballet: 'Why are you doing that? What does that step mean?' For Kenneth, used to dancers doing whatever he asked of them without questioning the reasoning behind it, it was a new, rather disconcerting experience but, as the filmed results showed, he was able to articulate his motivation fluently and the final result, which ended with a performance of the finished works, proved a fascinating insight into the choreographic creative process. Jack Gold allowed Kenneth to have considerable control over the finished product, participating in the cutting and editing which was, for Kenneth, so long interested in the technical side of film-making, an equally absorbing process. The film, entitled *A Lot of Happiness* (a quote from one of Kenneth's exhortations to his dancers), was transmitted by I.T.V. on December 15, 1981, and subsequently won one of the prestigious Emmy Awards in America. It had been intended that *Isadora*, which had been filmed in performance on October 26 by Granada, should have been transmitted that same evening, thus making a mini-festival of MacMillan works, but political events in Poland preempted by another programme, dealing with the Solidarity movement, arranged for transmission early in 1982. *Isadora* was postponed and the Polish subject substituted because of its immediate topicality.

The Royal Ballet began its North American tour in New York at the end of June, 1981, and *Isadora* had its American premiere there on June 24. In the main the New York critics did not like the ballet – one could sense, in several of the reviews, a feeling that Isadora Duncan was an American possession who had been appropriated by the British – but audiences responded enthusiastically to the drama of the production and the leading artists were given a tremendous reception.

In Toronto the critics were much more responsive and the audiences equally so, as indeed they were when the ballet was presented in Washington, D.C. After the conclusion of the tour – the repertoire also included *Gloria* which received great acclaim, especially in Toronto – Kenneth, Deborah and Charlotte travelled West again to spend a much needed holiday with Herbert Ross and Nora Kaye at their luxurious beach-house at Malibu. While they were there Charlotte celebrated her eighth birthday and Nora Kaye organised a real Hollywood party for her, a beach barbecue attended by several celebrities from the film colony as well as Mikhail Baryshnikov.

Kenneth and family began their return from Los Angeles by train, taking the famous Santa Fé Chief across the Rockies to Chicago, then continuing across the great mid-Western plains to New York, before flying back across the Atlantic.

*

After the autumn season had begun at Covent Garden (with *Isadora*) Kenneth flew back to New York to start rehearsals with Baryshnikov who had recently been appointed Artistic Director of American Ballet Theatre and who had asked Kenneth to do a ballet for him. Kenneth had suggested using a score by Gordon Crosse called *Wild Boy*, inspired by François Truffaut's film *Wild Child*, the theme of both film and ballet being based on one of those archetypal figures that have recurred throughout history, the human who has grown up in the wild in the company of animals, and his subsequent reaction to, and effect upon, sophisticated urban society.

Because of the company's various commitments Kenneth was not able to rehearse the new ballet continuously; after two or three weeks in New York he returned again to London then travelled to New York again a short while before the ballet's premiere at the Kennedy Center in Washington, D.C. on December 14, 1981.

Wild Boy had a jungly decor by Oliver Smith and costumes by Willa Kim – about which Kenneth was less than enthusiastic, remarking that they were 'not very helpful' to his conception of the ballet. The American critics – rarely on the same wavelength as Kenneth – were decidedly lukewarm about the work although the *New York Times* critic, who saw it both in Washington and New York, reviewed the ballet appreciatively. Following the Washington first night she wrote: 'Kenneth MacMillan's *The Wild Boy* . . . is a highly provocative ballet that will send tongues wagging for the wrong reason. . . . Sex is the leitmotif of the ballet but not its subject. There has been too much simulated coupling in ballet for anyone to become exercised over the few such moments in *The Wild Boy*. The dramatic jolt Mr. MacMillan achieves, then, comes from the occasional touches of verismo he drops like a bomb into his own stylised context. . . . As it turns out, the ballet is not so much the story of the wild boy himself, but of his effect upon others – what natural man instinctively reveals about socialized man. The cards are admittedly stacked. Civilised man in here embodied by two brutish louts who carry on with folk-flavored movements and flexed feet like two

Russian muzhiks. A woman, Miss Makarova, completes this coarse trio, with Kevin McKenzie identified as her husband and Robert la Fosse as his friend. When they capture the wild boy, Mr. Baryshnikov, the contrast between his pure state in nature and their own violence is inevitable. Contaminated by contact with them – including his sexual awakening with the wife – the boy is unable to return to his uncorrupted state, obviously preferable to that of the villagers.

'Yet the dramatic point about *The Wild Boy* is the revelation about the trio. The initial imagery is of a ménage à trois with the wife tossed – shared – by the two men. Yet it takes the wild boy to disclose the true passions involved, and here is the surprise. In a cleverly choreographed bit of timing the boy grabs the men's hair and smacks their faces together. They collide into a real and lengthy kiss on the lips .. Mr. Baryshnikov danced with fantastic intensity and Mr. McKenzie and Mr. La Fosse had a marvellous impact in their own performance. *The Wild Boy* is more a sketch than a finished work, but its very rawnness is what makes it stimulating.'

The critic was right. Kenneth had not been able to work out fully the ballet as he would have wished and the way in which it had been created in fits and starts was mainly responsible, but from long experience he was resigned to several of the American critics seizing upon the ballet's few moments of sexuality as its *raison d'être* (as the *New York Times* critic had prophesised), ignoring any deeper meaning in its theme of the culture shock between primitive innocence and sophisticated decadence.

On February 23, 1982, Granada TV transmitted its postponed tele-recording of *Isadora*, with the original cast. It was very well received by the television critics. It was generally felt that the work, with its spoken narrative – sometimes adapted as voice-over the danced scenes – was rather better suited to the medium than many ballets and the Director, Derek Bailey, made telling use of close-ups throughout the performance, particularly the last frozen frame of Isadora's face at the moment of her death in the Bugatti.

At this time Kenneth was concerned with ideas for his new work for Sadler's Wells Royal Ballet. He had also been approached by Peter Schaufuss, one of the world's great virtuoso male dancers, to create a showpiece *pas de deux* for him and the celebrated Italian ballerina Elisabetta Terabust, with whom he had established a renowned partnership, appearing as guest artists with various international companies. Schaufuss and Terabust had previously asked Kenneth if they might 'annexe' his comic Stravinsky *pas de deux*, *Side Show*, originally created for Nureyev and Seymour in 1972, and had danced it with great success as a gala piece, so Kenneth was more than delighted to devise something new for them.

The music that Kenneth selected was the first movement from Verdi's String Quartet in E Minor (he had once considered it as an 'extension score' when he was creating *The Four Seasons*). Rehearsals progressed at a studio at The Place, St. Pancras, home of the London Contemporary Dance Theatre. In making the piece Kenneth took full advantage of Schaufuss's tremendous technical virtuosity although there was also considerable lyricism in the choreography.

The first performance of the *pas de deux*, called *Verdi Variations*, took place in the Italian town of Reggio Amelia on March 1, 1982, at a gala given by Aterballeto – an acronymic title made from Associazione Teatri Emilia-Romagna – a dance company serving several theatres in that region and with which Schaufuss and Terabust often appeared.

The Times critic, present at the premiere, wrote: 'Terabust . . . has never looked better than she does in her solos, full of pretty little steps, and in the many off-balance poses of the adagio sections. Schaufuss, besides partnering her with unfailing strength and friendly attentiveness, tackles such wildly whirling leaps in his solos that there is no defining or even describing them; yet the most prodigiously abandoned moments are all carried off with astonishing accuracy.'

Simultaneously with *Verdi Variations* Kenneth had been working on his new ballet for Sadler's Wells Royal Ballet. It began with a score, *Noctuaries*, by Richard Rodney Bennett which Kenneth – so pleased with the music for *Isadora* – had commissioned. It was concerned with a metamorphosis of both style and mood, beginning in happy vein, almost ragtime, but developing into something darker, even tragic, in feeling. But the more Kenneth progressed with the choreography the more he felt it was not developing as it should. With very little time to spare, he decided to abandon the ballet; instead, he choreographed the second movement of the Verdi String Quartet for two couples. This second movement, in contrast to the pyrotechnics of the first, was much more lyrical – even romantic – in feeling for its series of double duets, with changes of partners, the dance patterns shifting and altering focus, sometimes in unison, sometimes in a mirror-image of each other.

Barry Wordsworth (who had been entrusted with conducting the first performances of *Isadora* and who was then resident conductor with the Sadler's Wells Royal Ballet) made an arrangement of the Verdi score for string orchestra and Deborah designed the costumes, body tights for the men, simple dresses for the women, in subdued colours in all-over patterns like the end-papers of a book.

During the making of *Quartet*, as the new ballet was titled, Phyllis Adams, Kenneth's first ballet teacher who had almost taken the place of his mother, died in Gt. Yarmouth on February 17. Kenneth, of course, was deeply saddened at the news; Miss Adams had been one of his lifelong fans, always travelling down to London to see Kenneth's new works. He had dedicated *Isadora* to her and had had the satisfaction of knowing she had lived long enough to see it. With two hundred or so other people he attended her funeral in Gt. Yarmouth.

Quartet was given its premiere at Sadler's Wells Theatre on March 2, 1982, and apart from the original *pas de deux* for Schaufuss and Terabust, was the most abstract pure-dance work that Kenneth had created for a long time. Most critics were aware that Kenneth intended to complete the ballet by choreographing the final movement and so considered it somewhat as a 'work in progress'.

The *Financial Times* critic wrote, briefly: 'MacMillan's four dancers – Galina Samsova and Desmond Kelly, Marion Tait and Carl Myers – are displayed in lyric encounters that suggest shifts in relationship, sorrows as well as joys. There seem traces of a theme, but more important is the eloquence of the performers and the generous pulse of the dances.' The *Daily Telegraph* critic thought that 'This piece had the great advantage of showing MacMillan doing what suits him best – the creation of *pas de deux* and also from the fact that it had two splendid ballerinas, Galina Samsova and Marion Tait For much of the time the two pairs of dancers moved in unison but sometimes they diverged; and Samsova and Tait clearly revelled in the chance of moving through its patterns of classical steps showing certain changes of mood adapted to changes in the music.' The *Observer* critic also liked the work: 'To the second movement of Verdi's only string quartet (now orchestrated by Barry Wordsworth) two couples . . . move in a series of confrontations which flow lyrically and reach moments of ecstasy in high melting lifts. If any emotional theme was intended it was not very clear but as a work in progress it was most agreeable and beautifully done.'

The *Sunday Times* reviewer also thought the ballet was good as far as it went but reserved judgement until the ballet was complete: 'It is good to see MacMillan inventing pure dance again,' he wrote, 'and its felicities will be best considered when his full setting of this music reaches the stage.'

Ten days later, on March 13, there was another television transmission of one of Kenneth's full-length ballets. This time it was *Manon*, with Jennifer Penney, Anthony Dowell and David Wall in the three leading roles, which had been recorded by BBC, TV at a performance of the ballet given at Covent Garden on January 19. This recording was one of the series produced by a newly-formed company in association with the Royal Opera House and made available to the public as a video cassette. The television critics praised it highly. *The Times* critic referred to it as '. . . one of the masterpieces of this magnificent company', adding that the ballet presented '. . . a treat of an evening'. In a preview of the programme the critic said that Kenneth was '. . . as finely tuned to Abbé Prevost's sensual tale as Puccini and Massenet were . . .' The *Observer* critic was most enthusiastic: '. . . let me record my, and I hope your, gratitude for *Manon*, the Kenneth MacMillan ballet transmitted from Covent Garden. Lately I have spent quite a lot of time hailing MacMillan as a man of genius and won't pile the bouquets any higher here, but it still needs to be said that Jennifer Penney and Anthony Dowell in the first *pas de deux* were enough to make you hope that Manon would see sense and stick with De Grieux, instead of screwing everything up and being shipped off to croak in Louisiana.'

The following month *Quartet* was given its first performance in the complete three-movement form at a Royal gala in Bristol on April 7, 1982. The first movement was danced by Sherilyn Kennedy and David Ashmole – with his role somewhat cut down from the extreme virtuosity created for Schaufuss, and consequently lacking the same impact – and the finale began with a fast, bright *pas de deux* for Sandra Madgwick and Roland Price with all the dancers conjoining for the last section. Most of the critics were not over-impressed with the work although their reactions were, to some extent, affected by having seen the ballet piecemeal.

Before the premiere of the completed *Quartet* Kenneth had begun work on his new ballet for Covent Garden. There was to be a programme celebrating Stravinsky's centenary and the new work was to be the centrepiece of an all-Stravinsky programme, beginning with Mikhail Fokine's *Firebird* and ending with Bronislava Nijinska's *Les Noces*. The score that Kenneth had chosen (there was, of course, practically nothing in the Stravinsky canon that had not already been used for a ballet) was *Orpheus*, written in 1947 in close collaboration with Balanchine and first produced the following year. The music represents Stravinsky in typically cerebral vein, nothing so colourful as *Firebird* or *Petrouchka*, so rhythmically incisive as *Les Noces*, so lyrical as *Apollo* or so violent as *Rite of Spring* – although practically all those elements are present in the Orphean legend.

Kenneth's approach was a stylised one, with a narrative addition of his own: after Orpheus's descent to Hades in search of Eurydice, and their rapturous, fatal gaze upon one another, he introduced an Angel of Light and a Dark Angel who struggle for the possession of Orpheus's soul. The Dark Angel triumphs over the hero's body but the Angel of Light retrieves Orpheus's lyre which, in turn, is taken by an enigmatic figure of Apollo. In the apotheosis Eurydice's original descent into Hades is complemented by the lovers' ascent to Elysium while Apollo plucks the lyre.

Nicholas Georgiadis designed a spectacularly beautiful set (for which he was subsequently given the *Standard* Award for the outstanding contribution to dance for 1982). Eurydice's coffin was lowered beneath the stage, suspended by gilded ropes and surrounded by flickering candles. Orpheus's descent to the underworld was by way of a series of golden ladders; the lovers' apotheosis was achieved via a glittering chainmail cylinder suspended from golden arms. The very striking costumes and masks were in black, gold, grey and shades of red.

Kenneth had asked for Peter Schaufuss as a guest star for the role of Orpheus and once again he exploited his dancer's astonishing technique to tremendous effect, particularly in the opening solo where Orpheus laments the loss of his wife. With Jennifer Penney as Eurydice, the central *pas de deux*, when the lovers are reunited, was conceived in Kenneth's most rapturously ecstatic, convoluted manner, using Penney's tremendous plasticity to full advantage. Apollo's role was the most stylised in the ballet with the sliding, jerky, mechanical movements of an automaton. This rather tricksy idea of Kenneth's confused and annoyed a number of critics, but Kenneth had done it deliberately to link the legendary god with the popular folk-heroes of our own time. As he subsequently remarked, 'Most of today's pop-heroes are automatons,' and the current craze for robotics was a further symbolic connection.

Orpheus was given its first performance at the Royal Opera House on June 11, 1982, and was fairly coolly received by the critics. The critic of the *Financial Times*, after observing that Stravinsky's 'austerity of means' had governed Kenneth's choreographic approach to the material, wrote: ' . . . the dancing for Orpheus and Eurydice stresses linear purity that, like the music, seeks control rather than emotional extravagance, albeit Orpheus' initial solo, when he has watched Eurydice sink into Hades, explodes into a whirlwind of steps that marvellously convey his desolation and anguish. For the two Angels who struggle for Orpheus' soul . . . MacMillan has made dances of extreme sculptural convolution as they lock in combat and suddenly – in a stunning theatrical coup – we see Orpheus and the Dark Angel skied high on a golden ladder . . . The music's restraint is never more potent, and MacMillan's response never more persuasive, than in the succeeding solo for Eurydice . . . and in her duet with the blindfolded Orpheus its economy of expression quite as subtle as that of the music . . . In the role of Orpheus MacMillan's use of Peter Schaufuss' virtuosity is never gratuitous; the dance feeds from his bravura but also enhances them, and emotion is vivid in the tearing and tormented leaps he performs as in the sustaining dignity of his style. Jennifer Penney is at her most fluent as Eurydice; Wayne Eagling's aggressive menace as the Dark Angel, the gentler strength of Ashley Page as the Angel of Light and the ferocity of the Furies are very fine.'

The reviewer in the *Daily Telegraph* thought that Kenneth had '. . . tackled the ancient myth . . . in the chic style favoured by Diaghilev in his final years. The result was a rather cerebral piece, ignoring all the profound, symbolic aspects of the myth, and concentrating on striking visual effects aided by the glittering decor of Nicholas Georgiadis. But there were certain sections in which MacMillan showed skill in devising remarkably difficult steps for the guest artist, Peter Schaufuss . . .' The *Sunday Times* critic, mentioning the '. . . eveness and astringency' of the score went on to say that it was '. . . mirrored by MacMillan in choreography of disappointing blandness', although he conceded that 'MacMillan makes good use of Schaufuss's virtuoso technique.' The *Sunday Telegraph* critic, however, found the ballet to be '. . . as full of surprises as anything (MacMillan) has done', and, after referring (as did almost every critic) to Schaufuss's tremendous virtuosity, added that the struggle between the two angels was done with such '. . . choreographic bravura, and so well danced, that they make a highpoint in this fascinating ballet'. He concluded by saying: 'In spite of this slightly underpowered emotion in the central couple, the ballet was mesmerising. The spare, cerebral music prevents it, perhaps, from being immediately popular. But this is a work we shall learn to savour as repeated viewings reveal its rich complexity.' The reviewer was too sanguine in his expectation of 'repeated viewings'; at the time of writing it does not appear as if the work will be revived.

*

During June and the beginning of July Kenneth engaged in a new venture. It was on a small scale but, for him, it was an important step in his career and a portent of bigger things to come: he began directing rehearsals of two one-act plays by Ionescu, *The Chairs* and *The Lesson*, produced in a pub-theatre, *The New Inn* at Ealing.

Kenneth had long wanted to expand his directorial experience into the 'straight' theatre; fortuitously, Keith Gray, the Stage Manager for the Royal Ballet at Covent Garden, had been associated with a number of productions at the small Ealing theatre and suggested that Kenneth might like to make his directorial debut in the legitimate theatre there, which he was very pleased to do. His cast of three was Peter Baldwin, Mary Miller and Harriet Thorpe. The productions which opened on July 17, 1982, were, in the main, well reviewed (critics were curious, of course, to see how this celebrated choreographer approached his material) but for Kenneth by far the most important part of the exercise had been the experience of directing actors. It was very different from what he had been used to for the past thirty odd years: whereas, while creating choreography, dancers would carry out his instructions or suggestions without question, the actors, of course, had their own interpretive contribution to make, querying the motivation for a particular move, look or gesture, suggesting a pause or a change of pace; it was a much more collaborative effort than creating steps. All in all, Kenneth found it immensely interesting and instructive – it certainly did not put him off the idea of directing more theatre.

A week or two later, at the end of the Royal Ballet season at Covent Garden, Kenneth and family travelled to Italy with the company for a short season which consisted of a triple bill and *Romeo and Juliet* which was performed with great success at the beautiful Fenice Theatre in Venice and then in the open air at the Caracalla Baths in Rome.

After the summer holidays the new ballet season at Covent Garden began with a revival of *Mayerling* during which a new young dancer, Alessandra Ferri, made her debut as Mary Vetsera. Ferri's qualities as a dramatic dancer had been brought to Kenneth's attention by one of her teachers at the Royal Ballet School, Julia Farron (who had, of course, been a distinguished dancer herself in the days of the Sadler's Wells Ballet). Kenneth was immediately struck with Ferri's potential and cast her as Vetsera while she was still in the corps de ballet. His confidence in her powers was rewarded with a performance that many critics called sensational: on that evening a new star was born and Kenneth had discovered a dancer to inspire him, just as he had discovered Lynn Seymour as his Muse back in 1960.

On November 14, 1982, Granada Television transmitted a performance of *Gloria* which had been recorded the previous June when the Royal Ballet had had a short season in Manchester. Unlike the T.V. recording of *Isadora*, *Gloria* did not have the same impact on the small screen as in the theatre, but much of its sad, haunting beauty was apparent, particularly in the long, lyrical duet for Jennifer Penney and Julian Hosking to the *Domine Deus*. This transmission of *Gloria* brought to a close a year of Kenneth's career which had been especially notable for the televising of his work, from the specially created duets of *A Lot of Happiness* to the full length *Isadora* by Granada TV and *Manon* by BBC, TV. And the Ionescu plays were portents of further things to come in the legitimate theatre.

26

A new muse and a knighthood

Before the beginning of 1983 Kenneth was immersed in his new one-act work for the Royal Ballet at Covent Garden. The theme, of an idyllic situation gradually turning into one of catastrophe, had had its origin in the abandoned score of *Noctuaries* by Richard Rodney Bennett. Kenneth still wanted to develop the idea and he now found material in a novel, *The Garden of the Finzi-Continis* by Georgio Bassani. The story, which concerns a rich, cultured Jewish family in Italy in the late thirties and early forties, during which time Mussolini's Fascist regime began the systematic deportation of Jews to Hitler's death camps, was also made into a film by Vittorio de Sica. Neither the novel nor the film actually dealt with the fate of the Jewish family, but Kenneth's intentions, before deciding on the novel as his basic subject matter, had been to develop the idea of halcyon days turning into a time of horror and so the scenes of the ballet alternate between the large, beautiful garden of the novel's title, in which a group of young people develop their relationships, and the concentration camp.

The music that Kenneth chose was from Tchaikovsky's incidental music to *Hamlet* (not the fantasy-overture *Hamlet*) and the second movement from the suite *Souvenir de Florence*, and Martinu's Double Concerto – a combination of composers that he had also used in *Anastasia*. Tchaikovsky's gentle, melancholy lyricism and Martinu's strong rhythms and dissonances served Kenneth's narrative purposes very well indeed.

For the garden scenes Yolanda Sonnabend designed a semi-abstract set suggesting a rather overgrown arboretum of Renaissance grandeur in which the characters – the young people in sports clothes of the period, their elders in more formal attire – disported themselves. The concentration camp was a bleak, grey area illuminated by harsh overhead lights, the costumes grey and brown striped and ragged tunics.

The main characters of the story were taken straight from the novel: Micol, the beautiful, wayward heroine; Georgio (only referred to in the first person throughout the book), her infatuated admirer; Malnate, Micol's lover and Georgio's somewhat ambiguous friend; Alberto, Micol's effete, mortally ill brother; Micol's Mother and Grandmother and Georgio's Father. In the novel the class differences between Georgio's Father and Micol's family were strongly stressed; in the ballet they could only be briefly hinted at.

Kenneth cast his new discovery, Alessandra Ferri, as Micol. Georgio was the first major role taken by Guy Niblett. Ashley Page played the sexual athlete Malnate; Derek Deane Micol's sophisticated brother Alberto; Sandra Conley her Mother; Julie Wood her Grandmother; and David Wall Georgio's Father – socially distant from the Finzi-Continis, but a man whose moral courage sustains them in the hideous environment of the concentration camp.

To portray the greatest horror of our century in terms of classical ballet was typical of Kenneth's conviction that the medium can be made to reflect the most serious of subjects – and probably takes this theory to its ultimate extreme. Certainly the concentration camp scenes were done with a power and force that many people found very harrowing indeed and which, as was to be expected, divided the critics even more than usual. But no one could say (though one did) that they were there for cheap sensationalism; they represented the choreographer's genuine concern, demonstrably developed throughout his career, with the fundamentals of the human condition and with man's capability of inhumanity to man.

Kenneth called the new ballet *Valley of Shadows* and it received its first performance at Covent Garden on March 3, 1983, in an all-MacMillan triple bill, beginning with *Orpheus* and ending with *Requiem* (receiving its first performance by the Royal Ballet) thus making a programme rather heavily overloaded with serious works.

Whether or not they liked the ballet (its very subject matter makes the word 'like' inappropriate) most critics considered it at length. *The Times* critic dwelt particularly on Alessandra Ferri's performance: 'The one thing that has to be said very definitely in the ballet's favour is that Alessandra Ferri is exactly right for Micol, the young heroine. Not only is her supple, pliant body ideal for the ingenious, contrived adagios that are MacMillan's speciality, but she has enough flair and commitment to convey emotion with her face even in the most back-breaking moments. Until almost the end she appears only in idyllic scenes in the garden . . . It is a serious drawback that from those episodes one would never guess the most important facts about the characters, namely where they are (in Italy) when (just before and after the outbreak of the Second World War) and who (Jews). Those have to be inferred from the alternating passages which take place in a concentration camp. The three movements of Martinu's Double Concerto, separately played turn and turn about with Tchaikovsky, accompany those, and a large cast (guarded by just one Nazi in uniform) gibber, shake and shudder unceasingly, while David Wall and Sandra Conley try energetically to give some depth to what looks like a cynical exploitation of

Scenes of *Valley of Shadows*, danced to music by Tchaikovsky and Martin■, alternate between the Arcadian setting of the garden and the bleak horror of the camp; the work itself represents the ultimate extreme of MacMillan's belief that narrative ballet is capable of being powerfully expressive theatre. *Above*: the young people in the garden: Guy Niblett as Georgio, in love with Micol, the spoilt, wayward heroine; Alessandra Ferri as Micol; Ashley Page as Malnate, Georgio's friend and Micol's secret lover; Derek Deane as Alberto, Micol's mortally ill brother. *Below*: David Wall as Georgio's Father and Alessandra Ferri as Micol in the final concentration camp scene. (*Anthony Crickmay*.)

history for trivial theatrical effect. Their head-knocking duet, and the rapid expiry of Derek Deane and Julie Wood provide moments of unintentional comic relief.'

No other critic found any part of the ballet unintentionally comic. The *Financial Times* critic, in a second review of the ballet, thought that the work '. . . returns to themes which have much concerned the choreographer in recent years: the matter of what a ballet may treat as a subject in the closing decades of the twentieth century (and not the nineteenth, whatever a conservative public may believe); the possibilities of narrative; the nature of emotional loss and isolation, which has ever touched MacMillan's rawest creative nerve; historical incident as a fit subject for dance, whether actual, as in *Anastasia*, or social, as in *La Fin du jour*. Indeed, this latter work now seems more significant than its surface brightness first suggested. When, at its end, Merle Park closes the door at the back of the set to shut out the encroaching night, it is that darkness which is to fall on the concentration camp of *Valley of Shadows*.

'*Valley of Shadows* . . . has set considerable narrative problems for MacMillan. These, I find, he has largely solved, with the alternating scenes in the doomed garden (Yolanda Sonnabend's poetic setting rich in symbols – urn, obelisk, statuary – evocative of death) and the concentration camp as shifts both in time and emotional viewpoint. The heroine Micol's tragedy is double, and MacMillan shows us a self-centred girl with her affections torn between her awareness of the young love offered her by Georgio (Guy Niblett very fine in his innocent passion) and her own physical response to the unambiguously sexual but ambivalent Malnate (Ashley Page broodingly sensual).

'Yet nearest to the centre of Micol's feelings is her love for her brother Alberto, an identification almost incestuous in its response to his *dégagé* charm and his sickness (he is dying of leukemia), presented with great sensitivity by Derek Deane.

'The ballet's progress is a study in Micol's increasing isolation, the garden depopulated as family and friends disappear into the death camp, as her brother succumbs to his disease, and as she loses Malnate to military service and Georgio flees Italy. A crucial moment comes when Georgio, in their last meeting, flings his Star of David armband at her feet, a doubly symbolic action in which he rejects his fate and reminds her of his identity as a Jew. At last, in the death camp Micol has to face everything that she has chosen to hide from in the garden, and identify herself with the destiny that has overtaken family and friends.

'In exploring this level of his narrative, MacMillan has devised choreography as inventive and lyrically passionate as any he has made in recent years. A ravishing quartet in which Micol soars through the garden on the arms of the three young men in her life has a rushing, impetuous beauty.

'The various duets are judged with acute perception of the differing nature of Micol's involvement with Georgio, Malnate, Alberto, and in them Alessandra Ferri shows uncanny sensitivity for so young an artist. Seeming never to give herself fully to Georgio; entirely aware of what Malnate means in purely physical terms, obsessive with Alberto, Miss Ferri lives her role with astounding communicative power.

'It is in the concentration camp scenes that MacMillan courts theatrical disaster. On the ballet's dramatic terms they need to be shown as the truth which Micol (and how many more) sought to ignore, and MacMillan neither capitalises on their bestiality nor sentimentalises them.

'MacMillan's imaginative resource here produces dance imagery that is even harsher and more penetrating than those raw, torn-from-the-psyche agonies that told of Isadora's grief at the death of her children; movement is reduced to its angriest, most anguished outlines, and presented by Sandra Conley, Julie Wood and David Wall with admirable sincerity. The scenes are profoundly disquieting; their triple repitition may diminish any shock value but they are essential to the exploration of Micol's story and to the emotional momentum of the piece.'

It has seemed worthwhile quoting this critique at length because it reveals an understanding of the aims and realisation of the work (and its relationship to other ballets by Kenneth) with unequalled perception – a perception, moreover, drawn almost entirely from the stage action. The only information not communicated directly by the dance was the nature of Alberto's illness, but that he was desperately sick was made perfectly evident. Besides this acute awareness of Kenneth's intention and achievement in *Valley of Shadows* most other criticisms seem somewhat superficial. The *Guardian* critic was unable to discern the relationships of the young people: 'From the choreography it was almost impossible to figure out that Georgio was the lover of Micol, that Malnate was the rival and, above all, that Alberto was her brother who seemed given to epileptic fits. The dancing, so much of it glorious, and the emotional concern of the girl, seemed so similar with all three. Mother, father and grandmother are hardly established until they bear the heaviest burdens of the persecution scenes. Sandra Conley's breakdown and exit at Nazi command, presumably to a gas chamber, is the most searing performance of all though David Wall sustains the anguish of the imprisoned father and Julie Wood is a credible grandmother in distress.'

214

The critic of the *Sunday Telegraph* found the ballet to have some relevance to contemporary times: 'Film, book and now ballet also spark off larger questions. Against the awfulness of the camps, the triviality and paltriness of much of the social round, the exchanging of one affair for another, seemed even more futile, and this gave the ballet its particular relevance.

'Much of our own feverish activity may seem equally pointless – just so much cracking of thorns beneath the pot. MacMillan fans will recognise this landscape. This is the world of the madhouse and the tyrannised; and the fact that 'they' wear Nazi uniforms makes yet another variation on the white-coated or uniformed symbols of authority in these desolate areas that MacMillan has frightened us with before. But it works as theatre, it shows off the dancers in a challenging way, confirms Ferri as a rising star and leaves us, as intended, with churned emotions.'

Two or three critics stated in their reviews that, in fact, the sexes were segregated in the camps. Not so. In many, if not all – including some of the most notorious – there was no general segregation except in places like bath-houses; indeed, even in such hideous circumstances, there were accounts of flourishing love affairs.

The performance of *Requiem* in the same programme brought almost unanimous praise. Concluding his review of *Valley of Shadows* the *Financial Times* critic wrote: 'About the welcome arrival of *Requiem* whose choreographic serenities and momentary acknowledgements of divine wrath (the men impelled by terror in the Libera Me) are exactly those of Fauré's music – little needs to be said, save to note the cool clarity of the Royal Ballet performance, and to salute Bryony Brind and Wayne Eagling in their debut performances. It is a beautiful ballet and eases the mind after *Valley of Shadows*, without diminishing the new work's impact.'

The *Sunday Times* critic wrote that 'The evening . . . concluded triumphantly with the Fauré *Requiem*, one of MacMillan's great works. . . . Wonderful music it is, beatific and tranquil; the dance marvellous, the dancers too – Bryony Brind, Wayne Eagling, and from Stuttgart as guest, Marcia Haydée who created the central role. In Haydée's poignantly innocent solo to Pie Jesu, a little girl playing in a pool of light, you see a magnificent artist, and a choreographer inspired.'

The *Sunday Telegraph* reviewer was equally enthusiastic: '. . . in *Requiem* . . . MacMillan is seen in a superbly confident and fluently inventive mood. A special inspiration is the solo to the Pie Jesu created, and on this occasion danced, by Marcia Haydée with exquisite tenderness and grace.'

It is interesting that several critics mentioned the *Pie Jesu* in

Twenty years after the first performance of the *Rite of Spring* in 1962, Monica Mason was still dancing the exhausting role of the Chosen Maiden. The photograph above shows her relaxing in her dressing room with Kenneth and his wife Deborah. (*Clive Boursnell.*)

Kenneth was knighted in H.M. the Queen's Birthday Honours list in June, 1983; the investiture took place in October that year. *Below*: outside Buckingham Palace with Deborah and Charlotte. (*Catherine Ashmore.*)

particular. When Kenneth came to create it he drew on his memory of Charlotte, aged three, dancing at a party to music by Bach. 'She did extraordinary things,' he told an interviewer. 'I tried to emulate them in the Pie Jesu.'

Requiem entered the Royal Ballet repertoire as part of a direct exchange with the Stuttgart Ballet which received *Gloria* in return, produced in Stuttgart in January, 1983, some two months before *Requiem* at the Royal Opera House. *Gloria* had a great success with the German audience who considered its anti-war theme of universal relevance rather than specifically related to the national antagonisms of the first Great War which had directly inspired it, and Birgit Keil, Reid Anderson and Christopher Boatwright in the roles created by Jennifer Penney, Julian Hosking and Wayne Eagling, each scored a personal triumph.

Early in May, 1983, Kenneth received a letter from No. 10, Downing Street, inquiring *if* he were to be offered a knighthood would he accept. Kenneth replied in the affirmative. For nearly a month he heard nothing more. On June 1, he opened his newspaper and learnt that he was now Sir Kenneth MacMillan. The investiture itself did not take place until October 20, 1983, when he went to Buckingham Palace accompanied by Deborah and Charlotte. What impressed Kenneth most about the occasion, he says, was the way everything was impeccably 'choreographed', the placing of the various relatives and friends around three sides of the ornate red and gold investiture room, the discreet manoeuvring by the ushers of those who were to receive the accolades.

This formal acknowledgement by the State of Kenneth's services to British ballet seems a natural place to conclude this necessarily incomplete chronicle of his career. He had come a long, long way in the forty years since, as a lonely but determined teenager, he had knocked upon Phyllis Adams's front door and announced that he wanted to be a dancer. Internationally accepted as one of the great choreographers of this century, the canon of his works runs the whole gamut of the art, from abstract lyricism to narrative expressionism, but undoubtedly his greatest contribution has been in two specifics: in developing the full-length ballet far beyond the formal, stylised conception that spanned the nineteenth and twentieth centuries, and in demonstrating that ballet can illumine with poignancy and subtlety the private and public problems of our time. From *The Invitation* to *Valley of Shadows* he has proved that the vocabulary of classicism is capable of not just pretty divertissements but is also an essential part of the expressive power of the theatre. For any choreographer there can be no greater recognition than that.

Envoi

Of course Kenneth's career continues with as much pace and panache as at any time in the past. He remains as the Royal Ballet's Principal Choreographer, having created *Different Drummer*, based on George Buchner's play *Woyzeck* and given its premiere at the Royal Opera House on February 24, 1984. He is preparing the long-postponed full-length production of *Prince of the Pagodas*, with music by Benjamin Britten. He has widened his experience of directing in the 'straight' theatre with a production of August Strindberg's *Dance of Death* for the Manchester Royal Exchange theatre, featuring Jill Bennet, Edward Fox and Peter Baldwin, and the first British production of Tennessee Williams's *The Kingdom of Earth*, starring Nichola McAuliffe and Stephen Rea at the Hampstead Theatre. An expanded version of *The Seven Deadly Sins*, specially created for television, was transmitted by Granada T.V. on April 22, B.B.C. T.V. relayed a performance of *Romeo and Juliet*, with Alessandra Ferri and Wayne Eagling as the lovers, filmed at the Royal Opera House and available as a video cassette, on December 29, 1984. On October 17, 1984, Kenneth's dances for the Venusberg revels in a new production of Tannhauser at the Royal Opera House, received their first performance with dancers drawn from London Contemporary Dance Theatre. Kenneth's collaboration with these artists was so successful that plans were mooted for him to produce an original work for this modern dance company. On September 4, 1984, after talks with Mikhail Baryshnikov in London, Kenneth was appointed Associate Director of American Ballet Theatre. *Romeo and Juliet* has entered that company's repertoire, having its premiere at the Kennedy Center, Washington D.C. on January 3, 1985. Later in the year the original one-act version of *Anastasia* was also produced by American Ballet Theatre.

And so it goes on: with Kenneth only in his fiftes and at the height of his powers it is obvious that, within a few years, a supplement to this chronicle will need to be written. Whatever the future holds it is certain that Kenneth MacMillan's creative projects will increase in number and diversity and, despite the brilliance of his past achievements, it would not be an idle prophecy to say: 'The best is yet to come.'

Ballets Choreographed by Kenneth Macmillan

Premiere	Ballet
1 2.1953	**Somnambulism** Sadler's Wells Choreographic Group, Sadler's Wells Theatre. *Music*: Stan Kenton. *Cast*: Lane, Poole, Macmillan.
14.6.1953	**Fragment** Sadler's Wells Choreographic Group, SW Theatre. *Music*: Stan Kenton. *Cast*: Neil, Page, Britton.
24.1.1954	**Laiderette** Sadler's Wells Choreographic Group, Sadler's Wells Theatre. *Music*: Frank Martin. *Decor*: Improvised. *Cast*: Lane, Poole.
4 7.1955	**Laiderette** (Ballet Rambert)
13.1.1955	**Danses Concertantes** Sadler's Wells Theatre Ballet, Sadler's Wells Theatre. *Music*: Igor Stravinsky. *Decor*: Nicholas Georgiadis. *Cast*: Lane, Britton, Poole.
25.5.1955	**The House of Birds** Sadler's Wells Theatre Ballet, Sadler's Wells Theatre. *Music*: Federico Mompou arranged by John Lanchbery. *Decor*: Nicholas Georgiadis. *Cast*: Lane, Poole, Tempest.
1.3.1956	**Noctambules** Sadler's Wells Ballet, Covent Garden (1st ballet for CG). *Music*: Humphrey Searle. *Decor*: Nicholas Georgiadis. *Cast*: Edwards, Lane, Nerina, Linden.
7.6.1956	**Solitaire** Sadler's Wells Theatre Ballet, Sadler's Wells Theatre. *Music*: Malcolm Arnold. *Decor*: Desmond Heeley. *Cast*: Hill, Page, Britton, Boulton.
10.12.1956	**Valse Excentrique** Gala, Sadler's Wells Theatre. *Music*: Jacques Ibert. *Cast*: Grant, Linden, Shaw.
1.3.60	**Valse Excentrique** (Royal Ballet)
28.6.62	**Valse Excentrique** (Western Ballet Theatre)
16.1.1957	**Winter's Eve** American Ballet Theatre, Lisbon. *Music*: Benjamin Britten. *Decor*: Nicholas Georgiadis. *Cast*: Kaye, Kriza.
6.5.1957	**Journey** A.B.T. Choreographic Group, New York City. *Music*: Béla Bartók. *Cast*: Kaye, Kriza, Bruhn.
2.1.1958	**The Burrow** Royal Ballet Touring Company, Covent Garden. *Music*: Frank Martin. *Decor*: Nicholas Georgiadis. *Cast*: Heaton, Britton, Seymour.
20.8.1958	**Agon** The Royal Ballet, Covent Garden. *Music*: Igor Stravinsky. *Decor*: Nicholas Georgiadis. *Cast*: Lane, Blair.
12.4.1960	**Le Baiser de la fée** The Royal Ballet, Covent Garden. *Music*: Igor Stravinsky. *Decor*: Kenneth Rowell. *Cast*: Seymour, Beriosova, MacLeary.
10.11.1960	**The Invitation** Royal Ballet Touring Company, New Theatre, Oxford. *Music*: Matyas Seiber. *Decor*: Nicholas Georgiadis. *Cast*: Seymour, Gable, Heaton, Doyle.
4.9.1961	**Seven Deadly Sins** Western Theatre Ballet, Edinburgh Festival. *Music*: Kurt Weill. *Decor*: Ian Spurling. *Cast*: Linden, Laine.
15.9.1961	**Diversions** The Royal Ballet, Covent Garden. *Music*: Arthur Bliss. *Decor*: Philip Prowse. *Cast*: Lane, Beriosova, MacLeary, Usher.
3.5.1962	**The Rite of Spring** The Royal Ballet, Covent Garden. *Music*: Igor Stravinsky. *Decor*: Sidney Nolan. *Cast*: Monica Mason.
14.7.1962	**Dance Suite** Royal Ballet School Performance. *Music*: Darius Milhaud. *Cast*: Derman, Cooke, Cragun.
15.2.1963	**Symphony** The Royal Ballet, Covent Garden. *Music*: Dmitry

Shostakovich. *Decor*: Yolanda Sonnabend. *Cast*: Sibley, Parkinson, MacLeary, Doyle.

13.7.1963 **Las Hermanas** Stuttgart Ballet. *Music*: Frank Martin. *Decor*: Nicholas Georgiadis. *Cast*: Haydée, Keil, Barra.

2.6.1971 **Las Hermanas** (Royal Ballet New Group)

12.2.1964 **La Création du Monde** Royal Ballet Touring Company. Royal Shakespeare Theatre. *Music*: Darius Milhaud. *Decor*: James Goddard. *Cast*: Wells, Farley.

2.4.1964 **Images of Love** The Royal Ballet, Covent Garden. *Music*: Peter Tranchell. *Decor*: Barry Kay. *Cast*: Beriosova, Seymour, MacLeary, Nureyev, Gable.

9.2.1965 **Romeo and Juliet** The Royal Ballet, Covent Garden. *Music*: Sergey Prokofiev. *Decor*: Nicholas Georgiadis. *Cast*: Fonteyn, Nureyev, Blair.

5.12.1969 **Romeo and Juliet** (Royal Swedish Ballet)

3.1.1985 **Romeo and Juliet** (American Ballet Theatre)

7.11.1965 **Song of the Earth** Stuttgart Ballet. *Music*: Gustav Mahler. *Decor*: Nicholas Georgiadis. *Cast*: Madsen, Haydée, Barra.

19.5.1966 **Song of the Earth** (Royal Ballet)

23.11.1978 **Song of the Earth** (Paris Opera Ballet)

30.11.1966 **Valses Nobles et Sentimentales** Berlin Opera Ballet. *Music*: Maurice Ravel. *Decor*: Jurgen Rose. *Cast*: Carii, Kapuste.

30.11.1966 **Concerto** Berlin Opera Ballet. *Music*: Dmitry Shostakovich. *Decor*: Jurgen Rose. *Cast*: Carii, Kapuste, Seymour.

18.5.1967 **Concerto** (American Ballet Theatre)

26.5.1967 **Concerto** (Royal Ballet Touring Company)

17.11.1970 **Concerto** (Royal Ballet)

25.6.1967 **Anastasia** (1 Act) Berlin Opera Ballet. *Music*: Electronic music produced by Fritz Winckel and Rudiger Rufer and Bohuslav Martinu's Fantaisies Symphoniques. *Cast*: Seymour, Holz, Bohner.

14.4.1976 **Anastasia** (Stuttgart Ballet)

8.10.1967 **The Sleeping Beauty** Berlin Opera Ballet. *Music*: Pyotr Ilyich Tchaikovsky. *Decor*: Barry Kay. *Cast*: Holz, Seymour, Kesselheim, Kapuste.

11.3.1968 **Olympiad** Berlin Opera Ballet. *Music*: Igor Stravinsky. *Cast*: Seymour, Beelitz, Kapuste.

21.2.1969 **Olympiad** (The Royal Ballet)

1.6.1968 **The Sphinx** Stuttgart Ballet. *Music*: Darius Milhaud. *Decor*: Dalton. *Cast*: Haydée, Cragun, Madsen, Clauss.

1.11.1968 **Cain and Abel** Berlin Opera Ballet. *Music*: Andrzej Panufnik. *Decor*: Barry Kay. *Cast*: Bohner, Frey, Holz.

14.5.1969 **Swan Lake** Berlin Opera Ballet. *Music*: Pyotr Ilyich Tchaikovsky. *Decor*: Nicholas Georgiadis. *Cast*: Seymour, Frey, Bohner, Barra.

8.3.1970 **Miss Julie** Stuttgart Ballet. *Music*: Andrzej Panufnik. *Cast*: Haydée, Frey.

27.11.1970 **Checkpoint** Royal Ballet New Group, Opera House, Manchester. *Music*: Roberto Gerhardt. *Decor*: Elisabeth Dalton. *Cast*: Beriosova, MacLeary.

22.7.1971 **Anastasia** (Three Acts) The Royal Ballet, Covent Garden. *Music*: Pyotr Ilyich Tchaikovsky and Bohuslav Martinu. *Decor*: Barry Kay. *Cast*: Seymour, Beriosova, Sibley, Dowell.

19.1.1972 **Triad** (orig: Trio) The Royal Ballet, Covent Garden. *Music*: Sergey Prokofiev. *Decor*: Peter Unsworth. *Cast*: Sibley, Dowell, Eagling.

25.2.1972 **Triad** (Royal Ballet New Group)

6.6.1984	**Triad** (American Ballet Theatre)
19.5.1972	**Ballade** Royal Ballet New Group, Teatro Nacional de S. Carlos, Lisbon. *Music*: Gabriel Fauré. *Cast*: Lorrayne, Clarke, Jefferies.
24.4.1972	**Side Show** The Royal Ballet, Royal Court Theatre, Liverpool. *Music*: Igor Stravinsky. *Costumes*: Thomas O'Neil. *Cast*: Seymour, Nureyev.
12.10.1972	**The Poltroon** Royal Ballet New Group, Sadler's Wells Theatre. *Music*: Rudolf Maros. *Decor*: Thomas O'Neil. *Cast*: Last, MacLeary, Jefferies.
13.1.1973	**Pavane** The Royal Ballet, Covent Garden. *Music*: Gabriel Fauré. *Costumes*: Anthony Dowell. *Cast*: Sibley, Dowell.
15.5.1973	**The Sleeping Beauty** (II) The Royal Ballet, Covent Garden. *Music*: Pyotr Ilyich Tchaikovsky. *Decor*: Peter Farmer. *Cast*: Sibley, Dowell.
19.7.1973	**Seven Deadly Sins** (II) The Royal Ballet, Covent Garden. *Music*: Kurt Weill, *Decor*: Ian Spurling. *Cast*: Penney, Brown.
7.3.1974	**Manon** The Royal Ballet, Covent Garden. *Music*: Jules Massenet arranged by Leighton Lucas. *Decor*: Nicholas Georgiadis. *Cast*: Sibley, Dowell, Wall, Rencher.
7.10.1974	**Elite Syncopations** The Royal Ballet, Covent Garden. *Music*: Scott Joplin, *Decor*: Ian Spurling. *Cast*: Derman, Park, MacLeary, Sleep.
10.2.1978	**Elite Syncopations** (Sadler's Wells Royal Ballet)
5.3.1975	**The Four Seasons** The Royal Ballet, Covent Garden. *Music*: Guiseppe Verdi. *Decor*: Peter Rice. *Cast*: Derman, Collier, Wall, Dowell.
29.9.1976	**The Four Seasons** (Paris opera Ballet)
9.10.1975	**Romeo and Juliet** Ballet for All. *Cast*: Ellis, Silver. (Ballet and Theatre).
11.12.1975	**Rituals** The Royal Ballet, Covent Garden. *Music*: Béla Bartók. *Decor*: Yolanda Sonnabend. *Cast*: Eagling, Derman, Wall, Seymour, Mason.
28.11.1976	**Requiem** Stuttgart Ballet. *Music*: Gabriel Fauré. *Decor*: Yolanda Sonnabend. *Cast*: Haydée, Keil, Madsen, Cragun.
3.3.1983	**Requiem** (Royal Ballet)
2.12.1976	**Feux Follets** John Curry. *Music*: Franz Liszt. *Cast*: Curry.
30.5.1977	**Gloriana** Royal Ballet, Covent Garden. *Music*: Benjamin Britten. *Decor*: Yolanda Sonnabend. *Cast*: Seymour, Eagling.
14.2.1978	**Mayerling** The Royal Ballet, Covent Garden. *Music*: Franz Liszt, arranged by John Lanchbery. *Decor*: Nicholas Georgiadis. *Scenario*: Gillian Freeman. *Cast*: Wall, Seymour, Park.
21.5.1978	**My Brother, My Sisters** Stuttgart Ballet. *Music*: Arnold Schoenberg and Anton von Webern. *Decor*: Yolanda Sonnabend. *Cast*: Keil, Cragun, Montagnon.
29.4.1980	**My Brother, My Sisters** (Royal Ballet)
26.6.1978	**6.6.78 (homage to N. de Valois)** Sadler's Wells Royal Ballet, Sadler's Wells Theatre. *Music*: Samuel Barber. *Decor*: Ian Spurling. *Cast*: Tait, Kelly.
23.11.1978	**Metaboles** Paris Opera Ballet. *Music*: Henri Dutilleux. *Decor*: Barry Kay. *Cast*: Khalfouni, Bart.
15.3.1979	**La Fin du jour** The Royal Ballet, Covent Garden. *Music*: Maurice Ravel. *Decor*: Ian Spurling. *Cast*: Park, Penney, Eagling, Hosking.
24.8.1979	**Playground** Sadler's Wells Royal Ballet, Edinburgh Festival. *Music*: Gordon Cross. *Decor*: Yolanda Sonnabend. *Cast*: Kelly, Tait.

13.3.1980	**Gloria** The Royal Ballet, Covent Garden. *Music*: Francis Poulenc. *Decor*: Andy Klunder. *Cast*: Eagling, Hosking, Penney, Ellis.
30.4.1981	**Isadora** The Royal Ballet, Covent Garden. *Music*: Richard Rodney Bennett. *Decor*: Barry Kay. *Scenario*: Gillian Freeman. *Dialogue*: Mary Miller. *Cast*: Park, Hosking, Deane, Rencher.
12.12.1981	**Wild Boy** American Ballet Theatre, Kennedy Center, Washington DC. *Music*: Gordon Cross. *Decor*: Oliver Smith. *Cast*: Makarova, Baryshnikov.
1.3.82	**Verdi Variations** Aterballeto, Regio-Emilia. *Music*: Guiseppe Verdi. *Cast*: Terabust, Schaufuss.
7.4.1982	**Quartet** Sadler's Wells Royal Ballet at Bristol Hippodrome. *Music*: Guiseppe Verdi. *Cast*: Samsova, Kelly, Tait, Myers.
11.6.1982	**Orpheus** The Royal Ballet, Covent Garden. *Music*: Igor Stravinsky. *Decor*: Nicholas Georgiadis. *Cast*: Penney, Schaufuss.
3.3.1983	**Valley of Shadows** The Royal Ballet, Covent Garden. *Music*: Bohuslav Martinu and Pyotr Ilyich Tchaikovsky. *Decor*: Yolanda Sonnabend. *Cast*: Ferri, Wall, Deane, Page, Niblett, Conley, Wood.
24.2.84	**Different Drummer** Royal Opera House, Covent Garden. *Music*: Anton Webern, Arnold Schoenberg. *Costumes*: Yolanda Sonnabend. *Cast*: Eagling, Ferri, Jefferies.

Television Performances of Major Works by Kenneth MacMillan

Somnambulism (retitled The Dreamers) BBC TV
Punch and the Child (Three-part series) BBC TV
Turned Out Proud (Dance suite for television) BBC TV
Elite Syncopations (Stage performance recorded for TV) BBC TV
Mayerling (TV documentary with performance excerpts) LWT
A Lot of Happiness (Two pas de deux created for TV) Granada TV
Isadora (Stage performance recorded for TV) Granada TV
Gloria (Stage performance recorded for TV) Granada TV
Manon (Stage performance recorded for TV) BBC TV
Seven Deadly Sins (Expanded version for TV) Granada TV
Romeo and Juliet (Stage performance recorded for TV) BBC TV
Triad (Stage performance recorded for TV) PBS USA
Manon (Stage performance recorded for TV) Swedish TV

Stage Plays Directed by Kenneth MacMillan

The Chairs and The Lesson	The New Inn, Ealing. *Plays*: Ionescu. *Cast*: Peter Baldwin, Mary Miller, Harriet Thorpe, David Taylor.
Dance of Death	Royal Exchange Theatre, Manchester. *Play*: Strindberg. *Cast*: Jill Bennett, Edward Fox, Peter Baldwin, David Taylor.
Kingdom of Earth	Hampstead Theatre. *Play*: Tennessee Williams. *Cast*: Nicola McAuliffe, Stephen Rea, David Taylor.

Index

Adams, Phyllis, 6–8, 192, 204–5, 217
Afternoon of a Faun, 120, 154
Agon, 50–5, 129
American Ballet Theatre, 42–3, 47, 81,
  99, 132, 202, 218
Anastasia, 98–100, 104, 114–18, 124,
  129–34, 164, 176, 199, 210, 213, 218
Anderson, Reid, 153, 217
Apollo, 114, 206
Ashmole, David, 144, 157, 206
Ashton, Frederick, 9–11, 14–15, 22, 28,
  34, 36, 41, 43, 46, 59, 61, 75, 79–80,
  91, 94, 110, 114, 117–18, 120, 124–7,
  150, 157, 163, 176, 181, 186, 190–1

Baiser de la fée, Le, 28, 53–7, 218
Balanchine, George, 15, 50, 60, 86,
  95–6, 114, 125, 128–9, 150, 157, 206
Ballabile, 15
Ballad of Reading Gaol, The, 122–3, 174
Ballet Imperial, 15, 95–6
Ballet Rambert, 17, 34–5, 39–41, 114,
  157
Barra, Ray, 73, 90, 92, 99
Bartered Bride, The, 10, 41
Bartók, Béla, 46, 148–9
Baryshnikov, Mikhail, 81, 147, 154,
  157, 202–3, 218
BBC, 24, 27, 35–6, 41, 147, 205, 218
Beagley, Stephen, 148, 155
Bejart, Maurice, 62, 64
Bennett, Richard Rodney, 181–2, 190,
  197–200, 204, 210
Bergsma, Deanne, 61, 67, 77, 157
Beriosova, Svetlana, 53–7, 61, 64,
  77–8, 112, 115–18, 157
Berlin Opera Ballet; KM director of,
  90–106; 108, 110, 176
Blair, David, 50, 129
Bolshoi Ballet, 6, 79–80, 84, 117, 122
Boulton, Michael, 39, 41, 52
Brahms, Johannes, 176, 190, 199
Brecht, Bertolt, 60, 130, 192
Brind, Bryony, 171, 215
Britten, Benjamin, 38, 43, 155, 199
Britton, Donald, 10, 22–3, 27–30, 39,
  48
Bunraku (puppets), 145, 148
Burrow, The, 47–9, 51, 55, 62, 72

Cain and Abel, 103–4
Capon, Naomi, 26–7
Carnaval, 11, 126
Carte Blanche, 23, 34
Cauley, Geoffrey, 77, 125
Chase, Lucia, 42–5, 99
Checkpoint, 112–15
Chopin, Frédéric, 31–3, 111, 144, 150,
  190, 199–201
Cinderella, 14, 36, 114, 155
Coleman, Michael, 111, 117, 122, 130,
  141–4, 155–7
Coliseum, 129, 145–7, 167–8
Collier, Lesley, 117, 144, 154, 157, 161,
  190
Concerto, 63, 93–4, 99, 125, 134, 183,
  189
Conley, Sandra, 190, 211, 214
Cooke, Kerrison, 66, 93, 116, 123
Cragun, Richard, 66, 73, 103, 154, 157,
  167–8
Craig, Edward Gordon, 177, 191
Cranko, John, 11, 15–23, 32, 36–9, 43,
  47–9, 72–3, 85–92, 95, 101–3,
  106–9, 122, 125, 129–30, 151–7, 168
Création du Monde, La, 74–5
Crosse, Gordon, 182–5, 201

Dale, Margaret, 20, 35, 41
Dalton, Elisabeth, 102, 106, 112–14
Dance Suit, 66
Danses Concertantes, 28–32, 40, 50–2, 62,
  185
Deane, Derek, 211–3
Death and the Maiden, 41, 46
Debussy, Claude-Achille, 11, 120
Derman, Vergie, 61, 66, 77, 92, 97–9,
  117, 130, 142–4, 148, 157
Diaghilev, Serge, 51, 62, 73, 128, 180,
  184
Different Drummer, 218
Diversions, 61–3, 180
Dowell, Anthony, 67, 81, 88, 91,
  110–11, 117, 120, 124, 127, 137–8,
  143–5, 150, 157, 163
Doyle, Desmond, 37, 52, 58–9, 67, 77,
  107
Drew, David, 122, 125, 148

Duncan, Isadora, 73, 86, 184; see also
  Isadora
Dupond, Patrick, 173, 175

Eagling, Wayne, 88, 120, 144, 148,
  152–7, 161, 171, 178–80, 188, 190,
  208, 215, 218
Edinburgh Festival, 20, 60, 184
Edinburgh, University of, 146–7
Elite Syncopations, 141–3, 147, 163, 167,
  172, 180, 183
Ellis, Wendy, 157, 188
Evening Standard, 144, 180, 193, 207
Eyden, Deidre, 88, 190

Fanfare for Europe, 127–8
Fauré, Gabriel, 33, 123, 127, 152,
  168–9
Ferri, Alessandra, 209, 211–15, 218
Feux Follets, 153–4
Field, John, 15, 99, 109–10, 125
Fille mal gardée, La, 114, 129, 154
Fin du jour, La, 177–81, 213
Firebird, 95, 206
Fokine, Michel, 11, 126, 206
Fonteyn, Margot, 7–9, 22, 42, 81, 84,
  104, 110, 122, 125, 140, 157
Four Seasons, The, 144–5, 173, 189, 204
Four Temperaments, The, 128–9
Fragment, 22–3
Frankfurt Ballet, 143, 154
Freeman, Gillian, 158–62, 165, 176–8,
  181–4, 196–8
Frey, Frank, 103–9

Gable, Christopher, 58–9, 69, 76–84
Genet, Jean, 46, 116
Gentele, Goram, 107, 151
Georgiadis, Nicholas, 30, 33–4, 38,
  41–3, 47–8, 50, 52, 56, 70–3, 84–5,
  90, 97, 104–5, 134–7, 161–4, 175–6,
  185, 207–8
Gershwin, George, 22, 200–1
Giselle, 9, 42, 104, 124
Gloria, 179, 186–90, 193, 196, 201, 217
Gloriana, 155
Goddard, James, 74–5
Gold, Jack, 200–1
Granada TV, 203, 209
Grant, Alexander, 41, 77, 150, 172
Great Yarmouth, 2–3, 6, 10, 120, 192,
  196, 204
Grey, Beryl, 7, 9, 15

Haydée, Marcia, 73, 88–91, 100,
  103–4, 108–9, 134, 152–4, 157,
  166–9, 215
Heaton, Anne, 10, 40, 48, 58–9
Helpmann, Robert, 9, 14, 36, 45, 75
Hermanas, Las, 70–3, 172
Hill, Margaret, 11, 20–1, 27, 39–43
Hosking, Julian, 157, 178–80, 188, 190,
  193, 217
House of Birds, 32–4, 38, 40–1, 47, 69,
  74
Howard, Andrée, 10–11, 41
Hurok, Sol, 81, 84, 140

Ibert, Jacques, 35, 41
Images of Love, 75–9
Invitation, The, 55–9, 72, 94, 172, 217
Ionesco, Eugène, 208–9
Isadora, 101, 176–7, 181–2, 190–204

Jefferies, Stephen, 123, 154, 167
Johnson, Nicholas, 116, 123
Joplin, Scott, 141–2, 199
Journey, 46, 188

Kay, Barry, 60, 78, 96–8, 100, 103,
  108–9, 117, 132, 173–4, 181, 196–9
Kaye, Nora, 42–7, 167, 201–2
Kchessinska, Mathilde, 116–7
Keil, Birgit, 166–9, 200, 217
Kelly, Desmond, 122, 172, 205
Kenton, Stan, 21–2
Kriza, John, 44–6

Laiderette, 23–4, 27, 34–5, 40, 48, 72
Lanchbery, John, 33, 67, 78, 150,
  159–62
Lane, Maryon, 11, 21, 24–6, 29–30,
  34–7, 52, 61, 69
Lavrovsky, Léonid, 79–80, 85
Lawrence, Ashley, 92, 99, 103, 126
Lifar, Serge, 95–6
Linden, Anya, 37, 41–2, 50, 60
Liszt, Franz, 153–4, 162–4, 190, 199
London Festival Ballet, 17, 154
London Weekend Television, 166, 200
Lorca, Federico García, 22, 72–3
Lorrayne, Vivienne, 61, 67, 123
Lucas, Leighton, 133, 138

MacLeary, Donald, 30, 39, 49, 52–5,
  61, 67, 77–8, 84–8, 91, 112, 115, 124,
  140–4, 157

MacMillan, Betty (KM's sister), 2, 7, 105, 196
MacMillan, Deborah (KM's wife), 119, 123–4, 127–9, 155, 158, 172, 191–2; and Charlotte (dau.), 131, 139, 145–6, 150–1, 166–7, 181, 185, 201–2, 216–17
MacMillan, Edith (KM's mother), 1–4
MacMillan, Jean (KM's sister), 2, 7, 105, 196
MacMillan, William (KM's father), 1–11
Madsen, Egon, 90, 103, 134, 157
Mahler, Gustav, 85–90, 155
Makarova, Natalia, 124–5, 129, 140, 147, 150–2, 157, 202
Manen, Hans van, 143, 150, 152, 157
Manon, 131–40, 142, 164, 193, 196, 205, 209
Markova, Alicia, 41, 81
Martin, Frank, 24, 48, 72
Martinu, Bohuslav, 99, 116, 210–2
Mason, Monica, 63–7, 77, 88, 111, 142–4, 148, 152, 157, 216
Massine, Léonid, 15, 62, 68–9, 86
Mayer, Laverne, 60, 66
Mayerling, 155–67, 172, 180, 193, 199, 209
Metaboles, 174–5
Milhaud, Darius, 59–60, 74, 102
Miller, Mary, 192, 198, 208
Miller, Patricia, 11, 24
Miss Julie, 107–9, 122
My Brother, My Sisters, 166–72, 180, 185, 190, 193

National Ballet of Canada, 143, 172
Neil, Sara, 22, 29, 39, 41
Nerina, Nadia, 37, 41, 77
Neumeier, John, 155, 157
New York City Ballet, 50, 96, 111, 120, 127, 129, 144, 150
Niblett, Guy, 211–3
Nijinska, Bronislava, 28, 206
Nijinsky, Vaslav, 62, 120, 175
Noctambules, 37–40, 47–8
Noctucries, 204, 210
Nureyev, Rudolf, 74–81, 84, 96, 104, 110–11, 124–6, 129, 140, 157, 203

Olympiad, 102, 104
Orpheus, 206–8, 211
Orwell, George, 112–14

Osborne, John, 47, 51–3, 158

Page, Annette, 22, 26, 29
Page, Ashley, 171, 188, 208, 211–13
Paris Opera Ballet, 62, 96, 173–5, 188
Park, Merle, 81, 84, 142, 147, 154, 157, 161, 178, 180, 184–6, 192–8
Parker, Monica, 134, 193
Parkinson, Georgina, 61, 67, 77, 86, 99–100, 105–7, 157
Patineurs, Les, 36, 115
Penney, Jennifer, 88, 117, 130, 134, 142, 145, 152, 155–7, 178–80, 188, 190, 193, 205–9, 217
Petipa, Marius, 9, 14, 96, 100, 181
Pineapple Poll, 17, 22, 109
Piper, John, 17–18, 38
Playground, 182–5
Poème de l'Extase, 122, 124
Poltroon, The, 126
Poole, David, 11, 20–6, 29–30, 34, 40, 52
Porter, Marguerite, 144, 157
Poulenc, Francis, 150, 179, 186–9
Praagh, Peggy van, 27, 172
Press (reviews of KM's ballets), 42, 45, 58, 65–6, 68–9, 73, 75, 78, 91, 117–18, 121, 125–6, 131, 135, 138, 143, 145, 148–50, 154, 164–5, 168–9, 172, 175, 180–1, 184, 188–9, 194, 196, 198–9, 202–3, 205–8, 211–15
Prince of the Pagodas, The, 38, 155
Prodigal Son, The, 128–9
Prokoviev, Sergey, 79–85, 120–1

Quartet, 204–6

Rake's Progress, The, 22, 109
Rambert, Marie, 34, 156–7
Rassine, Alexis, 9, 41
Ravel, Maurice, 94, 177–80
Rencher, Derek, 77, 117, 150, 194
Requiem, 152–3, 166, 168, 171, 188–9, 211, 215–7
Rite of Spring, The, 62–7, 148, 168, 206, 216–7
Rituals, 148–50
Robbins, Jerome, 111, 120, 125–7, 144, 150, 157
Rodrigues, Alfred, 15, 22, 26, 61
Romeo and Juliet, 79–85, 107, 129–31, 134, 139, 147, 154–6, 199, 209, 218
Rose, Jurgen, 94, 154

Ross, Herbert, 167, 175, 201
Rosson, Keith, 67, 77
Rowell, Kenneth, 34, 54
Royal Academy of Dancing, 11, 74, 177
Royal Ballet, 45–6, 49–51, 58, 69,
74–5, 78–80, 99–100, 104, 107, 143,
167, 171, 175–7, 186, 190, 201,
208–10, 217; KM director of,
109–56; School, 66, 155
Royal Danish Ballet, 62, 80
Royal Swedish Ballet, 81, 99, 107, 137,
193
Sadler's Wells Ballet, 9–17, 24–8,
32–41, 45, 49
Sadler's Wells Theatre Ballet (inc.
Royal Ballet II, Royal Ballet Touring
Company and Sadler's Wells Royal
Ballet), 69, 93, 109, 112, 154, 157,
163, 166, 172, 182–5, 203–4; as New
Group 114–6, 120; as Choreographic
Group, 20–4, 28, 34, 40, 120; School,
7–9, 45
Scènes de Ballet, 14, 143, 157
Schaufuss, Peter, 203–8
Schoenberg, Arnold, 167–9
Schubert, Franz, 41, 46
Searle, Humphrey, 37–8
Seiber, Matyas, 56–9, 151
Selner, Gustav Rudolf, 90, 98
Seven Deadly Sins, 60, 130, 142, 192, 218
Seymour, Lynn, 49, 54–9, 67–9, 76–84,
92–4, 99–105, 111, 117–18, 124–5,
130–2, 147–8, 150–7, 176, 183–4,
203, 209
Shakespeare, William, 75–80, 86
Shaw, Brian, 37, 41
Shearing, George, 17–18
Shostakovich, Dmitry, 67, 93–4
Sibley, Antoinette, 68–9, 110, 117, 120,
127, 134, 137–8, 157
Side Show, 124
6.6.78, 172–3
Slade School, 31, 68, 187
Sleep, Wayne, 128, 142, 145, 150, 157
Sleeping Beauty, The, 9, 15, 58, 95–9, 101,
105, 114, 124, 127–9, 155–9, 181
Solitaire, 39–41, 47–9, 166
Somes, Michael, 122, 186
Somnambulism, 20–7, 40, 69
Song of the Earth, 85–91, 143, 149,
152–4, 168, 172–5, 188–9
Sonnabend, Yolanda, 68, 147–9, 153,
167–8, 171, 183–4, 210, 213

Sphinx, The, 102–3
Spurling, Ian, 60, 130, 142, 173, 178–9
Stravinsky, Igor, 14, 28–30, 33, 41,
50–4, 59, 62–4, 95, 102, 203–4
Stuttgart Ballet, 66, 70–3, 85, 92,
99–104, 107–9, 124, 134, 151–5,
166–72, 175, 188, 217
Suite en Blanc, 95–6
Swan Lake, 22, 42, 58, 95, 100–1, 104–6,
109, 114, 126, 140, 147, 157–8
Sylphides, Les, 15, 26, 115
Symons, Oliver, 60, 66
Symphony, 67–9, 147
Symphonic Variations, 114, 157

Tait, Marion, 173, 205
Taming of the Shrew, The, 154, 157
Tchaikovsky, Pyotr, 28, 53, 95, 116–18,
133, 154, 181, 191, 210–2
Terabust, Elisabeta, 203–5
Tetley, Glen, 114, 125–6, 134, 150–2, 157
Thorpe, Harriet, 208–9
Tooley, John, 106–7, 110, 151
Trecu, Pirmin, 20, 24, 52
Triad, 120–4
Tudor, Antony, 34, 42, 86, 104
Turned Out Proud, 35–6
Twiner, Anthony, 65, 148

Valley of Shadows, 210–7
Valois, Ninette de, 7–11, 16–17, 20–4,
28, 31–2, 37–9, 43, 50, 61, 64, 75
Valse Excentrique, 41, 66
Valses Nobles et Sentimentales, 11, 94
Verdi Variations, 203–4
Vernon, Gilbert, 29–30, 35–6
Vision Scene, 96, 100

Wall, David, 111, 117, 122, 133, 138,
142–4, 148, 152, 154–5, 161–4, 167,
193, 211–4
Webern, Anton von, 167, 169
Webster, Sir David, 94–5, 99, 106,
110–11
Weill, Kurt, 59–60, 130–1
Western Theatre Ballet, 59, 66, 130
Wild Boy, 202
Winter's Eve, 44–5
Wordsworth, Barry, 197, 204–5
World of Paul Slickey, The, 51–2
Wood, Julie, 211–4
Wright, Peter, 47–9, 68, 110, 115, 124,
128–30, 139, 192